Neespaugot

The Legend of the Indian's Coin

a novel by

John Mugglebee

BRANDT
STREET
PRESS

Neespaugot – The Legend of the Indian's Coin

by John Mugglebee

© 2017 John Mugglebee

Published by
Brandt Street Press
5885 Bartlett Street
Pittsburgh, PA 15217
www.brandtstreetpress.com

ISBN: 9780974260792

Book Design by
Mike Murray
Pearhouse Productions
Pittsburgh, PA
www.pearhouse.com

Front Cover Design by
Chris Hyatt

Printed in the United States of America

To David P and Sarah H,
my reason why

The greatness of man is that he is a bridge and not a term. What you can love about man is that he is transition and perdition.

FRIEDRICH NIETZSCHE
THUS SPAKE ZARATHUSTRA

Contents

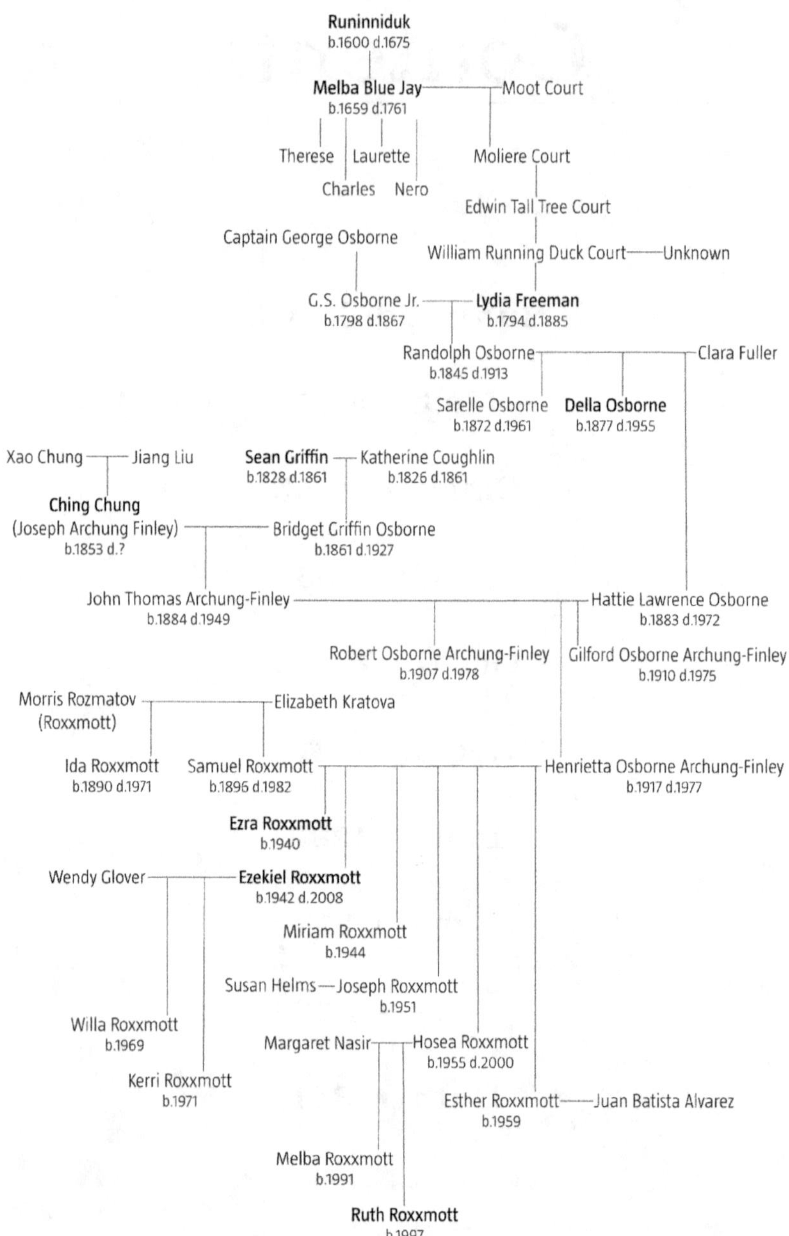

Runinniduk
b.1600 d.1675
Melba Blue Jay
b.1659 d.1761
Moot Court
Therese
Laurette
Charles
Nero
Moliere Court
Edwin Tall Tree Court
Captain George Osborne
William Running Duck Court
Unknown
G.S. Osborne Jr.
b.1798 d.1867
Lydia Freeman
b.1794 d.1885
Randolph Osborne
b.1845 d.1913
Clara Fuller
Sarelle Osborne
b.1872 d.1961
Della Osborne
b.1877 d.1955
Xao Chung
Jiang Liu
Sean Griffin
b.1828 d.1861
Katherine Coughlin
b.1826 d.1861
Ching Chung
(Joseph Archung Finley)
b.1853 d.?
Bridget Griffin Osborne
b.1861 d.1927
John Thomas Archung-Finley
b.1884 d.1949
Hattie Lawrence Osborne
b.1883 d.1972
Robert Osborne Archung-Finley
b.1907 d.1978
Gilford Osborne Archung-Finley
b.1910 d.1975
Morris Rozmatov
(Roxxmott)
Elizabeth Kratova
Ida Roxxmott
b.1890 d.1971
Samuel Roxxmott
b.1896 d.1982
Henrietta Osborne Archung-Finley
b.1917 d.1977
Ezra Roxxmott
b.1940
Wendy Glover
Ezekiel Roxxmott
b.1942 d.2008
Miriam Roxxmott
b.1944
Susan Helms
Joseph Roxxmott
b.1951
Willa Roxxmott
b.1969
Margaret Nasir
Hosea Roxxmott
b.1955 d.2000
Kerri Roxxmott
b.1971
Esther Roxxmott
b.1959
Juan Batista Alvarez
Melba Roxxmott
b.1991
Ruth Roxxmott
b.1997

Runinniduk

June 8, 1675

The storm had finally passed at first light, but it was still raining inside the cabin. The old sorcerer watched water seep through cracks in his crooked roof and plop against his worm-eaten table and three-legged stool. A rum jug he'd long ago drained and set aside was overflowing with the runoff. The hay-covered floor was sodden, and the small cabin reeked like a barn. Runinniduk lay on his feather bed, loath to move and stir up another day's pain in his ancient bones. But urgency is the mother of movement, and he had a strong urge to piss. He rose with a grimace. His blundering first step carried him against the table, and he smacked his shin. *Megerchid!* he cursed, kicking over the stool. He limped to his crooked door, unlatched its crooked hook and stepped out into sparkling daylight.

The Praying Village—fifty-seven cabins, a small chapel and a schoolhouse planted in a clearing in the coastal woodland—was resplendent in the damp morning light. The heavens rose high, blue and cloudless.

The air, warm and salty, carried the scent of the ocean, the perfume of the forest, the bicker of birds and the laughter of children. Native boys and girls were kicking a sopping ball of furs along the communal vegetable gardens. Runinniduk turned aside his loincloth and emptied his bladder into the mud. This was splendid! The cessation of the rains meant a sojourn to the white town to do business. He folded his pizzle back under his skins and returned to the cabin to prepare for the trip.

Doing business with the *wonnuxug* always warranted special accouterments: his rabbit-skin breeches, yellow doublets, buckskin moccasins and green London cape. And his coin! Goodness, he couldn't forget *that* when going among the Coatmen. Hanging by its strap against his English doorframe, the coin was imprinted with the pitiful image of a lone Indian, naked but for a girdle of leaves and cowering under the light of the Gospel. The engraved figure pleaded for the white man to "Come over and help us!" Demeaning as the imprint was, Runinniduk had always accepted the coin in the spirit in which it was intended: as a gift of thanks and as a symbol of goodwill between peoples. Some forty years back, when he was all of thirty-five, he had pounded a nail through it, sanded the sharp edges and pulled a leather strap through the hole. That way, he could wear the coin to all meetings with the *wonnuxug*.

Runinniduk descended his rickety steps sideways to spare his sclerotic knees. His medal gleamed in the bright light, as did his white head of hair, wispy as the desiccated wings of a dead insect. Old as he was, Runinniduk was still large and lumbering—a head taller and a foot broader than his door frame. And no sooner had he hobbled into the road than the children spotted him and ran him down like wolf puppies.

"Please, Master, stay and play with us!" they yelped in English. Runinniduk had taught them, their parents and their parents' parents the white man's tongue, for it was his firm belief that his people's salvation was only possible through the white language.

"*Gersuggayoh*," answered the old man, a kindly reminder that the children must not lose their own tongue either. "It is muddy. And I have business this day with the Puritans."

Disappointed, the children dispersed, and Runinniduk trudged up the puddled road toward the peninsula.

A straight week of rain had turned the marshland passage into a bog, and in no time Runinniduk's moccasins hung off his feet like a pair of dead raccoons. The Neespaugot River, usually a narrow lazy brook, flowed wide and fast, and there was no longer a rope bridge in sight, so Runinniduk waded across the torrent. Such was his craving to do business in the white man's town.

On the opposite bank began the *wonnuxug* farmlands, stitched like their clothing by long picket fences used to corral their fat shit-laying cows. Runinniduk remained on the road to the peninsula before taking the footpath up its eastern flank. At the top of the ridge, he had an unimpeded view of the North Bay. The Coatmen's town stretched around the bay in an unbroken line, and their harbor burst with boats of every size. Their lives were protected by an eighty-cannon fortress on the opposite point, while their livelihoods and souls were vouchsafed by two structures at the center of their enterprise: a house of law and a great white church with a towering steeple. Over a hundred thousand *wonnuxug* now invested the land—more souls than all the tribes of Massachusetts put together.

Runinniduk eased onto a rock to catch his breath. His gaze carried him far out to sea, then, in the opposite direction, across an equal expanse of forest. His regard turned inward, offering an unimpeded view of the past as well as a dark outlook on the future. In truth, the old sorcerer held little hope for the survival of his people.

He thought of a time before white towns and farms and their legions of black-clad Coatmen, when the North Bay burgeoned only with the Great Spirit and the pull of the tides, the whispering of the woodlands and the chant of the Atlantic. One day in his twentieth year of life, he had been fishing in the North Bay when a lone ship pushed through the fog and dropped anchor. Even at that time, *wonnuxug* ships were nothing new to the young Runinniduk. The previous years had brought an increase in white warships, always three at a time, and overflowing with over-sexed soldiers with long knives and exploding sticks. But the lone boat that day was different, for it bore not soldiers and cannons but civilians, many of them women and children huddled and shivering along its deck. Runinniduk's first fear was of the *Muttianomoh*.

The *Muttianomoh* had occurred two years prior, when white soldiers had sickened the entire Nipmuck village of Kowasset, killing every last man, woman and child. Runinniduk's tribe had blamed him for the tragedy, since he, too, was "white." As punishment, the tribal council had ordered him to go into Kowasset, burn the corpses, sleep among the spirits for a period of two moons and serve as a sacrifice should the bloodthirsty gods of the whites still require one.

When he was born, Runinniduk's pale flesh had proved a great mystery to the tribe and even to his own parents, both of whom were as brown as Indian corn. No one had a definitive answer to why the Wampanoag baby was born as white as the sap of the milk plant, with hair as bright as the sun and eyes as blue as spring violets, or why, as he got older, he was taller, broader and thicker-boned than other natives, his eyes closer together, his nose long and sharp. Tales of white visitors stretched back hundreds of years. The tribal elders often recounted the story of Geshanni. One hundred years before, Geshanni, an eleven-year-old Lenni Lenape girl, had survived a thousand-mile trek from Delaware to Massachusetts to become Runinniduk's great grandmother. Perhaps she had been the carrier of the white man's blood.

Before the *Muttianomoh*, Runinniduk's physical oddities had never caused him any problems. On the contrary, the tribe respected his difference, called it *mekegoo jeebi* (strong spirit) and, on his eighteenth year, had made him a *pawwaw*, a sorcerer, *because* he was different. The elders had named him *Runinniduk,* or Snow Hare, as that animal was revered for being steadfast and perseverant.

Following the *Muttianomoh*, all that changed. Runinniduk was viewed with suspicion, and for the first time in his life, his skin made him an outsider among his people. But because he had slept for two months among the dead of Kowasset Village and no evil had come to him, the tribal council still considered him a *pawwaw* and accorded him a vote on whether to annihilate the People of the Boat before their white demons could annihilate the tribe. "What shall it be, Snow Hare? Life or death for the *wonnuxug*?"

Runinniduk was still troubled by the power he had wielded that day. Yes, he could have helped condemn a hundred white men, women and children to death. And why? His sole reason at the time would have been simply to regain the trust of his tribe. It made him shudder to think about it. But he had voted for life, a decision which, in light of the past fifty-five years, had quite possibly helped condemn an entire nation. This, too, made him shudder.

Over all those years, Runinniduk had tried to be a good friend to the white man. After marrying Weetamoo, a Nipmuck, and with Chief Massasoit's blessing, the couple had gone to live in the Praying Village for six months of each year, where the chief felt that Runinniduk could be of use in quelling quarrels with the *wonnuxug*. Runinniduk had built a *wonnuxug* house with a stone floor and fireplace, a Londonian doorframe, and beds with feather mattresses for his wife and children. He had even erected a latrine, though he never used it himself. He deplored the white man's practice of shitting shamefully inside a closet. Instead, he always did his business in a ravine downwind of the village, shaded by elm, sycamore and maple trees, rich in rose leaves, assorted vines, sage, elder, skunk cabbage and wild spinach, where a cool brook bubbled by, narrow enough to straddle, unload and clean himself with handfuls of cool water and lard.

By this point, he had made several sojourns to Boston, to a Puritan institution of learning called Harvard, where he had helped a minister named John Eliot translate the King James Bible into Algonquian. The book was called *Up-Biblum God, Nukkone Testament, Wusku Testament* or the Massachusetts Bible. In gratitude for his help, the Massachusetts Bay Colony had given Runinniduk one of the first ten coins minted in the new world. The only other native recipient was Massasoit himself.

And for so many years thereafter, and despite more and more contention, Runinniduk had held out hope that his native population and the *wonnuxug* might work through their differences and create one strong people. But that dream seemed doomed after Massasoit's death in 1661. No sooner was the Sachem buried in the Sacred Grounds of Chiefs on Mount Hope than the white colonies unlawfully seized fourteen square miles of Nipmuck land for the farming and the grazing of an ever-burgeoning herd of their cattle. Runinniduk himself went before the High Court of Neespaugot to argue the Nipmuck grievance, but the head judge had refused to hear the case.

"And what of the leagues of covenant?" argued Runinniduk.

"Null and void!" thundered the judge. "Its terms died with the Sachem."

From that moment, white farms began to overrun Indian lands with impunity. Tribal territory was possessed and cleared, and cattle left to stomp across sacred grounds. Natives were systematically shot at, thrown out of the white man's court, or paid off with alcohol, the last of which was Runinniduk's case. Since Massasoit's death fourteen years before, Runinniduk had sought escape in rum. The once-proud *pawwaw* had become an inveterate drunk.

Which explained his business in town that day. He sought an appointment with a jug. The old tippler entered Neespaugot and hobbled up Cabot Street to North Bay Commons, a peaceful square rimmed with white-columned municipal buildings, straight-angled shops and neat double-walled houses with two floors and bay windows. Runinniduk appreciated *wonnuxug* carpentry and masonry, about the only thing he still respected about the white man. He crossed the Commons to the corner of Beacon and Grove Street and went about finding a tavern. He had three favorites: the Turtle and Egg, the King's Court and the Maid and Butler.

He found each one closed, boarded up as tight as a coffin.

"What tomfoolery is this?" he wondered aloud. He looked about and realized that the establishments of the seamstress, the cloth merchant, the livery man and the blacksmith were likewise shuttered. The habitual buzz of Yankee industry was nowhere to be seen or heard that late morning. The shutters on all of the white man's commerce hung as low as the eyelids of the guilty.

And then it hit him. Of course, you old fool, it's the *wonnuxug* Sabbath. From six o'clock Saturday night to sundown Sunday, no travel was allowed and taverns refused all patronage. The constables forbade ninepin games. Two *wonnuxug* caught talking in the street could be arrested for a breach of religious etiquette.

Frustrated and now doubly thirsty, Runinniduk sank onto a bench in the Commons. *Wonnuxug* customs were like the recent rains. They could flood an otherwise fine day with depression. Runinniduk was seventy-five years old and still understood so little about the Puritans. They were, to his mind, incomprehensible in argument and deed. Their very existence was based on a construct that repudiated the natural forces around them. They had been victims of persecution, flight, starvation and sickness in their own land across the water, yet instead of embracing the Great Spirit, they had settled their old demons into the new world. Worst of all, they feared change. It was the root of their problems. The Puritans desired a state of absolute stasis. They worshipped a river that did not move, seasons that did not change. They woke in the morning, praying to find the day exactly as they had left it the night before: a constant din coming from the crowded harbor, the town crier making his rounds, the watchman calling out the hour, the Ancient and Honorable Artillery drilling on the Commons. The sun set and the shutters fell with a crack, and the following day the Puritans streamed from their homes in mortal fear that, sometime during the night, Satan had changed things around.

Those who did not toe the Puritan line—meaning those of independent mind, those who spouted off about change and innovation, those of excitable and ambitious talk who could not confine their lives to the Puritan way— were shunned and driven from the commonwealth.

Why, he wondered, could not the Puritan hear the whispering stone, the singing plant? All is life. Life is the cascade of spirits, it is phantom and runs like the water. It is ever-changing.

But such talk only infuriated the Puritan.

"Godless Indian, you! Plants and stones have no soul. Only a man hath a soul, and God is the only truth. The law of the jungle is Satan's way."

The Puritan demanded no less than total conformity to his customs, meaning the total annihilation of the native belief in the Great Spirit.

Runinniduk grew very thirsty.

He knew of men at the docks, smugglers they were called, who imported illegal ale, and he headed for the harbor. As he cut through the courthouse square, he saw four of the King's soldiers abusing a slovenly woman whom they had shackled inside a pillory. She was what the white men called a trollop.

"Speak, bitch!" ordered the captain of the guard, kicking her backside.

"Three heathens, I tell ye, one a half-breed light as mayweed," she shouted, breaking the law of whispers required by the Sabbath. "It was them what killed the census-taker."

A soldier smacked her leg with the flat end of his musket. "And you was a part of it. Own up and confess!"

"God be my witness, I had nothing to do with it. But I seen the whole thing. One held his arms, another his legs and the third, the filthy half-breed, did to him what Canon Fulbert's ruffians did to poor Peter Abelard. They snipped off his balls. Then they twisted his neck."

The oily woman's terrified eyes landed on Runinniduk, who was glued haplessly to her interrogation. She readily accepted Satan's gift. "Why, that's him, guv'nuh! That's the half-breed!"

Instinct told Runinniduk to flee. But he was no longer the Snow Hare of yore. The soldiers caught him and knocked him to the cobblestones. To preclude any further idea of escape, they splintered his hip with the butt of a musket.

Just after sundown, Runinniduk and two other Christian Indians were carted into North Bay Courthouse, tried for a crime they had not committed and sentenced to hang within the hour. It was a beautiful spring day, and twilight still burned like daylight as the three men were carted to Gallows Hill, a short distance from the Commons. As the rope was being tightened around Runinniduk's neck, someone in the crowd recognized him.

"Hold on there, guv'nuh executioner. That's Running Duck!"

"Running who?"

"You know, the savior of the colony."

A restless murmur swept through the crowd. They had all been children once and had grown up with the legend of the beneficent Running Duck.

The town alderman called for silence to address the gathering.

"Here ye now, good brethren. This heathen hath been condemned for murder. Moreover, his half-breed features are recrudescent proof of adultery with savage women, and no sin, be it hundreds of years old, escapes the Almighty. Running Duck is the product of that original sin. Legend or not, this heathen must die. His execution serves its place in the intricate workings of a moral world. Sin of any kind bequeaths a sinner's fate. Hang him!"

The latch was kicked, the trap doors opened, and three natives plunged with a loud crack of only two spines.

Runinniduk's rope, not his neck, had snapped, and he now lay on the ground, crushed but still breathing. It took five men to put him in a cart and take him to the Frog and Egg Tavern. They set him on a drinking table still sticky with twenty-four-hour ale, while the garrison doctor made a perfunctory examination to determine whether he was conscious enough for another go at the noose. A stiff stein of trough water was splashed in his face, bringing him to his senses. "Good," said the doctor, "We have our answer. Take him back."

A quarter of an hour later, Runinniduk was back on the gallows, tied to a rope.

"Any last words…again?" asked the executioner.

Runinniduk tried to speak, but his vocal cords had been severed in the first hanging. He wanted to hold his coin, but his hands were bound. He wanted to ask the executioner to take the coin from around his neck and place its leather strap in his bound hands. The executioner grew impatient. "The prisoner hath nothing to add."

The alderman nodded. The executioner released the lever. The trap door sprung.

"This day," began one farmer's journal, "an Injun was twice kilt in the colonies."

Melba

June 11, 1675

Smoke permeated the loft, chasing Abigail Lawrence from a restful slumber. Had the cinders in the hearth been rekindled? A true blessing if they were. Nothing like a warm hearth to get a head start on the breakfast and morning chores. She crawled over her sleeping husband, draped a shawl about her shoulders and, eight months pregnant, descended the ladder to the dirt floor of her Cabot Street home.

Fiddlesticks! The chimney was cold. But there was no mistaking the presence of smoke. It hung below the rafters like the devil's veil. Abigail thought she heard a shriek coming from outdoors. A dying cat, perchance? She looked through the gun hole, saw nothing and unlatched the door. The air outside was thick with smoke and ash. One hundred feet away, in the middle of the road, Goodman Driscoll, the fruit merchant, made a ghostly figure, leaning over his fruit cart. "I say, Mr. Driscoll," called out Abigail. "Whence cometh this smoke?" He made no reply but continued in the study of his wares. She recalled that the poor fellow was going deaf. Barefooted, Abigail advanced toward the street. "Mr. Driscoll!" she shouted. Still he made no sign, but now she was close enough to see why. The fruit merchant was not leaning over his cart but was being suspended above it by the shaft of an arrow imbedded in his chest. His face was gray. A two-foot skein of bloody saliva linked his mouth with his peaches. Abigail shot a look at King's Hill, hoping for the comforting sight of Fort Charles. Instead, she received the shock of her young life. The fort was gone. Obliterated like a great tooth torn from the gums of the hill. All that remained of that edifice was a bonfire and a great spillage of flame and smoke darkening the rising sun.

"Attack!" she cried out to no one in particular. Then, holding her belly between two hands, Abigail ran back toward her house. A few feet from her door, someone seized hold of her long hair and yanked her back. As her feet left the ground, she caught a flash of light, and that was her last image.

Sam Quanohit had been concealed behind Abigail's house. A young Narragansett man with a wife and three children of his own, Sam had come to Neespaugot to punish the Coatmen for killing the great *pawwaw* Runinniduk, who had taught Sam to read and write Algonquian and English. First, he had killed the fruit merchant, and now he would slay Abigail. Sam had never attacked a woman before, much less a pregnant white one, and the situation made him uneasy. But he steeled himself, for she would soon be inside her house fetching a musket. She never saw him. Sam caught her from behind by her hair—white women had nice soft locks, and it was a shame they trussed and hid them under cloth—and before she hit the ground, Sam had most of her scalp in his hand. He slammed her head against the walkway, then stabbed her in the throat and screamed to dispel his revulsion. When her husband came outside, Sam was waiting and plunged his knife into the man's eye and split his head with a tomahawk. He sliced off the couple's garments and left their bodies, naked and without respect, in their doorway. Their clothing, Sam piled in the middle of the road. He stripped the fruit merchant and added his vestments to the pile and lit it on fire. He returned to the house with some burning garments and set the place ablaze. Then, he walked out and looked for other *wonnuxug* to kill.

Minister Kenneth Barnes ran past Sam Quanohit's burning pile, pursued by screaming demons clobbering and butchering folk as they went. The minister reached the Commons, where he ran headlong into a smiling demon with an arrow ready and waiting on his bow. Armed only with his Holy Bible, the minister used the Good Book as a shield and cried out, "Please, Lord Jesus, save me!" The arrow pierced the Bible and carried paper and print into and out the back of the minister's skull. As he lay dying like a skewered turkey, his killer, Tokansint, a Wampanoag, stood over him and taunted: "Come, Lord Jesus, save this poor Coatman if thou canst!" Tokansint scalped the minister and stripped his body of clothing.

The attack on Neespaugot raged all day and into the night, and a suffocating veil of scarlet smoke blanketed the town, holding in both heat and a hellish glow radiating off the rubble and its thousands of cadavers. Bodies lay everywhere, across the Commons, slumped over picket fences, piled in doorways and dangling out of windows, pierced with arrows, bludgeoned with tomahawks and cudgels, stripped, disemboweled, decapitated. As the wailing of the injured, the whooping of the attackers and the bonfire of garments—skirts, bodices, doublets, cloaks, breeches, caps, women's shoes, men's boots and children's booties—died down, a dry snowfall of ash settled far and wide over tide pools of gore.

A macabre silence reigned over Neespaugot, until a single horse and wagon trundled up Cabot Street, the wooden wheels churning over the blood-stained cobblestones. "Get on there!" prodded its driver, a sixteen-year-old girl of fair cheeks and blue eyes. She punched at the reins, determined to keep the skittish horse moving forward. Sitting in the buckboard were two men in their early twenties, each dressed in English clothing, both of them dark-faced. Joe Bear and Jack Wolf were brothers. The driver, her white flesh, gray bonnet and coarse dress to the contrary, was also native. The three cousins had ventured from the Praying Village to collect the body of their grandfather, Runinniduk.

They passed the blackened remains of the North Bay Church, where they had each been baptized, catechized and confirmed. The town hall and the royal governor's house also lay in charred heaps. Every shop, inn and cottage in the town center was smoking rubble. The only structure still standing inviolate was the gallows, rising in the square. The bodies of the three executed men still hung there like sacks of laundry, eerily silhouetted against the amber fog.

The girl positioned her wagon under the dead men and steadied the horse, as Joe Bear cut down the corpses one by one and Jack Wolf lowered each into the buckboard. Then, the six travelers, three living and three dead, headed south out of town toward the Great Woods.

Under a moonless sky, the dirt road gave way to woods and then to black forest. Joe Bear and Jack Wolf grew fretful. The two brothers, colorful names aside, had been raised as Puritan Christians, and they saw evidence of Satan and his minions in each demonically shaped bit of vegetation, each screeching airborne predator. But the girl had spent half her youth in the wilderness with her grandfather, and her concerns were of a more earthly nature: running into a vengeful white militia or a Wampanoag war party with little sympathy for Praying Villagers. Even in peaceful times, the Christian Indians were looked at with suspicion and contempt by the Puritans and the tribes. The Praying Villagers had learned to read, to pray and to wear English dress, yet the whites acted horrified by the result, while the Great Woods tribes considered their converted brothers unnatural beings, like eunuchs. The Christian Indians lived in limbo—part of neither world, detested by both.

As the girl steered the wagon into the depths of the forest, she pondered the irony of the catastrophe: a war had broken out over the deaths of three Praying Village Indians whose lives were an abomination to both warring sides.

That night, the cousins buried the other two corpses and then continued on with their grandfather's body. The goal was to reach Mount Hope—a three-day journey south—and lay him to rest in the Sacred Grounds of

Chiefs. But decomposition had gotten a fierce head start on his old heavy body, which had been left to swing in the elements for two days. The girl had no choice but to bridle the horse in a glade and start the ceremony there. The brothers collected stones for a barrow while the girl prepared her grandfather for an Algonquian burial. While removing his shirt, she made a startling discovery. "Cousins, come," she called. Both came running to see what she'd found. "Behold! Grandfather's coin. The Coatmen didn't take it."

"Praise the Lord," said Jack Wolf.

Joe Bear, the elder, slipped the leather strap over the dead man's head. But instead of keeping the coin, he poured the strap into the girl's hand. "It's yours, Melba Blue Jay. Grandfather always meant for you to have it."

Both men returned to their task. The girl pulled the strap over her head and tucked the coin down the high collar of her dress. Then she undressed her grandfather and sharpened her knife. She began by incising his torso, arms and legs, skinning him and pulling off the outer layer as one did with hares. Her cousins helped her set his remains inside the barrow and cover him with stones. She chanted a quick prayer to Manitou, and together they recited the Lord's Prayer.

Melba Blue Jay fetched her satchel and bow and arrows from the buckboard and told her cousins to take the horse and wagon back to the Praying Village and collect their family. "Promise me," she entreated, "that you will ride north and not stop until you reach the French land."

"The English mean us no harm, Melba. We are Christians as they."

"Cousin, from now on, all Indians are heathens to the white man."

"What are your intentions, young one?"

"I shall fight the Coatmen for what they did to Grandfather. I go to join Metacom."

Melba Blue Jay traveled by night, dressed in buckskin to avoid being killed accidently by a Wampanoag or Narragansett warrior eager for another white scalp. But once the sun rose, she donned her English dress and bonnet and entered the white towns and camps for reports of the latest news of Philip-alias-Metacom. Thus did she see with her own eyes the burned-out shells that had been the vibrant towns of Groton, Sudbury, Middleborough, Seaconcke, Rehoboth and Swansea. The destruction stretched as far west as the Connecticut River, where the towns of Deerfield, Hatfield and Northampton smoldered on the plains.

In a meadow outside of Dartmouth, Melba happened upon a zombie cow. The beast stood staring at her without expression. She saw that its underbelly had been slit open and its guts hung to the ground. The animal had wandered hill and dale, trailing its viscera like a tail. Melba understood the message: we hate your stupid cattle, which ramble through our villages and sacred grounds and deaden great stretches of prairie with their insatiable chewing and incessant shitting. She doubted that the white man understood as much.

Another day, on a ridge, she found fifty birch poles stuck in the ground, each mounted with the severed head of an Englishman, hair stirring in the coastal breeze. The macabre scene looked like an absurd council of talking heads. Again, Melba doubted that the Coatmen would understand the message beyond its barbarism and its appeal to the white man's fears. For a native, the soul resided in the head, and the line of heads was telling the white men that they would be denied entry into the afterlife. Some of the heads were so decomposed and wormy that Melba concluded they'd been dug from graves.

Such carnage and desecration left Melba conflicted. The Coatmen had murdered her grandfather, and for that she wanted them dead. Yet her grandfather himself had somehow believed in these people and had felt protective toward them. He had worn his coin like a shepherd his horn, and he had suffered Metacom's barbs about "giving importance to cheap white trinkets," because the coin and his copy of the Massachusetts Bible were strong symbols of a lasting marriage between unlike peoples. *His* message to *her* was that the coin meant a better world to come, a world of tolerance and acceptance. He admitted his doubts to her, but he also said that his narrowing vision did not nullify the existence of a wider vista. "Maybe it is for you or your children's children to see it."

Chased into a swamp one night by a group of militiamen who had spotted her shooting at a turkey, Melba Blue Jay hid in the overgrowth and clutched the coin as she would her grandfather's hand. Her assailants came close. She studied them between black branches groping like angry fingers at the yellow moon, their rifles loaded and ready, murder on their tongues. "We'll never catch anyone in this accursed swamp. These fucking

Injuns live with Satan!" And yet there she was, literally under their noses. Another few inches and they'd have blasted her into the soggy earth. When they finally moved on, she released her grip on the coin. Her palm was bleeding.

The next morning, dressed in her English clothing, Melba Blue Jay ran headlong into a war party of Narragansett. Taking her for white, they charged, tomahawks raised. She whipped off her bonnet and spoke commandingly to them in their own tongue. "Brothers, I am native, the granddaughter of the *pawwaw* Runinniduk." The warriors stopped in their tracks. "I am called Melba Blue Jay. *Wishbium*! Take me to Metacom."

Metacom's palisade lay deep in the heart of the Great Swamp, invisible to the untrained eye and impenetrable except by fire, thanks to a tree-high barrier of brambles and thickets tangled around dead trees stacked forty yards deep. A well-concealed passage led through that natural fortification into a square mile of cleared land and a village twice the size of the Praying Village. Hundreds of wigwams ringed a pond. A thousand Wampanoag and Narragansett men, women and children were going about their daily chores, tending their vegetable patches and corralling their turkeys, geese and pigs. One of her Narragansett envoys boasted, "Only the birds in the air know we are here."

Two warriors came for Melba. They laid rough hands on her and jostled her to where Metacom and his closest advisors awaited and threw her to the ground at Metacom's feet. One of the warriors emptied her satchel on the ground. Out poured her victuals, knife, buckskin tunic and gray bonnet. Metacom picked up the bonnet and looked at it with disdain. "*Mergerchid*," he spat. *Shit!*

The Sachem had the fierce demeanor of a wolf, the cold obsidian eyes, the wide brow and cruel mouth. Tall and tautly muscled, he was known for his violent temper. He always carried his cudgel—a petrified piece of wood with a large deadly knuckle—with which he would just as soon smash a man's brain to mush as look at him. The line between friend and foe was often only a matter of his mood. He was unpredictable and feared by all, and few natives, not even the most hardened warriors, had the nerve to meet his eye.

"Who this girl be?" he said. "Be she Blue Jay, granddaughter of Runinniduk, counsel to my father? Or be she that weak *wonnux* whelp called Melba? Speak, you worthless white-skinned *gung-shquaws*. Today be you native or mealy Christian slave?"

She tried to raise her head, but a warrior stepped on her back and pushed her prostrate. The moment the pressure slackened, Melba sprang loose and punched the man in the face. Before he could do her harm, Metacom signaled the warrior to let her alone. "Let white female dog speak."

"Great Sachem, I come to avenge my grandfather."

"You lie!"

He came at her. Melba stood her ground, did not flinch, did not turn from him, for to do so would signify weakness and result in her demise. He towered over her, and she could smell the blood of his most recent victims on him. For several moments, Metacom's anger swelled until it seemed all but certain that her brains would soon be lying outside her skull. Then, he broke out laughing. Her character pleased him.

"You have warrior heart. How old be you?"

"*Nobnecuddusk*, Sachem."

The Sachem considered this and warned her, "Maybe, but I still sure you spy. If I think this tomorrow, you die." And he strode away with her bonnet.

That night Melba Blue Jay was kept in the stockade with two captive white women from Lancaster and Middleborough. They didn't know what to make of her fair flesh, white clothing and perfect Indian tongue. When she spoke to them in English, they too accused her of being a spy—for the Indians and Satan, and they recoiled from her.

The next morning Melba was dragged into Metacom's wigwam, where he tested her resolve.

"How a shitty little white squaw help me?"

"I can read and write English, Sachem."

"Bah, we no fight with words."

"I know how the Coatman thinks."

"And I do not, worthless *mergerchid*."

"Sachem, your cudgel splits a man's head and makes his kin angry and wanting to fight with you. But I can write words that infect their hearts with fear and make them weak against your armies. And I can deliver these messages in person, without raising suspicion."

Metacom seized her by the arm and swung her to the ground. "A fool you take me! I let you go and you tell the *wonnuxug* where we hide!"

"Sachem, I hate the *wonnuxug* as much as any here."

Metacom dragged her outside by her hair and called

all of his people to gather round so that they might know his will.

"This girl be slave, so treat her like one. But remember, she my slave. Harm her and I eat out your heart."

Over the next several weeks, Melba cleaned, skinned, cooked and weaved, waiting for the Sachem to decide whether or not to use her skills. She was always the last person to eat, following even the two white captives. Only the dogs ate after her. She was fed the leftover turkey carcasses, rodent entrails and cornmeal fallen in the dirt. She was whipped, not hard enough to do her bodily harm, though sufficient to bruise her pride. At times of high anguish, Melba considered escaping. But to where? The land was aflame, the natives wanted nothing to do with her, and she truly did hate the Coatmen. Her family was in the French land—or at least she hoped they were—because word had come that the English army had destroyed the Praying Village and imprisoned its people on a cold merciless chunk of rock called Misery Island, fifteen miles off the coast of Neespaugot.

One morning, some warriors came for her. The first stop was the icy stream, where they threw her into water so frigid she thought her life would leave her. "Ahh!" she cried and shivered.

"*Qutshetush!*" they said. "Undress and clean the shit off your face, *gung-shquaws*." They tossed her a blanket and some other woman's English dress. It smelled of death.

"*Chawgwan ne?*" she asked.

"Ask the Sachem."

Metacom waited alone by the dying light of his wigwam fire. He pointed at an English chest beside the fire. "*Yunjonum,*" he ordered. Melba opened the chest and found some sheets of parchment, quills and jars of ink. "You say you know writing to make fear to the *wonnuxug.* Prove it. Take this." He handed her the bonnet.

That fall and winter, colonial towns awoke to find mysterious parchments nailed to the doors of their churches:

> To the townspeople of Bridgewater, beware, for today Harold Johnson will be crushed by a wheel, Betty Mackey will catch a bullet to the head and Billy Shrivner will have his throat cut.

> To the people of Providence, beware. Winston Brattle will collapse and die this morning.

> To the folk of Dartmouth, beware. In three days' time Margaret Rollins shall take a spear in the heart and fall down her well.

> To the townsmen of Taunton, this very afternoon Constable Hackenworth shall be seized by abdominal pains and perish before nightfall.

> To the people of Plymouth, beware! This night the Warner infant will suffocate in his crib.

All of the messages were signed "Blue Devil."

Who was this Blue Devil? Townspeople believed that Satan had been among them, for who but the Beguiler could know the names of their fellow townsfolk? The fact that none of the predictions ever came to pass was lost in the subsequent Indian attacks that always followed a visit by the infamous Blue Devil.

Melba's propaganda sowed much hysteria in the colonies, yet those successes went unacknowledged by her own people, who knew nothing of the havoc she was wreaking in the white world. In the tribe's eyes, she remained a good-for-nothing half-breed slave living off their victuals and under Metacom's protection. Many of the tribe lived for the day the Sachem lost interest in her. They would tie a rope to each of her arms and play tug of war until they had torn her limb from limb.

That winter, the cruelest on record, Melba was spying in the town of Warwick when James Sharp Bone, a Narragansett, was captured and tortured. They crushed him under heavier and heavier stones and scalded his body with burning oil until he gave up the whereabouts of Metacom's palisade. Melba rushed from town in a blizzard. By the time she reached the Great Woods, the white winds had cowered tall trees and obliterated landmarks under a heavy blanket of snow. The Coatman army was equally confused. Twice she crossed their fresh tracks, as they turned in circles. She could distinguish the crisp cut of leather boots, the half-moon of hooves and the imprints of skins. The soldiers were on foot, walking their horses, guided by Pequot scouts and the Massachusetts Bay Colony militia. She caught up with them at Wompshauk Pond and took cover upwind, behind the knuckles of a fist of bogwood. A Pequot scout appeared from the frozen swamp, a man of wild hair and great size, and clothed in the skins of large beasts that don't die easily. He held his furred hand against the shooting snow and sniffed the air several times, before issuing a bird cry. The Coatmen army arose to the bank of the pond. Many were soldiers, their ragged red jackets stuffed with rough, twined cloth for added warmth. The militiamen wore buckskin but their stench was indistinguishable from the regulars. All were unshaven, their faces etched with aggravation and a desire to kill. They carried their long flintlocks in both arms, pinned like prayers to their chests.

They and their horses pressed east, following the perimeter of the pond, adding five miles to their purpose. Melba collected her courage and stepped onto the pond. The ice creaked. She hesitated. The only thing she feared in life was falling into icy water—a childhood accident. *Go!* she commanded herself, and she set out across that exposed expanse, battered by the wind, the snow swirling in all directions and stinging her down to her petticoats. She reached deep water, her heart stopping with each creaking step. After half an hour, an eternity, she made solid ground and now had her first head start since leaving Warwick.

The palisade seemed deserted but for the lookout, a toothless old sack of sticks whom she had to awake to get his attention. "What are *you* doing out here, Qannipin? Where are the young lookouts?"

"All the fighting men left this morning."

"*Debecornug,*" she cried, but there was no time to lose in whining. Melba grabbed the old man's bony shoulders. "The white army comes. What does a lookout do if he needs to gather the tribe quickly? Is there a horn? A drum?"

"The youngsters whistle."

"Then whistle, Qannipin!"

"One needs teeth to whistle and I have only my gums."

Melba left the old man and ran to the center of the compound. The only thing she could think of was a game that her grandfather had taught her: "Come out, come out, wherever you are!" she screamed in English.

Women, children and *cochises* like old Qannipin spilled out of their wigwams trailed by their pigs and ducks. At the sight of Melba, the tribe turned from panic to hostility. Wootonekanuske, Metacom's wife, raged at her.

"Slave dog, you call us out into this cold for what?"

"Wootonekanuske, it's the white army. They know where we are and they'll be here soon to massacre us. We must abandon the village!"

"Are you are mad, white girl? None fight in such a storm, especially Coatmen, who are afraid of the cold."

"*Wemooni!*"

"The truth. Ha! What would you know of that? You are nothing but a walking lie. Your pale skin is a lie. Your blue eyes are a lie. Begone to your pen and be glad we do not poke out your eyes and cut out your tongue."

Metacom's nine-year-old son went to kick her in the shin, a practice the Sachem often encouraged with splendid mirth. Melba seized the boy and put a knife to his throat. "I will kill this child if one of you comes near me. Now listen to me, you hovelling hares, I am leaving with the boy. If you try to stop me, he is dead. If you do not leave this palisade in three hundred heartbeats, he and all of you will be dead. Now, grab your warmest furs but nothing else. I will await you on the Mount Hope Trail. Hurry or we are all dead!" To show she meant business, Melba cut the boy's chin, and his blood and tears ran.

Melba dragged the crying child from the palisade and up a ridge. After tying him to a tree, she waited for what seemed an eternity until the tribe came into view, a slow-moving serpent consisting of a thousand women, children and old men blackening the west bank of the Kickimuit River. Mindful that the villagers would now tear her to pieces, she left the boy and headed back into the swamp to find Metacom's army.

Not a month before, a white army had ambushed a palisade south of Narragansett Bay, setting fire to each longhouse and wigwam and shooting down men, women and children as they ran out, "bashing in their burning heads with our rifles," Melba had overheard a soldier say in the Marlborough square. "We killed and torched them with such relish that, had we been cannibals, there might we have ate."

A great black billowing cloud now rose in the direction of Metacom's palisade, followed shortly thereafter by volleys of gunfire. Who were they shooting at? Along the river, the air thickened with the smell of gunpowder and burning wood. Melba stayed along the ridge and saw that Metacom's warriors had stumbled upon the Coatmen as they were busying themselves with burning the palisade. The whites were now trapped between the fire they had started and the people they had come to kill. Metacom's army was mowing them down with arrows. Those soldiers still alive knelt in groups on bended knee firing blind and azimuthal volleys, creating skeins of smoke. But the arrows descended upon them like snowflakes. Melba heard an English captain trying to rally his men.

"Fight on for God and King!"

As he spoke, an arrow lodged in his throat and blood spilled down his red tunic and across the new snow. Some militiamen tried to flee on the soldiers' horses, and they too were brought down like deer.

As the fight finished, Metacom went through the fallen Coatmen, dashing the brains of any who weren't dead. "*Gordunch skwishegun!*" he shouted. *Take off their heads!*

That night, Metacom named Melba to his counsel, the tribe's first female *pawwaw* in two hundred years.

By the end of that winter, more natives had perished of European diseases—cholera, smallpox and whooping cough—than white weaponry. Then, in the spring, when it couldn't have gotten worse, it did. The Mohawk crossed the Connecticut River and joined up with the Mohegan and Pequot to fight their ancestral enemies, the Wampanoag and Narragansett. By summer, Metacom's army had the English in front of it and enemy natives behind it. Metacom was surrounded.

One steamy night in August, the dense and silent air swirling with bugs, the Sachem called for his seventeen-year-old *pawwaw*. "I need your counsel, Blue Jay. You who know the *wonnuxug* best, how must I become invisible to them?"

"Sachem, the Coatmen know you by your long hair. They consider long hair a badge of cruelty and cannibalism. Short hair is your best disguise and will protect you from the white man's bullet."

On the afternoon of August 12, chased to his last stand on Mount Hope, Metacom faced his enemies in the hammering heat. Insects swirled about the gashes in his flesh. His left knee was twisted into a misshapen mess, so he favored the right one and leaned on the infamous cudgel with which he had dashed the heads of so many. Naked but for small breeches and stockings, he lifted the club, encouraging his enemies to shoot, but the ragged soldiers and militia, their long rifles trained on him, held their fire and a long silence reigned on Mount Hope.

Neither the Sachem's stature nor his defiance had stopped the execution. Rather, it was the idiot fact that, as one militiaman later put it, "For fourteen months we put lead in thousands of heathens, but hain't none of us never killed a short-haired Injun. None of us wanted to go to hell."

The honor of killing Metacom fell not to a white man but to a native, a young ambitious Algonquian named Alderman. Impatient and greedy for the bounty on the Sachem's head, Alderman fired a ball charged with burning powder into the great man's chest, and Metacom fell dead.

Captain Benjamin Church ordered the Sachem beheaded and quartered. Metacom's arms and legs were hung in four different trees. His severed right hand was given to Alderman, who already envisioned himself storing it in a bucket of rum and showing it for pennies. Metacom's genitals were shipped across the ocean to Windsor Castle to the King of England. His head stayed in the colony, was nailed on a pole and marched around

New England. Eventually the head would wind up back in a newly built Neespaugot, and there, stuck high above the courthouse square, it stared down at squeamish tourists.

White women returning from Indian captivity were given chilly receptions. Raped or not, they had lived in the company of savages, thus were sullied embarrassments to their families, communities and themselves. An honorable woman should have made it her solemn duty *not* to survive.

The militia that caught Melba Blue Jay never questioned her race. To them she was just another dishonorable captive, and they eyed her the way she had looked at that eviscerated cow in the meadow—she was nothing more than a walking piece of dead meat, good to no one. She was carted back to Neespaugot and turned over to the parish, which in turn passed her on to a deeply religious farm couple named Collins. The couple set her to chore in their barn, milking the cows.

Melba played well her role of the repentant pariah. She worked hard, read the Bible diligently, spoke contritely of the sin of having survived and attended services religiously. In the meantime, she was snooping around the white man's records, to know if Joe Bear, Jack Wolf, her mother and two small brothers had managed to escape to the French land.

Downtown Neespaugot had been thoroughly destroyed at the outset of the war, and now all public buildings were either makeshift or under construction. Finding documents was a maddening enterprise, especially given that Melba had but two days a month of free time away from the Collins farm. However, she had managed to forge a friendship with a thin pimply clerk named Grimby, who was smitten with her and eager to be of service. The problem was his boss, a miserable old bag who worked in archives and considered it her religious duty to remind Grimby that he was wasting his time in conversation with a fallen woman, "loins sullied with the filth of the heathen seed." But Grimby's crush was sturdier than the gossip's calumny, and one day outside the half-built Hall of Records, he handed Melba a sizeable register of names. "They'd hang me if they knew I'd taken it," he said, proud as a young cock.

Melba sat on the Hall of Records steps and opened the book. In it was a record of the names of the Praying Villagers who had boarded the HMS *Gallagher*, destination Misery Island, between the twenty-fifth and twenty-seventh of June 1675. Melba's chin quavered as her eyes located the names of Mary Nemasit, her mother; Peter and Jethro Nemasit, her little brothers; her uncle Richard Mashpee; her aunt Nahmeokee Mashpee; her cousins Joe Bear and Jack Wolf and others. They and all their kind had perished on a grim rock in the Atlantic. "All of their carcasses," went the entry, "were dumped in the sea."

Rage got the better of her, and she heaved the register at the gobsmacked Grimby. Before he had recovered, she had her knife at his windpipe. "*Wotone!* Go fetch your soldiers. Tell them Blue Devil awaits them here."

The trial of the century got underway in February 1677, in a vegetable storehouse allocated as a courthouse. Blindfolded, gagged and bound, the accused was jostled through a gauntlet of hecklers stretching all the way down to the port. The first witness for the prosecution was one of the white women from Metacom's stockade. (The other had done the honorable thing and flung herself on an Indian lance.)

"I, Willa Carlisle, do swear upon the eternal souls of my loving family, butchered at Lancaster, that this creature, handsome though she be, is the Blue Devil spoken of. She tried by devious means to recruit me and Agatha Haynes into foul actions, but Agatha killed herself, and I sought the light of the Lord, and in His hands did my soul place."

The charge against Melba was treason. The prosecution assumed, as did all who saw Melba, that the accused was a white woman who had taken up arms against her own people. But that argument quickly unraveled under the testimony of Minister John Eliot, the Boston reverend who had translated the Massachusetts Bible with Runinniduk. Now greatly wizened and liver-spotted, Minister Eliot told the court of his long efforts to save native souls. "A half-century of labor I fear now failed. Today I present myself before this court to swear under oath, and as God is my witness, that I baptized this child and that she is not white, but full Algonquian."

"Nonsense!" cried out one of the English lay prosecutors. "One need but look at her."

"I registered her name and date of birth," said Minister Eliot, drawing out his Bible. "I had been invited for that purpose to the Praying Village by her grandfather Runinniduk, the Indian most instrumental in translating the Massachusetts Bible. And I read: *Melba Blue Jay, begat 5 May 1659 to Mary Nemasit (a Narragansett) and Tom Bold*

Falcon (A Wampanoag), son of Runinniduk (a Wampanoag) and Weetamoo (a Nipmuck). Let the records show as well that her grandfather Runinniduk was also fair of flesh, though his own parents were Wampanoags of this land before the arrival of us settlers."

The clergymen prosecutors chose not to counter the word of a man of the cloth. The treason case was dead in the water, so the prosecution would need to find a new angle, preferably one more incendiary. At the next session, the staff of prosecutors opened the proceedings with a new accusation: witchcraft.

"If the accused be Injun-born," said the chief religious prosecutor, "then where art that dusky skin, the devilish body piercings, tattoos and other self-mutilations of the dark heathen? How came she to resemble our sisters, mothers, aunts? The only answer possible is that Blue Devil is an aberration, something not of this world, a witch, a demon answering directly to Satan."

The Carlisle woman was called back to the witness box where she gave proof of the prosecution's claim. "Yea, I saw her mix and minister a demon brew that got the heathens whooping and dancing," said Willa Carlisle, her bluish face a plaster of righteous indignation and bitterness. "The concoction did put new life into the injured. They frothed at the gills and itched for more fighting."

The prosecution then produced Metacom's widow. Confined to a box of bars on small wheels for her own protection until the trial's end, Wootonekanuske was rolled into the courtroom/storehouse. Starved beasts in cages knew a more humane fate. King Philip's wife was a mound of suppurating wounds from repeated beatings and defilements. A soldier had caved in the left side of her face. Someone had crushed her legs and torn out her hair. The chief prosecutor showed her nothing but scorn.

"Tell this court, bitch, of Blue Devil's magic."

Through the bars of her wagon, Wootonekanuske addressed the audience mechanically, a guest to her own words. "She know the wind come."

"You refer to the hurricane of last year. What exactly did she predict?"

"She say storm smash Coatmen house and killem many."

"How long before the storm did she say this?"

"Many days."

"And that devil of a husband of yours, did he or did he not foreswear the attack of those towns in the storm's path?"

"*Nye.*" Yes.

"Why?"

"Sachem say Blue Jay the devil," she mumbled by rote.

When it came the accused's turn to take the witness box, a mortuary silence fell over the storehouse. An English journalist sent from London to cover the trial tried to describe the defendant to his English readership (with a ten-day lag): "This particular devil is quite comely. They say that she is full Indian, yet her English countenance maketh sunlight of a dreary dress. Difficult it is to detect evil in such maidenhood. The audience's mixed feelings of vengeance and uncertainty is expressed in a collective stirring of discomfort."

The chief prosecutor ordered the accused to answer the charges brought against her. "Do you admit to a covenant with Satan?"

"Based on what? That I used plants to ease suffering? Those plants are of this world, not another."

"And is it also natural to predict the weather, witch?"

"If you, sir, took the time to observe the wind and animals, you too would know whence comes the storm."

"Yet you chose to call yourself 'Blue Devil'."

"I admit this, but I was a cheap imitation. The real devil is so much more cunning and destructive."

"Then you *do* admit to a covenant with Satan!"

"No. But I met the devil many times in Puritan Neespaugot."

The courtroom stirred, and anxiety rippled through the dense crowd outside the storehouse, traveling like wind over tall grass. The examining prosecutor could barely contain his sense of triumph. "So tell this court of these meetings with the Beguiler."

"Well, let me see… It started with my first menses. Satan saw my bleeding and shoved me behind the church where he warned me that blood, holy inside the body, becomes excrement once released. And, on another occasion, Satan scolded me for not wearing enough clothing. He said that my body was a church to the spirit but despicable to look upon unclothed and must be trussed up like a corpse."

"Do you mock this court?"

"I merely answer your question, sir. Satan, working through men like you, taught me to fear chaos and worship control, to fear God and create devils with every new temptation to the spirit. Those were the lessons of my youth spent in Puritan Neespaugot. I learned early on that Satan is unnecessary when a society such as yours is so gifted at creating hell."

The court exploded in outrage. One councilman could be heard screaming for the accused's head. Minister Eliot clamored to be heard.

"Quiet! Hear me now, good brethren. This young Algonquian is rash, but she speaketh truly. The late war did not happen without the approval of God. Why would the Good Lord bring such death and destruction to our doorstep, if not to punish us for our sins and excesses? If we hang this girl for reminding us of our failings before the Lord, are we to hang many of our finest preachers who are at this moment making similar discourse in the colonies?"

A lynching was averted. Deliberation began. A committee of magistrates, clergy, politicians and merchants gathered in a back room of the makeshift courthouse, rife with the odor of onions and fresh lumber, to debate Melba's fate.

"She was eviler than the demon Philip," argued a magistrate. "She made war against the whole world of God. *Salva republica*, she must be adjudged to die."

He was joined by a clergyman who cited Psalms 137:8-9: "'O daughter of Babylon, who art to be destroyed.' I too vote for her public execution."

The merchants and politicians feared killing her "lest it serve to unite the heathen under her martyrdom."

"No treaty," reminded Cotton Finley, the owner of a small shipping operation in Neespaugot, "has yet been signed with the Abenaki Indians, and hostilities are ongoing in the north and the northwest. I think I speak for my fellow merchants when I say that a public hanging would be bad for business. Cannot we simply decide to ship her from the colonies, into foreign slavery?"

"But she is the Blue Devil!" protested a clergyman.

"If she is a devil," said Cotton Finley, "then killing her will simply send her home to the evil brew that spawned her. 'Twould be a far greater punishment to ship her to a hell on earth and there leave her to rot."

The trial reconvened, and Melba was ordered to rise. She expected a verdict of death, and she welcomed it. Her family members were dead, her nation exterminated, and it was clear that the colonists would not be happy until every dusky face was erased from New England. The chief judge perfunctorily pronounced her guilty, then, clearly disgusted by what he was about to say, delivered her sentence through gritted teeth: "It is the decision of this court that you be shipped from these colonies to a faraway bondage where earthly darkness shall be your punishment."

The public roared its disapproval, and Melba felt her legs give out and braced herself against the rail. By chaining her to some foreign rock, they were condemning her soul to *jeebicornug*, the Great Emptiness. She tried to usher forth a protest, but both of her languages failed her. So she leapt from her chair and ran at a soldier to incite him to stab her. Instead, he dropped her with the butt of his musket.

Wrote the London journalist: "Today, Melba Blue Jay was chained to one hundred eighty other heathen malefactors—men, women and children—and marched to the Neespaugot docks where a slave ship bound for the West Indies awaited. An ironic circle was closing, for back in 1620, the native peoples had welcomed the passengers of a boat named the Mayflower. Fifty-six years later, a slave ship called the Seaflower lifted its sails and departed Neespaugot stuffed to the bulwarks with deported Indians."

Clarisse

August 22, 1697

1

Her seventh and last client of the day wanted it fast and missionary. The sweaty brute made no effort to spare her his crushing weight as he ramrodded his cock into her raw and tired loins. She kept the pain to herself. No customer was ever going to derive that satisfaction from her. Mercifully, this one was quickly spent and pulled out with the same crudity as he'd gone in. As he stood to draw up his breeches, she wondered how the man made his money. His leather doublet and shirt were of good quality. The sea had tanned him like a boot, but he smelled neither of fish nor rum. And, he could afford her. Villa La Seine was the most lavish brothel in Cap-Français. The Villa, a French colonial private hotel on the Caribbean waterfront, offered a stable of fifteen handpicked prostitutes (including two boys) receiving customers in clean silk sheets, Parisian lingerie and perfume. After twenty years in the profession, Clarisse lay, as it were, atop the pecking order, in a third-floor room down the hall from the boss himself, Monsieur Jean.

"*Ce n'est pas toujours qu'on culbute une blanche sur cette isle de negre,*" said the man on his way out. *It's rare to fuck a white woman on a nigger island,* is what he had said. And then it hit her, his line of work: he was in the cruelty business, a slave runner just into Saint-Domingue with a load of chattel.

Clarisse's bedroom went dark. She lit a candle and dragged a chair and a basin of soapy water onto the balcony. Dusk was falling across the harbor, the setting light imbuing the ships, water and rooftop tiles with a luminescence that seemed self-generating, like the candle burning inside the room. As she squatted over the basin bathing her sex, she cast an eye down the long porch. Monsieur Jean's French windows were open, and the light breeze was stirring his drapes. "It's almost time," she muttered to herself.

She slid the chair under her bottom and paid herself the rare luxury of scrutinizing the waterfront. Normally, she couldn't bear the sight of ships offloading their human cargo and reloading stores of sugar, tobacco and indigo. The process was too depressing, too much a reminder of her lost world, annihilated culture and enslavement. But this night, the waterfront provided a semblance of hope in the form of a ship, the *Roi Louis*, moored at Pier Three, where its sailors were loading crates of distilled sugar for imminent departure, just as Monsieur Jean had promised.

Two decades had passed since she was dragged onto that miserable malarial island, stripped, beaten and herded with other slaves to the auction block where an infestation of loud lewd men had amassed like jellyfish, white and stinging. Two men with a mutual dislike for each other became locked in a bidding war for her, until the astronomical sum of eight hundred Louis d'Or brought both men back to earth. The competitors struck a deal and purchased her as a joint venture—the slave of double owners, a half-slave to each. The French colony's *notaire* drafted the deed and officially changed her name to Clarisse. Whereupon she had been tossed in the back of a wagon and transported along rugged trails into the island backcountry. The driver took pleasure in whipping the mules and making the ride unbearable for her and the three naked Africans to whom she was chained. Every bump and bend sent them careening across the splintery floorboards and ramming into the side planks. Their backsides were raw, peppered by splinters and plagued by mosquitoes. Despite the discomfort, one of the Africans showed an erection.

The wagon had trundled onto the grounds of a sugar plantation and stopped at the slave compound. A white man the size of a bear snapped his lash and growled, *"Degagez!"* When they didn't move fast enough for his liking, he seized their chains in one of his enormous paws and yanked the four of them from the wagon. He whipped them to the slave hut where a stocky, yellow-eyed African woman waited in the doorway. She handed Clarisse a sack with armholes, then slapped her in the face so hard that Clarisse would feel it for days.

The white giant dragged Clarisse across the compound to a barn where a suspended oil lamp illuminated four stakes driven into the ground, with ropes snaking away from each. The giant's unwashed face broke into a lascivious grin of missing teeth. She understood what was to happen and struck first, aiming a knee at his crotch. She missed. His hot smelly laugh washed over her, before he punched her in the ribs and kicked her legs out from under her. His meaty hands locked around her throat, choking her to the verge of unconsciousness before releasing her and tying her limbs to the stakes.

"*Elle est prêt,*" he called over his shoulder and moved away. *She's ready.*

Out of the shadows stepped her co-owner, the puny one with a mop of greasy hair dangling like swamp vegetation over a rough-pocked face. His mouth was a cavity of missing and rotting teeth, his expression a cesspool of foul intentions. She would learn later that his name was Veucq and that he, like the wild hogs of that island, was born on Hispaniola, the son of a French pirate and a captured Spanish woman. When Veucq was a boy, his father was hanged by the Spanish, just after killing his mother for who knows what reason. All that Veucq remembered was his father's method of punishment, one that Clarisse would see employed on uncooperative slaves. "What he did was he stuffed her alive in a barrel studded with spikes and rolled her down the hillside." Unlike his pirating father, Veucq possessed a sedentary disposition and some very good luck; in 1659, Spain ceded Saint-Domingue to France, and Louis XIV wanted sugar and tobacco farmers.

Dazed by her beating, Clarisse couldn't defend herself, and when Veucq grabbed her by the hair and smacked her head against the earth she feared he would dislodge her grandfather's coin, which she had embroidered with tresses and had smeared with her own feces. Veuqc stepped between her legs, unbuckled his breeches and let them drop into a pool around his boots. His shirt hung to his knobby knees, and he lifted it to expose a puny bloodless appendage, which he then aimed at her belly. And he urinated on her. It wasn't a rape but a defilement.

The next day, she was put to work in the boiling house, stoking the furnaces and feeding sugarcane into kettles. There were four furnaces, each with seven kettles, each one smaller and hotter than the one before it. She had to skim and channel the juice from the largest kettle to the last one, called the *teache*, where the cane became syrup to be poured into a cooling trough, where it crystallized and could be shoveled into barrels called hogsheads. Then it was shipped as raw sugar or rum to New England and Europe for manufactured goods to be taken to Africa. There, the goods were bartered for slaves who were thrown into the disease-infested bowels of ships and transported to the colonies for more sugar and rum—a monstrously effective, financially sound cycle of cruelty.

The temperature inside the boiling house hovered at one hundred degrees, and the slaves who worked there were given two short water breaks in fourteen hours of labor. Her first weeks on the plantation, Clarisse had passed out several times a day. She would come to, lying in the dirt like a dog. At night she slept on a mat with forty-five other slaves in a cabin smaller than a typical Wampanoag family wigwam. The head slave was a woman, Kula, the Ivorian who had slapped her. She whipped all of them with a switch and decided who ate and in what portions. Kula had two jobs: emotionally emasculate the African men (tyrannized by a woman, the men became listless, more phantoms than men) and torture Clarisse. Veucq despised the fact that Clarisse could escape his control two weeks a month, and he made her pay upon her return. He had Kula whip her with redoubled gusto. "Let that whoremonger dress you up all he wants," said Veucq. "Here, you aren't worth the dirt you're standing on."

Joint ownership was all that had stood between her and greater bodily injury or death.

Clarisse's official introduction to her second slavemaster had proceeded in much the same way as with Veuqc. Four henchmen had fetched her off the plantation and carted her back to the port where they had jostled her into a courtyard behind Villa La Seine brothel and into a windowless storage room lit by burning flambeaux. They chained her to a bench by her wrists and ankles and waited. Finally, a tall vulture-like man walked in and bowed gallantly. "Jean Rastignac at your service," he said. Then, he lifted her sack dress and began poking around her sex. Apparently pleased by what he found, he explained what he was about to do. "Understand, *c'est pour ton bien*, Clarisse, for your own good." Without emotion, he freed his sex and aroused himself while still speaking clinically. "You must never take pleasure in this, *ma cherie*. It's a job. You'll need to get off on the right foot, *demarrer comme il faut*."

He mounted her. She spat in his face. Without anger, he wiped the spittle from his bony chin. "I will remove the pleasure, so that you can protect yourself, Clarisse. One day you will thank me, *tu veras*." With that, he shoved himself inside her and shot a look at his men as if he had just discovered gold. *"C'est incroyable! Elle est vierge!"* A virgin! He couldn't get over it. "I can charge triple, quadruple…" But he changed his mind. *"Non, je vais me payer ça.* I think I deserve it." With that, he dashed her hymen. *"Retournez-la,"* he ordered his men, who flipped her over on her stomach. Then, he sodomized her.

She was taken to the first floor, to a large communal bath, and thrown in a wood tub of twice-used bathwater and scrubbed from head to toe. While cleansing her hair, one of the men discovered the coin. She tried to fight him off, but he held her head under water until she gave up the struggle. As she gagged and vomited over the edge of the tub, her owner was summoned. The vulturine Rastignac reach into her hair and yanked the coin out, along with a fistful of her hair. He cut the strands from the coin, rinsed it in the tub water and read aloud its inscription: *Sigillvm Gvb Et Societ De Mattachvsets Bay In Nova Anglia. Come over and help us.* The engraving of the naked Indian amused him and his men. Then, to her surprise, Rastignac handed the coin back to her. "Keep it. Whatever it is, you just do your job and I'll leave you in peace."

Jean Rastignac always seemed to her more suited to the salons of Paris than to Caribbean prostitution. He dressed impeccably and was clean and cultured. But his looks were deceiving. At the end of her first week in Villa La Seine, Clarisse had witnessed him plunge a dagger in a customer's neck for credit default. *"On n'est pas une banque ici, monsieur,"* he explained rather superfluously to the dying man. *We're not a bank here, sir.* Then he cleaned his blade on the man's breeches.

For the past twenty years of her life, Clarisse had followed the same routine: two weeks slaving on the plantation, two weeks whoring in the brothel. Filthy as a harbor rat, she would arrive at the brothel, be bathed like a queen, then dirty herself figuratively between silk sheets. Two weeks later, she would throw the cane sack over her head and sully herself (and the coin) in fish slops and mud for her return to the plantation. Coming or going, the one given in her routine was that she was perpetually dirty.

She had known pregnancy nine times in those twenty years—four times with success, none wanted. By dint of a simple coin toss, Veucq had acquired the rights to the first male and female offspring. Rastignac didn't care. To him, children were an unfortunate accident of the trade. "Children are elephants," he said. "Elephants take years to grow up and be productive. If that execrable little sugar fucker sees a long-term business plan in elephants, so be it. For me, a knocked-up whore is an unproductive whore, and you will take every precaution to avoid that state, am I clear?" He made her ingurgitate all manner of concoction, from catnip, savory, sage soapwort, cyperus and pennyroot to the so-called "prostitute root": worm fern mixed with crushed ants. She had done as much vomiting as fucking in Villa La Seine.

None of those remedies had stopped her first pregnancy at the age of nineteen. She had begged Rastignac to help her terminate her condition but he had refused. *"Pas de question, cherie!* You *must* have your elephant. Need I remind you that the same contract that insures Veucq's property rights also protects you on his plantation? If I meddle in the pregnancy, nothing prevents him from hurting you. Not to mention that I will owe him double, and if that happens, I swear that I shall take that Indian coin of yours faster than you can say Neespaugot, *compris?"*

At the plantation, she had bribed the African women with her meals, measly as they were, to squat on her belly, press their forearms into her abdomen and tighten ropes around her midsection to wring her like a husk. The techniques led to her vomiting and shitting blood but not to termination.

And so it was that on September 22, 1680, she gave birth on the plantation to her daughter Therese. Veucq refused to let the suckling leave the plantation, and Rastignac and the colony notary had to come out to threaten the sugar baron with a breach of contract. "What breach?" said Veucq. "Nothing is stopping *her* from leaving."

"A baby needs its mother's milk."

"I know nothing about what babies need, messieurs. All I know is that this baby's leaving is a question of liability. If Monsieur Rastignac is so concerned about the whelp's welfare, perhaps he should consider leaving the mother here with her child."

Three years later, Clarisse had a second child, a boy who by rights also belonged to Veucq. Five more years and two miscarriages passed before she gave Rastignac his first "elephant." He had thanked her by forcing her to fuck until the day her water broke. And Veucq, knowing the child had nothing to do with him, had kept her toiling away in the boiling house. But against all odds, she delivered a daughter on the fourth of March, 1688. The child was registered under the name Laurette Rastignac.

Her fourth and last child to date had been born prematurely, a boy with a stump for an arm, a club for a foot and a hole for a brain. Rastignac, bitter about his own worsening syphilis, named the hairless, shapeless pink creature Nero.

First-born Therese reached puberty a filiform, chestnut-haired cynosure whose beauty came to Rastignac's attention via his henchmen. One day, he himself came to fetch Clarisse from the plantation to see with his own eyes what all the fuss was about her daughter. He had to admit that he had been wrong about elephants. "I want the girl," he told Veucq. "Name your price." Veucq promised to consider the offer, and Clarisse knew that her daughter's days were numbered.

Back at the brothel, she had begged Rastignac to act within the hour. "You must go back and get her. You have no idea, Monsieur Jean, what Veucq will do to spite you."

Rastignac wasn't buying it. "You exaggerate, Clarisse. Why would he harm her? Veucq loves his money more than he hates me."

Two weeks later, Clarisse returned to the plantation and couldn't find her daughter. Frantic, she ran from hut to hut until she found her eleven-year-old son Charles. Sobbing, the boy told her that his sister was dead. Veucq had strangled her in the slave hut in front of him. Clarisse spotted him crossing the compound and tore after him. She sank her nails into his face. The giant ran to his screaming master's defense, pulled her off and pounded her. A blow to her head sprang loose her grandfather's coin. The giant released his grip on her and picked up the coin. "*O! La salope a de l'argent!*" The bitch has money. Veucq wiped the blood off his face and had a look at the object. "Worthless," he said, handing the coin back to the giant and spitting on Clarisse. "Killing your little bitch cost me several thousand *sous*, but it was worth every penny. Fuck Rastignac!" The giant laughed and stuck her coin in his pocket.

Nightfall settled over the waterfront, and the lightkeepers lit the port lamps. Out at the shoals, the lighthouse sprang to life with flame. Clarisse gave a look over the rail before emptying the basin into the square. The water hit the cobblestones with a loud splat. She stepped back inside her room and grabbed a jug of rosewater.

Rastignac saw only three people now: his *notaire*, his doctor and her. She tapped lightly on the open door and entered without waiting for an invitation. He lay in bed, hidden from view by a silk netting protecting him from flies. She parted the netting and was briefly overcome by the stench. His face was devoured by syphilis. His hands, reposing on his chest, made mounds of suppurating sores. He looked three-months buried and decomposed. She poured the rosewater on a cloth, dabbed at his face and neck to cool and ease his suffering, picked up the fan on the escritoire and waved away the heat.

"A just end for a pimp," he croaked.

True, it was a fitting demise for a hard, treacherous, murderous procurer. But Monsieur Jean had also proved himself decent enough to Laurette and Nero, and he had given her certain liberties, condoning visits into town to meet with whomever she wished; he didn't care if she was earning money on the side as long as she was capable of performing her task at the brothel. Monsieur Jean had even taught her and the children French and had discussed the philosophies and sciences of the Enlightenment with her.

"All is arranged?" he asked, groaning.

"*Oui*, Monsieur Jean."

"I want the three of you on that boat, Clarisse."

"The *four* of us," she said, rinsing the cloth.

"We have been through this, Clarisse. I can do nothing for Charles. He is Veucq's property."

"No, he is my son and I shall not leave him there."

With the pluck that defined his existence, Rastignac found the strength to tighten his grip around her wrist. "Madame, I give you the best chance you will ever have of leaving this island and saving at least two of your children. Do not compromise that."

She left the wet cloth on his forehead and closed the screen.

Downstairs, two of Rastignac's men came to fetch her chest, while two others accompanied the children. Rastignac had left nothing to chance—his men were jailors as much as bodyguards. They led the family down the candlelit boardwalk to the ship, up the gangplank and to their quarters, and locked them inside. A moment later, another key could be heard turning in the door, unlocking it. Time would be short from there on out, and she did her best to explain the situation quickly to nine-year-old Laurette. "You will stay here with Nero and await my return. Men have been paid to protect you. Keep your brother safe. I will be back, *nerternees*."

She opened the door, leaned her head into the corridor and found the coast clear. She slipped out, locking the door behind her and sneaked off the boat. As per her instructions, a horse with saddlebag was waiting for her behind the livery. She mounted the steed and raced out of town, taking the backroad into the black jungle.

Within sight of the compound, she dismounted, opened the saddlebag and removed two daggers sharpened to a whisper. She also had some beetroot, bootblack and spare clothing in the event she made it back alive to the ship. She ripped off her sleeves and petticoats and painted her face. Twenty years after disappearing, Blue Devil was back.

She sneaked onto the plantation and hid behind a copse of hardwood near the slave drivers' outhouse. The giant's digestion had never been a hard read. He lived on rum, poorly cooked pork and maggot-filled cheese; his exercise, apart from crushing the bones of slaves, was waddling several times a night to the outhouse, carrying a bucket of lime in one hand and a bushel of shucks to wipe his ass in the other. The moon had long since reached heaven's summit when she spotted his broad and baleful silhouette rising twenty-five yards up-compound, hauling bucket and shuck. As he passed, she leapt out and shanked the first knife into his lower back to bring him down to size. The second blade slit his throat. He whirled and flailed but could not make a sound and collapsed shuddering in the dirt until he bled out. She lifted her grandfather's coin from around his bull neck. Then, she cut off his head.

She burst into the slave hut, painted in gore, the giant's severed head in one hand, the two knives in the other. Such was her state that her own son did not recognize her. "Go!" she shouted at the slaves. "Seek your vengeance!" Kula, the head slave, had been dead now some eight months, and the slaves had no real leader to approve or disapprove. As the slaves bolted from the shanty toward the slave drivers' quarters, she spoke to her son. "You are thirteen, Charles. You are a man. You must leave the compound alone. Follow the road and you will see my horse. Wait there for me until the moon is over the valley. If I am not back by then, go to the ship we spoke about and find your brother and sister and sail to the French land and take care of them, especially Nero who cannot tend to himself."

"What about you, Mama?"

"I have some unfinished business to see to."

Veucq's *poteaux-en-terre* villa was situated at the north end of the compound, its lamps still burning on the porch and in the parlor, where the foul wretch sat swigging alone at a long table strewn with empty bottles of all shapes and sizes. She sent the foreman's gory head bowling down the length of the table, knocking over bottles left and right. Startled, Veucq tipped backward in his chair and fell. Before he could recover, she had bounded onto the table, a knife in each hand. He bounced up like a flea, shaking and screaming for help. She called his attention to the window, where the vermilion glow of flames was just then topping the magnolia and hardwood trees. He held up his hands in surrender.

"Okay, you win. *Laisse moi te liberer*," he said. "I will free you."

"Get my son's papers."

"*Bien sur, bien sur.*"

He opened a chest and pulled out a pistol.

"*Tu vois, eh, Clarisse!* Now, we are even, eh?"

"There is no Clarisse, *wonnux* scum. I am Melba Blue Jay."

She flew at him and drove a knife into his ear with such rage that its point came out through the opposite ear and she could not extract it. She had to leave it imbedded in his head as she decapitated him with her other knife. She mounted Veucq's and the foreman's heads on stanchions and set them upright in the yard. Now, neither of their worthless souls would be making the voyage to the afterlife. Then she set the villa aflame and went to join her children.

2

As arranged, Monsieur Jean's brother, Guy-Pierre Rastignac, was there to meet Melba and her children when they disembarked in New France. The man standing at the base of the ramp could not have been more different from the dapper vulturine pimp. Guy-Pierre was a trapper, short and stout, covered in whiskers and clothed in offal-stained buckskin. He stank of ale and, being a nervy sort, swore at everything, with a *putain* (fucker) this and *putain* that. However, he did resemble his older brother in one respect: he was unsentimental. "I'm not doing any of this out of the goodness of my heart," he warned Melba, loading her trunk into his buckboard, next to a slain bull elk, the blood in its nostrils not yet congealed. "That is to say, if my brother hadn't paid me good money… You must be one hell of a—" She shot him a murderous look, and he didn't dare finish his sentence.

They headed out of Ville-Marie north to Hochelaga, once a Saint Lawrence Iroquois village, where Guy-Pierre lived a reclusive existence in the company of rusty bear traps, muskets and band saws. He pointed out his porchless house in a glade, before carting them deeper into a densely packed wood and stopping before an abandoned cabin on stilts missing a good portion of its roof. The front door, riddled with holes, hung by hemp like a gate. "This cabin's not much," he said. "And you might need to run out some raccoons, but you do have yourselves half an acre of land, if you can make something of it." He dragged the trunk out of the wagon bed and moved it from the dirt road, before making his pitch. "You might need some help, madame, and I might even be willing to offer some, in exchange for you being"—the cheeks above his sprouting whiskers blushed—"nice to me in a woman's way, if you see my meaning." Melba pulled a knife on him. "Whoa, there!" he said, recoiling. "We do what we do, bartering, and I just thought—"

"Thought what *exactement*, monsieur?"

"*Bien*," he said by way of an apology, grabbing hold of his slain elk by its antlers and tugging it out of the wagon, "It's yours. Killed only a few hours ago." He climbed back up onto his buckboard. "Just make sure you gut it downwind because of bears and wolves."

She tossed him a piece of silver. "If you want to show good faith, monsieur, bring me some supplies. We'll need a band saw, hammers, nails, rope, some empty barrels, a sack of salt, a broom and some skins to sleep on."

"GYAH!" he shouted, striking the horse to action.

"Where's the nearest fresh water?" she yelled.

"Over there, about thirty yards," he shouted back, riding away.

The first chill off the Saint Lawrence River made the children ill, but by then they had a roof, a proper door, caulked walls, barrels of dried berries, hard apples and a stone kiln full of smoking meats. Melba relieved their aches and pains with crushed antler velvet.

Spring brought the constant crack of ax to wood, the creak and crash of falling trees, the singing of band saws, the sloshing of wagon wheels, the raw barking of carpenters come to the wood for the material to build Ville-Marie's houses and missions. To get her own lay of the land, Melba ventured into town.

The townspeople were mystified by the sight of a single white woman with three dissimilar charges in tow, the one a swarthy Spanish boy, the second an Indian girl and the third a hairless retarded runt. The woman was both refined yet able to hunt, skin and fix a roof. Some in town believed she was a widowed *bourgeoise,* undoubtedly the wife of a disgraced Huguenot. Others were convinced she was a high-class criminal or political *intrigante* exiled to the New World by Louis XIV. The mission priest convinced her to send the older boy and the girl to his Jesuit school—he in a white class, she in a female indigene class.

The following year, at age fifteen, Charles quit the French missionary school and became an apprentice trapper under the tutelage of Guy-Pierre Rastignac. Two years later, the two of them set out with their traps west into Mohawk country. Neither was heard from again. After thirty-six months of daily agonizing, Melba fetched everything of use from Guy-Pierre's cabin and then nailed it shut like a coffin.

Daughter Laurette remained at the mission school. The priest spoke of an *élan sacre*, a blessed energy, regarding Melba's dusky daughter. It was true that, back on the island, Laurette had been a sickly and listless child, but in Canada she had become a robust young woman, her small black eyes charged with a stubborn goodwill. A head shorter than her mother and of stout ill-fitting limbs, Laurette spoke tough and was tougher than she spoke, doing most of the chores, making the meals, hunting, fishing and caring for Nero. Laurette became a teacher at the missionary, lecturing children both white and brown in a stone-and-timber room alongside the church refectory. She wore a stiff dress, tied her Indian hair into a bun and was adamant about not leaving Ville-Marie. "*Maman,* you must give up this idea of a return to Neespaugot. I won't go, and Nero would never survive the passage."

That much was true. Outfitted in oversized settler clothing, Nero danced in the meadows like a one-legged bear cub, happy to be happy without knowing or caring why. Melba sometimes wished she could know such mindless peace. She had turned forty-one at the turn of the century, and with each passing year the ache of homesickness had only grown stronger. To free her spirit of such torment, she made repeated retreats into the wilderness to meditate. It helped but never lasted. She was in many ways still a slave, shackled to the single-minded goal of taking back what the white man had snatched from her people. Her grandfather's coin was a nagging reminder of unfinished business, and sometimes she thought of throwing it in the Saint Lawrence River.

Nonetheless, she knew that one day she would attempt a homecoming, and she kept up her health and strength for that day of reckoning by cleaning her teeth three times a day with stream silt and wintergreen, preserving her back and sitting out her menstrual cycles.

One fitful night, Melba woke up trying to snatch a fleeting dream of Neespaugot. Laurette was lying uncovered on her pallet bed, a tangle of hair and bunched limbs. Nero's prune-like head lolled from side to side, his misshapen mouth a gaping tragedy. Melba rose and covered herself with a fur, lifted the latch and stepped onto the porch. Above the high rising forest, millions of celestial fires burned in the arching night. The dark fields were radiant with glowing insects and the eyes of rodents. Winged predators made darting letters against the clear night. The cry of a hawk, the screech of an owl, the whistling of a jay. The cool air dried her sweat. She shook her moccasins for bugs and put them on.

As she was stepping off the porch, she spotted something moving, an animal awesome in size yet indistinct, certainly of canid origins but too big to be a fox, coyote or even a wolf. It bolted behind the woodshed and made a branch-cracking retreat back into the forest. Melba gave chase, whistling three times. It had left an odor: the smell of a man's cologne.

When she got back, Laurette was standing in the cabin door, holding a rifle.

"Was it digging in the vegetable garden again? One of these nights, I will get off a clean shot and blast it dead."

Melba smiled at the irony. Her dark little Wampanoag daughter made the perfect picture of a proud Coatman. Laurette was a deadly shooter with scant regard for the spirit of what she blasted. She had renounced all native and English words, choosing to speak French only. She was a pious Christian and a devout churchgoer, and she feared nature like a Puritan.

The next morning the animal did indeed make a clear target in Laurette's sight. Melba barely had the time to tip the barrel before the blast reported across the land and into the woods. The creature froze, met their stares and scampered off.

Disappointed, her daughter lowered the gun.

"Why did you do that, *Maman*? I had it dead to rights."

"Have you ever seen anything so majestic? It was blue."

"Who knows if I will get a better chance at a shot?"

"A magnificent blue beast," Melba thought aloud. She went into the cabin and returned with some provisions and a knife. Laurette was confused.

"You cannot kill a monster like that with a knife, *Maman*."

"I'm not going to kill it, Laurette. I'm going to talk to it."

She patted her daughter's cheek and set out.

The animal wasn't hard to track. It meandered through woods and meadows, leaving a twitter of prairie moths hovering a foot off the high grasses and thistles. Melba followed it down into a dale where it stopped to look at her, as if to make sure she was keeping up. It was then that Melba understood that she wasn't tracking it; the creature was in control, and it had fetched her for a purpose.

Its brindled coat shone blue in the dew and sunlight. It traveled with a timber wolf's elegant gait, but this was a dog the size of a deer, three feet at the shoulder, gangly, barrel-chested, shaggy and a hundred and fifty pounds of muscle. Its snout was as pointed as a pike's. Like Melba, the creature had been imported from some faraway place.

The animal wended into a valley that the Iroquois called *Mishian*, or Little Rain, and disappeared behind a spurt of hemlock and dogwood trees. Melba smelled smoke. A hundred yards on, she found the dog lying on a man's cape beside a campfire. It eyed her with a certain detachment before reposing its massive head on the cape and ignoring her altogether. At that moment, another exotic creature appeared from behind some nearby bushes, still pulling up his violet breeches. Visibly embarrassed, he dragged a bum foot over to Melba.

"Madame, I am chagrined by the timing. Nonetheless, your presence honors me. Moot Court, at your service," he bowed.

Genteel manners notwithstanding, the man was a dark-skinned Indian wearing a silver wig. Middle-aged, handsome and tall even without the red high heels on his feet, he sported a leather jerkin, silk cravat and stained vanilla leotards under his knee-breeches, which he finally managed to clasp. A black-and-white handkerchief overflowed a small chest pocket in his threadbare vest. He finished limping to the fire and lowered himself with some difficulty onto a large log. "I twisted my ankle," he said and smiled, stating the obvious.

"This land is not much suited to high heels," she said.

He laughed. "A point well-taken, madame. These heels are *de rigueur* at the court of Louis XIV but of little use in this rugged place. I'm afraid that I had nothing else to put on my feet. I'm no hunter. No gatherer, either. I wouldn't know a snakeroot from skunk cabbage. Alas, I have forgotten how to be an Indian."

"If you stay out here, the wolves will teach you fast enough."

"Oh, I doubt that, my good lady. You see, I am most fortunate to have Monsieur Bleu there." He glanced affectionately at the resting dog. "This hairy fellow is both cherished companion and faithful protector. He has been shot, stabbed, lanced and whipped. He has tangled with Asian tigers, fought a clan of Steppe wolves, been mauled by a brown bear, bitten by a cobra and sent flying by a bull elephant. He has more lives than a litter of rats."

"Well, you almost lost him at my place. My daughter shoots straight. What sort of dog is he?"

"*O, la!* The king of hounds! The most complete combination of wiliness, feistiness, meanness, grit and perseverance ever assembled in a canine. Part Arabian stallion, part Siberian tiger, and bred and trained to outfight the formidable tundra wolf. Why, old Monsieur Bleu is none other than a cross between the Russian wolfhound and the German Leon Berg. He has been with me in my travels across three continents and countless countries."

Later that morning, Melba hiked back to the cabin, hitched Guy-Pierre's horse to his wagon and, by the end of the afternoon, had carted Mr. Court and Monsieur Bleu back to the defunct trapper's house, where the guests would stay for several weeks while the man's ankle healed.

During the convalescence, Melba made twice-daily visits to Guy-Pierre's cabin. She soon learned that the incongruous Mr. Court was indeed a hunter of sorts—his focus was on one game alone: women. He was a fifty-eight-year-old Mohegan philanderer with a penchant for contracting pneumonia and hookworm, who had spent a good two-thirds of his life in Asia and Europe, mostly in France where the Sun King had invited him to Versailles on four different occasions. Had she read Moliere? Racine? They were friends of his.

Melba wasn't dupe to his tricks. But as philanderers went, he wasn't so bad. His spirit was positive; his charm, wit and verve, infectious. By and large, he broke down her resistance to men and sex, and she surrendered herself to him one night out of doors, where they had made camp a few miles from the trapper's cabin. He freed her of her trappings and lay with her naked on a bedding of pelts. The dandy proved himself more than just talk. He tasted her the way certain guests of Jean Rastignac had sipped special wines: slowly constructing delight rather than overindulging in it. He probed her parts like a scientist after proof and, locating it, played it like a musician his cords, coaxing music and release. When she could no longer hold on, she sang out the notes of joy for the first time in her life. A lasso of thrushes whipped above the plain.

He lay back, panting, and spoke to the bright firmament. "I knew it!" he said. "Until a moment ago, you, madame, were a virgin!"

She laughed. He was right. She was a forty-two-year-old virgin. She had never made love before. Moot got on an elbow to look at her. He fingered her coin, tried to make out its design in the weak flickering light of the campfire, before setting it back between her breasts. "It seems to me," he said, "that after such a—how to put it—*earnest* orgasm, you might be prevailed upon—without my pushing you, of course—to release some of your darker secrets?"

Melba spoke of her childhood in Neespaugot, of growing up an outcast to both Puritan and native societies. She spoke of her grandfather and what they'd done to him and how she'd fought against them and the punishment they had exacted. Of toiling in the boiling house. Of reading *Dom Juan* between doing customers in the whorehouse. Of the murder of her firstborn and of the rage that had no outlet. "I killed him." She said it so softly it came out as a whisper. "I killed him," she repeated more forcefully. "I killed him!" She began to weep.

The dog brought them a rabbit, and Melba skinned and cooked it, and they ate it. Over the howl of wolves and Monsieur Bleu's cracking of brittle bones in his powerful champing jaws, Moot conversed:

"Madame, you have a lot in common with Monsieur Bleu. He too has lived a dog's life, but look at him now. At one with himself, eh?" His levity brought a smile to her countenance. "*Le voila!* Such gaiety stirs me anew."

He eased her back on her rump and climbed between her thighs and inserted himself in her loins. "There is no amount of pain that cannot be put right with a little love and affection, *n'est-ce pas?*"

Her moaning sent the dog seeking quieter pastures.

As sunrise stretched across the plain, the aging dandy was still chirping.

"We are an odd pairing, eh? An old Injun Frenchie dressed like a Versailles vizier, and a lady of distinction wearing skins. I believe we are much like that coin of yours. There are not ten such as us, madame."

On the walk back, Melba was worried for him. "You are on the run, are you not, Moot? That is why you had no shoes, only heels, the first time I saw you."

"You are a keen observer, madame."

"What did you do?"

"It is ever the same crime with me."

"An angry husband?"

"Several angry husbands, I fear. A trifling matter among the great crimes of the world, but man is wolf to man, and so I am pursued."

"Stay with us, Moot. I'll protect you."

"Your invitation warms the cockles of my heart, my dear, but I cannot. I was born to move and should I stop, I shall surely die."

"Should they catch you in the wilderness, you'll surely die."

"Madame," he said with profound emotion, "being killed and dying are not at all the same thing."

The following week, Melba found the cabin vacated save for a note left on his pallet bed:

Madame, you have given me some of the very sweetest moments of my existence. I know that I am but a long-winded old dandy, but I hope you will give some consideration to what I should care to impart to you. Life, my dearest Melba, is a great weather report, full of highs and lows. I would like to believe that your depression has run its course, replaced by fair weather. Pray remember, whenever your spirit flags, a phrase of Mr. Bacon in his Novum Organum: *"They are ill discoverers that think there is no land, when they can see nothing but sea."*

Several mornings later, Monsieur Bleu dragged his useless hindquarters onto the porch, the bullet wounds in his hide oozing infection. A chewed-off noose dangled around his neck.

Melba spent the better part of the morning tweezing buckshot out of the animal's flesh. She applied compresses of vine water, pinkroot and pipsissewa, and prepared him a stew of thorn apple and dormouse. The next morning, supplied with a gourd, hardtack, her buck knife and a bow and arrows, Melba set off into the wilderness in search of Monsieur Bleu's master.

It took her four days to find the body. It might have taken her longer had it not been for the rounds of buzzards and the trail of stench. His killers had strung him up like her grandfather, in this case to the branch of a shagbark hickory. His putrefying corpse was black with flies. They had sheared his clothes and cut off his testicles and penis and nailed the package to the tree trunk.

On the same branch dangled a second rope, tooth-cut, drawing into relief what was missing, the non-execution, the hanging of empty space, freedom. Melba wanted to believe that, before he died, Moot Court had lived the final satisfaction of seeing the dog with more lives than a litter of rats, biting its way to breath and life.

Melba cut down the corpse and buried it under a barrow of stones. Then she went home.

The great beast—half stallion, half tiger, that nothing could kill—regained the use of its back legs. It slept on the porch, watchful for whatever ill will might be blown against their door. One night Monsieur Bleu bloodied a wolf. On another it chased away three intruders, almost chewing off the leg of one. Bears stopped foraging around the cabin. Drunken trappers seeking sex steered clear.

Nero took comfort in squatting beside the animal, petting him, calling him Misser Blue. The beast paid the eleven-year-old little mind, but neither did it discourage the daft darling's caresses.

Only once did the dog enter the cabin, when it heard Melba's dire screams. It pushed its muzzle through the door and regarded with rather more interest than usual the wriggling bloody infant whom Laurette was just then guiding from Melba's womb.

"Shoo, you!" said Laurette.

Melba raised her sweaty head off the mat.

"No, daughter, he can stay."

At the sound of her voice, the animal came to her side, sat and stared at her and the newborn.

"Monsieur Bleu, meet Moliere Court, your master's son. He requires your absolute devotion and protection. Can you do that?"

The dog's cold lupine regard seemed to relish the idea.

Mother and daughter finished loading their canoe. They had gourds of fresh water, a pannier of corn, beans, squash and sunflowers, a fishing spear, canisters of powder and lead, a musket, steels and flints, a bow and quiver, ropes, blankets, a sheet of oil linen for a tent or sail, and an oilskin bag containing maps and scribbled notes concerning their route. The smell of waterproofing— heated spruce resin and grease—mixed with the musk of the river.

Monsieur Bleu was already aboard, stretched out in the center of the canoe as Melba had trained him, taking up a third of all available space, his great pointy head higher than the bulwarks, surveying the shore. Melba climbed in and extended her arms for the baby. Laurette balked a last time.

"I don't understand this adventure, *Maman*. How will we hide from the English?"

"We won't hide, *nerternees*."

"The English will torture us and eat Moliere with their marmalade."

"Laurette, get in or go back, but give me the baby. Moliere at least will grow up in the place of my ancestors."

"That place no longer exists, *Maman*!"

Melba waited for the young woman to decide. Flustered and ill-humored, Laurette handed over the child, pushed the canoe off the bank and climbed in.

That past autumn, Nero had died while their mother was away preparing this insane journey. Laurette had shrouded her little brother in winding sheet and carried him, light as windlestraw, to a moosewood tree behind the cabin, where she buried him. She, alone, his preacher, congregation, family and undertaker.

To anyone watching from shore they made a strange sight, a white woman dressed in skins and a dark-skinned Indian habited in a starch calico dress from Rouen, France, paddling downriver with a giant dog and an infant. A multitude of ducks and geese took flight, filling the crepuscule with a deafening chatter. The clack and bray of elk and moose came through the morning mist. The baby, penned in by Monsieur Bleu and the supplies, tapped the dog's head and giggled with delight. Using the dog as a support, the child stood on unsure bowlegs and squealed at the herd of deer gathered along the shore. Melba handed him his toy, a small totem carved in wood, but he preferred to slap at the medal dangling from her neck.

"*Wemoo*," sang Melba to her child. My light. "Laurette, my spirit blooms. We are going to Neespaugot!"

Her disgruntled daughter made no response. Laurette had been dreading this voyage since she first heard her mother questioning trappers about the Champlain Valley. A southern route to the English colonies existed, the trappers had explained, but it meant paddling several hundred miles against the current, portaging between two river rises, and surviving encounters with wolves,

Mohawk Indians and the dreaded *Dark*, as the trappers called the deadly and unavoidable rapids on the downhill side of the Green Mountains.

"You heard them, *Maman*. It is foolhardy."

"I heard it was possible, Laurette."

The Saint Lawrence swept them along to the mouth of the Richelieu River, and the upstream battle commenced. The two women paddled until they could no longer feel their arms, so they got out and towed along the banks. They steered the canoe into a cove and made camp for the night, having covered only ten upstream miles.

They made twenty miles the following day. They beached along a bank so plentiful with coots that even the baby managed to touch one. That night the dog chased away a large but inoffensive bear.

The sparkling vista of Lake Champlain appeared at midday, and they battled the boils and swirls at the mouth of Lake Richelieu. The weather worsened. Melba sheltered the baby from the heavy spring downpour. Laurette was as glum as the horizon, for they were now in Mohawk country.

They paddled into a sheltered cove and prepared for another night. Conifer wood was plentiful but smoked too much, so they made do with small kindling. The air hung heavy with humidity and insects. Laurette gummed the baby with mud, then lit into her mother.

"I am so sick of this! What are we doing out here, tormented by mosquitoes and ticks? We are lousy, grimy and not fit to be seen by civilized folk. Why, *Maman*? Why did we have to leave? We had a life. You are selfish. *Oui, egoiste!*"

Melba fed the baby and rocked him to sleep. Only then did she answer her daughter's question.

"*I* am here, *nerternees,* because the spirit calls me home. Why are *you* here, my daughter?"

"Oh, you know why!"

"I do not. You could have stayed in Ville-Marie."

"You need me. Moliere needs me."

"I want you, yes. But I don't need you, darling. You are free. You can do as you please."

"Free to be alone. It's not that easy, *Maman.*"

"Of course it isn't, my sweet. Yet you seem to think it is easy for me to live without my homeland, my people and the customs I was born to. No, *nerternees,* it is anything but easy to wander the earth without an identity, to turn the other cheek while the Coatmen rub out your race and all trace of the Great Spirit, to accept oblivion. You say you are fed up with this sojourn, but I am sick of exile," she said, throwing a last log on the fire before coming over and sitting down next to her daughter. "I only want to breathe the air of my ancestors." Laurette fell into her mother's arms and they both drifted off to the sound of lapping water.

That night the Mohawks came among them, a small war party moving so stealthily that even the dog did not hear them. Melba opened her eyes and saw them standing on the other side of the campfire, ghostly silhouettes sprung from the flames. She gripped the dog by its nape to steady him, before she chanced to rise and speak with them.

"Welcome," she said in English.

Three young warriors stood on the other side of the fire, each about Laurette's age, all powerfully built and heavily armed with knives and lances. Their facial paint shone green in the cinder glow, lengthening and disfiguring their actual features. The centerpieces of hair ridging their respective crowns bristled like the shag between the angry dog's shoulders. One of them stepped closer.

"English?"

"Yes, English," she answered, hoping her daughter would remain asleep.

"What you do far from settlement?"

"Trapping."

"You trapper woman?" Derision colored the question.

"We English squaws make good trappers. Look, I have trapped this beast." She spurred Monsieur Bleu into rising. The dog fixed the Mohawks in its baleful glare. His magnificent mass awed them.

"What manner the beast?" The bravado had disappeared from the intonation.

"Half tiger, half stallion," she said. "The spirit of the Great Bear flows in its veins. No bullet, arrow, hangman's noose, snake or wolf pack can harm it."

"How trap you it?"

"Magic." And as if on cue, the full moon passed between clouds and shone its light on Monsieur Bleu, giving the animal's coat an otherworldly blue hue.

"You give him?" asked a warrior.

"He would eat you," answered Melba.

The plausibility of such a thing gave the warriors pause. "What have you else give?"

Melba offered to each a woolen cloth and they accepted the gifts with gratitude. In return she asked them about the *Dark*. The young men told her what she already knew, that there was no way around those rapids and that the chances of survival were slim for those brave or crazy enough to challenge them. "Make you ready when eyes no more see and your ears crush." The Mohawks receded back into the darkness, but not before one warrior left a parting warning. "If you survive *Dark*, no go west of Connecticut Valley. Still much dangerous to English. Abenakis kill English."

Lake Champlain, which the Abenaki called *Petonbowk*, or Middle Water, was the size of a small sea, and it took Melba and Laurette most of a day just to paddle to Grand Isle, halfway down the lake. There, they put ashore, concealed the canoe with bushes and then made camp two hundred yards inland, away from the maddening mosquitoes. The women's blistered hands could no longer hold the paddles, so it was decided to rest the following day. Melba spent the next morning preparing a harness for the dog—Monsieur Bleu would be of great help in the portage. That afternoon Laurette wanted a bath. "Moliere could do with one, too," she said, setting the baby inside his *tikinagan* and hoisting the contraption on her back.

"Take Monsieur Bleu for protection, *nerternees*."

"I desire no part of that animal. I am sick to death of its stink and I don't trust it. With you not around, the beast will devour Moliere and me faster than I can say Neespaugot." Laurette strapped on the cradleboard and shouldered her flintlock. "This," she said, tipping the rifle, "is all the protection I need."

Laurette found a comfortable strip of beach and spread a blanket upon which she undressed the baby. Then she carried him in her arms through the reeds and viscid shallows into clear water. She made a loud game of dunking him and lifting him high in the air and he screamed with delight. She bathed him and took him back to the blanket to dry in the warm sunlight as she shucked her own miserable clothing. Laurette waded to midstream and soaped herself with lard. From the water she kept a vigil on the baby. A beautiful boy, she told herself, brown and plump and brimming with good health. She rinsed and trudged from the ooze and ran to the blanket and kissed the baby on his black hair. The boy reached for the wet glistening jewels of her pubic tresses.

"Time for some laundry," she cooed at the child. Laurette took her dress out into the lake, a stone's throw from the blanket. She got scrubbing, tossing an eye at the baby. A stubborn stain occupied her attention, and when next she cast a look at Moliere, her heart nearly stopped. An adult wolf was crouched on the blanket, sniffing at the baby who was tapping on its muzzle. The animal playfully hunkered and pawed at the blanket. Laurette shouted "Shoo!" and splashed. The animal threw her an expression of yellow-eyed detachment. Just then, three other wolves trotted from the bushes. A moment later five more cantered from downshore. Nine wolves surrounded the child on his blanket, where the rifle lay uselessly gleaming in the sun.

"God preserve us!" shouted Laurette, racing toward the shore.

As screams reached Melba, Monsieur Bleu had already bolted toward the commotion. Melba seized her bow and quiver and sprinted for the lake, coming out to the shore several paces north of the attack. Down the beach, a ring of frenzied wolves were attacking something. She saw Monsieur Bleu lunge into the pack, snapping a wolf from the maul, then another and another. Melba aimed and shot arrows as she advanced, trying to pick off single targets or at least dissuade those wolves from rejoining the fight, and it was only by chance that, while reloading, she spotted the blanket off to her right, behind a knuckle of twisted driftwood. The baby was on it, sitting there alone, calm as day, his contented gurgles drowned out by the sharp crack of canid rage.

"Laurette!"

Melba seized her daughter's gun by its barrel and charged the maul, hammering at the remaining wolves, clearing them off the prey at the center of their attack. Bloodied and gashed, Laurette continued to ward off invisible claws and teeth long after the wolf pack was gone. Shock finally put a stop to her mad antics, and she collapsed into unconsciousness.

"Monsieur Bleu, stay with Moliere!" The dog, missing whole chunks of blue coat and skin, limped to the baby and lay down.

Melba carried Laurette to the lake to clear the blood and mud to see how deep the wounds were. Her daughter's head was open to the skull, her right cheek shredded, just missing the eye, and both arms and legs were lacerated to the bone. Back at their campsite, Melba stanched the bleeding with the dress from Rouen, France. Infection was now the principal concern.

Within an hour, a high fever developed, and Laurette's flesh went scarlet with inflammation. Melba salved her wounds with herbal pastes and fed her hot soups of boiled trout. And the wait began.

They remained on Grand Isle for a week. Laurette had been touch-and-go for several days, but she was a robust woman and finally rallied. Seven nights after the attack, she gritted her teeth and declared through a mask of hideous scabs that she had no intention of dying on that God-forsaken island. "What is the *Dark* to me now."

They set out the next morning. The Winooski River was a serene passage through some of the most beautiful countryside Melba had ever seen. They stopped often along its banks to gather the wild onions that had given the river its name. From there, Melba steered the canoe into the Mad River, which they traveled to its rise in the Green Mountains.

The portage to White River covered two miles but took two days of pushing and pulling a three-hundred-pound boat across bedrock, screed, basin, swamp and loam, all with a baby strapped to one or the other of the women. They might not have made it at all but for Monsieur Bleu. Tied into the harness that Melba had sewn, the dog yoked the canoe inch by inch. They greased the bottom of the boat with a deer's entrails, making it easier to slide. They got tangled in swamp grass, cut by cat o'nine tails, had to burn bloodsuckers off their legs, kicked away cottonmouth rattlesnakes, slipped on water lilies and almost drowned the dog in the White River rise. Laurette's scabs cracked and bled. Melba strained a knee and her bowels gave her trouble. Both she and her daughter suffered from menstrual cramps. But they made it, and for the first time since they had left the Saint Lawrence River, they were now traveling with the current.

Their joy was short-lived. The current quickened and the horizon darkened and drummed. The young Mohawks called it *ungertug*; the Montreal trappers, the *Dark*. "One moment you are floating under warm bright skies," said the trappers, "and the next, all creation disappears, buried in a coffin of frosty mist and blackness. Worse, a rumbling invades your ears, as if the whole world was breaking apart."

They rowed to the bank and tied down their gear.

"In two bends, we shall be in the river's jaws," Melba shouted over the din.

"Have you already visited this place, *Maman*?" asked Laurette, her long hair matted to her face—there was as much water in the air as in the river.

"No. Three weeks ago, a band of Mohawks spoke to me while you slept."

"*Oui, bien sûr!*" said Laurette, thinking her mother was teasing her.

"Switch places with me. I'll take the bow," said Melba, tying Moliere to Monsieur Bleu. Affectionately, she caressed the hound's massive head. "Take good care of him, Monsieur Bleu."

"Can't we just go around the rapids, *Maman*?"

"The cliffs are too steep, *nerternees*. We would have to leave everything and hike for a month. No, the rapids it must be."

"Then God help us!" Laurette made the sign of the cross.

Coming round the penultimate bend, the roar of the river made further talk useless. The canoe started to run, and the women fought the current to remain on track. The jolts increased in frequency and violence. They were hit hard by spray. The explosions of water muffled Moliere's shrieks, but nothing could mask the fright in the baby's eyes. The sight broke his mother's heart. *"Ne sewortum,"* Melba cried. "I am sorry."

At the ultimate bend, the river no longer seemed to move under them but rather to envelope them, sweeping high above both sides of the canoe and crashing down on their heads, swamping the inside of the boat and threatening to overturn it. Then, the world seemed to drop away and they found themselves plummeting, fighting to hold on, water beating against their faces, blinding all but the dog, immovably focused on his sole task of saving the child.

Then, as abruptly as it had started, it ended. The river tired, the roar calmed and the mist lifted. The canoe came into smooth water. Melba steered the boat to shore and untied Moliere. She clasped him to her chest and cried uncontrollably. Laurette hugged her, and the three of them huddled for many minutes. The dog climbed out and pissed.

From there the river grew fat and lazy with a wide, slow current. Dawn broke red and slate across the eastern sky, the pink of skinned meat. Female voices sweet with song drifted from downstream. *"Canakisheun, weekchu? Wotone doddi gung-shquaws peormug."*

"What are they singing, *Maman?*"

"Where are you going, my handsome young man? Going to a place where the pretty girls fish. The last time I heard it, I was sitting on my grandfather's knee, gutting cod on Neespaugot Beach."

Around the bend, they encountered a group of Abenaki women cutting up trout. The girls thought they were English and dropped their catches. Melba called to them from the middle of the river. "*Mud ger-tee wheezig.* Do not be afraid, we come in peace."

They were a clan of fifteen families living on the run from the English and Mohawks. Their leader, Wamsut, had a disagreeable face like pebbled dirt. His wolverine eyes were bloodshot from drinking the pilfered stores of Coatman whiskey. He spat words as if they had a bad taste, confusing pride with idle boasting. "I am Sachem of the world and will soon crush the English and destroy those Mohawk dogs." The grandiloquent Wamsut hadn't yet been born when the war started.

Melba's plans to return to Neespaugot disappointed the young blowhard and his clan.

"I do not believe my ears," said Wamsut. "Why go back among the Coatmen?"

"I intend to have back my spirit and the land of my ancestors."

"Foolish squaw! You expect the English to tell you, 'Here, take what is yours. We gladly return your lands and will send back to Africa our black men.'"

Melba did not react to the hothead's impertinence.

"Wamsut, I mean no disrespect. It is true, I am but one woman. But the faith of one is sometimes enough. My daughter and I thank you for your hospitality."

The next day, Melba and her family reached White River Junction in a lightning storm. At the outpost, Melba traded trappings for stores. Outside the shop, a drunken sex-starved mountain man made a nuisance of himself until Monsieur Bleu bared his teeth.

From there, the settlements multiplied along the Connecticut River: Greenfield, Deerfield, Hatfield, Holyoke. They paddled to Springfield and bartered a new dress for Laurette. Melba reminisced to Laurette that the last time she'd been in Springfield, Metacom's army was burning it to the ground. Now, there was no sign that there had ever been a war. The Coatmen were a resilient people. What must they have done with Neespaugot? Melba suddenly went quiet with despair.

"*Maman*," said Laurette, "what troubles you?"

"Oh, I was just thinking of the war. In particular, a young Mohegan man we captured. He was a fellow native, and I asked him why he fought with the English against his brothers. He answered that it was easier to hate a brother than an enemy."

"I don't understand such thinking."

"*Nerternees*, when your great-grandfather Runinniduk was your age, his Sachem refused to help the Mohegans in their struggle with Rhode Island. A native never forgets. A great tree sometimes has poisoned roots."

"So what did you do to the young man?"

"Metacom dashed his brains out."

Days later, and a month in total, they made Old Saybrook, where they caught the sweet smell of ocean brine and could hear the chatter of gulls, terns and cormorants. "Saltwater!" cried Melba, leaping from the canoe into the ocean. It was a cleansing by salt.

That night on the Atlantic shore, Melba rigged a sail with the sheet of oil linen. The next morning before sunrise, they caught the earliest tide. Then, for the better part of three days they crawled toward Massachusetts, battling heavy seas and steering clear of a multitude of heavy ships, English brigs coming into New England with cargo, much of it human, and leaving with bellyfuls of prime colonial raw material. At night they beached their canoe and camped along the narrows and dunes. On the third day, Melba's heart grew heavy as the swell swept them past Misery Island, the prison and tomb of her family and so many other Christian Indians. Some minutes later, Neespaugot rose on the coastline, its rebuilt fort on the promontory, its church spire and its hundreds of clapboard houses making like seashells clustered to the rocky shoreline. North Bay Harbor bustled with brigantines and barques. Not even in Montreal had Laurette seen so many ship masts. The thought of the English world's collective weight crushed Laurette's morale.

"*Maman,* these people are too many!"

"Yes, *nerternees,* they are. But it changes nothing about our goal."

They rode the tide into a deserted section of South Bay Beach. Melba leapt out and threw herself into the sand. "We are home, *nerternees!*"

"*Ah, oui!*" said the irritable Laurette. "If home is a prison or gallows."

The next morning they entered Neespaugot via Cabot Street, Melba transporting Moliere in his *tikinagan,* Laurette so nervous her jaw hurt, the dog advancing stop-and-trot, sniffing and pissing on the rebuilt fence posts. Neespaugot's rebirth was truly impressive. Its administrative buildings, businesses and individual dwellings stood well-weathered and ship-shape with finely shingled roofs, weather vanes and porticos. The downtown area was now entirely cobblestoned, and gorgeous elm and maple trees rimmed the Commons. It being daybreak, merchants were just getting their day started. The green grocer was putting out his vegetables, some fishermen were laying out their catches, and a woman and her cow were delivering milk.

"*Maman*," said Laurette, "where is the dire raiment of the Puritan you told me about?"

Her daughter had a keen eye, for it was true—Puritan clothing was nowhere in sight. Nor were those instruments of humiliation and torture, the stocks.

"I don't know, *nerternees*. I too am mystified."

Outside the courthouse stood the town constable, a small man with teacup-handle ears, a burnished nose and a sinister regard. Perfunctorily, he tipped his tricorn hat. "Good morning to you folk. Quite a beast you have there." He eyed all four of them with suspicion.

"Where are gone the Puritans, sir?"

"Puritans? Why, they burnt themselves out with their witches," he said, as if he himself had never been one of them. "Come to see the head, have you?"

Melba did not understand the question and did not care for the way the man looked at them. She tried to move on, but the constable ordered them to stop. He looked Laurette up and down with ill-disguised contempt.

"Much illegal transaction these days," he said to Melba. "I suppose you have her papers?"

"Her papers?"

"She is your slave, is she not?"

"She is my daughter."

"Ah, a half-breed, then?"

"She is native, as am I." Melba stared down at the man, whom she dwarfed. "Are we free to go?"

He bowed contemptuously. Laurette exhaled. "You see, *Maman*. The Puritan is gone."

"No, *nerternees*, the Puritan is not gone. He has merely changed form."

As they rounded the corner of the courthouse, the constable's question about "coming to see the head" flew in their faces. Laurette saw it first and threw her hand to her mouth. High atop a pole against the leaden sky, a desiccated human skull stared down at them, much of its leathery skin still clinging to the bone. It was the head of a short-haired native.

"*Maman*, what kind of frightful place is this? They are barbarians. No, worse—they are cannibals!"

A gaunt but kindly gentleman with long thin mustaches and a velvet waistcoat saw their distress and asked if he might be of assistance. "Have you come to these parts to grieve relatives lost in that distant war?"

"An entire nation lost," Melba shot back. "Why, pray tell, have you people left his head up there?"

The man laughed, aware of the trophy's anachronism. "I'm afraid Metacom's skull still makes amusement for passing pilgrims. It's just business."

"Bad business. Tell your council that whilst the Sachem's head remains out of the ground, he will haunt you. But if you bury it, your colonies will at last find peace."

The man stood there, much perplexed by the sound of her voice. "Should I know you?" he asked.

"No, I am merely a passing pilgrim, as you said. We desire to find a trace of this young woman's native relatives in this land. Where are your Wampanoag people, sir?"

The gentleman frowned. "Those people are extinct. One must needs venture beyond the Connecticut River to find an Indian these days. There are no more such heathens in these parts."

Once the man had taken his leave, Laurette argued with her mother.

"You heard him. There are no more Wampanoag. There is no longer a need to push your claims if there are no longer the people to inhabit the land. We can go back to Canada."

"*Nerternees*, our people are still here, I can feel it. They are in hiding, invisible to the Coatmen."

It dawned on Laurette that her mother might be touched, and her fear reached new heights. Had she followed a mad woman into hell?

They continued down roads rumbling with settlers' wagons. They traversed rolling farmlands stretching half a day inland, where the arched backs of black slaves toiled in the stony New England soil. They crossed covered bridges, drank from water wheels and took nourishment beside the Coatmen's cattle pastures. The great forest had receded like an aging hairline.

After two days' travel, they arrived at Assawompset Pond, the tribe's winter settlement at the time of her grandfather. Melba expected to find more farms there. Instead, what they beheld was a ghost village. Wigwams and longhouses lay rotting around the pond. Broken hatchets and arrows littered the topsoil, and the acacia, sycamore and birch trees bore the holes of many bullets. Her childhood paradise was funereal.

"Why has no one touched this place, *Maman*?"

"I don't know. My guess is that the Coatmen are still superstitious."

"About what?"

"Disturbing the dead."

"If the English are afraid of this pond, *Maman*, they must have their reasons."

"They have their guilt, *nerternees*. Anyway, there is no sign of the living here."

Laurette was reassured to hear her mother admit the obvious. "Does this mean we can return to Canada?"

"It means we shall go into the Great Swamp. That is where we will find our people."

They reached the Great Swamp the afternoon of the following day. That tangled morass had only gotten thicker in the thirty years since the war, and the two women had to take turns holding Moliere while the other shielded his face and limbs from the razor-sharp branches and thistles.

"I understand perfectly why the English cursed this awful place, *Maman*."

Melba's voice deepened into a Coatman's masculine grumble. "These heathens, why, they are three parts vegetation!" she said out loud, the memory making her chuckle. "Sometimes we were buried only inches from their noses."

"You speak about this swamp with reverence, *Maman*, when everything in here is dead or being choked to death. It is repugnant."

"You think like a Coatman, *nerternees*. You see only the appearance of things. Life is vibrant here. Our people are here."

"If they are, then they have become the trees and vines and roots."

"Perhaps you're right."

"That gives me small comfort."

They took rest in a glade. Laurette sat Moliere on a fur and stretched her aching back. A brisant bird whistle broke the moist silence. Laurette watched her mother hurry to the edge of the glade and whistle into the dense growth.

"*Maman*," she called, "let's leave this bog before it gets dark, no?" Her mother ignored her and resumed a series of strident cries. The dog turned in circles, while the baby fiddled with his sculpted totem. "Moliere will need to be fed soon, *Maman*."

Suddenly, her mother was gone, vanished into thin air.

"*Maman!*"

Unquiet took root. It spread into Laurette's thoughts like the tree-killing vines all about her. So her mother was going mad. She had left her and the baby to fend for themselves in this nightmare of vegetation. "*Maman!*" All she managed to do was excite the dog, who took off into the morass.

Laurette sat down with Moliere to wait. Light and heat began to fade as her panic mounted. The air cooled and thickened with swamp musk. After an unbearable wait, Laurette heard something heavy and powerful closing quickly from the left. Laurette loaded her rifle and stepped in front of the baby. The dog burst out of a wall of vegetation, dragging behind it a long train of barbed prickers, thistles and swamp grass. Her mother was in close pursuit.

"*Nerternees*, come now."

Laurette snatched up Moliere and followed her mother into the thick of the swamp. They came to a narrow passage that dead-ended into an impenetrable wall of growth both dead and alive. There was nowhere to go. "It's a dead end, *Maman!*"

"No, daughter, it's a living end."

Her mother again vanished before her eyes. Then, she reappeared.

"What are you waiting for, *nerternees*? Come on!"

Laurette closed her eyes and pushed through the natural wall. What she saw next was a palisade as large as a farmer's field, with hundreds of *wetus* and several longhouses spread across the immense clearing. An irrigation system of wooden paddles churned in a canal dug from the bog. The scent of warming cornbread sweetened the air. And all about were people, beings who turned into shadows once Laurette tried to focus on them. The inhabitants of that clearing were like certain landmarks, often passed, ever invisible until the numb grip of routine slackened.

"*Aque!*" they hailed her.

The shadow people were clothed in Indian leggings and breeches, yet they were not Indians. They were as black as cow's teats, their bony crowns tufted with sheep's wool. Her mother had found a people all right: Africans!

"*Maman, ils sont noir*. They're runaway slaves."

"Africans do not speak Algonquian, *nerternees*. These are our people, a new people. They are the descendants of Africans, but they are also the children of Massasoit, of Metacom, of Cahotet the great Narragansett. Like us, these good people have done what was necessary to survive."

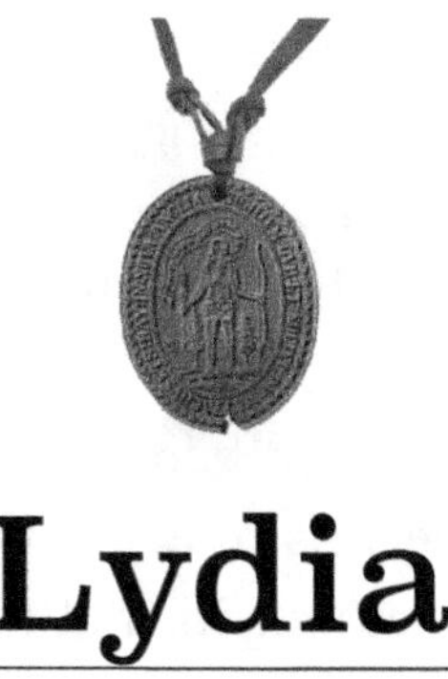

Lydia

April 13, 1828

The Captain paced nervously in the parlor window, a watchful eye on Franklin Street, as he made repetitive glances at his pocket watch. She's late, he thought to himself. No, she isn't, you old fool. Stop second-guessing yourself! But a faith healer, of all things? With my own son a Harvard-educated physician. What was I thinking? I'm a practical man, for God's sake! A man of rules and regulations. I have led men into battle on the high seas. I must've been mad to agree to such hocus-pocus. You're not mad, you worn-out boot, you're in pain. The acute headaches. You'd try anything that didn't involve bleeding.

He watched a two-horse cabriolet clop to the curb. The coachman shouted "Whoa!" and climbed down as the horses shuddered and shat. Franklin Street began in town, between the Old Port and Grover Wharf, but made a soaring rise up Sentinel Hill from sea level to Revolutionary Park, a two-hundred-foot elevation gain in one hundred yards. The coachman naturally had some difficulty securing his livery before opening the coach door for his passenger. A young, spindly mulatto woman the color of dark ale stepped down. Her hair was shorn like a sheep's wool, with only a thin tuft of black winkles on her head. She wore a purple robe, like some kind of Gospel singer, and looked barely twenty years old. The Captain decided she was much too young to be of any good to him and caned outside to the stoop.

"Coachman," he called to the driver. "There's been a mistake. Take this young lady back to where you fetched her."

The passenger ignored the Captain's directive and sent the driver on his way. Then, the brazen moll came up the walk and hailed him like an old friend. "Hullo, Captain George!" On the stoop, she grabbed his hand and shook it forcefully. "I'm Lydia Freeman, sir, and I mean to get you well."

Polite but firm, he disengaged his hand. "Well, Miss Freeman, you heard what I told the driver. I'm no longer interested in this mumbo jumbo."

Playfully, the mulatto popped open her large bag and began rummaging around inside. "Good news, Captain," she said. "Seems I'm fresh out of mumbo jumbo today."

"Are you mocking me, young lady?"

"Only funning you, sir. I believe that amusement is the best medicine. And rest assured, Captain, there'll be no bleeding."

He was dumbstruck. "How did y…? Who have you been talking to about me?"

"Just you, Captain. Your scalp rash and age tell me everything I need to know about what's ailing you. I'll bet you're having headaches."

"Why, yes—"

"Any doctor worth his salt would diagnose arthritis and prescribe bleeding. Except you'd sooner be shot than bled, am I right?" She winked, knowing the answer already. "I read up on you, Captain. Fifty years ago you almost bled to death at sea, the famous fire fight at Flamborough Head. 'Surrender? I have only begun to fight!'" she said, her voice dropping comically. "What did your son have to say about it, sir?"

"You really have been studying up on me, miss."

"Call me Lydia, Captain. You've had words, I suppose, the two of you?"

"Every blasted conversation with George Jr. ends up in the shoals. The last time we spoke, he warned me that my stubbornness would cost me my eyesight. Is that true?"

"Stubbornness causes grief, not blindness, Captain. You know, we can do this here on the stoop or perhaps I can come in…"

The visit lasted most of the afternoon. The Captain was thankful that Miss Freeman wasn't there to fill his ears with God and religion. In fact, he did most of the talking, as she plied him with tea, a concoction she made from walnut and birch bark grounds. The Captain hated tea, but he quaffed plenty of her elixir between frequent trips to the privy. When his bladder would allow it, he recounted personal stories he had never shared with another human being. His father's drowning off the Maine coast. His commission in the Continental Army at age twenty. His guilt over raiding the Irish coast like a two-bit pirate during the War of Independence. (He did not hold his commander, the hero John Paul Jones, in high esteem.) And, of course, the drama on the high seas, particularly the cannonball that ripped his ship in two and drove a piece of mast the size of a broom handle through this hip and kidney. "We were thirty miles off the English coast, on a burning ship," he said, pausing in reflection. "Nonetheless, it was nothing compared to losing my dear Alice to tuberculosis."

"Tell me your happiest memory, Captain."

"Probably the day my son was born."

"If I could grant you any wish, what would it be?"

"Grandchildren!"

"How did you make your fortune, Captain?"

Following the war, he started a fishery. By the turn of the century, his enterprise had become so lucrative and his reputation so respected that Finley Sons, Transporters, a reference in the slave trade, offered the Captain a large stake in their company. Finley transported lightly levied wheat, meat and lumber to the West Indies, where it bought French and Spanish molasses to make rum to be shipped via Finley vessels to the west coast of Africa, where it bought slaves. Finley vessels had shipped a hundred thousand African slaves to America before the international slave trade was prohibited.

"The ban cut their commerce in two, and they needed me a lot more than I needed them," said the Captain. "I agreed to come aboard on one condition: that they get out of the slave trade. I told them the Far East was the place to be. The Chinese wanted furs in exchange for tea and silk at low prices. When they accepted, I drew up a business plan to send Finley ships around Cape Horn and up to trading posts along the Pacific Northwest, where they picked up beaver and sea otter pelts and continued on to China. Our foray into China and Indonesia made Finley more money than the slave trade ever had."

"Are you still on their board of directors, Captain?"

"No, no—I retired five years ago. Transferred all my shares to George Jr. Believe it or not, my son actually resented the gift. He told me quite bluntly that he had no interest in anything to do with Finley. What you need to understand about G.O.—my nickname for my boy—is that he was quite young when his mother died, so he was raised by nannies. He was always an odd, solitary sort. The sea made him wobbly, its fishes gave him rashes, and wharf life in general bored him. He grew up despising travel of any sort—"

"Ironic for a fella nicknamed 'G.O.'"

"Indeed, I should have nicknamed him S.T.A.Y. He shunned social contact, had no head for numbers and showed not the least inclination for running a business. In short, my boy had no get-up-and-go whatsoever. But he did have an affinity for science and chose the study of medicine. After long and earnest endeavor, G.O. became a licensed physician. He's a capable practitioner with a decidedly poor bedside manner. He can cure you but not his own shyness and awkwardness. He comes across as cold, aloof and severe.

"Anyway, two years ago, I razed a warehouse I owned on Onion Road and built him a house and medical practice. I kept it simple and sturdy. The interior walls are wainscoted in oak and elm, and the rooms furnished with Colonial-era tables, chairs, beds and desks. G.O. has a fully stacked library of medical texts and all the medical linen and supplies he needs. Five of the seven downstairs rooms are for surgical procedures. I put in six bedrooms and baths on the second and third floors. As a personal conceit, I had a widow's walk constructed on the roof, so that I might go up there for a smoke and a gaze out to sea. The only thing I asked in return was that he take a wife and give me grandchildren. What a hullabaloo that caused—you'd have thought I was suggesting the landlubber set sail around the world! I suppose that women and children are like traveling to him. The very thought seems to infect him with a disabling listlessness.

"Alas, he's no handsome man by any stretch. He's as long and lank as the Ancient Mariner, with big ears and distended fingers and toes. And his oddness bewilders folks. He's a loner. But, as I said, my George is a fine physician."

The Captain spoke and spoke, and when he heard the carriage come for Miss Freeman, he was already wistful that she would soon be gone.

"So when will you return, my dear?" he asked, paying her fee and cab fare.

A mischievous smile spread across her face, a not-terribly-pretty face but one imbued with light and energy. "Why, the very next time you need me, Captain George."

"Well, I need you now for these damn headaches."

"You sure about that, sir?"

When she had gone, the Captain realized that he was headache-free for the first time in two years.

Miss Freeman had made him well, and the Captain wanted to thank her personally. But he didn't know where she lived; contact had been made originally via the post office. So he asked around, starting with his old associates, the Finleys. They recognized neither the name nor her description—young, half-breed, twentyish, outlandish clothing, little-boy haircut. Nor had his son G.O. ever heard of her, though he did say that the South Bay was full of quacks.

The Captain recalled that, before Independence, South Bay had counted a thriving population of so-called Swamp People, made up of Indians and runaway slaves. After the war, those people were either dispersed or sold back into bondage, leaving nary a non-white face in all of Neespaugot, north or south. Still, it stood to figure that Miss Freeman's roots had to be in South Bay.

The pastor of the First Baptist Church of South Bay claimed to know Lydia Freeman but made no bones about his disapproval of her healing practices. "She has removed God from her work and stopped coming to church altogether after Thaddeus and Abigail Lovejoy passed on. *They* raised her. Good God-fearing folk—"

"I thought her name was Freeman."

"The Lovejoys were a white family. Lydia was adopted."

The Lovejoys had lost two sons in the War of 1812. However, their daughter Eloise Frampton lived in Boston. The Captain paid her a visit. Eloise Frampton was a sound-spoken, heavyset woman in her early thirties. She told the Captain her parents had adopted Lydia at the age of eleven. "Poor thing had been passed around like an old book," said Eloise. "First the orphanage, then several years living with a crazy old Indian woman, the two of them so poor they were feeding off swamp roots. But Lydia, bless her young heart, knew plenty already about plants and their remedies. Then she taught herself Latin and medicine. She even made her own clothing—without nearly the same success, I might add. I don't know why she prefers those robes. Take it from me, she has a comely enough figure," Eloise said, winking. "But Lydia's not interested in marriage. She's dedicated to her work." Lydia Freeman followed a farmer's lifestyle, turning in just after dusk and fast asleep a moment later. She rose every morning before dawn, made herself a cup of hot water and honey, her only nourishment till noon, read medical texts and case studies until sunrise, bathed five times a day and washed her bristly hair once a month. "A real stickler for routines, that big sister of mine."

"Did you say your *big* sister?" The Captain was puzzled. "The young woman I met looks barely out of her teens."

Mrs. Frampton hooted. "Lydia Freeman is thirty-four, sir! Three years my senior. But she does look young, I'll give you that."

On Eloise's advice, the Captain continued his inquest at the Blessed Mary Orphanage on Rantool Street. The orphanage was a filthy, sordid establishment situated in the eye of a storm of cheap inns, bars, brothels, run-down apartments and raw sewage. The headwoman brought out the records and confirmed Lydia Freeman's date of birth: July 12, 1794. But the records revealed nothing concerning her origins. "Inquire at the hospice on Lawrence Street," said the headwoman. "She was born there."

The Lawrence Street Hospice was a block away and smelled of decomposition. A stale Quaker clerk got out the ledger in question. "Yes, here it is. The midwife was Gladys Harper. She died about fifteen years ago, but you can still see her notations about Lydia Freeman's mother. 'African, no name, possibly a runaway slave, little spoken English, perhaps sixteen years of age, only one possession: a fusty coin of strangeful currency. Hour of death: 1:34 a.m., 12 July 1794. Posthumous birth.'"

The Captain eventually located her address but now faced a dilemma. He wanted to spend time with Miss Freeman, but to do so would require that he pretend to be sick. Such subterfuge flew in the face of everything he lived by, his entire code of behavior. It was difficult enough for him to admit he was truly ill. As his crew was yanking out the shank of mast buried in his right kidney, Captain Osborne's only remark was how pristine the Irish Sea looked, before he passed out from the pain.

But a seaman adapts to the elements and changes tack as needed. And thus the game began. He contacted her about sharp stings he was experiencing in his fingers and toes. Next, it was an earache. Then belly pain, urinary infections, fevers, back pain, chest ailments. Miss Freeman wasn't dupe to any of it, and after months of the charade, she called his bluff. "Captain George, some advice, please. I have a problem patient. A dear old man, but a dreadful malingerer. I adore him, I do, but he's taking up time better used on the legitimately sick."

The Captain took on a pensive frown. "Sounds to me like the poor fool needs you, my dear. Just not in the conventional way."

"Maybe I should insist that he stop malingering, or else I must refuse to see him."

"Yes, I suppose you could, dear."

But she didn't insist. And he didn't stop malingering. They both knew that the aged get their fun and games where and when they can. They also learned that no game lasts forever. Life always catches up with art. At the end of the year, the Captain developed dropsy.

"And what in blazes is that?" he asked Lydia.

"It's a kidney problem," she explained while examining him.

"You do remember that I have but one kidney left to me. The other is somewhere in the Irish Sea."

"Yes, I know. Now, lie still, would you?"

She checked the inside of his eyelids, listened to his neck with her fingertips, and had him lie down on his stomach while she kneaded his extant kidney and the scar above the missing one. "So," she said at last with her habitual good humor, "I'm going to put you on a diet of liquids composed of goldenrod, juniper, sugar and caffeine. It'll help clean out your system, Captain."

"Anything, so long as it doesn't require an operation."

Miss Freeman looked him kindly in the eyes. "No, dear, an operation would be unnecessary."

He stared into her oak-colored irises and got her meaning. "Are you saying what I think you are?" he asked. She nodded. Funny, but his death sentence didn't have nearly the effect on him that he might have expected. "My dear, I've been waiting to face the angel of death my entire adult life. I just never expected her to be so graceful. How long have I got?"

"A few months, Captain."

He struggled to right himself on the bed—she never helped him if he did not ask for it—and reached for his shirt. As he buttoned it, an epiphany broke his funk.

"Listen here, young lady. I'm firing you as my visiting healer. From now on, I'm paying you one hundred dollars a week to be my full-time caregiver."

"Maybe I should examine your head as well, Captain George. That's more money than I make in a year."

"I'm aware of that, but it's the price I must pay to get you to leave your other people."

"You know I can't do that."

"Did I fail to mention that the contract will be good for the rest of *your* life?"

"Do I strike you as that venal, sir?"

"Oh, nonsense, everyone is venal, young lady. The difference is that you deserve every penny of it."

"Then you don't know me."

"Dear, I'm offering you the finest deal in town. You'll be set for life, whereas you only need put up with me for six months. Before you know it, you'll be back among your other patients, wealthy to boot."

"You don't just drop people and then go back to them, Captain George. They need me as much as you do."

"Look, my sweet child. I've lived a good life. I've got no complaints, except for not having a grandchild. But that's beside the point. I'm rich. And, as you know only too well, I'm also very lonely. You're about the closest thing I have to a friend. All I'm saying is that my money might as well serve me *and* you. And how's this? You and I can dig into those mysterious origins of yours."

The Captain knew from Lydia Freeman that she had two passions in life: medicine and making sense of the strange coin her unknown parents had bequeathed to her.

"Captain George, your son needs to be part of this— and don't you squint at me, sir, I mean business. If he's not involved, neither am I. Now, I will start by giving you four days a week, on the condition that you ask to see your son every day and that I don't hear any more palaver about lifetime contracts."

The Captain had free access to the Finley ledgers, and he and Miss Freeman pored over pages long into the evening. When he became too sick and poor-sighted to continue, Miss Freeman went at it alone, until her own eyesight and emotions began to flinch. There were just so many listings, thousands upon thousands of nameless slaves categorized by sex, price and age. Expecting to uncover a nameless female runaway who may or may not have been pregnant at the time of her escape defied reason.

The one object tying her to her origins—the coin—was equally shrouded in mystery, figuratively and literally. For instance, it was nigh impossible to tell head from tail on the coin. One face showed an engraving with some kind of image, which time had robbed of all intelligibility; the other face had a faint scribble that may or may not have been some kind of inscription. The midwife who delivered her thought it said *Nana Lydia*. "It doesn't look much like *Lydia* to me," grunted the Captain.

"I suppose she saw what she wanted to," explained Lydia. "I understand that her own mother was named

Lydia. Mrs. Harper was a religious woman who abhorred the institution of slavery, so to insure that I would not wind up in bondage, she wrote 'Free Man' on my birth certificate. That's all I know."

The first time Lydia met the Captain's son, she was taken aback by his physique. G.O. was a skeletal giant with barely enough of him to hang a shirt on. His glaucous eyes—the color of poplar leaves—were pressed into a gaunt, lightly bearded face. That first meeting, at the Captain's Sentinel Hill home, G.O. balked at shaking her hand. Lydia took no offense since she had never met a doctor who wasn't hostile to her profession, race and sex. In time, however, she understood that Doctor George Osborne Jr. was neither hostile nor condescending. He was merely morbidly shy around women.

One fall afternoon, G.O. braved a hurricane to look in on his father. He hadn't been upstairs long when he bounded back down the stairs, as perturbed as Lydia had ever seen him. "Damn that stubborn fool!"

"The old walrus got under your skin again, did he?" she asked, bemused, while preparing a pot of tea.

Her bluntness tongue-tied him, as if the table had just spoken. He pulled up a chair without answering the question. She brought her clay teapot to the table, where she had set out two mugs, and aimed a stream of boiling liquid into each.

"No, thank you," he mumbled. "I'm not in the mood for tea."

She slid it over to him anyway. "Tea is always in the mood for us, Doctor George. You go on now and drink a little. It'll steady your nerves."

Her offer brooked no refusal, so he drank. She sat opposite him at the table.

"How can he be so damnably obstinate?" he said. "Granted, he's earned the right. War hero. Entrepreneur par excellence. But does he seriously expect to defeat this malady through sheer guts? Why won't he let me help him?"

She took her own sip without proffering a response.

"If only he trusted me," he continued. "Tell me, Miss Freeman, is he angry at me? Is he disappointed? You were quite blunt with me, so I shall be equally frank. What has he said to you on my subject?"

"To tell you the truth, the Captain talks mostly about sailing."

"Sailing?"

"Yep, says the trick to sailing is using what's given to you. You don't try to control the wind and the swell. You're patient in the doldrums and you never fight a storm."

The doctor understood the message and wasn't pleased to hear it. "That's thinking from caveman days, Miss Freeman. Science is not hostage to the elements."

"The Captain says that sailors, more than those in most professions, accept when it's their time, Doctor George."

"Rubbish!" he said. "That's not good enough, ma'am. I thought you were a healer. You should know better." He thanked her for the tea and stormed out of the Captain's house.

After that, it became a sort of routine. The doctor would drop in full of vinegar and certainty, sit with the Captain long enough to lose his sense of control, then beat a retreat through the kitchen, where he engaged Lydia in a teacup debate.

"He acts mule-headed to cover up his fear," said G.O.

"So, what's he afraid of?" said Lydia.

"What do you think? Why, life and death, of course."

"Both?"

"No, you're right. My father has no fear of death."

"And you, Doctor George? Is it life or is it death that scares you?"

The question embarrassed him, and he didn't respond.

Lydia pitied G.O. He was more than a mere loner. He was a castaway, an inherently good man banished to his own island. She suspected that he, like any good Puritan, feared life.

Lydia and G.O. were at the Captain's bedside when death came. The Captain mumbled "Ahoy," and the ghost left him. She closed his eyes and drew up the sheet, and G.O. broke down weeping.

"I am alone."

"No, sir," she said, "You will always have my friendship."

A month after the Captain's death—a July afternoon heavy with humidity, gnats and something altogether novel: factory pollution—a carriage stopped on the dirt road out front of Lydia's South Bay cottage. Its red-faced young coachman leaned over the fence and practically through her window. "Are you Miss Freeman?" Her nod brought him a sigh of relief and the latitude to continue his message. "Doctor Osborne asks that you come with me at once."

Onion Road was a track of warehouses and liveries running parallel to the old port, with only two recent houses to recommend it. One of them was the doctor's clinic. Osborne House was a queerly shaped Gregorian structure that seemed too narrow at the foundation and too high in the flank. Its three floors, widow's walk and weather vane looked like acrobats balanced one atop the other, battling gravity. The stone gateway was engraved with "George Osborne, Jr. MD," but no street number had yet been assigned to the lot.

Lydia released the latch on the wrought-iron gate and made her way up a red-brick walk. The front garden was nicely composed, with a lawn of chamomile and thyme neatly scythed and sheared, two young sycamores, a shingle oak, willow, American elm and Douglas fir, and a marble birdbath held by a sculpted Cupid on a Tuscan order pedestal, which Lydia didn't care for. The front door was open, but she called in first.

"Doctor George? Hullo?"

There was no reply. She thought she detected weeping coming from down a long corridor, so she hurried inside toward the sound. Ahead, a spillage of light fell into the corridor from one of the rooms, illuminating a staircase and, seated on its first step, a young woman, weeping miserably. "Miss?" said Lydia. The young woman didn't respond. She was a pretty girl in penny-poor clothing. Her face was a grim mask of filthy tears, and she clacked her teeth. "Sit tight, dear, I'll be right back."

Lydia entered the room—a surgery, in fact—where the smell of excrement and burning oil hung heavy. George Osborne stood beside a bed in disarray, taking the pulse of a girl lying twisted in a pile of sweaty sheets, panting like a winded hunting hound. The physician's eyes were bulging from fatigue and frustration. Lydia approached and untangled the sheets. "Oh, my," she said. The girl was pregnant.

"Twelve years old," said Osborne, scowling. "That's the mother in the hall there, barely twenty-one herself."

"Let's forget those kinds of details for now, Doctor George." Lydia submerged a cloth in cool water, half-wrung it and dabbed the child's milky face. "Everything's going to be fine, sweetness." The child's eyes seemed to reach out to Lydia through layers of pain and fear. "That little rascal doesn't want to give up, eh?"

"Neither of them speaks English," said G.O. "They came off some boat."

"Don't you worry, sweet baby," Lydia said to the girl anyway, but mostly for the benefit of G.O., who had clearly reached the end of his tether. "We're going to make things right, darling."

"A word, ma'am," said Osborne, clutching Miss Freeman by her elbow and prodding her away from the patient. "Miss Freeman," he said under his breath, "this labor has already endured thirty-six hours. She's condemned."

"Why would you go and assume that, Doctor George? A Caesarian birth doesn't have to be a death sentence."

"Is that so? And just when in your experience *hasn't* it been?" To his credit, he suddenly heard his own desperation and gathered himself. "Forgive me, Miss Freeman, I'm tired."

"No offense taken."

"I cannot bring myself to cut up a twelve-year-old, knowing it will kill her."

"You have to save the baby, Doctor George."

"I know."

"Neither is dead yet."

"Miss Freeman, I am incapable. Do you understand that? It's why I sent for you."

"You didn't think that I—"

"I did."

"Doctor George, I am no surgeon. I'm not even a midwife. I have never so much as removed a splinter from a finger."

"I am in no condition, I say."

"You just need a moment to settle yourself, sir."

"No, ma'am. You must help me. I will guide you through it."

Lydia looked from Osborne to the child and back to Osborne. She understood that the child would live or die by her hand. "Well, I'm not a complete imbecile, not yet anyway. Where's your alcohol?"

He thought she meant his sterilizing alcohol and pointed to a tray of medical supplies.

"No, sir. I mean your nastiest drinking alcohol."

Too fatigued and flustered to try to comprehend, G.O. did as she asked and returned with a bottle of rum and a glass. Lydia quarter-filled the glass and handed it to him. "Have the young woman in the hall drink this. She'll be needing it."

When G.O. returned, Lydia was force-swilling rum into the pregnant child. The idea of plying one so young with whiskey dismayed the doctor. Lydia spotted his confliction. "This, Doctor George, is a minor transgression compared to what was put into her to put her in this state."

"I'm… well, I'm not judging you. Perhaps I should have thought of it first."

"Well, that's about as much rum as I dare give her. It'll be a calamity if she gets sick."

As the child drifted into inebriation, they strapped her arms and legs to the bedposts. Osborne prepared his instruments, and then they washed each other's hands and the child's belly. Osborne showed Lydia where to incise, then sank his weight on the child's thighs and told her to begin. Lydia steadied her hand and cut into the child's abdomen. The child's cries produced even louder agony from the hall.

"She barely has pubic hair," said Osborne, squirting alcohol on the child's belly to keep the incision visible through the blood.

"Stay focused, Doctor George."

"All right, reach in… that's it… that's the uterus. All right. Now, it's very important that you incise north-south. No, you're not following what I'm saying. North-south. No, hold the scalpel… Miss Freeman, turn your hand, you're not— What are you doing?! Not that way! Careful of the bladder…"

His yelling brought the girl's mother into the room, but by then Lydia had already cut the uterus up high, east-west, with only a minimal insertion, all steps contrary to Osborne's instructions. The girl's mother nearly fainted at the sight of her daughter cut open. Osborne ordered her out, but Lydia overruled him.

"You can help us, miss. Step closer."

Lydia motioned the mother to approach. Deathly pale and jittery, the twenty-one-year-old grandmother reeled to the side of the bed. Lydia removed the fetus, but the mother saw only the butchery, not the baby, and began to wail.

"Take the baby," ordered Lydia.

Osborne started to move, but Lydia waved him off. "Go on, sweetness, take your grandson."

The pronouncement of grandson knocked the grandmother from her agony. Lydia placed the newborn in her hands, then snipped the umbilical cord. At the instant the newborn began to cry, the grandmother brightened. Lydia congratulated her and led her with her grandson to a basin of warm water. "You go on and bathe him now."

Back at the bedside, Osborne was readying the sutures and watching Lydia with stupefaction. "My God, Miss Freeman, you saved her life. Where did you learn that technique?"

"Books. Certain African tribes in Uganda have been performing the traverse Caesarian for centuries, with good results."

"She is hardly bleeding. What did your reading tell you about the vertical mattress suture?" The question was his idea of a joke. As Lydia began to suture, G.O. said, "I owe you a debt of gratitude, Miss Freeman."

"And I'll collect it when I'm done. I should like to see the Captain's perch."

An hour later, they were standing on the widow's walk. Twilight was falling over the eastern marshlands, and the Pickworth Point lighthouse lantern was starting to glow. Out at sea, a single-mast ship, shining through the soft obliteration, appeared to collide in parallax with the lighthouse.

"I see why your father was so fond of this perch. It's some view."

"I suppose," he said, sighing miserably. "'Water, water, everywhere. Nor any drop to drink.'"

"I take it you don't care for being up here."

A soft breeze lifted a few strands of his honey-colored hair. "This is only my second trip to this lofty space. I recall that the first outing lasted all of three seconds."

She laughed. "It wasn't my intention to test your courage, sir."

"That's quite all right, since I tested yours." The doctor paused. "I am mortified by what transpired here this night. I beg you to accept my apologies."

"None needed, Doctor George."

"Regardless of what you must think of me, I am a conscientious physician. But my nerve fails me on occasion. Lord knows I try to prepare for the worst, but the unpredictable…"

"Nobody can anticipate everything."

"Quite right, Miss Freeman. But the fear of change is a very real sickness for me. A phobia, if you will. It's called misoneism, this fear of change. When I can't head it off, well, you witnessed what happens. Thank you again for your aid. Father always said you were steadfast and loyal."

"We all have our weaknesses, Doctor George."

"Yours are still a mystery to me, ma'am."

"Really?" She found that funny. "I'm a thirty-seven-year-old spinster for a reason."

"Do you fear a relationship?"

"Oh, Lord, no! I just do not know how to slow down long enough to attempt one. I am driven, sir, and at times it almost drives me out of my skin. Your father thought I must be running from grief."

"What kind of grief, Miss Freeman?"

"My mother died young and nameless. I was cut out of her dead womb. My father's identity lies at the bottom of a sea of oblivion. The Captain claimed I keep moving, patient to patient, illness to illness, taking care of others' lives while neglecting my own, so that I don't have to face the fact that I'll never have any answers to where I come from. I think he was right. The more I move, the less real seems my grief. But sometimes I feel like Coleridge's idle painted ship on a painted ocean."

"I assure you, there is nothing idle about what you did tonight."

Lydia edged toward the trap door. "If you don't mind, I'll just have me a last peek at the girl and be on my way."

Down on the ground floor, the newborn rested calmly in a crib beside his sleeping mother and grandmother, whose combined age was thirty-three years and two hours old. Lydia pinched the door closed. "Tomorrow," she whispered in the hall to Osborne, "I'll be back with plenty of baby formula. The poor girl isn't going to have enough milk of her own. I also have some herbal paste for her sutures. My own concoction."

As Osborne walked her to the front door, he plucked up his courage. "Miss Freeman, would you consider working with me on a full-time basis?"

"My word, you Osbornes and your skylarking notions! I have my own patients, sir."

"I'm talking about traditional medicine. You told Father you would have studied medicine if it wasn't barred to women and coloreds. Well, I'm a pretty good teacher, and I have an extensive library."

"Why, Doctor George? Why me?"

"You complement me, ma'am. You have something I do not."

"Whatever would that be?"

"A sense of humanity, Miss Freeman."

Lydia was moved. Not so much by the personal sentiment as by the fact that a man of Osborne's profession would admit he was deficient. "Well, the opportunity to learn medicine is tempting, Doctor George. Give me a day or two to think about it."

The Osborne-Freeman collaboration began in fall of 1832. She was an earnest student; he, an eager professor who taught better than he practiced. But the experiment nearly died in its infancy, carried away by a viral bigotry, the vehemence of which neither had anticipated. Onion Road was a busy byway, trodden the day long by all manner of sailor, builder, liveryman and fishmonger with an unobstructed view of the clinic's front garden, which was even visible from the masts of ships in port and the construction scaffolding going up in the area. Word spread of an unmarried white man and an unmarried colored woman having lunch as equals beside the Tuscan birdbath, and in no time a daily diet of verbal and, on occasion, physical abuse—tar, sewage and horse manure—was flung over the garden wall.

G.O. believed the dirt would blow away on its own, once the community recognized the team's professionalism. When it didn't and his practice continued to suffer, Osborne still resisted the urge to *kowtow*—a Chinese word just then in vogue, thanks to the Finley trade—to "Lilliputians who clearly do not deserve our care."

Lydia, more concerned for his practice than he was, wanted to quit, but Osborne wouldn't hear of it. "No, ma'am, we won't be dictated to by a mob."

"Be practical, Doctor George. We aren't doing anybody any good if we can't work. Either we come up with a solution quickly, or I must go."

One mild Sunday afternoon while the two associates were trimming the rose bushes, Lydia suddenly dropped her clippers, clasped her bosom and performed a strange dance, as if a bee had gotten under her robes, a most unlikely event considering the amount of crinoline enveloping her from chin to ankle.

"Goodness, what's wrong?" said G.O.

"Lost something," she said, grunting, clearly embarrassed by what was transpiring under her dress.

"Where?" he asked rather lamely.

"Here's a hint. Somewhere between my skin and clothing." She laughed uncomfortably. "If you would have the courtesy of turning around, I will try to rectify the matter."

Osborne did as told and turned to face Onion Road. But he wasn't deaf. He could hear the evocative swishing of her stiff robes and petticoats, and as the color deepened in his cheeks, he thanked his lucky stars he had his back to her.

"All right, it's done," she said at last. "You can look at me."

Her raiment and composure were back in place. His, not so much. "Here," she said, placing into his hand the object that had caused all the fuss: an old brown coin attached to a broken leather strap pulled through a hole nailed in the alloy. The coin still radiated her body heat, which ramped up his own temperature. "The strap snapped and the coin went trickling down the front of me."

"What an insolent piece!" he said, holding the coin between thumb and forefinger. "My goodness, the underside is rather sharp where the hole comes out. It must be awfully aggravating against your flesh."

"Flagellant as it sounds, I welcome that light sting. It's a reminder."

"Of what?"

"Call it unfinished business. This coin, Doctor George, is the only connection I have to my ancestry. My mother was wearing it when I was born."

With renewed interest, Osborne perused the trinket. Time and happenstance had burnished it to a fine sheen. "It's almost blank."

"Just like me. Traces of its past are almost gone forever."

"We'll see about that," said G.O. He trotted into the house and returned with his magnifying glass, set the coin on the marble birdbath and studied it. "Its inscriptions and diagrams are illegible but there might be enough to work with. Did Father know of its existence?"

"Yes, but he couldn't make heads nor tails of it, pardon the pun."

"Father was a sailor, Miss Freeman. Getting to the bottom of this sort of mystery requires scientific procedure. I know a man down at the wharf, an expert metallographer. With your permission, I'd like to show it to him."

The next morning, the man in question, Mr. Langtree, put the coin under a microscope. But the artifact stubbornly guarded its secrets. The waters of time had smoothed it like a brook stone. "I cannot decipher its words or shapes," Langtree mumbled into his instrument. "What I can say is that it is a composite of silver, copper and manganese. Probably two hundred years old, give or take a few years."

"Any idea what country it comes from, Langtree?"

"No. I've never seen another like it."

Outside the shop, Osborne did his best to cheer her up. "At least we know the coin's age. Surely that fact will lead us somewhere."

It led Lydia to tears, for which she apologized immediately. "Forgive me, Doctor George. It's the emotional investment…"

Osborne sympathized from a distance, at a loss for an appropriate show of compassion. "No need to explain, ma'am. It's disappointing, I understand, but…"

At that moment, a passing coach saved Osborne. The horses slowed and a voice hailed from the cabin. "George, my good fellow!" Out stepped William Finley, stovepipe hat in hand. "What a coincidence. I was just thinking about you," he said, clamping his hat upon his head. William was a fair-haired man of thirty-six, broadening with age and self-importance, his enormous mustaches a fitting testament to his ego. "I dare say, George, it is a rare day indeed to see you in these quarters."

"Will Finley, my good man! I don't believe you've met Miss Freeman."

"Never had the pleasure, but the Captain spoke glowingly of you, Miss Freeman—"

G.O. said, "Will and I were classmates at Harvard."

"That's right. You went to class and I was your mate," joked Finley, until he noticed Lydia's sad disposition. "Is something wrong?"

"No, sir," she said, blowing her nose. "I'm just a mite perplexed."

"Well, if it's Osborne here perplexing you, join the line. I've sent the rascal enough requests to wallpaper his clinic."

"My apologies for not responding, Will, but—"

"Nonsense, George. I understand completely. You're a doctor, for God's sake! My mundane affairs mustn't distract you. That's why I intend to unburden you of your shares in the company, old man. Name your price, and this time next week you'll be free as a bird and a hell of a lot richer." The stout Finley clapped a firm hand on the shoulder of the much taller Osborne, who considered the offer capital news.

"You're a godsend, Will. Listen, while you're here, be a good fellow and have a look at this coin. Have you ever seen another like it?"

William Finley held the coin up to the sun, lowered it to waist level and thumbed it into the air, all without much interest. "Sorry, George, can't say that I have." He handed it back. "Your shares, George. Let's settle things by week's end, old friend."

The walk back to Onion Road was done in silence, though their respective gaits spoke loudly. The doctor sauntered sprightly, while Miss Freeman dragged. As they entered the clinic, Osborne seemed ready to break into song. "Do you know what this means, Miss Freeman? This is the answer to our problems."

"No, it isn't," she said, gathering her belongings to go home. "Money isn't going to save your practice."

Osborne was stupefied. "It will buy us time."

"It will buy you regret for having cast away your father's legacy for expedience and short-term gain."

"A legacy built on human bondage, Miss Freeman— and one I want no part of."

"That's the Finleys' legacy, sir. The Captain got them *out* of that trade."

"And into a different sort of plunder," he shot back, immediately regretting his choler. "Forgive me, Miss Freeman. It is not my intention to settle old scores with Father at your expense. The simple truth is that I find the Finley business as dry as horse hay. Finley mail accumulates on my desk until exasperation allows me to toss it out."

"Shame on you, Doctor George. Finley sends ships all over the world. It carries on trade with the most mysterious empire in the world."

"Yes, and in the meantime, my own affair here in Neespaugot is foundering. Selling those shares might just keep this ship afloat, ma'am."

"Come on, sir, we both know what will keep your ship afloat. If I leave—"

A child's panicked petulance came out in Osborne's face and voice. "I won't let you go! No, I won't! Better Father's legacy than you!"

Lydia set her bag on the floor and drew the skinny giant into her warm embrace. "It's all right, George. We'll figure out something." Lydia did what she always did— she went to the kitchen to boil water for tea.

Over a warm cup, Lydia sought solutions to their dilemma in the past. "Did you know, Doctor George, that the Captain faced something of the kind before he died. I had been visiting him daily and oft-times spending the night. His neighbors didn't care for a colored woman in their vicinity."

"So, what did *he* do?" asked Osborne, with a mix of jealousy and admiration.

Lydia smiled. "You know what he did? 'Load the cannons, boys!'"

"Well, I'm no warrior, ma'am."

"You don't need to be, Doctor George. As a businessman, your father taught me that equal strength makes for an equitable trade. Your problem is that no one perceives your strength."

"I have no strength to speak of, Miss Freeman, that much is abundantly clear."

"Not true. Your Finley shares are strength."

"I'm not following you, Miss Freeman."

"Write William Finley a letter, thank him for his kind offer but tell him that you have *other* uses for your shares."

"What uses, Miss Freeman?"

"Does it matter, sir?"

Osborne began to understand.

A reply followed a week later. William Finley reminded his "Harvard brother" of the Finley's rich tradition dating back to the colonies and of "your own father's immense contribution" to the continuation of the company's survival.

"Oh, boy," said Osborne, whistling. "He's steaming like your teapot, Miss Freeman. He thinks I'm involved in a hostile takeover."

"Exactly."

"Now what? How are these shenanigans supposed to help the clinic?"

She smiled at him like a parent would an innocent child. "You don't keep up enough on current events, Doctor George. Neespaugot's richest woman, greatest gadabout and principal organizer of parties and fundraisers is pregnant."

"Elizabeth Finley?" Osborne got the picture and grimaced. "I wouldn't know where to begin, Miss Freeman. I don't possess that courage."

"Doctor George, you trusted a novice to perform a Caesarian on a child. Would you also entrust that same novice with the use of your good name? Allow me to draft the letter for you."

My Dear Friend William,

For more than a century, Finley Sons has been our young nation's vessel, an invaluable enterprise in which, as you were so good to remind me, my beloved father, himself an insightful entrepreneur, chose to place his capital. I for one would be loath, even heartbroken, to see the Finley endeavor ripped apart on the high seas of competition. As you know, my own enterprise, as dear to me as yours is to you, is traversing a different strait, a storm of bigotry, and I shall do what I must to save it. But before I take a definitive decision, perhaps you and I, Harvard brothers for life, can find a way to batten our respective hatches. Seven years ago, I assisted your dear Elizabeth in the birth of your first child Terrence. It would thus be an honor and the proof our friendship, as well as the bonds that link us, to deliver your new child at my clinic.

Your devoted servant,

George Osborne Jr., MD

Before a horde of indignant onlookers, Elizabeth Finley, the twenty-eight-year-old wife of the scion of Neespaugot shipping and the town's most popular socialite, waddled nine months pregnant into Osborne House. She emerged four days later, a wan smile on her face and a newborn son, Rutherford, cradled in her arms. Her husband William and several large-boned men of the sea accompanied her to a carriage waiting on Onion Road. Before boarding, she and her husband addressed the expectant crowd.

"At the risk of disappointing those of prurient expectations," she read from a written statement, "I say once and for all that the working relationship betwixt Doctor Osborne and his midwife Miss Freeman is of a highly professional order. Miss Freeman is infinitely competent, and I shall not hesitate in the future to call upon their services in all matters related to the health of my family. Thank you." The couple mounted the carriage steps and rode off.

Osborne Clinic entered its halcyon years, a twelve-year period of peace and prosperity stretching from 1832 to 1844. In deference to the Finleys, the inhabitants of North Bay adopted a see-no-evil-hear-no-evil attitude regarding the mixed-race, mixed-sex partnership. In public, the Osborne-Freeman relationship was referred to as "cousinly," and only complete strangers gave more than passing notice to the odd couple relaxing in the front garden, reading across a garden table from each other, devouring the writings of Emerson, Thoreau, Hawthorne, Longfellow and Whittier. William Finley explained to offended traders newly arrived in town, "It's nothing— only a dusty, sexless bachelor and spinster. Centaur and sphinx, if you will. No sap in either of them. Both dry as beach wood."

In spite of the favorable turn of events, Dr. Osborne grew progressively grimmer and gruffer, treating all except Lydia to his characteristic indifference, even rudeness. Around town, where his long faces were as predictable as the weather, he became known as Dr. Grump. "If Dr. Grump smiled, his face would crack." In his twenties, Osborne's practice of medicine had sufficed to counterbalance those dark moods that the times were ill-suited to define psychologically. In his thirties, his meeting Miss Freeman and becoming her mentor had been enough to sustain him, but she was such a fast learner that he finally reached his limits as her teacher. Now in his forties, a massive weight descended on him, and he trudged under it and tried to bear it, but he knew it was only a matter of time before he stopped moving altogether, and the full load crushed him to dust.

As always, Miss Freeman came to his rescue with the right remedy. She declared that she was ready to give her mystery another crack and charged him with the mission. "Are you up to the challenge, Doctor George?" The undertaking required that he first grapple with one of his demons: his repulsion of travel. Miss Freeman's coin was, according to the metallographer Langtree, around two hundred years old, while town records went back only about one hundred fifty years to when Neespaugot had been rebuilt, so Osborne would need to go to Boston.

Over the next few years, he would spend considerable time away in Boston, poring through archives in the Massachusetts State Hall of Records and the Boston Library. A scientific man, he had begun his research looking for particulars to prove the big picture. When that method turned up nothing, he changed tack for a deductive methodology, starting instead with the general picture and deducing the particulars. The night of her death, Miss Freeman's mother was in her teens and spoke no English, meaning she hadn't been in the country very long. She didn't conceal the coin from the midwife, meaning that it was probably a gift, not a theft. No one on a slave ship would have given her a gift, which meant that the coin originated from someone in America. Another slave or poor immigrant was unlikely since they would have kept the coin for themselves. Thus, her benefactor had to be an American, and the chances were good that the coin was American, too. Osborne followed that lead and learned that the young colonies had suffered from a scarcity of hard money coming from England. So, in 1652, they had started minting their own coins. The first ten coins ever minted in the new world had born a special inaugural stamp, that of the Massachusetts Bay Colony seal.

"Take a look," Osborne told Miss Freeman, rolling out a wax paper sketch on his desk. They were looking at a naked American Indian begging for help, ringed by the inscription "SIGILLVM GVB ET SOCIET DE MATTACHVSETS BAY IN NOVA ANGLIA."

"And you think this is what's engraved on my coin?" she asked, eyes darting between sketch and medal.

"For me, the lines match," said Osborne. "What stumped the metallographer was that all Colony coins after these original ten bore only 'New England' on the obverse and a plant on the reverse. Miss Freeman, I'm convinced that your coin is one of those first ten. But I have more, my dear. Eight of those original ten coins went to Puritan notables. But two were given as gifts to Indians."

Miss Freeman held up the coin and scrutinized it sideways.

Osborne continued, "I don't know about you, Miss Freeman, but I cannot see this coin around the neck of a Puritan. Those self-righteous folk didn't go in for personal ornament. And there's the matter of this nail hole here. It's a rather crude alteration, and I doubt a Puritan would have done this."

"So what you're saying is that this coin—and perhaps my ancestry—dates back to an Indian?"

Nodding, he told her that the first Indian recipient was Massasoit, Sachem of all the Massachusetts tribes.

But none of Osborne's research turned up any colonial writing linking the chief and the coin. "If Massasoit had worn it to meetings with the Puritans, surely some colonial scribe would have made mention of it, if only as a testament under God to the white man's superiority. And the same goes for Massasoit's two sons, Alexander, who was poisoned after becoming Sachem, and the younger and more formidable Philip. Philip in particular, with his penchant for strutting around naked, I would think that at least one of the many survivors from his captivity would have mentioned the coin. After the war, the dead Sachem's belongings—including his head, limbs and genitals—were inventoried and divided up. But there was no coin in his possession. Which brings us to the second Indian recipient."

Miss Freeman was on tenterhooks. "Please, Doctor George, you're killing me!"

An uncharacteristic giddiness escaped Osborne's sunken gray regard. "I'm quite confident the second fellow is your man. A Puritan minister, John Eliot, wrote about an extraordinarily long-lived native named Runinniduk, who also received a coin for his work in translating the Bible into Algonquian. He was executed."

"But you said he lived a long life."

"He did. The colony hanged a seventy-five-year-old."

"My Lord, what was his crime?"

"Murder."

"Murder? At seventy-five?"

"Sounds fishy, I agree. There are gruesome details I won't trouble you with. Suffice it to say, when they strung up the fellow in the Courthouse Square, no one mentioned a coin. And before this Runinniduk could be cut down, King Philip's War broke out, Neespaugot was burned to the ground and all the records went with it."

"But that was a good one hundred seventy-five years ago, Doctor George. What about all that came afterward? The people?"

"I'm afraid that's as far as I've gotten for now, my dear. But I promise you, I shall get to the bottom of your origins."

She smiled wanly. "You're a dear, Doctor George. And at least I know the origins of *you*," she said, cupping the coin in her palm. "*You* have a name. The Indian's coin. *You* have a history."

While G.O. immersed himself in discovering her roots, Lydia had a side project of her own. It had started by convincing G.O. of the absolute necessity of holding onto the Captain's Finley stocks in order to guarantee protection for Osborne Clinic. G.O. argued, rightly so, that having the stocks necessitated showing an interest in the company, and he wanted no part of the affair. "Then let *me* do it," Lydia said. "Using your name."

The idea both amused and fascinated G.O. "Why not? You did such a fantastic job of it the first time. You were the me I could never be."

Thus the halcyon years became entrepreneurial for Lydia. When she wasn't delivering babies into the world or helping the old and frail depart it with dignity or assuaging the myriad human ills that fell between, she was busy burning the midnight oil in her South Bay cottage, studying business sheets and drafting letters to Finley. She combined the Captain's sageness with her own brand of folksy wisdom, studied the doctor's handwriting, modified her own calligraphy to make it less feminine and signed all her letters "Dr. G. Osborne, Jr."

Osborne correspondence began arriving at Finley headquarters in 1836, shortly before the battle of the Alamo. William Finley and his board of directors were impressed enough to read Dr. G. Osborne, Jr.'s letters at board meetings. Lydia learned this one morning at the fish market, when she ran into William Finley himself and some other dapper gentlemen in long coats and tall hats. William was quite excited to see her and made a point of introducing each gentleman, all members of the board. "Miss Freeman," he said, "works with the genial sawbones." The fellow on Finley's right insisted she tell Osborne thank you from all of them. "His participation has galvanized our meetings." "Hear, hear," the gentleman to Finley's left chimed in. "He has given us good insight with regard to the company's overseas operations," pointed out yet another gent. Said another, "And for a doctor, he has a sound grasp of venture capitalism, price indexing, bond trading and this newfangled science of publicity." "Yes, his letters are a must-read at our meetings." Finley quipped, "Guess the Captain's commercial savvy rubbed off on junior after all! Would it trouble you, Miss Freeman, to convince him to attend a board meeting now and then? Letters are fine, but we'd all like to pick his brains in person."

Lydia promised to do her best.

At no time during that period did William Finley ever question the authorship of the Osborne letters. On the contrary, by the 1840s, the company was acting on Lydia's suggestions. For example, the board voted unanimously in favor of her motion to establish additional outposts in Oregon "for the day when that fertile trail becomes a river of emigration and is annexed into the nation." Three years later, the Great Emigration began, opening up the Pacific Northwest to Finley commerce. Lydia also insisted on the absolute necessity of William Finley's presence in Canton as the United States government bore down on normalizing commercial regulations with China. On her recommendation, Finley sailed with Caleb Cushing when the diplomat negotiated his famous trading treaty with the emperor. Thereafter, Finley Sons, Transporters enjoyed *quid pro quo* privileges in all major Chinese seaports.

G.O. himself derived a vindictive pleasure from Lydia's success. "Such poetic justice!" he said, laughing. "The daughter of slaves transported to America in the bowels of a Finley ship is now spinning the company's fate."

Her singular accomplishments as an advisor were bittersweet for Lydia. Each success was shackled to the lie about her true identity. She was not Doctor Osborne. Legally speaking, she wasn't even a doctor. She was just another invisible colored woman. Worse, she was *that woman*. Her race, bright robes, shorn head and sunny disposition made her fellow Neespaugotans nervous. Lydia considered herself as steady as rain, but somehow the townspeople saw her as unpredictable, and unpredictability bred contempt. Like Hester Prynne in *The Scarlet Letter*, Lydia became a depository for their bile and shame. Fortunately, even contempt turns bland with time, and spite and malice lose their teeth, as long as nothing stirs up the bile.

When Lydia arrived for work that warm, muggy morning of July 12, 1844, she found a note attached to the iron gate: "Dear Patients, the medical practice is closed today due to extraordinary circumstances. With our apologies, George Osborne, M.D."

As Lydia hurried up the walk, G.O. sauntered from the house, as cheery as she had ever seen him. He was hiding something behind his back. "What would you say to a picnic at the shore?" he bandied.

"Have you lost your marbles, Doctor George? It's a workday."

"Wrong. It's your birthday, ma'am." From behind his back he produced a popping bouquet of roses. "Happy fiftieth, my dear Miss Freeman!"

Osborne had thought of everything: a tippet for Lydia, a blanket, towels, two stools to sit on, a parasol, a basket of food and some reading material. He had even hired a horse and buggy from the livery at the bottom of the street. The doctor wasn't much good at handling a horse, so Lydia took the reins. They clopped out of North Bay heading north for Stanley Cove, a deserted area of gray dunes, tall grasses and stubby shrubs, mostly leatherleaf and laurel. Lydia stopped the buggy at a cluster of stunted white oak and red pines, and Osborne hopped off to unbridle the horse and set down twin buckets of dry meal and water. Once the animal was securely hitched to a tree, the two of them hoisted their stores and set off across the dune for the beach.

The early morning haze dulled the horizon. The temperature was mild, and the smell of musk sweetened the air. Low tide stretched its mucky tongue almost a mile out to sea. There was no one else on the beach, only a thick gathering of gulls, terns, peetweets, cormorants and egrets.

They settled themselves in behind a dune, spreading a blanket, poking the stools in the sand. Each had his respective reading material. G.O. sat on his stool and dove into Goethe's *Roman Elegies*.

"Shame on you," said Lydia, teasing. She was no stranger to that erotic work.

"I will tolerate that only because it's your birthday, ma'am." He saw that she had an issue of *Graham's Magazine* folded on her lap. "And what might you be working through today?"

"A recent story of E.A. Poe."

"Isn't he that *Grotesque and Arabesque* writer?"

"That's right, and I must say, it's right up your alley."

"How so?"

"It's about solving a mystery using deductive reasoning."

"Do tell."

"The police break into a room locked from the inside and uncover the mangled bodies of two murdered women but no sign of their killer. The windows are also locked and located high above the street. The neighbors heard the killer's voice but can't agree on his nationality. The police are stumped. Enter Monsieur Dupin, a brilliant crime solver who espouses the principle of ratiocination. I haven't reach the end yet, but I'd bet my coin that Dupin will deduce what happened."

"He'll visualize the entire puzzle and work back toward its individual missing pieces. It's the process I'm applying to discover your origins."

"If only it could work as well as it does in stories, Doctor George."

"It will, ma'am. Of that I am certain."

The morning haze burned off, leaving a beautiful blue day. Gulls gathered on the loamy shore as the encroaching tide, time made visible, erased more and more land. At noon the couple nourished themselves on cold meats, bread and fruit, and they drank beer out of steins. Both became lightheaded and in need of a move. Osborne rolled up his trousers, Lydia removed her shoes, and they took a stroll along the beach.

The key to their partnership had always been frank conversation. Lydia and Osborne thought alike on so many issues that their discussions were more often exercises in common sense than debates. Still, they enjoyed airing their opinions to each other, there being no one else in Neespaugot with whom they could do so. As they walked along the shoreline, their conversation transported them along a variety of topics: the growing number of grand-scale ore and oil industries in America, the weakening of the Fugitive Slave Act in Prigg vs. Pennsylvania, the Underground Railroad and immigration.

Back at their picnic spot, they nibbled on the rest of their lunch, quaffed more beer and ventured into a more personal subject.

"Ma'am, do you ever regret not having children?"

"Sometimes. It's a regret I can live with. What about you?"

"I would have liked a son."

"Heck, it's not too late, Doctor George. You wouldn't be the first gent your age to marry a younger woman and start a family."

The thought made him scoff. "You'll find your ancestry before I wed a younger woman and have a child."

"Be bold, Doctor George."

"You do like teasing me."

Half an hour later, they took another walk, this time along a sandbar that looped out to sea and hooked back toward the shore like an enormous claw. Lost in thought, conversation and time, they reached the tip of the claw before they knew it and now faced a forty-five-minute hike back the way they had come. The other possibility, if they didn't mind getting wet, was to wade across the gulf between the claw and their beach, which stretched out before them only fifty yards away as the crow flies.

"Let's cross it," said Lydia.

"We'll catch our deaths."

"Come on," she taunted, tugging him by the arm into the water. They were both amazed to find that the water got no deeper than thigh level. "Look, Doctor George, we're cutting a path through the middle of the ocean. When I was little, I used to dream about being stranded at sea."

"My own *bête noir* was a nasty black dog. It chased me all over hell. Lanky and slow as I am, I got bitten a lot," he chuckled, the alcohol making him talk fast and slur. As they waded, G.O. pointed at the beach ahead. "Speaking of childhood recollections, my English nanny used to bring me here."

"You were a boy once, Doctor George?"

"A mindful boy at that!"

"The patience your nanny must've had, getting the likes of you to the beach."

"And how much trouble was I this morning?"

"If your nanny contented herself to wait until she turned fifty, I suppose you weren't much trouble at all."

He spent a moment in quiet reflection but did not lose his train of thought. "I recall that Miss Templeton brought me here quite frequently. I must admit I had a terrible crush on her."

"Ooh, the plot thickens!"

"Well, that's it, really. A foolish boy's first crush. I was very sad when she left."

They forded the rest of the way across the inlet to the opposite bank. The wet had crept up Lydia's skirts like a miniature tide, reaching her waist. They climbed the beach and plunked themselves down to catch their breaths. A pleasant breeze blew over them. The water in the inlet began to widen and deepen. He reached over and took her hand in a gentle embrace. Suddenly, he made a motion to kiss her. She recoiled.

"The tide's coming in, Doctor George. We'd best head back to town."

"Lydia," he pleaded, still gripping her hand.

"Goodness, the liquor has gone to your head."

"One of us could drop dead tomorrow."

"Or wish she were dead. We must stop this game before it goes too far."

"It's no game. Not for me."

"Doctor George, you have always known the limits. You must get a grip."

"Lydia… look at me."

His expression was so filled with yearning and stark male carnality that it struck her like a fist, dazing her. He leaned forward again. She leaned back on an elbow, her last buttress between him and lying flat on her back.

"This is getting out of hand, Doctor George. We're too old for this malarkey."

"Can one ever be too old to love, Lydia?"

"Love?"

"I am not deluding myself nor am I drunk. I love you, Lydia Freeman."

Her elbow tired and she dropped on her back. He fell on her and kissed her, peppering her face with odd quick pecks before settling his lips on hers. She came up panting. "George, please stop before we bring ruin on ourselves. I still have my menses."

"The chances," he cried, fumbling under her skirts.

"I beg you heed that favorite quote of yours from Emerson. 'Only shallow men believe in luck.'"

"Emerson be damned," he said.

He sheared her of two robes and a petticoat, until she lay naked under the sun, her exquisite brown flesh a godsend to his unbelieving eyes. "Lydia, I have been such a fool." He nosed her damp, cotton-scented skin. As his fingers played with her labia, she felt a sensation so overpowering that for a moment she was sure she had fainted. She felt his hardness against her thigh, witnessed the strange dance in his face, mirroring what transpired between their hips. She felt herself melt, wondered if it was even possible for a woman of her age to be so receptive. And then her answer came, for his penetration, though rough and rash, did not cause her nearly the pain she had anticipated. And, almost at once, her body surprised her by rushing still more balm to soothe the act. A great shudder hoisted her. She thrust forward against his weight, lost contact with the beach, and never remembered the descent.

Only when she opened her eyes again did Lydia realize that her index finger was punctured with her own toothmarks. Her loins oozed and her thighs squeaked. She didn't recall his having climbed off her, but he now lay beside her, on his back, panting, his trousers pushed down around his knees, his sated sex shriveled asleep. The sea breeze cooled the sweat on her dark belly. His hand found hers.

"I am sorry." His voice was raspy, and not completely as content as it had been a moment before. The alcohol and elation had abandoned him. "I was a beast."

"Say no more, George. A half-century of suppression had to come out somehow."

"But my feelings for you are sincere, Lydia." To prove it, he got to an elbow so that she might look into his eyes, his heart. "I am in love with you. Are my sentiments reciprocated?"

She squeezed his hand.

An old wives' tale of the time went that a woman might know whether she was pregnant by urinating on a coin and then holding it up to the light of a full moon. It was the kind of hokum invented *by* old women *for* credulous young ones. But one midsummer's night, a woman both old and possibly pregnant could be seen on Onion Road, squatting behind a sycamore tree in front of the medical clinic, peeing on a small piece of copper and manganese, and holding the wet coin against the firmament, waiting for a sign. Metal and urine met moonlight, and lo and behold the figure of an Indian materialized on her medallion, pleading, *Come over and help us.* "We are doomed," she muttered.

Some weeks later, Lydia found G.O. sitting at his desk in the parlor, ruminating. "George," she announced, "I am pregnant." He did not react immediately. His long skeletal fingers remained pressed against his lips, his depth of thought seemingly unreachable by the sonar of her message. But he had heard her, and after a time he rose to the surface and spoke. "Then let us wed."

Lydia grew cross. "George, you're not thinking straight. It's the end of everything. I must go away."

"To end up like your mother? A pregnant colored woman on the run, dying in childbirth? Never! I shall not allow it. You will stay put where I can protect you and our child."

"Noble of you, George, but who will protect you?"

"Bah! I need no protection nor do I give a farthing for this practice or its inhabitants. You and our child will be my only concerns."

"Without a practice, you'll have other concerns. How will we make do?"

"My Finley holdings will tide us over."

As word of Lydia's condition spread through the North Bay, the practice's clientele dried up like drops of sweat on a summer sidewalk. Late nights brought lewd effigies strung up on the branches of the sycamore tree outside the gate. Empty ale tankards and bottles of piss sailed into the garden. G.O. delivered his own son in June 1845, a healthy, light-skinned mulatto baby with orange freckles and honey-colored frizz. They named the child Randolph, Randy for short, in honor of Runinniduk, who had perished on a similar June day one hundred seventy years before.

Driven more by pride than necessity, G.O. stumped the wharf for needy patients, distributing leaflets advertising inexpensive medical care, but his action drew hostility and heckles. People, he concluded, were spiteful creatures preferring sickness, scandal and the preservation of their reputations over their own welfare. The devil take them all! He steeled himself inside his home, a good doctor reduced to tending to sick rose bushes, cedar hedges and a dying chamomile lawn.

Randolph's birth had been fraught with complications and had lasted close to eighteen hours. Lydia recovered slowly, but once on her feet, she took her skills into the poorest parts of South Bay, where she bartered medical consultation for food, clothing and household repairs. People, she found, were more comfortable exchanging for help than receiving it for free.

The first five years following the scandal, Lydia made the South Bay trip three times a week, catching the morning coach that crossed the Neespaugot River into the factory district. When Randy was old enough for grammar school, his skin color excluded him from all North Bay public and parochial schools, so Lydia enrolled him in South Bay and set up daily consultations in her old cottage until the school day was finished. Mother and son rose at 4:30 a.m. in order to be at school at 7:30. In the early 1850s, they would gain some time with the establishment of a ferry service linking Grover Wharf with the South Bay port-of-call.

The daily grind was tough on the boy; worse was growing up in a climate of danger and fear. From the pre-dawn moment when he and his mother stepped onto Onion Road to sunset when they closed the clinic's iron gate behind them, they could always expect some sort of verbal or physical harassment. They were denied access or kicked off the coach and ferry for bogus reasons, and shoved and heckled and pelted with any number of vile substances as they crossed the wharf and port-of-call. "Mama," asked Randy, "Why do these people hate us?"

"It's like a cold, son. They are ill."

"But you heal them and they still call us names. Why bother?"

"Ignorance is a most intractable virus, sweet boy. But giving up is not the answer."

The boy's father had given up. The doctor stood in the parlor window, a self-made prisoner in his own home. His once proud garden, a mirror image of himself, was going to seed. "Mind you," Randy's papa said to his mama. "They'll be coming back in droves one day. And when that day happens, I shall say my piece."

"And just what will you say, dear?" said his mama.

"Shove off, that's what!"

His mama called it the fantasy of an Apollonian world. Sounding off gave his papa a momentary pleasure that disappeared like daylight in the parlor window.

Randy loved fishing, so his mama braved the community's abuse and took him to the wharf, where they hooked night crawlers on a bent nail. The boy was a patient fisherman, and his mama told him that he would have made his grandfather, the Captain, very proud indeed. The boy already knew plenty about the Captain but nothing about his mama's kin. "Tell me something about your papa," begged Randy.

"How's this?" said Mama. "We'll play a game, a detective game." She sat down beside him on the pier. "If you walked into a room and found an apple missing a slice, what would you deduce?"

"Someone had cut it."

"With what?"

"A knife."

"But what if the knife was missing? Would that change your mind about what kind of object was used to slice the apple?"

"No."

"Good. We don't have to see it to know it was used. All right, let's start. There was once a very old Indian man named Runinniduk. That we know. He was very probably the first owner of this medal I'm wearing. Maybe he was our ancestor, maybe not. What we do know is that he liked wearing the coin whenever he came into town. He died in town, so he was probably wearing it then, but no townsperson had the chance to take it off his body before Metacom's army attacked the town. But someone retrieved his body and kept the coin, even though it had no monetary value. What does that say about the person?"

"He liked the strap?"

She chuckled. "No. But probably Runinniduk and his coin meant a lot to this person. Now, Runinniduk was very old, so he probably had grandchildren, and one of them might be this person. For the sake of argument, let's give this grandchild a name."

"Great Eagle!"

"Ooh, yes, I like that. Great Eagle was very brave and strong, but King Philip's war went badly for the Indians, and Great Eagle was killed, so one of his sons collected the coin. What shall we name him?"

"Swift Arrow!"

"Swift Arrow it is. Let's suppose that Swift Arrow survived the war and escaped to Canada. The years passed and Swift Arrow's great-nephew Long Hair desired to see the land of his ancestors, so he brought the coin back to Neespaugot. Long Hair became wealthy fishing for cod. He sent his son Fighting Bear to Dartmouth College to become a lawyer. After college, Fighting Bear sued the colonials for native land. Fighting Bear was imprisoned, but the Revolutionary War broke out. Fighting Bear fought on the side of the revolutionaries, but he was killed in battle. His son Kenneth Silver Bird saved the family coin."

"He's a great big Indian, Mama."

"Right you are. So the great big Indian returned to Neespaugot and took up his grandfather's fishery business right over there," she said, pointing to a Finley warehouse. "One day, while Kenneth Silver Bird was out on the water, fishing, he saw a boat run aground off the coast of South Bay. It was a Finley slave ship abandoned by its crew because of a cholera outbreak. Kenneth Silver Bird could hear the cries of the sick and dying coming from the galley. Should he steer clear of the infected vessel?"

"No, Mama. He must save them."

"You're right, Randy. Kenneth Silver Bird came to their rescue. He climbed aboard, took a hatchet to the locked hull, lifted the hatch and was thrown back by the stench. He sent a burning torch into the monstrous cavity of human swill and disease. The dead were everywhere in the hull of that ship, outnumbering the living by four to one. Kenneth lowered a rope and, one by one, pulled to the deck those with the strength to hold on."

"How many did he save?"

"Fourteen men, eight women and three children. He got them all to shore. But then a heavily armed mob turned up."

"What's a mob?"

"A group of people wanting to do violence. The mob wanted to kill the survivors to protect the town. Kenneth told the slaves to run for their lives. After much shooting on the beach, the mob set the Finley ship ablaze."

"Did Kenneth Silver Bird get away, Mama?"

"Yes! He managed to save a fifteen-year-old girl. She's African, so we'll call her Teya Bai. Along with her sick mother. Neither knew any English. Kenneth hid them deep in the Great Swamp, where the mother died. But Kenneth took good care of the girl. Teya Bai was a thin but strong Senegalese, very black, with beautiful eyes and cheeks. In no time, Kenneth was in love with her. He feared taking her back to town, so he made runs for provisions. On one such run, late at night, his wagon overturned and he was crushed to death."

"What happened to Teya Bai?"

"She was left to fend for herself. And she was going to have a child, Kenneth's child. Famished, she made it into Neespaugot on the eve of July 11, 1794. She died the next morning, giving birth to me."

The boy hooked a flounder and pulled it in. As he was gutting it, he said, "I want to know the real story, Mama."

"So would I, son. But we may have to live with the possibility that we will never know who my ancestors were."

Griffin

November 21, 1860

1

Mayhem was Mad Dog's religion. Kelly's Bar and Saloon, his place to preach. The infamous Kelly's, one of a half-dozen sleazy cathouses piled at the west end of Grover Wharf, catered to a clientele of drunken Irishmen, swabbies of all nationalities and peacekeepers such as Mad Dog, who was merely a glorified thug with a club. The establishment offered a large storage area off the back alley, a perfect area for Mad Dog to "question" suspects. That meant beating the shite out of someone, dragging the person down the alley to the pier and throwing him into the black current lapping at the pilings. One loud plop, two Hail Marys, and Mad Dog was usually back at the bar before the froth on his pint had settled. "A fecking baptism in the bay," he called it.

But this particular November night, something was detaining Mad Dog. It had been a good hour since he'd run a Portuguese sailor out back for questioning, and his mates Paddy and Ian were getting concerned. With barely a brain between them, the two peacekeepers stumbled off their stools and wobbled out the front door to the wharf. They howled Mad Dog's name against a waxing moon. No response. Maybe he had taken the plunge along with his suspect. Such a happenstance, they agreed, would be a benediction, for Mad Dog was without a doubt the evilest mick in New England. "We'd best keep a-looking fer the bastard anyway," said Paddy. "Case he's still breathing."

"That'd be prudent," said Ian. "Wouldn't want him mad at us."

They found Mad Dog lying in the storage area behind Kelly's, unconscious, his face planted in his own vomit, his skull cracked open. Stellar detectives, Paddy and Ian deduced that the suspect had gotten away. Based on that evidence, as well as the fact that Mad Dog was too big and mean to lose a fight, Paddy figured Mad Dog's interrogation was no doubt interrupted by the desire to retch, at which point the Portuguese sailor had had the good sense to seize the moment and whack ol' Mad Dog on the crown with his own billy club, which Ian spotted lying a few feet away in the light of a whale-oil lamp dangling over Kelly's garbage racks.

The two geniuses requisitioned Kelly's wheelbarrow and trundled Mad Dog down the dark boardwalk. Slightly less than a mile away, the Nigger Doctor's clinic on Onion Road bartered medical care against food and clothing. Neither peacekeeper intended to give the doctor anything, for they knew from experience that even if you had nothing to barter, the Nigger Doctor always saw to your ills.

They made Onion Road around three in the morning and stopped at the broken gate. Ian pushed the gate aside with his boot, and they rolled their charge up the walkway to the house.

Mad Dog was a brawny brute, and it took all of Paddy and Ian's collective strength to hoist him out of the wheelbarrow and up the steps to the front door. The knocker was broken, so Ian used his fist. They heard the deadbolt draw, and a grizzled half-breed with a sheep-sheared head opened the door. She held a candle in one hand and gripped her buttonless housecoat about her bony frame with the other.

"Wounded constable," said Ian. "He's bleeding bad from the head. Fetch the doctor, woman."

"You men wait here and don't any make noise," she said. "There's a thirteen-year-old youngster upstairs who needs his sleep, even if the rest of us got an eternity for that." And she closed the door.

"Don't make any noise, she says," said Ian, annoyed at being told what to do by a Negress. His vexation turned to mischief, and he broke into song.

As I went home on Monday night
as drunk as drunk could be
I saw a horse outside the door
where my old horse should be
Well, I called me wife and I said to her:
Will you kindly tell to me

Who owns that horse outside the door
where my old horse should be?

Paddy joined in:

Ah, you're drunk, you're drunk,
you silly old fool,
So drunk you cannot see
That's a lovely sow
that me mother sent to me!
Well, it's many a day I've travelled
a hundred miles or more,
But a saddle on a sow
sure I never saw before.
As I went home on the Tuesday night—

"Shush!" The woman was back, cutting their vulgar week short. "Shame on the two of you!" She had changed out of her bed rags into a royal blue choir robe. Beads of water shone on her jaw line and forearms. "Bring him in."

Neither Ian nor Paddy had ever set foot inside the Nigger Doctor's house, though they had left plenty of suspects slumped at the front gate. They followed the half-breed down a long, musty corridor running straight through the gut of the house to a small, frowsy chamber. It was a simple room, wallpapered in tawny poppies and daisies. There was a sink with a pump faucet, a dusty cabinet of yellowed medical supplies and, in the opinion of the two Irishmen, a conspicuous lack of religious paraphernalia.

"What's keeping the doctor?" asked Ian.

"Put your man on the bed there and take off his boots," she said.

"What for? The rest of him is just as dirty."

She gave them a look that compelled them to remove Mad Dog's shoes.

The woman opened the cabinet and took out a bottle of whiskey and some linen washcloths. The stale air accentuated the stench of the men's body odor and prior imbibitions.

"This fellow is dead drunk," she said.

"Naw, he stinks from the fight. You see, what opened his skull was a full bottle of corn liquor."

She wasn't buying their story. "Your man is fuller than an egg."

"The doc is taking his flipping time about getting here," said Ian.

"Gents, Doctor Osborne is sleeping. I'm the only doctor you're getting."

"Whoa! Now hold on there. This man needs a doctor, not some potato peeler."

"Fine by me. You can take him elsewhere."

Paddy was hesitant. "Where else is there, Ian?"

The woman upped the ante. "I suggest you gents make up your minds before he sobers up."

Paddy and Ian, two heads with one brain, nodded at the woman.

She poured good whiskey on Mad Dog's skull, stitched him up and bound his noggin. When Mad Dog came to, he took one look at her, reared up and grabbed her by the neck. Ian and Paddy figured it was curtains for the Negress, but Mad Dog suddenly went woozy and fell back on the bed. "You filthy black hell-cat bitch!" he said. "You keep yer bloody hands off me!"

"Get him out of here," she said, massaging her neck.

Paddy and Ian each climbed under an arm as heavy as sheetrock and edged Mad Dog, who was still spewing invective, toward the door. "I'll be back, nigger, and I'll skin you and yer whole fecking family alive!"

2

Like a Samson or Hercules, Sean Griffin was a physical freak of nature with little to redeem him. Raised in Limerick by an abusive alcoholic father for whom all communication had started and ended with a fist, Sean had been conditioned to crave a daily dose of violence, and his incredible size supported the habit. By the time he was eighteen years old, Sean stood six feet three inches, weighed close to twenty stone, and had already sent countless men and boys to the hospital—two to the morgue. His father convinced him that his potential to extort money was lost on that woebegone county of stick-and-bone paupers, and that he might as well give America a try, "where they call crime public office."

Sean took to the road, beating and extorting his way south, arriving at Cobh Harbor on September 17, 1847, still a few shillings short of a ticket on the frigate *Miles Standish.* He roamed the quadrant, strong-arming steerage hopefuls, but eventually he realized his father was right: shaking down misery and desperation was like trying to squeeze juice from leather. Steaming like hot gas and ready to explode, Sean received a tap on the shoulder. He swung round prepared to rip the nose off someone's gob when he found himself looking at a small, young woman with a belly like a barrel of beer. "What!?" he said.

"Me name's Kate. Kate Coughlin. I was told yer out a few farthing, lad."

Sean eyed her with suspicion. "What the bejasus would it be to a north-country bitch such as yerself?" He wiped the filth from his chin.

"It'd be worth plenty to me *and* you. You see, lad, they're not letting unmarried pregnant Catholics board this boat, nor be they letting ticketless louts from Limerick aboard. Should you be neither Catholic nor married, we could be of mutual benefit to each other."

"Feck no, I'm not married! And I hate Catholics almost as much as the bloody Protestants—"

"Then are ye willing to part with yer last name fer some money?"

The freckled-faced lass, aside from a belly's worth of baby, was quite comely, with emerald eyes and sunset hair. Sean's rough face, its bone structure bearing the blows of diverse objects, sharp and blunt, widened with a lecher's grin. He ogled her bosom as if he possessed it already. He imagined the little minx supplementing him in all kinds of ways across the rollicking North Atlantic. "All right then, me lass, show us the quid."

Before doing so, Kate requested he lower his head, him being twice her size, so that she might have a word in his ear. "Just so's we're clear, lad," she whispered. "If I have the money to share with you, it's because the rotter whose throat I slit won't be needin' it." Her breath wafted off her lips sweet as death, and her soft voice was as chilling as a North Sea wind. Sean, no stranger to murder himself, recognized the music of death when he heard it. "Don't look so surprised, lad. Cuttin' throats is what I was born to. First it was chickens and rabbits and sheep, then bitch nuns and now bastards what make the mistake of thinkin' they own me. Are you followin' me? Good, now be a gint and collect me bags. We're going to see the dockside priest."

On the crossing, Kate Coughlin miscarried. Calm as a wash maid folding linen, she rolled the fetus in a ragged bedsheet and tossed the bundle overboard. If she was grieved about it, she didn't show it. Sean wondered if the fetus's father was the luckless dolt who had unwittingly funded their voyage, but he didn't dare ask. The truth was that he didn't want to know. What good was such information to him? All that counted was that the witch he now called his wife had disgorged the fecker like a swine. Now that they were halfway across the Atlantic, the thought struck Sean that Kate might slit his own throat and dump him overboard with less compunction than she'd shown her fetus. But she allayed his fear. "Not to worry, lad, we'll be needin' each other for a while to come."

Kate allowed him a nightly poke. Steerage was overcrowded and stank of the emanations of a wretched humanity, so he and Kate fucked on deck, the crew watching but none daring to open his trap. She lay under him, neither pleased nor displeased, and let him get about the business until he was done.

To Sean, his new missus seemed old, though not in a physical sense; years-wise, she wasn't much older than Sean. But there was something stale about her. Her lovely face emitted no light of its own and, but for the occasional and accidental brilliance of her rush of rusty curls, her demeanor remained cold, a magnificent sculpture changing hues according to the sunlight, dead to the heart. She was an enigma to him, and it was her enigmatic personality that scared him to death and subjugated him.

After favorable winds and an eight-day crossing, the *Miles Standish* reached Neespaugot's deep-water harbor—the Industrial Revolution had rendered North Bay's historic Old Port obsolete—where the ship disgorged its hundreds of destitute Irish men, women and children onto Grover Wharf and into the hands of processing agents who studied, stamped and funneled the lot toward the South Bay slums surrounding a host of factories. Neespaugot Cotton Manufactory was a water-powered, cotton-to-cloth textile mill and New England Machines produced the machines for making the cloth. Neespaugot Iron and Wire fashioned barbed wire for the Wild West, U.S. Iron pounded out railroad girders and canal locks, and American Envelope ran off twenty-five thousand envelopes per day. There was a water and coal refinery and a glass factory. The steam-powered United Shoe Machinery, or simply the Shoe, pumped out army boots and uniforms.

Kate Coughlin and Sean Griffin went to work sixty hours a week in a poorly ventilated seven-story building at the mouth of the Neespaugot River. Sean was lazy, shiftless and ill-humored, and didn't last a year. He had turned up at the mill late one dawn, drunk and surly, and when the foreman demanded that he account for himself, Sean lifted the man and heaved him over a spinning jenny. He then hoisted a warping machine and hurled it through a wall. It took six peace officers to restrain him. That incident earned him the sobriquet Mad Dog.

Sean's time in jail proved beneficial because he discovered what he wanted to do for a living: wear a badge, bully people and call it "law and order." Needing to contend with two hundred thousand newly immigrated Irishmen, the municipality was only too happy to entrust a bloke such as Sean with a nightstick and a license to commit mayhem.

Kate worked six more years in the mill, until 1856, when her employers, the textile moguls Cabot, Brown and Thorton, noticed her punctuality, meticulousness and barren household, and transferred her to their Pickworth Point estates to housekeep, mind their children and run errands for their rich wives. A fourth scion, Mrs. William Finley, hired Kate in 1858, to do chores at her mansion.

Between 1856 and 1860, Kate Coughlin Griffin learned three things about rich people and their attics: what went up never came down, the dross was worth a small fortune to poor folk and skeletons abounded. The Finley attic in particular was a gold mine of bric-a-brac, sculptures, trinkets, tribal weaponry, baubles inlaid with gold and gems from all corners of the globe—from Zanzibar to Shanghai, New Guinea to Hawaii—all of it brought back as gifts by generations of tasteless men to appease sedentary women with no patience for any of it. Kate's rule of thumb was to filch only what she could comfortably conceal. Silk cloth, books, bits of silverware, small pieces of china and, whenever she could find them, jewels and money. The booty went straight to Grover Wharf, to Irish middlemen selling to outgoing vessels. The income from her thieving, Kate would smuggle back into the Finley attic and hide it with the lifesavings she had brought from Ireland. The Finley mansion attic was her shelter from Sean.

One day while sifting through the Finley attic, Kate discovered a finely crafted dark-wood chest about the size of a toolbox. It was unlocked—and this was a mild disappointment to her, because a chest of valuables would normally be locked. And she was right, for the case contained only business correspondence: invoices, bills of lading and business ledgers, some dating from colonial times. Their numbers and figures followed by dollar signs piqued Kate's curiosity, so she examined the papers more closely. That was how she learned that the Finleys had been slave traders.

Kate wasn't surprised. More often than not, the bloody rich were more crooked than locust branches. Still, how could she exploit this trove? Perhaps she could make a few pennies selling the papers to those fanatics calling themselves Abolitionists? Unconvinced, Kate continued rifling in the chest for something more concrete and came across a letter from a certain Edwin Tall Tree, also called the Black Injun. This Black Injun fellow was writing to his "Dear friend Paul (Finley)," thanking him for "sharing such an important book, which doth render me happy in heart that a record exists of my grandmother's extraordinary life and quest to recover our tribe's homeland. I herewith return the book with glad tidings, Signed, Edwin Tall Tree, the Black Injun, 1772."

Intrigued, Kate rummaged for the aforementioned book, which she found at the bottom of the chest, bound in oilcloth and string. With her claw knife, she snipped the string, drew back the cloth and found a slim book with a pistol-colored leather cover and a faded title: *Blue Devil: the Trials of a Wampanoag Woman*. Above the author's name (Daniel Hillard) was an embroidered picture of a Punch-and-Judy Indian pleading for help that, the back cover explained, was on the seal of the Massachusetts Bay Colony. Across the inside cover page was a handwritten dedication: "My dear Colin, This Injun woman's exploits might hearten you in your bitter economic argument with the Crown. With great respect and devotion, Your loving father, Andrew. Neespaugot 1725."

The bloody book was one hundred thirty-five years old! Its pages were as spare and brittle as dried maple leaves. Figuring it had to be worth something, Kate pinched it and took it home where she began to read it.

The nuns of The Little Sisters had taught Kate enough about reading the Bible to know that she had never wanted to read anything ever again. So it surprised her when she had devoured *Blue Devil* in a sitting, the first book she had ever read that wasn't the Bible. The fact that she understood the book told her that it had no doubt been written for laggards like herself. Nonetheless, it was a fascinating education into the history of early Neespaugot and its Puritans, Runinniduk and his coin, King Philip and his war, and Melba Blue Jay and her long legal battle over ownership of the Great Swamp.

But as interesting as the story was, *Blue Devil* offered Kate minimal gain, perhaps twenty cents on the wharf, if that. Still, money was money, and Kate promised herself to hawk it at the first occasion down at Grover Wharf.

Then, an incident changed her mind. As Kate was serving tea and crumpets to the chattering patronesses of privilege at the Finley mansion, she overheard a conversation pertaining to the so-called Nigger Doctor and his midwife, Lydia Freeman.

"There I was," said Elizabeth Finley, "ready to give birth to Rutherford at their clinic when that crazy-fool doctor came in and announced he was going to Boston to research the origins of that stupid old coin of Miss Freeman's."

Kate's ears pricked up at the mention of "old coin." Surely those fattened cows of fortune weren't referring to the coin she had spent her afternoon reading about? Kate lingered longer in the salon.

Several of the guests moaned in unison. "Ah, *the* coin!"

"I swear, she never takes it off," said Mrs. Brown.

"But why should she?" said Mrs. Thorton. "After all, it's her *link* to her Indian ancestors." The parlor burst into nasty giggling.

"Oh, spare me!" said Elizabeth Finley. "The woman's an African. That coin is just some cheap trinket from the dark continent. Osborne showed it to my William years ago, and there's simply nothing to it."

"I think the metal rubbed off on her brain," said Mrs. Carlyle.

Mrs. Lowell-Townsend agreed. "That silly Negress has always been obsessed with that worthless curdle of tin. My goodness gracious, she's the spawn of slaves!"

The woman had a point. It was highly unlikely that Melba Blue Jay's medal had wound up around the neck of a sixteen-year-old African slave. And yet the book did speak of Melba Blue Jay's Swamp People, whom the colonists called Black Indians. Also, the letter in the chest was from *the* Black Injun.

More than just coincidence, these facts warranted some research. The next day, on one of her hired errands into North Bay, Kate stopped by the Neespaugot Bureau of Archives, Records of Births and Deaths, where a fellow countryman, Danny O'Shea, clerked. And Danny was kind enough to dig up everything he had on black Indians, specifically those with the last name of Court. Moliere Court, a cabinetmaker, had been survived by one son and two daughters. The son's name was Edwin Tall Tree Court. *Edwin Tall Tree, The Black Indian.* Edwin Court had fallen at the battle of Saratoga and been survived by three sons: John Eagle, Benjamin Wolf and William Running Duck, the latter a known derelict and thief. William Running Duck had been charged with desertion during the Revolutionary War. He had abandoned the field of battle to haul the remains of his father Edwin back to Neespaugot. Out of respect to his friend Edwin, Commander Paul Finley had spared young William's life, but several years later, in 1794, William Running Duck was hanged for murdering a white man during a drunken brawl. His record showed prior arrests for drunkenness, surliness, disturbing the peace and… "aiding and abetting runaway slaves."

Wasn't 1794 the year of Lydia Freeman's birth? Mary, Mother of God! thought Kate. This William Running Duck was Miss Freeman's father and the missing link between Lydia Freeman and the Indian's coin! Unknown to anyone in Neespaugot save Kate, Miss Freeman was the only living member of the oldest family in Neespaugot, the great-great-great-great-granddaughter of Runinniduk, savior of the colonies and a trusted *pawwaw* of Chief Massasoit. She was more blueblood than the bloody bluebloods who enjoyed making light of her. Now the blooming book had value!

But Kate was still stumped about how to use it to her benefit. As she awaited inspiration, she put the book back in the chest, along with the letters, the slave-trade logs and all the archive documents Danny O'Shea had given her, and sneaked the trove out of the attic and over to Grover Wharf, where she placed it into the custody of a lawyer named Arondale, a wharf-side clerk with a sizable paunch and three dribbled chins but reliable ethics and trustworthiness.

Shortly afterward, Kate discovered she was pregnant. It was a monumental error she would have to abide by, for she refused to think about an abortion. With all the killing she had done, she wasn't about to compound her bleak eternity with the murder of her own child. As the weeks went by, Kate grew obsessed with the idea that the child growing within her was feeding off her life, sucking out her spirit, as if the fetus was the vengeful composition of the souls of her victims. Over time she sunk into depression and thought of nothing but suicide. One late morning, Kate climbed to the Finley attic, tied a rope around the rafter and stood prepared to kick the stool out from under her feet.

Two ideas stopped Kate from taking her life. First, killing herself meant killing the fetus, thus doubling down for eternity on all the murders she had committed. And second, inspiration struck about how to use the contents of the chest.

The next day on her way to work, she burst into Mr. Arondale's office.

"I need you to write up me last will and testament. The chest I put into yer keep, and all that's in it, shall go to the child what's growin' in me, boy or girl, is that understood?"

"Yes, ma'am—"

"And somethin' else. You'll put in a clause for Lydia Freeman."

"For whom? I don't follow…"

"The Nigger Doctor's assistant. You will write a clause sayin' that if she opens a trust for me baby and puts into that trust two thousand four hundred fifty-six dollars, then me baby's chest and all the documents therein shall go to Miss Freeman."

"Let me get this straight. You desire that the contents of the case, which are the property of a child yet unborn, be delivered to this Freeman woman provided she can prove that she has opened a bank account in the name of your yet-unborn child, containing the—how much?"

"Two thousand four hundred fifty-six dollars. Can you put that in the will or not, sir?"

"Of course, but what happens to the case in the event of the child's death?"

That possibility had never crossed Kate's mind. But he was right. With her bad luck, chances were high that death might very well deal her that card. She stared at

Arondale's three chins, so angry that she thought of ripping out his throat. But she collected herself and said, "If neither the child nor I survive, give the case to Miss Freeman anyway."

3

Groaning like a bad actor, Mad Dog straggled into their tiny apartment, his skull swabbed in a dirty bandage. Kate was cooking in the alcove, her swollen belly pressed against the stove, her long apple hair hanging over the copper pot she was stirring. She shot him a quick look then ignored him. The only sounds were of the wooden ladle scraping the sides of the pot and the clamor coming from other apartments. Mad Dog snuggled up against her buttocks and set his massive hands on her belly, making sure she saw the skeins of blood and vomit on the sleeves of his navy-blue pea coat. "Sorry about last night, m'love. Miscreants attacked me while I was doing me rounds."

"A bloody liar you be, Sean Griffin. You was liquored to the gills."

"Feckin' hell, Kate, I was a victim! Ask Ian and Paddy." He lowered his hands from her hump to her rump.

"All right now, you can just stop that nonsense. It won't get you nothin' but a pair of swollen knockers."

His hands climbed back up to the belly. "I just better not go catchin' nothin' from that she-devil."

"The only thing you ever catch is trouble. What she-devil?"

"The Nigger Doctor's nigger."

Kate came alive as if Mad Dog had just met the bloody Duchess of York. "What was she like?"

"A right cunt, I tell you. I ought to have strangled her!"

Kate stopped stirring, removed Sean's enormous paws from around her waist and turned around to face him with a searing indictment. Her rotundity imposed an ample and welcome cushion between her and the cruel fool whom fate, in its immutable asininity, had thrown into her path.

"Now you listen to me, Sean, me feckin' love. Tomorrow you shall take those poor folk one of m'cakes and thank them properly. And you will remind Miss Freeman of yer miserable feckin' name, and you will tell her that I shall be along a day to request her services. Is there any part of that what's unclear, you witless churl?"

"No, Kate, I got it."

"Fine, yer a corker. Now then, go wash up. We sup in five."

4

The following day, Mad Dog did as instructed and transported Kate's cake to Onion Road. He was met at the front door by the Nigger Doctor himself, a tall scarecrow with a scraggly beard and dire demeanor. The old fecker just stood in the doorway like King Nebuchadnezzar, staring at Mad Dog but saying nothing.

"You the croaker what runs this kip?"

"What do you want?" asked the gint.

"The nigger what lives here with you, she sewed up me feckin' head last night."

"That's my wife you're talking about, you idiot!"

"Bejasus, yer wife, is she?" Sean set down Kate's cake and yanked the man off his feet and dangled him in the air. For an instant, Mad Dog considered ending the doctor's days but remembered that the fecker still had some use to Kate. So he set down the scarecrow, who tried to slam the door, but Mad Dog inserted his boot in the jamb.

"Every muscle in me body is feckin' screamin' to tear that beard of yers from yer bloody face and shove it up the nigger's—ah, me excuses, yer wife's—twat. But today I've come round peaceably to give you this." Mad Dog forced the cake into the croaker's claws. "Me wife baked it for you rodents." Mad Dog bowed derisively, bid adieu and headed back the way he'd come. Feck! How he hated having to pluck up his manners and express himself to people unbecoming of such efforts.

5

Two weeks later, the thirty-three states went to the polls and delivered 1,866,452 winning votes to Abraham Lincoln for president of the United States, and Kate Coughlin-Griffin, eight months pregnant, left the Finley estate on Pickworth Point, a pilfered package of quality meat hidden under her skirts.

She reached the beginning of Grover Wharf, where normally she would catch the North Bay-South Bay ferry home. But that day Kate meant to reach Onion Road. Stingy about money spent on horse cars, she had one of two options. Sentinel Hill was closer as the crow flies, but presented a half-mile climb at a twelve percent gradient over uneven cobblestones. Harbor Road circumnavigated the hill, but that meant a detour of several miles via the wharf. Kate didn't care for the wharf and its bustle, barnacles, bloody blubber and merchant marines slinging horny catcalls at her. Not that she paid the sailors much mind. The problem was Sean. If he was walking his beat and so much as imagined a bloke ogling her, the crazy fool committed literal murder. He often beat the bloke to within a hair-width of his life and tossed the bloody carcass into the harbor. His police reports read "accident" or "suicide." Once, he pounded into unconsciousness a crew of five and left them all to drown. "Squelching a riot," he wrote in his report.

Kate chose the hill. It took her forty-five minutes to reach the summit. Steel gusts of ocean wind, harbingers of another harsh winter, jostled the juniper and elm trees in Revolutionary Park. Kate tightened her cloak, adjusted her bonnet and took in the panorama. The harbor was a white forest of masts, crosstrees, spreaders, crow's nests and binnacles, dories, one-masted cutters, two-masted brigantines, barques, clippers, corvettes, frigates, three-decker warships and whaling barquetines. Boats hugged every available mooring like ants around a crust of bread. Vessels bobbed at anchor from one side of the bay to the other, almost a mile across South Bay. She let her eyes wander along the vast stretches of shoreline, from tidy

North Bay to Industrial South Bay, from the Pickworth Point lighthouse, taking the slapping surf on both cheeks, to the Thumb Point lighthouse far to the south, and from the blackened stacks of United Shoe Machinery to Great Misery Island, protruding like a minor imperfection on the vast plate of the Atlantic.

Blue Devil had taught Kate that this particular stretch of Massachusetts coastline was pregnant with an alternative history few, if any, Neespaugotans knew anything about: that the original colony had hanged its most important Indian benefactor, that his centenarian granddaughter had rallied the remnants of her people and had died more popular than any New Englander not named Adams, and that her own great-great-granddaughter was alive and doing good deeds for a community that took spiteful pleasure in shitting all over her. Kate herself derived a sneaky pleasure of her own in knowing these things while the chattering patrons of privilege remained ignorant.

Kate cut through Revolutionary Park, its grassy promontory and long-silent cannons facing the sea, and picked up State Street, which took her down the north side of Sentinel Hill to the Old Port. She crossed Cabot Street and came to Onion Road. According to *Blue Devil*, the road was named after an onion warehouse that had existed there in the first decades of the colony until the town was burned to the ground following the hanging of the Indian benefactor.

The iron gate lolled ajar, broken. The name plaque was now the palimpsest of any number of attempts to degrade it by use of acid, hammer, knife, buckshot, paint and India ink. It read "NIGXXXgeR born MaD."

Though Kate had never laid eyes on Miss Freeman, she had done enough eavesdropping to feel that she knew the old caregiver. If nothing else, Kate could identify with the poor woman's situation, the two of them having entered life as orphans and outliers. But Kate was clever enough to know that they were also polar opposites. Miss Freeman had been extracted from the womb of an unidentified dead slave and raised by a white family, had taught herself medicine, had become the personal caregiver and confidante of the Revolutionary War hero Captain George Osborne, had joined the medical practice of the Captain's son, and had been treating the poor her entire life. In other words, Miss Freeman was good. Kate was anything but.

Kate dipped in her bag, pulled out her package and knocked. Footsteps approached from inside. She was anticipating a man or woman and was surprised when the door was opened by a lad of thirteen or fourteen years of age. The boy was an unusual physical specimen, with nappy hair the color of wheat, gray eyes and a barley complexion too brown to be white and too white to fit the role others would expect of him. So, thought Kate, here was the cause of so much animosity.

"Would yer mum be in, lad?"

Hardly was the question out when the old woman appeared behind the boy, settling a kind sinewy hand on the lad's shoulder. Kate wasn't so much shocked by Miss Freeman's age as by the disparity of years between mother and son. Fifty years' difference, to be exact.

Miss Freeman noticed Kate's bulging belly. "Are you experiencing contractions, dear?"

"No, m'lady. I have some time yet. I just wanted to bring you this." Kate extended the offering. "It's a very good cut of beef meat, m'lady."

Miss Freeman was perplexed. "Whatever is this for, child?"

"You might call it a downpayment."

"No need for that, dear."

"No, it's not for the birthin'." Kate looked emphatically from mother to son and back to mother. Miss Freeman took the hint and asked her son—Randy, she called him—to go back indoors. Once the boy was gone, Kate reached in her skirts and retrieved a wad of greenbacks, several hundred dollars' worth. "I need you to take this." She tried to put the money in Miss Freeman's hand, but the woman refused.

"I can't accept that, dear."

"Forgive me, m'lady, but this money's not for you. It's for me baby."

"I don't understand—"

"Me name is Katherine Coughlin Griffin. You sewed up me husband a while back. A loutish policeman?"

"Good Lord!"

"Exactly, m'lady. And me money must stay out of his stinkin' hands."

"And you expect me to hide it from him?"

"Yes, m'lady. And I have more. Much more."

"I'm sorry, dear, but you should deposit it in a bank where it'll be—"

"No banks, m'lady! If somethin' was to happen to me, that worthless husband of mine would end up with all of it. I'm beggin' you. I don't know where else to turn."

Kate whittled at Miss Freeman's reticence, using the old woman's kindness against her. Miss Freeman finally broke down and took Kate by the hand. "Come in, Katherine, and let's have us a chat over a warm cup of tea, shall we? Then you can tell me everything."

"Very kind of you, m'lady."

"And do stop this m'lady nonsense. I might just start getting a hankering for it."

6

Lydia found the Irish woman to be the saddest person she had ever met. No light shone in Katherine Griffin's eyes. Her pale flesh, of a rare purity, was dead to the touch, and her expression was as lifeless as a tomb. Her mind was afflicted with black thoughts and certain terrible deeds performed in her youth. She told Lydia that she was bound for hell, a destiny she seemed to relish. She was convinced she would die in labor, but what scared her was taking the baby with her. Lydia asked why she thought such things. The despondent young woman answered, "Because I deserve it."

Katherine's depression ran so deep that Lydia could only assume a spleen infection. Well into January 1861, Lydia massaged her, fed her plants and beverages, and tried to bolster her body and morale by getting her to open up about her troubled past. Lydia also tried to convince her to open a trust fund, but to no avail. Katherine wanted nothing to do with banks. "They'll just try to dig up the origins of me bounty. Please, mum, you must hold onto me money."

"Why do you trust me, Katherine?"

"Because there's no one more trustworthy in this whole bloody town, mum."

Katherine was full of secrets, and Lydia couldn't shake the idea that the woman seemed to know more about her than she was letting on. Eventually, Lydia finally agreed to do as Katherine wished on condition that she open up about her life. It was not curiosity but therapy Lydia had in mind.

Katherine Griffin had grown up in a Londonderry orphanage, watching other children come and go through adoption or death. She herself had been a healthy, pretty child, but her sullen disposition repulsed potential foster and adoption families. Still unclaimed at puberty, she was shipped off to a convent, the Little Sisters of Charity in nearby Ballykelly. There, Katherine became a difficult warder, balking when ordered to rise or pray or read the Bible or sing hymns or sweep the immense vaulted corridors of the Little Sisters, an old military garrison. The nuns did everything within and beyond their rights to break her will. One nun in particular, Sister Cloris, took dark and daily delight in correcting Katherine with a shillelagh, beating her black and blue.

One fine spring day while Sister Cloris was sponging the third-floor windows, Katherine crept up behind the habited nun and shoved her out the window. Katherine watched Sister Cloris plummet belly-up, arms flailing, mouth twisted, wimple fluttering, all the way down to the courtyard stones. Her head cracked open like a cantaloupe.

Katherine crept down the steps and placed herself demurely among the throng of wailing hypocrites gathering around the body. As the other girls turned away from the crushed body spilling its blood over the stones, Katherine's focus fell on Sister Cloris's hands. They were still soapy from her last chore.

Katherine was thirteen years old.

Sister Cloris's death was ruled an accident.

Katherine ran away at fourteen and, claiming to be nineteen, found work as a charwoman on a large farm outside of Dungannon. The brother of the woman who ran the farm got her with child. The farm woman helped her rid her body of the baby and then whipped Katherine off the property.

"Thereafter, I knew many lads, mum. Cruel men. That brute of a Sean is a choirboy compared to most of them. And I murdered me share of them, mum. I cut out their stinkin' throats with me claw knife, watched them gag for air, splutter in their own ooze. Abominable acts, mum. And I'm fully expectin' to rot in hell for what I done. Me soul's been ripped from me heart. To take a life is to lose yer own, mum, even if it be a gobshite's life you've took. I am dead many times. I am dust now."

Lydia attempted to give her hope. "You were young, abused and terrified, dear. This is a new country, a new start."

For the briefest moment a charming color rose into Mrs. Griffin's wan cheeks, before dying out like a gaslight.

"The baby's me new country, mum. Tell her I did me best."

"Dear girl, you must tell her yourself."

"The best I can do is make sure she gets that money. Sean will only drink it up."

"Katherine, you must be honest with me. Does your husband know about this money?"

"O, no, mum! I wouldn't put you, yer family or meself in that danger."

And Lydia believed her.

7

Only days before her due date, Katherine Griffin made her final cash delivery into Lydia's safekeeping, bringing the sum total of her haul to $2,456, all in small denominations of greenbacks. A small fortune for the times. "Blood money," Katherine said matter-of-factly. "Pried from the dead grip of thieves and fellow murderers."

The loot had come to America in pound notes and been converted little by little to dollars. Katherine admitted to Lydia that the exchanger at the wharf had swindled her out of a quarter of it. "I made the mistake of tellin' him I was hidin' it from Sean."

Secret money and deception never led to any good, and Lydia feared for all concerned. "I still think we should put this in a bank, Katherine. If you like, I can do it for you."

"Not yet, mum. Sean could get wind of it."

"But how?" Lydia asked, confounded once again by the woman's opacity. "You told me he doesn't know about the money."

"He's got his informants, mum," she said.

From then on, Lydia tried to persuade Katherine to stay at Osborne House and build up her strength. But Katherine was unwilling to change her routine. "I'm fine, really I am, mum. The minute I feel a contraction, I'll make haste."

Three days passed without a sign of Katherine. Lydia decided it was time to do something, and she hired a horse car to take her to South Bay, to an area the old-timers called the "Indian Village" but that was now an overbuilt slum housing the factory workers and their burgeoning families. Katherine's building was less than twenty years old but the front steps were already broken, the interior walls smashed, the floors buckled, and a stench of squalor inhabited the corridors. Lydia located Katherine's apartment, turned the knob and let herself in.

"Katherine?"

The small parlor resembled a crime scene. What little furniture there was lay in pieces. Broken glass littered the floor, and Lydia saw bloodstains leading into the kitchen. She expected to see Katherine's corpse on the floor. Instead, the woman was squatting on the edge of a chair, Buddha-like, her massive belly billowed between splayed thighs. She was attempting to induce birth. Her fattened cheeks had become gaunt, her unwashed red hair was painted to the sides of her head by fever, and her eyes, once so lifeless, now burned with an acute agitation.

Lydia pressed a hand to her head. "Sweet Lord, you're burning up."

"I've not had one feckin' contraction."

"You must come with me now, dear. Let me help you up."

Katherine pushed her away and glared at Lydia, her green eyes wide with murderous intent. "How much longer?"

"I can help induce, if you come back to the clinic with me."

"Help me induce here."

"I can't, dear. If we leave now, we can be at Osborne House in the half-hour."

"Tomorrow. I shall come tomorrow."

"Why tomorrow?"

"Tomorrow, I said. I promise. Now, go. And cheers on you, mum." Katherine nudged her back out the door and slammed it shut. Lydia heard the deadbolt snap.

8

The glacial day was sunless but imbued with an intense light that hurt the eyes. Snow flurries the size of bonbons pelted Kate as she waddled along Cabot Street, shivering with fever. She turned up the hood of her calash, intensifying the solitude that had been her baggage since childhood. Despair, anguish, fear—each was a separate pulse concerting with the beating of blood in her ears. She was weak. With any luck, her death and the baby's birth would coincide like passing trains.

Kate had done her best to time her death, subjecting herself to all manner of madness short of killing her baby. She had starved herself and bled herself out of holes poked in her thighs. On the coldest nights, she had crept out of doors naked and rolled through the snow until almost passing out. Each time, she pulled back, teasing death. Yes, she had to die, but the child had to live.

The heavy fluff-bowed fir trees in the Nigger Doctor's yard seemed to bend the house, too, with its splintering clapboards, its crooked eaves and downspout, and porch trellis damaged by drunks. At the foot of the house lay broken bottles and frozen horse droppings, projectiles hurled with hatred and derision, reminders of the attackers' refuse for brains.

Kate was coughing fitfully when she reached the porch. She tossed off her calash and knocked, pausing to take a last look at the intense and gloomy world she was leaving behind. It seemed only fitting she should disappear and her child appear on such a stark day, white as blank paper, clean as a slate.

The floorboards squeaked as Miss Freeman led Kate down the dark hall. The old woman walked with a noticeable limp.

"Would you be ailin', mum?" asked Kate.

"I hurt my ankle tagging after Randolph," she said, chuckling. Miss Freeman seemed to let nothing drag her down.

"Mum, harbor you no malice toward this community? You have given people so much and received so little in return."

"I guess I don't bargain so well."

Yes, thought Kate, you don't. Kate couldn't have found a better host to do her dirty work.

They entered the living room, with its smell of enclosure and stale pipe tobacco. The doctor, a lanky sixty-three-year-old man with a fierce white beard and severe look, was reading a book by kerosene lamp.

The boy, reading beside his father, smiled at Kate. The doctor set a page marker in the book, closed and posed it. He removed his bifocals and rubbed them with a handkerchief.

Miss Freeman patted her arm affectionately. "You wait here where it's warm, dear. I'll only be a minute, lighting the coals in your room."

She left Kate with the doctor and boy. A protuberant vein twitched on the doctor's forehead, as he gestured Kate to the divan. Once she was seated, the doctor abandoned her for the fireplace, where he stoked the fire and emptied the ash from his pipe into the cinders. The doctor placed his pipe on the mantel and went to the window, hands in the pockets of his tatty trousers.

"It's fallin' by the bale, sir," said Kate.

"Yes, I can see that," he mumbled.

"I haven't seen such a white dust-up since I worked in the cotton mill."

He didn't respond to her attempt at humor.

Kate supposed that the humorless Osborne and his family wintered in that one room. The stink of melancholia and decrepitude permeated the surroundings, from the mahogany desk to the divan on which she sat, from his winged chair to the Windsor chairs by the fireplace. Everything in the room was both grand and had seen its day, including the doctor, whom she found bold but shabby.

Miss Freeman came for her. "Your room's ready, dear. Follow me."

It was a small but comfortable chamber a few doors down the hall from the living room. The heat had begun to take, but the room was chill and smelled dusty and crypt-like. Kate started to hack. The cough pounded her like a fist.

"When did the cough start?" asked Miss Freeman, helping Kate out of her wet coat.

"Yesterday."

"And the fever?"

"Yesterday," lied Kate. The fever, like the cough, had been with her for a week and a half, since she had taken to crawling through the snow at three o'clock in the morning.

Kate undressed to the skin. Her milk-bloated breasts reposed on her belly like sacks of booty. She had the belly of a kangaroo, the hump glowing with the kindling growing inside her. Her dewy flesh was sprinkled with silver pinheads of transpiration. While toweling her dry, Miss Freeman noticed the wounds on her thighs but said nothing as she lifted a nightdress over Kate's head. The touch of the coarse material against Kate's swollen nipples made her wince.

Miss Freeman removed the warming pan from between the sheets and turned back the covers. "Lie down, dear, so I can examine you." As Kate got on the bed, Miss Freeman stirred the coals in a scuttle under the window. "It's a bit nippy in the room yet, Katherine, but it'll soon be toasty."

Miss Freeman lifted Kate's gown and set her barky hands on Kate's white belly, pressed around its perimeter. She told Kate to bend her knees while she examined her cervix.

"No signs of dilation, dear. Any contractions?"

"Yes, mum, many," said Kate.

The news astonished Miss Freeman. "Can you describe the pain? Did it feel like throbbing or cramping?"

"Throbbing, mum."

Miss Freeman drew the blankets over her and left the room.

Kate released a cache of shivers. Tears ran down her temples. A coughing fit took her again, originating in a region much too removed to contemplate.

Once the hacking and melancholia had settled, Kate lay in sweaty reflection, reasoning away her fear of eternity. Could the beyond be any worse than her life had been? Thirty-one horrible years spent alone, without a single family member or friend, enduring humanity's wickedness, half-starved in an orphanage, beaten daily in a convent, raped in a ditch, the fruit of her womb twice sucked out of her and thrown in the garbage and the sea, hobnobbing with thieves and killers, murdering four other human beings in cold blood and settling into a marriage with a scourge of a man. If there were a God above, and if He were wondering what a stupid girl from Ulster was doing dying in a house that an entire community avoided like the plague, Kate would tell Him that, the way she saw it, the Nigger Doctor's home was the perfect venue for her demise. There was no better exit point for one such as she, born under a star of desperation and error, and pursued her whole life by the Furies of hatred and stupidity.

What little comfort she experienced from her eye-to-eye with God soon passed, and another dark thought possessed her: by being born in that despised venue, would her baby be condemned to a similar life of desperation and error?

Her blood money had never seemed so worthwhile.

Kate perused her surroundings. The brown-daisy wallpaper gave her the impression she was lying inside a dead bouquet of flowers. The painting posed on the mantel depicted a storm at sea, the swell rising into an awesome force to challenge the dark heavens. The violence of the painting clashed with the staid mood of the wallpaper. But the more Kate thought about their differences, the more she saw their similarities. The common denominator was death.

She broke the silence with a new wave of coughing.

Miss Freeman returned with a cup of tea and a strange rubberlike tool clamped around her neck. She stuck the clamps to her ears and set the tool's metal washer over Kate's heart. "Breathe, dear. Deep breaths." She moved the metal down to Kate's belly.

"What are you doin', mum?"

"Listening to the insides of you. It's called a stethoscope. Here, listen to your baby's heartbeat." She put the clamps to Kate's ears.

Kate could hear the tiny thumping of her baby's pulse. "That's really it, mum? Is me baby well?"

"I hear a good strong regular beat," said the old healer. She set her hand on Kate's forehead. "You, on the other hand, are suffering. I've put something in your tea to bring down that fever."

"I suppose you think I should try to live, now that I've heard me baby's heart," Kate said.

"Yes, dear girl, I do."

Kate drank her tea and fell into a deep sleep, and when she woke Miss Freeman was there, applying a cold compress to her face. "How do you feel, dear?"

"Lost, mum."

Miss Freeman took her pulse. "Sweetness, you've got pneumonia."

"You'll be able to get the baby out in time, mum. Say you will."

"Katherine. I can't do this alone. You must help me."

Kate made a feeble effort at a smile. "I need to clear me conscience, if yer willin' to listen. A sort of confessional."

"Speak your mind, dear."

"I'm a bad person, mum."

"Katherine…"

"I know about you, mum. I heard me employers talk about you. So I played you, mum, and I'm sorry for it. I'd have cheated someone else if I could. See, I lied to you. Sean knows about me money."

"Dear Lord!"

"He doesn't know where it is, but he'll figure it out, once he reads me will. You see, yer in me will, mum." Miss Freeman looked at her as if she were delirious. Kate swallowed the distaste for what she was about to say. "Forgive me, but I have somethin' you want. I know the answer to the origin of yer coin and yer entire family line. I have the proof. And believe me, mum, it's a story worth knowin'. You descend from greatness. Not the highfalutin kind, but the genuine stuff. And I promise to get you this proof, but only if you protect me money from Sean and see that it gets to me baby."

"But I said that I would, Katherine."

"Sorry, mum, but good as you are, I know that promises fade like that wallpaper, once the motivation has dried up."

"And you think blackmailing me is better?"

"Sean can be very persuasive. They don't call him Mad Dog for nothin'."

Miss Freeman slapped Kate across the cheek. Kate was too sick to care.

"I don't blame you for that. I'd have done worse. But it changes nothing one way or the other. If Sean gets the money, you get nothin'."

"Why should I believe you?"

"You shouldn't. But you can believe me lawyer. There's a letter in me sachel. Open it when I'm dead and follow the instructions. One day you shall be very happy, mum." Kate looked Miss Freeman in the eyes and made a feeble smile.

9

Seven pounds and screaming, Bridget Coughlin Griffin entered the world at 11:14 p.m. on February 8, 1861. Her mother survived six minutes in her company—the time to name her—before her own life receded behind her green pools for eyes, leaving a leaden shore.

Lydia, exhausted and close to tears, closed Katherine's eyes. "I cannot fathom the depths of such despondency, such will to self-destruct," she said to G.O.

Osborne rubbed her shoulder. "You did everything you could, my dear."

"It was a suicide, George, pure and simple."

"Yes, I've heard of such things," he said. "Suicide by childbirth. I just never…" Osborne no longer knew what to say, so he took the infant from the room while Lydia arranged the body.

Katherine's satchel lay on a chair under her garments. Lydia found the letter destined for her and had to read it three times before she understood its gist. A book and some documents proving her ancestry were in the possession of a lawyer named Arondale, who would relinquish it to her upon the opening of a trust account of $2,456 in the name of Katherine's child.

Lydia set down the letter and looked at Katherine's bloodless face. Death had left a mocking rictus stretched across it. Nothing, Lydia now understood, had been coincidental in this woman's decisions. In effect, the vixen had managed to restage the circumstances of Lydia's birth, right down to the mother dying in childbirth. Katherine had cast herself in the role of Lydia's mother, a runaway like her, pursued by demons and possessed by an obsession to deliver her child and booty into the hands of the one person who was bound to take responsibility for both: *I know about you, mum. I heard me employers talk about you.*

Lydia wiped her tears away and threw the sheet over the corpse.

Until well past midnight Lydia and Osborne discussed what to do with the body, the baby and the bounty. The doctor was for contacting the city morgue and the orphanage. "Let that maniac deal directly with them. And the same goes for the woman's money. Just give it to the lawyer and be done with it."

"No, George, I gave my word."

"To a miscreant."

"It's still my word. The money is for the baby. Nor will I contact the morgue until I've had a chance to speak with Mr. Griffin. He deserves that at least."

The following day Lydia bundled herself in an old coat and hired a horse car to the police station, where she asked for Sean Griffin. A desk sergeant yelled out for "Mad Dog," who lumbered down a flight of stairs, scruffy, bleary-eyed and stinking of stale liquor. Seeing Lydia brought no positive side effects to his general state of loutishness.

"If you come here to settle up for me wife," he said, his invidious temper all ablister, "you won't get a cent from me, nigger woman."

"Mr. Griffin, is there somewhere we can talk?"

"Why sure. Step into me feckin' stateroom."

Griffin escorted Lydia outside to the station-house stoop where the first thing he did was evacuate a wad of brown spit into a mound of pristine snow. "I'm listening."

Lydia tightened her tippet. "Sir, Mrs. Griffin came to us yesterday—"

"Shite, I know that. Did she or didn't she drop that kid yet?"

"You have a daughter, Mr. Griffin."

"Feck! I wanted a son."

"There were complications, sir."

"Eh?"

"Your missus was gravely ill. She died last night, sir."

Sure that he hadn't heard her right, Griffin told her to repeat what she had said, which she did. Contempt and rage rendered him speechless and apoplectic. He began beating his thighs.

"Mr. Griffin, she was so weak from pneumonia."

Griffin took a threatening step toward Lydia but slipped on some ice and landed on his rump. He remained sitting in the snow for a moment, trying to get his thoughts around what was gone, what had been irrevocably snatched from him.

He rose, fueled by the only genuine emotion in him: vindictiveness. "Me Kate went to you. She put herself in yer hands." Griffin shoved Lydia into a snow bank. Not willing to leave the matter there, he trundled after her, intent on pushing her head into the bank and suffocating her.

"Hey there!" yelled the cab driver, still standing in the snowy road beside his horse.

Griffin redirected his rage. "Clear off, you gobshite, or I'll give you some of the same!"

"No, sir, I stand here till I get my fare."

Griffin reached into his trouser pockets but came up empty. "Wait there, you bloody Jew. I'll pay yer feckin' fare, but you leave this witch where she lies, hear me?"

When he was gone, Lydia called to the horseman for help. "Please help me, I've injured my hip."

But the man was too scared to approach. "Sorry, ma'am. He's the law."

Two policemen arrived from down the street and, seeing her trying to crawl to her feet, helped her up and to the cab. Griffin reappeared on the run. One of the policemen advised him to calm down and was promptly rewarded with a ton of fist to the head. The other policeman pulled his club and whacked Griffin on the jaw. Griffin spat out a tooth, picked up the clubber by the chin and threw him onto the station-house steps.

By now, other policemen had been drawn outside by the commotion and, finding the habitually irate Mad Dog going wild on all and sundry, joined in the fracas. They pounded him, but he gave them back twice what he received. His brawn and brute force mesmerized both Lydia and the cab driver. It was like watching a tornado ripping a path toward them, and if they didn't move in a hurry, they too would be sucked into the vortex. The scuffle ended from sheer exhaustion on all sides. Nine officers and Griffin lay in the snow, panting and staunching bloody lips and noses.

"For the love of God, make haste, sir!" Lydia yelled at the dawdling driver. She stuck twice the fare into his hand. "Now go!" He lashed his horse a good one.

10

Mad Dog knew that Kate had a cache of money and assumed it was hidden in their apartment. Before long the dwelling, never homey to begin with, resembled the losing ship in a broadside cannon battle. The floorboards were ripped up, the walls stripped and the cabinets turned to kindling. When there was nothing left to tear asunder, Sean came to the enlightened conclusion that Kate's money was elsewhere. But where?

In the meantime, he took out his anger and frustration on the Nigger Doctor's family, taking a perverse delight in keeping them holed up in their monstrosity of a house. Onion Road became his beat, and if he managed to catch any of the three trying to sneak out, he swung his shillelagh and chased them back inside like scared sheep into a barn. In the wee hours, after a night spent drinking at Kelly's, Sean laid siege to the premises, bombarding the clinic with empty booze bottles and a barrage of curses. "May yer arse hairs turn to hammers and beat the shite out of you! May yer feckin' house burn and roast you alive. May five-hundred foot soldiers sodomize yer half-bred whelp. I shall cudgel yer brains out for what you done to me Kate!" His monologues never mentioned money.

Dawn would find him at the station, sleeping off his binge. He slept through his wife's burial in Neespaugot Cemetery's potter's field. He ignored the pleas of the orphanage to come fetch his daughter. And, only rarely setting foot inside his apartment, where he feared running into the ghost of Kate, he ignored a letter pertaining to Kate's last will and testament sent from a wharf-side lawyer named Arondale.

11

Osborne had had enough of Sean Griffin's intimidation and somehow managed to reach the police station without being spotted by the maniac. When it was his turn in line, he stepped up to file his complaint with the desk sergeant. The sergeant sported two black eyes and a swollen left jaw, and Osborne assumed the man, being likewise victimized by Griffin, would be sympathetic to his plight. But the sergeant was only half listening to his complaint, and the man's confounded nonchalance finished by riling the doctor.

"Am I to assume you do not take this grievance seriously, sir?"

The sergeant tapered his mustaches and fired off a barb. "Oh, but I do. Very seriously. You took Mad Dog's wife from him."

"I what? Are you suggesting—"

"I don't suggest, laddie. I uphold the law."

"So uphold it and call off your man."

"From doing what? Has he entered your property? Has he attacked you?"

Osborne groaned. "For the love of God, he beat up my wife on those steps there. He beat up the whole precinct."

"But has he attacked *you* personally?"

"I just told you. He's threatening me and my family."

"Prove it."

"Fine. Send a man between two and four a.m. and you'll have your proof."

The sergeant smiled crookedly. "We'll do that, laddie. The police of Neespaugot have nothing better to do than waltz out to yer place in the middle of the feckin' night."

"My God, man, does someone have to be hurt or killed to get the appropriate response from you?"

"We're not in the scuttlebutting business. Now clear off."

Osborne left the police station angry and determined to do something about it. But what? What was one to do when one's complaint was with the law itself? The only person who had the necessary clout with the local judges, politicians and police was William Finley. Fat chance there. Will and Elizabeth Finley had refused to speak to Osborne for the past fourteen years. Their public beef was Randy's birth: "Elizabeth and I feel misused by the immorality of Doctor Osborne and Miss Freeman." But the real reason they hated Osborne was his threat to go public with proof that Lydia had been the author behind a decade of business advice to Finley Sons, Transporters.

"Help the clinic and I stay quiet."

"No, you nigger-loving bastard. You breathe a word and I'll have all of you murdered!"

Fearing for his wife and child, Osborne had remained silent. But the damage had been done, and now obtaining a helping hand from William Finley was about as likely as receiving an apology from Mad Dog Griffin. Still, what choice did Osborne have? He left the police station and headed for Grover Wharf.

Finley Sons, Transporters, its headquarters and hangars, took up the first five piers. Nervous to the point of shivers, Osborne entered the main office on Pier Five and asked a clerk if he might speak with Mr. Finley. The clerk left his desk and disappeared into a deeper office. A moment later a handsome young man in his early twenties stepped out to meet him.

"I'm Mr. Finley. You requested to speak to me?"

Osborne's jaw dropped. "My word! Rutherford?"

"Indeed I am," said the young man, reddening because he was not sure who was addressing him.

"I'm Doctor George Osborne. You were born at my clinic, young man."

"Oh my, of course. Doctor Osborne! I've heard so much about you, sir," said Rutherford, a bit carried away with youthful exuberance.

"Yes, I suppose you have," said Osborne. Young Finley reddened more, but Osborne reassured him with a friendly pat on the back. "Don't fret. I'm used to it. My, but you have done your parents proud. Listen, are you busy? Can you give me a few moments of your time?"

"I'd be most honored, Doctor."

The young man showed him into a stately office—in fact the chairman's office, with its tri-odors of wood, leather and power. He took Osborne's coat and offered him a seat in a comfortable leather chair beside a polished teak desk. The oak-paneled walls were covered in splendid images, paintings, portraits and daguerreotypes. There were pictures of Grover Wharf and the Finley sailing fleet, of the distant harbors of Hong Kong, Canton, Shanghai, Taipei, Tokyo, San Francisco and Hawaii, and several images of the Finleys themselves, taken in the company of local, national and foreign dignitaries, including Millard Fillmore, the latest (and last) Whig president of the United States. There were also artist-commissioned portraits of past members of the board. As Osborne glanced through the likenesses, he came face to face with his dear father, the Captain, stern and heroic.

"My word!"

"Sir?"

"That's my father," blurted out Osborne like a star-struck child.

"You don't say!"

"Yes, he was quite the seaman and naval hero, as well as a member of the board back in the early days of the republic."

"Yes, he was." Rutherford was very polite, if not quite convincing. No one had ever told him about the

Captain, that much was as plain as the bit of egg stuck in the corner of the young man's mouth.

Missing, Osborne noted with melancholia, was the most influential member of the board from 1835 to 1845. There was no image of Lydia Freeman on the Finley wall of fame.

"Have you traveled much, Doctor Osborne?"

Osborne grinned and sighed. "No, Rutherford, I've never been much of anywhere. I had none of the Captain's true grit." Then, shifting the subject, he said, "You, I take it, are being groomed to succeed your father."

Rutherford was too young to dissimulate his sense of self-importance, but he did possess the class to shine a modest light on his good fortune. "Only because my older brother Terrence preferred to run the San Francisco operation. I've only just graduated from Harvard."

"Well, we have that in common. I'm a Harvard man myself."

"Do tell!"

"Class of '22."

That was the extent of their shared experience, and an awkward silence wedged its way between them.

Osborne explained his predicament regarding Sean Griffin. "I was hoping to solicit the aid of your father in this matter."

Rutherford showed compassion but admitted he was at a loss. "My father, you see, is in China at this moment, and Mother and I are terribly worried. Apparently he's caught an illness there."

"My word. If you have a list of symptoms, I'd be glad…"

"We're hopeful he'll be back in late spring," the young man barreled on, apparently anxious to extricate himself from any notion of the doctor lending a hand.

"Late spring, is it? That's a shame, really."

"Perhaps I could write him a letter."

"No, don't trouble yourself," said Osborne, crestfallen. "The spring is… well, I'm sure things will have worked themselves out by then."

Rutherford accompanied the doctor to the door and, as they shook hands goodbye, the young man had a sudden thought. "Would it help if I spoke to Mother? She might intercede in the name of Mrs. Griffin, whom she was fond of."

Osborne was suddenly incensed. Yes, Katherine Griffin, a conniving murderess, *she* you're fond of, but not the health-givers who delivered your babies. Still, he would be damned if he would let it show now. "Thank you for your kindness, Rutherford, but I shall see to it myself. So long and best to you."

The doctor trudged out to the wharf, dazed and clueless. His family was in grave danger, yet he had no solution. All right, yes, he had thumbed his nose at everyone and now no one gave a damn about him. But it was all so unjust concerning Lydia. She had spent her whole life staying involved, helping people. Where was the moral in that? Even Hawthorne's great-suffering heroine from *The Scarlet Letter* was eventually vindicated. But Hester Prynne was white, whereas Lydia's own scarlet letter was planted in her skin. Shame was pronounced upon her by history. She was tawny, half-caste, muddy, colored, neither this, that or the other. She didn't register in society's sympathy. To right that wrong would take a century of future history winding back against the current.

His thoughts returned to the Captain. What would Father have done? And he heard his father's voice: To hell with others' sympathy! He is helped best who helps himself!

Osborne strode down several piers of icy boardwalk to Gaines Street, entered an armory located a block from Kelly's Bar and Saloon and purchased a .36 caliber Navy revolver. The clerk was kind enough to teach him how to load it. "How many boxes of ammo?" asked the clerk.

"The minimum," replied the doctor. "This gun has a one-time use."

12

Among Sean Griffin's many flaws was a resistance to reading—not just books but anything inscribed with letters of the alphabet. And so it was that his wife had been dead already a month, and the letter explaining the terms of her will still lay unread under greasy dishes in his kitchen. Eventually, a tinge of curiosity and a lump of boredom convinced Sean to unseal the envelope. But he got no further than the sender's address before stuffing the letter pell-mell back inside its cover. "Feckin' lawyers! Always wanting somethin'," he said, without bothering to confirm his assumption.

Weeks later, again motivated by boredom, he took another stab at the letter. He read a line and stopped, content with his effort and convinced that a line of reading every now and then was the right dosage, a patient and not overly taxing approach to messaging between human beings. After a further few weeks, he reached the end of the correspondence but was no closer to understanding it than when he'd started. He stuffed it in his coat, carried it to the precinct and asked the staff sergeant to have a crack at solving the lawyer talk. The sergeant, no genius himself, had the good sense to admit that he couldn't make much hay out of the gibberish.

"Sorry, mate. It's all blarney to me. If I was you, I'd get meself a proper what-for from the bloomin' barrister himself."

So Sean headed for the wharf to pay a visit to Mr. Arondale.

The lawyer was feeling windy that afternoon and had just let escape a vociferous fart when his office door banged open and Sean Griffin burst in.

"Yer goin' to tell me what the feck this means!" Sean's balled-up letter landed in Arondale's face.

The lawyer kneaded the ball back into an identifiable sheet of paper and had himself a look. "Ah, yes. Mr. Griffin. So glad you came in. As I stated in the letter, all property shared with your poor defunct wife will now become yours. I'll just need you to sign a few documents—"

"What did she leave me?"

"Everything she owned…sir, with the exception of a certain chest—"

"And what's in the feckin' chest?"

"As I stated in my letter, sir, just some documents of no use to anyone but Lydia Freeman."

"Who the bejasus is *that*!?"

"I'm not at liberty to share that information with you."

"Where'd me bloody money go, you fat barrister bastard?" Sean slammed the table, sending feathered quills into the air like the plumes of shot birds.

Arondale finally understood the kind of man he was dealing with. For self-preservation, he deflected. "I'm afraid you'll have to take up the money matter directly with Miss Freeman."

"Why the feck would I do that, you gobshite?"

"Well, it's stated very clearly in the terms of the will. For Miss Freeman to recover her case, she'll need to open a trust fund for your baby. Ergo, she has your money."

Sean pulled out his club. "I will crack yer crown in two, so help me, if you don't start talkin' English. Now who is this Freeman bitch?"

The lawyer wilted. No client, especially a colored one, was worth scrambled brains. "She works with the Nig— with the doctor on Onion Road."

"That bloody nigger woman!" A sudden thought sparked in the cold, empty chamber Sean called a brain. "And what if the bitch don't want the feckin' case no more? What's to stop her from keeping me money, legal speaking?"

"Well, nothing," Arondale said. Talking to Sean Griffin was like playing fetch with a hungry tiger.

"Them Osbornes knew this when they murdered me wife."

Despite his better judgment, Arondale tried to reason with the fool. "Your dear wife was confident that Miss Freeman would do anything to have the case, sir."

"Well, we'll see about that. Where's this feckin' case?"

Arondale was cornered and made a yellow smile. "Mr. Griffin, first Miss Freeman must open—"

Griffin loomed over the lawyer. Fetch was finished, the feast was about to start. "I want that case *now*, you gobshite."

"I cannot. The law restricts my—"

Griffin grabbed the lawyer out of his chair and swung him across his own desk.

"May worms crawl up yer arse and eat out yer liver, man. I said I want that case!"

"It's in a bank vault."

"Have it here in an hour." Griffin hammered a fist into the lawyer's belly, producing a spout of sour air from both ends of him. "One hour, you fat skank, or they'll be fishin' you in pieces from the feckin' harbor."

13

Osborne was reading under a gas lamp when the clangor of metal against stone invested the parlor. He went to the window, parted the curtains and felt ill. Down at the street stood Griffin, giving the front gate the boot. In his hands was some kind of small chest. Osborne was sure it was a box of gunpowder to blow them to smithereens, and he rushed to fetch his gun.

The racket brought Lydia to an upstairs window. Down on the street, she saw Griffin hulking at the gate, twice as broad in his filthy blue police overcoat, cradling something in the platter of his enormous hands. He spotted her in the window and yelled up.

"Does this box mean anything to you, woman?"

"It means no good if you've got it."

"It's me Kate's case. What's inside I believe holds some material interest to you and yer kin."

"Begone, Mr. Griffin. You're not welcome here."

"That's too easy, now that you gobshites got me money. But I'm willin' to offer you a deal. Give me what's mine, and you get yer case."

"That money belongs to your daughter Bridget."

"Well, I'll see she gets it."

"Will you now? Your daughter has been in this world for close to three months, yet you've never even set eyes on her. Your own wife didn't trust you, sir, so why should I?"

"I swear on yer mongrel hide, I'll burn this case and everythin' what's in it."

"I can't stop you from doing that, but I can keep my promise to your wife."

"We'll see about that."

Griffin kicked open the gate. Lydia ran into the hall and called to her son. "Stay upstairs and hide, Randy. Promise me!" She hurried downstairs and managed to bolt the front door just as the first wave of fury struck the structure, shaking the entire wall. Griffin's vile voice violated the sanctuary. "Open up, you gobshites, and gimme what's mine!" A second blow cracked the door frame.

Osborne's lank figure appeared from deep down the central corridor, lugging what looked like a pipe the length of Lydia's lower arm. Into the light he strode, the dull sheen of the long-barreled revolver in his right hand, chilling Lydia's blood. "George, no! He'll kill you!"

"Forgive me, dear," he said, panting hard. "But it's time I took a stand."

The front door caved in. The darkened entry was suddenly and absurdly illuminated by the glow of sunset, before Griffin's massive frame forced obscurity once more upon the scene. Osborne lifted the gun with two hands and pointed it at the intruder. "I'll shoot you dead, Griffin!"

Griffin grinned and set down the case. With murderous deliberation, he opened his coat and pulled out his nightstick. "Go on then, fecker, pull the trigger. But aim true because I aim to mash yer brains like so much Irish stew up and down these black halls."

Osborne's hand shook. Griffin struck first, rapping the hand with his stick and knocking the gun to the floor. He punched the frail doctor in the face and clubbed him to the carpet. He swung high to better crack the doctor's skull, but Lydia cried out "No!" momentarily, causing the stick to remain suspended where it was. Lydia positioned her body to shield her unconscious husband from harm. As Griffin prepared to deliver the blow, the boy leapt on his back.

Randolph Osborne might just as well have tried to tackle a wall. Griffin shook him off like rainfall and squeezed him in a choke hold till the fight left him. Still clutching the spluttering youth, Griffin picked up the gun and cracked it open to check it was loaded. It was. He snapped the barrel shut and swung renewed contempt at Lydia.

"Thought you'd use me child against me, you feckin' half-bred cunt. See how you like it." Griffin stuck the gun barrel to the boy's head. "Click!" he said through rotting teeth.

"Please, Mr. Griffin, I'm begging you not to hurt him. His name is Randolph—Randy. He's only fourteen."

"Fetch Kate's money now, or feckin' Randy is due for an accident. I'll be on yer roof." He dragged the boy kicking up the staircase.

Lydia helped Osborne sit. The blows had opened a gash under his beard, shattered his cheekbone and fractured his left hand. "Forget about me, dear. Go get him the money."

Katherine Griffin's booty was stuffed in a cloth bag hidden under the floorboards of a broom closet on the third floor. Lydia retrieved it and continued climbing on a sore hip up the pulley ladder. She hobbled out to the widow's walk where she was buffeted by a freezing wind. The roof lay patched with old snow and sheets of ice. Griffin stood at the edge, dangling Randy over the abyss. The brute and boy made darkened silhouettes against a crimson sky. "About time," he shouted at her. "Me arm was getting tired. Ha!"

Lydia took a stack of greenbacks from the bag to prove its contents. "Now please let him go."

"Throw it over here." She did as ordered, but Griffin did not release her son. "You give me one good reason to spare yer mongrel. You murdered me wife and stole me money."

"For the love of God, Mr. Griffin, you're the law."

"Yer feckin' right I am! And I say this devil's patchwork you call a son fell off this here roof. Yes indeed, seems the little fecker crawled here to play, slipped on the ice and took himself a head-first tumble down there. Splintered his skinny neck, he did. Terrible accident. A right pity you niggers cannot look after yer whelps."

Lydia needed to think fast. "Mr. Griffin, what town in Ireland was she from, your poor wife?" Griffin looked cockamamie at her, thrown off by the question, which she repeated. "Name the town, if you can, sir."

"Don't you feckin' talk to me about me Kate."

"Randy, tell Mr. Griffin what town his wife came from."

"Londonderry," the boy said, shaking from cold, fear and defiance.

"You see, your Kate liked my son enough to tell him where she came from, Mr. Griffin. She told him many stories of your emerald country. Think about that as you're doing him harm. And think about this. You know same as I that your wife was a witch, the dark witch Hecate. And believe me, she will haunt your miserable soul till the end of your days for hurting a boy she cared about."

In truth, Griffin was already being haunted by Kate. She had him screaming into the bitter, dull morning, raking her cold blue hands over his liquor-entranced view of vomit-gunked gutters.

Griffin heaved the boy back over the rail and shoved him at his mother. Then, he scooped up the bag. "It had better be there, every last penny, or I'll be back, ghost or no ghost."

Lydia smothered her son in an embrace, and the two of them stood there trembling from shock and the bitter cold until long after their tormentor had quit the premises.

14

Sean Griffin had his wife's booty at last. But he was soon to learn the hard way why such assets are called liquidity. It took him only two months to piss away Katherine's blood money on booze, cards and a fraudulent land-investment scheme out west that disappeared with the con man. Returning to dead-broke made Sean touchy. Touchiness led to brawls and property damage. Eventually, even his abettors in the police turned against him. In July 1861, he was removed from duty and given a choice: jail time or fighting for the Stars and Stripes against the Stars and Bars.

Sean didn't consider it much of a dilemma. It was common knowledge the Northern armies, superior in manpower and resources, would make fast work of a bunch of cotton-growing huckster delta drunks. He'd be back in Neespaugot before the plums were out. A bona fide war hero, he'd run for fecking mayor!

In that foolish frame of mind, he and an entire battalion of underprepared overconfident nitwits marched into the first battle of Bull Run. Waves of Confederate soldiers with fixed bayonets broke through the battalion's left flank. Sean tried to run, but the indiscriminate explosion of cannon fire leveled all and sundry, and blew Sean off his feet. As he lay in that Virginia field, peppered with falling grit and other men's entrails, he realized that the world had lost its sound. His eardrums had disintegrated. As if waking from a long sleep, he struggled to stand. A passing bullet tore off the small finger of his left hand. He felt something warm flapping against his cheek. It was his right ear, what was left of it. Even his rifle was snapped in two. A frenzied pack of gray-coated men charged at him, and Sean sensed his end had come. He howled at them. "Come on, you maggots! May yer bowels boil and yer shit run red!" Using his broken rifle barrel as a club, Sean expressed himself in the eloquence of violence, bashing and felling attackers in twos and threes. For an instant he lost himself, a foretaste of the eternal nothingness that awaited him, until he was literally shot back into the present by the stinging jolt of bullets tearing him to pieces. He kept clubbing until he dropped from fatigue. His last vision was of boots. They were walking on him, trampling him down into the gore-moistened earth.

15

Many days after the break-in, Lydia had been too afraid to open the chest, though it had beckoned her with its implorations: *I have somethin' you want, mum. I know the answer to the origin of yer medallion and yer entire family line. I have the proof.* But all she could do was stare at its cakebox-sized dimensions, pine panels, gilded latches and hinges and engraved initials "FST." She was convinced the chest was Katherine's posthumous cheap trick, and that she would find only an empty chest or one stuffed with hay. What Lydia feared most was crushing disappointment leading to hope-killing despondence. If her worst fear were to materialize, it would mark the end of the road for any chance of finding an answer to the riddle of her life.

When at last the drip-drip of fear spilled over the brim of expectations, Lydia finally raised the lid. Moments later, her boy Randy raced down the stairs in the direction of his mother's screaming.

Hours later, outside the parental bedroom, Lydia cautioned Randy not to make a fuss. "We don't want to startle your father." She carried in a tray rattling with a pot of analgesic tea and a cup and saucer. Randy was cradling the chest in both arms.

Inside the musky room, the cadaverous Osborne lay strung out in bed, his swollen head heavily bandaged, his broken right hand plastered and posed on a pillow. He was awake and made a wan smile at their soft entrance. The boy took his father's lucidity as a license to herald the good news. "Papa, we know!"

Osborne met Lydia's bright countenance with a weak but optimistic grin. "Capital news," he said hoarsely.

Lydia set the tray on the bedside table and helped the doctor sit up. She sat beside him and edged the cup to his parched lips. "It's not hot," she assured him. He took a sip but declined a second.

"It's perfect, but the best elixir is what you've come to tell me. Isn't that right, son?" He winked at Randy.

The boy reached into the chest and fished out a pistol-colored hardbound text. Osborne retrieved it with his left hand and read aloud its title: "*Blue Devil: the Trials of a Wampanoag Woman* by Daniel Hillard." He weighed it by feel. "My word, for something so valuable," he said, "it's quite spare." It did indeed appear inconsequential in his huge, bony hand. Osborne flipped to the last page. "Sixty-five pages," he muttered. He read the editor's note. "'The author, Mr. Hillard, was shot and killed last year in a duel over this important work of journalism. His book is now into a second publication in *The London Gazette* and Term Catalogues.'"

"May I, George?" asked Lydia, repossessing the book to find the passage she had in mind. "You must read this."

Today, the seventeenth of April in the year of our Lord 1725, marks the eleventh time in fifteen years that the High Court of Neespaugot is to hear the arguments of Melba Blue Jay, now in her sixty-sixth year of life. Melba has come to petition the court for the retrieval of all land lying between West Neespaugot River and the Hamminsett Hills—formerly known as the Great Swamp—for the benefit of a clan of Negro Indians referred to as the "Swamp People."

The bleak weather today has not deterred the damp and ill-humored masses from filling the courtroom, and the stench of fusty raiment rises like a cloud over the proceedings. All attend for one reason and one reason alone: to look upon the woman who has become something of a folk hero in these parts and has come to symbolize the colony's own discontent with the Crown and its unjust taxing policies. Little matter that Melba Blue Jay is an Indian. The attitude of these New Englanders is no longer "the only good Indian is a dead one." In fact, present-day colonists are more inclined to identify with extinct New England Indians than with their British brethren across the ocean.

The court officer tells all to rise, and all rise as the magistrates doth sit.

The court scribe reads aloud the claimant's curriculum vitae. After each detail, a massive hurrah breaks out, followed in short order by the knocking of the chief magistrate's gavel, lending the session a Punch-and-Judy ambience which has the judges scratching their wigs.

"Born in Neespaugot on the fifth of May, 1659, into the Wampanoag tribe"—hurrah! bang!

"A former enemy combatant in King Philip's War"—hurrah! bang! bang!

"Exiled in the West Indies. Illegally re-entered the colony from New France. Never married, two offspring, a daughter Laurette Court, now deceased, and a son, Moliere Court, eighteen years of age.

"Jailed five times for contempt of court and vandalism"—hurrah! bang! bang! bang! "The claimant chopped down the high pole in Courthouse Square to steal Metacom's skull, but before she could be apprehended, she gave the skull to a large blue dog against which the constable's bullet had less effect than a tick. The dog disappeared into the forest. The skull was never recovered"—hurrah! bang! bang! bang! bang! bang! bang!

At this point in the proceedings, the claimant herself rises to deliver her brief:

"I, Melba Blue Jay, being of sound mind, act today as my own counsel, confident in the guidance I have received from the texts of Bartolome de Las Casas, Grotius, Francisco de Vitoria, Hobbes, Locke and the reverend John Eliot. Herewith my claim: Denying Indian sovereignty is a matter of arbitrary, religious and racist principle. It is neither God's way nor the way of international justice among nations. The court must nullify on ethical grounds the confiscation of the Great Swamp and have said land returned to its rightful owners, the Wampanoag Indians."

Hurrah! bang!

I would be remiss in my journalistic duties were I not to give, at this juncture, the critical point of view. So let it be *noted that her critics believe that Melba Blue Jay owes her notoriety solely to prurience. In short, if she hadn't been a fair-fleshed beauty running around in short furs, she would have no following. The critics explain this as a recrudescence of lust following the stringent Puritan reign.*

And yet, how explain that this day in court — as I mentioned, her eleventh to date — all records for attendance are broken, yet the native beauty of fair flesh and firm principles is nowhere to be seen in the hall. Yea, in the witness box stands a shriveled avatar of gypsy-moth hair and dubious hygiene. The former beauty is now a leathery old woman. I and every other person of good sense must reach but one conclusion: in the absence of prurience, the populace has come for the principles!

The questioning begins promptly at a half past two in the afternoon.

Magistrate Collins: Madam, this tribunal has been listening to your appeals for fifteen years now. It has become a sort of rite.

Melba Blue Jay: A rite I could live without, sir. I do not undertake any of this lightly or without financial hardship.

Magistrate Collins: Madam, this court has told you before and respectfully states again: we magistrates have no competence in the apportioning of land. Only King George can decide what the Crown is willing to surrender.

Melba Blue Jay: How convenient for this court, sir. Must I really undertake a voyage to Buckingham Palace to deal with a problem a few miles from this building?

Hurrah! bang!

Magistrate Collins: We have no Privy Council in Massachusetts, so, yes, you would have to take up the matter directly.

Anonymous voice: *A lot of swine dung, that!*

Another voice: *Do you magistrates sail for London every time you need your arses wiped?*

Magistrate Collins: *Order, or I'll have you all removed!*

Crowd: *BOO!*

Melba Blue Jay: *I should like to ask the court a question.*

Magistrate Collins: *Proceed.*

Melba Blue Jay: *Other than brute force, by what authority does England base its own claim to Neespaugot and the entire colony?*

Hurrah! bang!

Magistrate Collins: *Madam, other than demagoguery, your question lacks sense. The Crown rules the Commonwealth. The Commonwealth is part of the Crown. Why, it is as if you would know by whose authority your fingers belong to your hand.*

Melba Blue Jay: *Sir, my fingers belong to my hand by the authority of the Great Spirit. It is nature's law. If you are saying that the Crown appropriated my people's land based on natural law, then I see not why you gentlemen masquerade in wigs and gowns and hold hearings in a court of law. Natural law demands no such pretense. It suffices to be king of the forest.*

Anonymous voice: *You tell them, mum!*

Magistrate Collins: *Come, come, madam. This very day you benefit from our system of justice.*

Melba Blue Jay: *Justice, sir? Forgive me, but I barely recognize the word. It's more of an elaborate insult, a fifteen-year rite, as you said, of getting the royal runaround. I would beg you to consider the facts. The great Sachem sold you some land, and that land became yours. Then, you seized all the land, without a deed of ownership and without a penny's compensation. Where is the justice in that? If I took your cow and you came to claim it, how could I refuse to give it back, knowing it is your cow and that I had not paid for it?*

Magistrate Collins: *Your cow was forfeited in the war, madam. War knows its own justice.*

Melba Blue Jay: *You speak of war, sir, but I believe what you mean is conquest. The war was over, yet those you hadn't annihilated you banished. Then, you took what belonged to them. There was no settling of grievances, sir. There was no justice.*

The courtroom rumbles.

Anonymous voice: *She is right. One hundred years ago this woman's grandfather was serving our grandparents their first hot meal in the new world. Today we serve her a load of mush!*

Raucous laughter.

Magistrate Collins: *Order or we shall end this session now! Madam, you have our sympathy but there is nothing this court can do for you.*

The claimant removes from around her neck a copper coin, stamped with the colony seal. Presented many years ago to her grandfather Runinniduk, the coin has succored her in her darkest moments.

"Eureka!" said Osborne.

Melba Blue Jay: *My grandfather loved your people and insured their peace, though many of his own tribesmen felt about you the way many in this court today feel about the Crown. In gratitude, the colony hanged him. That injustice set off a terrible war that brought the colonies to the brink of* destruction. Today I hold this token before you as a simple reminder of a simple truth: injustice only leads to conflict and bloodshed.

Magistrate Collins: And such seditious talk will lead you and your Swamp People straight to gaol and gallows.

Melba Blue Jay: Oh, the Crown has nothing to fear from us, sir. We are small and inconsequential. Your problem lies with a much bigger tribe. I look about this gathering and I see a people who have never set foot in England and who outnumber Europe-born Englishmen by a hundred to one. How long before they tire of being treated like second-class citizens? How long before they, collectively, form a new identity, as we Swamp People have done? How long before they choose to break the shackles of a distant authority with an unjustifiable claim on their lands and livelihoods?

Voice: Well-spoken, good lady!

Voice: Bravo!

Magistrate Collins: Order!

Voice: Order, my arse!

On a nod from the bench, the court officer and two armed guardsmen rise with muskets loaded and clear the courtroom, bringing to a close another royal runaround, as Melba Blue Jay so eloquently put it.

Osborne set the book in his lap and asked, "What happened to her?"

Randy blurted, "She lived to be a hundred and two, Papa."

Osborne was incredulous, until Lydia proved it by showing him a census report taken of the Great Swamp in 1771: "2,372 free Africans and 31 Indians, including the oldest person in New England, a 102-year-old female Sachem…venerated on both sides of the Neespaugot River."

"I stand corrected," said Osborne, grinning. "A chief, no less."

"More than a chief, G.O. Those Swamp People were considered freeloaders and squatters, but no authority moved against them. She must have had quasi-deity status."

"But no legal victory?"

Mother and son shared a wink.

Lydia handed Osborne a faded legal writ from April 1773.

The Great Swamp Reform Act

Pursuant to the non-continuation of colonial tax collecting, the governance of the land between the West Neespaugot River and the Hamminsett Hills is no longer tenable, said area costing the town of Neespaugot more money and men than the town and its officials can afford. Also, pursuant to the Neespaugot Mercantile Act, "What cannot be taxed shall be excised and rendered redundant." Henceforth and as of this day, the aforementioned territory shall be a separate and distinctly self-governing district under Indian supervision.

"I'm not sure I follow," said Osborne.

Lydia said, "The Great Swamp Reform Act came into existence between the Neespaugot Mercantile Act and the War of Independence. The Neespaugot Mercantile

Act was the harshest act enacted on the colonies. It made the Crown the only producer of anything in the colonies, raised the import-export duties from two and a half to five percent overnight, and shut out foreign and colonial competition. It was economic warfare before the real war. So the Swamp Act was the colony's counterpunch. It told the Crown in so many words that if the colonies were to be gutted, the colonies would no longer collect the taxes in an area like the Great Swamp. Thus, the Great Swamp passed back into Indian hands. The Great Swamp Reform Act would inspire the Boston Tea Party."

Osborne chuckled. "So let me get this straight. No Melba, no Swamp People. No Swamp People, no Swamp Act. No Swamp Act, no Boston Tea Party. No Boston Tea Party, no Declaration of Independence."

"I wouldn't go that far, G.O."

"But the thought is delicious. As delicious as that of a colored woman named Lydia Freeman making economic policy for the slave-shipping company that had dragged her mother into bondage. So, what happened to this Swamp Act and the Swamp People?"

"What you'd expect," she said, handing him letters written between Paul and Lionel Finley.

Neespaugot, 11 May 1777

Dear Lionel,

Neespaugot is now under patriot control. As per General Washington's orders, we have conscripted all able-bodied Black Indian males from the swamp and sent them south to New York. They are a bedraggled bunch, but they are disciplined fighters, led by a man of great character, Edwin Tall Tree. He's the son of Moliere Court, the French-Indian cabinetmaker. Edwin Tall Tree is a personal friend of mine and a hard man to miss, standing six foot five, weighing two hundred sixty pounds, and as dark-skinned as the wharf water. He wears a long frizzy mane of black hair, and his attire, both over and under, make an odd compendium of shirts and trousers shorn and re-stitched together to his size. The Swamp People call him Muggayoh Metoog, but in town he's known as the Black Injun. He is a good leader and will not let you down.

Your brother, Paul

Saratoga, 20 October 1777

Dear brother,

Sadly, your friend and mine, Edwin Tall Tree, was felled today. He fought bravely and died an honorable death, a fact which even our enemy must surely vouchsafe. He was to have been buried with full honors, but his son William Running Duck (an angry headstrong young man) absconded with his father's remains and one Continental Army wagon and horse. The Swamp fighters have told me in good faith that this boy will be passing your way with the intention of laying his father in the ground on Mount Hope, alongside the Ancients Massasoit, Wamsutta, Canonicus, Miantonomi and the women chieftains Weetamoo, Askamaboo and

Melba Blue Jay. If you happen upon William Running Duck, apprehend him and try him as a deserter.

Your brother, Lionel

Neespaugot, 12 November 1777

Dear Lionel,

Will Running Duck was apprehended last night and brought to me. I was inclined to have him shot, but I must admit, the sight of his father's coin about his wretched shoulders stayed my hand. Instead, he was given thirty lashes of the whip and four week's menial labor. The boy—he is but nineteen years of age—had trained his father's remains three hundred miles back to Mount Hope, battling buzzards all the way, to bury his father in sacred grounds. But he found only farmland, he said. Even Melba Blue Jay's barrow is now a carrot patch, he said. Apparently, he tried to bury his father there anyway, until some farmers shot at him and he fled. The young fool ended up having to burn his father's rotting corpse.

Your brother, Paul

Lydia said, "I'm guessing the last Swamp People were dispersed at the end of the war. Or rustled up, separated by mulatto, quadroon and octoroon, and sold like livestock to the southern states. As for William Running Duck, there's this document from the city archives."

Hanged this day, 7 April 1794, William Running Duck, Negro Indian, aged 36. Time of death, 7:48 a.m.

"Katherine believed, and now so do I, that this man was my father. He was known to the authorities as a troublemaker who abetted runaway African slaves. He must've taken in my mother and lain with her. Then, one fateful day he left their sanctuary in the woods, went into town, got drunk and beat a white man to death. He was hanged in the town Commons, one hundred nineteen years after my great-grandfather Runinniduk.

"Three months later my mother staggered into Neespaugot, starving to death, pregnant and going into labor. Her English was poor, and the hospice midwife couldn't get a name out of her. My mother's only possession was a weathered coin on a wretched strap. She perished just after midnight, and the midwife cut me out of her uterus, saving my life."

Lydia grew quiet, then her introspection turned to tears streaming down her cheeks. Osborne draped his good arm over her shoulders. "My dear, dear wife," he said softly. "Now, at least, you know."

The three family members sat in silent communion for several minutes. At last, Lydia rose off the bed and lifted the tray. "She was good to her word, George. You have to give her that."

"She was a master pilferer."

"Yes, but it's now my duty to pay her back. Randy, I have someplace I need to get to. Want to come?"

"Sure, Mama. Where are we going?"

"The orphanage."

Archie

April 15, 1861

1

Crossing the Philippine Sea, *The Neespaugot* hit the doldrums. The wind died, the seas flattened, and time itself ceased. The schooner's nine sails hung from their crosstrees like wilted lettuce. The world of water and sky turned silent but for the creaking cadence of the ship's hull bobbing like a cork in a vat of whale oil.

The doldrums would last three days, and by the end of it, the deck hands were whiling away their boredom with pissing contests and teasing the only boy on board, a Chinese tyke.

"So, tell us your name again, boy."

"Ching Ah Chung," answered the nine-year-old.

"Well, which is it, you little bastard?"

"Ching Ah Chung," he repeated.

"Bloody hell, the runt cannot decide what his own name is. So, Ching-*or*-Chung, what think ye of going to America?"

"Rord bress thee, my damn fine ord ferrows. I frigging joy to go America if it prease God. I eat pissing good mutton, and a Jane's soft frou-frou to unbutton."

"Fucking hell! Comes out the same every time."

The laughter spread like contagion across the deck, and not a dry eye to be found.

The boy had come aboard at Shanghai. His daddy, some damn herbalist on Xanghing Street, had saved Master Finley from a staph infection. The Master made biennial visits to China for business and, unbeknownst to most, had a craving for Chinese twat. To show his gratitude, the Master had agreed to take the herbalist's wayward son to America and away from Mama Sung's brothel, where the boy ran errands, waxed boots and played poker with Balmoral-booted gamblers, rum-runners, whale men, pelt peddlers, frock-coated missionaries and monkey-jacketed sailors.

At Mindanao, a husband-and-wife team paid a pretty penny to come aboard. Naturalists, they called themselves. Said they observed and recorded nature without the bias of ideology or sentimentality. Thereafter, *The Neespaugot* made periodic stops at various atolls in the Caroline and Marshall Islands to allow the overeducated fools the chance to study what they called flora and fauna. The couple let Ching-or-Chung tag along. Returning to the ship, the boy would try to translate his wonder to the crew, but the only thing he managed to communicate was his piss-poor speech. If, as the Naturalists claimed, the natural world was a great testing ground for the survival of the fittest, Ching-or-Chung represented the dodo bird of children. He couldn't even make up his mind about his own name. What chance did he have in the world at large?

"Come closer, you brainless little shit, and let ol' Gunner educate you," said the sailor. "Bet you ain't never heard of the Kraken. You see, the Kraken be a beast both reptile and proboscidean, as big as ten Finley ships and perfectly capable of swallowing an entire vessel and its crew with nary a hiccup. Aye, Ching-or-Chung, heed me warning and don't let them science folk lead you astray. The next time they take you to an atoll, tread lightly, for it mightn't be what you think. Go on, Fat Charley, and tell the urchin here what happened to old Smythe."

"Well, old Smythe, yer see, he gets too friendly with some science folk. Especially the missus, heh heh. And that be his undoing. One day he goes ashore with them on what they think be land. But it ain't. It be the Kraken's back. The monster wakes up and gobbles Smythe and the science lady like they's bacon. Shat 'em both out days later near Hawaii."

The boy was used to a good ribbing. Got plenty of it back at the whorehouse. He didn't take it personally. Besides, it beat spending time with the ship's chaplain. Five times a day since the ship left Shanghai, that dried-up pikestaff of a chaplain had been yanking the boy's orchid ears toward the Scriptures and riving his rump with the rod. "You sloe-eyed, heathen guttersnipe, you *will* learn the language of the Lord!" Switch, switch! The boy's howling education echoed from the East China Sea to the North Pacific.

The boatswain rang the assembly bell. "All hands on decks! The Captain would have a word with you buggers." The Captain addressed the crew. "Men, the war has started. Three days ago, the Confederates attacked Fort Sumter. That's in Charleston, South Carolina, for you morons. I suspect we'll make fast work of those cotton farmers and the whole thing will be over by the time we get home. That'll be all."

A week later, *The Neespaugot* put in at Honolulu to unload spices and silks. Honolulu was a strange mix. The native population looked Chinese. The Naturalists had told Ching Ah Chung that the Chinese had been master sailors long before the Europeans and had explored great distances of the Pacific. But the city didn't look Chinese. According to the crew, Honolulu resembled New England, with its white picket fences, missionaries, docks, whalers and seamen. Ching didn't know what to make of the city, so he followed the Naturalists' advice and trusted only what he could see. And what he saw was beards. All the white male adults in Honolulu wore beards. The Finley sailors were clean-shaven to a man and seemed genuinely flabbergasted by the new trend. But by the time they took to sea again, most of the deck hands, the boatswain and the Captain himself had sprouted whiskers of their own. Only Master Finley continued to shave.

The ship reached Neespaugot in late July, and the war, by all accounts, was not as quick as the Captain had predicted. Ching understood that a blue army of untrained soldiers had met a gray army and been routed. Now, warships and transport vessels filled South Bay's newly constructed deep-water harbor. Grover Wharf rumbled under wagons of artillery, ordnance and provisions being loaded onto three-mast ships, their gangways trembling beneath the legions of new troops embarking for the fight. Ching noticed that many of the recruits lacked uniforms and were dressed in street clothes. They were quite young and spoke in a variety of accents and languages. No one looked eager to be going anywhere.

That autumn, talk of the war—its battles and fallen sons—occupied every conversation from shop to street corner. Yet there was little consensus about what the fighting was about. Some said it was to "teach Dixie a lesson." Others said it was to keep the country together. Few people spoke about the issue of slavery. The exception (at least in Ching's sphere) was the Master. Quite often at the dinner table, he would tell his grown son Rutherford "Ford" Finley that slavery was an abomination that needed to be stamped out. "This war, Ford, is a moral one." That line of thinking contrasted sharply with what the Naturalists had explained to Ching: "In war, moral issues are like a dog's drool. They hang around at the whim of a tongue and gravity. What matters is teeth."

Ching wondered who the slaves were and where they were hiding. In North Bay, black faces were as scarce as Asian ones. There was an old colored woman who hobbled across the Commons, pushing a pram with a white baby in it. Sometimes she was accompanied by a light-skinned colored teenager who could have been her grandson or grandnephew. On rare occasions, the woman and her grandson were accompanied by a lanky old white man with a severe disposition and bandaged head. Ching often saw the colored woman belittled with pointed fingers and harsh insults, making him wonder if he had gotten it backward; maybe it was the North that was *for* slavery, and the South *against* it. When he asked the Master about the colored woman, the Master said, "She's not worth the breath needed to explain the situation to you, boy."

For much of his first year in New England, Ching lived a double life. He spent his mornings from sunup to noon in the company of the chaplain, who spared no switch in the boy's unsentimental education. The afternoons were long, dull passages to be bided like the doldrums. His backside still smarting, Ching would take long walks, meandering along the Pickworth Point peninsula to Grover Wharf and the Old Port. But once the sun went down and the blessed evening began, he consumed himself in debauchery. East Gaines Street, at the far side of the wharf, was where the action was. Drunken seamen, gamblers and whores. Upstairs in Kelly's, Ching lost his virginity to a fifty-three-year-old prostitute who smelled of vaginal thrush and old yarn. He was eleven years old.

The whores of Kelly's protected the boy from buggers and brutes. And it was those ladies who solved the mystery of the boy's waffling name, Ching Ah Chung. *Ah* was the Chinese term for "mister." All along, the boy had been presenting himself in the politest way possible in Chinese: Mr. Ching Chung. The ladies continued to call him "Our China Doll."

In the winter of 1862, Ching's antics reached the ears of the Master, who decided that an American name would help straighten out the imp. The boy was marched by the seat of his pants to the courthouse and his name legally changed to Joseph Archung-Finley. "I fully expect you to live up to your new Christian name, Joseph," said the Master. "Do you know who the Biblical Joseph was?"

"Yes, sir. He was sold into slavery in Egypt, but he became a potentate."

"Correct you are, Joseph. A potentate, not a whoremonger. The chaplain has done his job and maybe you don't need him any longer. So here's my deal. You lay off the brothels, and I'll give the chaplain the boot."

It was difficult to give up his carousing at the cathouse, but he intended to live up to his new name. A promise was a promise. He didn't know it then, of course, for he was too young, but Joseph Archung-Finley would never be the sort of person who makes good on a resolution. But in this case, he was absolved of his promise when his new name failed him first. His stepbrother Ford took to calling him "Archie," short for Archung. The nickname possessed neither the exoticism of Ching Ah Chung nor the nobility of Joseph, but the wharf workers liked it, said it fit him like a glove, and treated him better because of it. "Come on, Archie," they said. "Let's step into Kelly's for a drink."

2

In the winter of 1862, the Master delivered what he expected would be disappointing news to Archie. He wouldn't be making the voyage back to Shanghai that spring. The Union cause needed the help of every available Finley vessel. "I've wired your father, Joseph, and hopefully I can take you next year."

Archie drew a long face, for show. In truth, he was overjoyed. He wanted to stay in America where, despite the war, he had it decidedly good. His bedroom in the Finley mansion on the peninsula was as big as his family's entire apartment above his father's shop. He was given three square meals a day. His new name had brought him a certain respect on the wharf, where the mariners now taught him their craft instead of teasing him. His school lessons were now dispensed by a kindly spinster who didn't own or need a rod. He had even learned to ride a horse. In addition to all that, he was back to leading a double life: Joseph by day and Archie by night, sneaking out at dark to join his "girls" at Kelly's.

But a year, especially a year of war, makes a lot of difference in a boy's attitude toward his surroundings, and the following winter, 1863, Archie became truly homesick. Maybe it was the coffins arriving by the thousands at Grover Wharf from places with funny names like Chickamauga and Chattanooga. Maybe it was seeing whole families crushed under the weight of army casualty lists tacked to the pilings each sunrise. "Sir, when should it all be over?"

"I wish I knew, Joseph," said the Master.

"I should like to return to China and work with my father, sir."

"I know, and I'm sorry, Joseph, but my hands are tied. We're both stuck here for now."

Another year passed, and the cute tyke whom the sailors had loved to tease and whom the prostitutes had considered a China doll, was gobbled whole by the Kraken of a voracious adolescence. Archie was no longer adorable, but a lanky youngster slightly under six feet and needing a shave. A graceful symmetry of fine facial bones gave him the look of a cat, though he was more dog-like in temperament, being persistent, often infuriatingly so. He wore his lick of shiny black hair short and sported a cap, and his cracking voice was imbued with mischief. He took to wearing sideburns and looked much older than his thirteen years. But for his slanted eyes, Archie might have passed for a westerner. Most incoming sailors took him for Hawaiian.

By the spring of 1865, Archie's return to Shanghai was all but a moot point. The war was over, the nation had prevailed and slavery was dead, but so was the President, so were several thousand of Neespaugot's favorite sons, so was Archie's dear stepbrother Ford Finley. Poor Ford had perished in the naval battle of Plymouth, off the coast of North Carolina. A few months after his death, Mrs. Finley succumbed to grief and the Master suffered a stroke. The left half of his face seemed to be sliding off his head, to the dazed consternation of his right eye. He mumbled that he was done with living, and had his elder son return from San Francisco to run the company.

Terrence Finley was known for two things: obstinacy and a tendency to drive everything he touched into the ground—or, in this case, the sea. That was why the Master had sent him to San Francisco, to keep him at arm's length as he groomed Ford to take the reins. But fate had determined otherwise, and Terrence was now the last brother standing.

Physically, Terrence looked a lot like the Master, being stout, ruddy and round-faced. But his demeanor was full of impatience and choler. He wore a shaggy, yellow mustache that covered his upper lip and was always wet with lathered spit after his frequent tongue-lashings. He wasn't in the mansion ten minutes when he put things straight to Archie. "I do not like Chinamen. I'd as soon call a ship rat a brother as a yellow bastard such as you. And yes, you'll go home to that squinty land of yours, but you'll do it at your own damn expense. Your days of being treated like the fucking Kublai Khan are over. Prepare to be buggered, you fish-eyed fuck."

Archie was thrown out of the Pickworth Point mansion and into a bunkhouse on the wharf where he was put to work loading and unloading ships at dawn and dusk for a few pennies a day. His kindly spinster teacher was let go. Fortunately for Archie, the Massachusetts Education Law of 1852 made schooling for any child under sixteen years of age a requirement. Being fifteen, Archie was enrolled in South Bay Public School. "But the minute you turn sixteen," said Terrence, "you're out on your ass."

Archie's teacher at South Bay Public School was only five years older than he was. Mr. Randolph Osborne had honey-colored skin, caring eyes and a mulatto's hair and features. Archie immediately recognized him as the teenager from the Commons. "Sir, didn't you used to take walks with a colored lady and a white baby?"

"That's right, Joseph. The woman is my mother and the baby, now five, is my adopted sister."

"There was a tall man with a bandage around his head."

"Yes, my father. You certainly do have a memory, Joseph."

Mr. Osborne taught a little of everything—mathematics, poetry, philosophy and history—but he seemed most animated lecturing about geography, exploration and population movements. His motto was, "What moves improves." He often tried—and usually failed—to coax the students into sharing their own family stories. His "melting pot" metaphor, a term in use since the 1790s, was, in the words of one Irish smart-aleck, "privies blarney."

South Bay Public was a poor school populated with poor kids of varied origins, boys and girls with last names like O'Connell, O'Keefe, Blyleven, Steinbrenner, Kirchen and Thibidault as well as Johnson and Haley. There were three Negro children, all named Lincoln, none related. Archie was the only Asian.

Mr. Osborne told the class that he himself was the product of three continents: North America, Africa and Europe, in that order. Sometimes he would bring to school an old coin tied to a broken leather strap. "This belonged to an ancestor of mine," he said. "A Wampanoag Indian man named Runinniduk, who was hanged in North Bay two hundred years ago."

The teacher's efforts to make history tangible generally fell as flat as sails on a windless sea. Most of the students weren't interested in learning history but in making some of their own. They mocked Mr. Osborne behind his back. Certain Dutch kids had a name for him: "doat," they called him. The derisive term was derived from the Dutch *doopen*, meaning a mix. "Osborne's half-dog, half-cat, stinks like a goat and looks like a dope. He's a fikken doat."

Archie did very well in school that year, and Mr. Osborne felt it would be a shame if he dropped out for his last year. Archie tried to explain the ultimatum he was given by his stepbrother Terrence Finley, but Mr. Osborne called that nonsense and hired a carriage to the Finley mansion to convince Terrence Finley to fund the young man a little longer. The young teacher was sternly rebuffed. "The law says sixteen," said Terrence. "Well, the bastard's sixteen and can fend for himself. I won't pay another cent for his food and lodging."

"In that case," said Mr. Osborne, treading on thin ice, "I suppose he should be receiving his part of your father's inheritance."

Terrence bounded out of his chair like a red devil toy on a spring. "You listen to me, you pale-mongrel bastard! Never—I repeat, *never*—will that worthless fish-head see a cent of my family's money!"

"Very well, sir, but there are courts for this sort of thing."

"Then, by all means, try your luck. Now, get the hell out of my house, tar baby, before I rip that rug you call hair off your black skull."

Mr. Osborne suspected there was more than simple bluster to Terrence's dare, so he procured a copy of the Master's will. The Master had indeed left Archie an inheritance, and a choice: either a three-thousand-dollar payout *or* a commission as first officer on a Finley vessel. Neither choice was binding before Archie's eighteenth birthday.

For his last year of school, Archie boarded with Mr. Osborne, his mother and six-year-old sister Bridget—the father, a doctor, had just died. Archie paid the mother, Miss Lydia, what he could from the money he earned at the docks. The Osborne family lived on Onion Road, in a funny-looking building that was a bit of an onion itself, with layered rooms and a living room serving as a deep core. Their house had once been a medical clinic, but Mr. Osborne's birth had caused a scandal that had shuttered the practice. Archie could not understand how a birth could be a scandal. Confucianism, the Scriptures and the Naturalists shared at least that point in common: every new life is a miracle. The first rule Archie had learned from his true father Xao Chung was: *Never impose on others what you would not choose for yourself*. It was the sine qua non for any society that hoped to survive. A community chooses spite at its own peril.

Miss Lydia loved to pick Archie's brain about his father's herbal trade. "Tell me everything you can remember about Chinese medicine, Joseph," she said, preferring his Biblical name to his nickname. Archie surprised himself with how much he actually did remember. There was the fat book on his father's desk called the "Bencao Gangmu," the most comprehensive medical book ever written about traditional Chinese medicine. He remembered that. He also remembered the varied textures and odors of shiitake and lingzhi mushrooms, of ginseng, wolfberry, cinnamon, ginger, peony, stringbush and golden larch. He recalled various animal parts and crushing dried herbs and animal organs into powder, and rolling them with honey into pellets.

And certain principles were revived in his mind: the four natures, the five tastes, the meridians and *qi*, the Chinese term for universal energy and balance.

After many discussions with Miss Lydia, Archie got the distinct impression that he wasn't telling her anything she didn't already know, and he asked her if she had been a "healer." She chuckled and told him no—not in name, anyway. She admitted to a bit of "dabbling." But Archie wasn't fooled. The unassuming Miss Lydia was a healer in her own right, and Archie suspected that the former clinic must have been a good one before it was shut down.

Archie graduated school in June 1867. He was seventeen and would need to wait a year before collecting his inheritance. Rather than waiting around Neespaugot, Archie took a job out west with a railroad company looking for a translator. He made his farewell to Miss Lydia and Mr. Osborne at Mr. Osborne's marriage to Clara Fuller in the Osborne House garden. More than one hundred guests attended, most of them Miss Clara's relatives, ex-slaves playing banjos and horns, dancing and belting out ballads and spirituals the afternoon long. The aroma of mutton chops, pig's feet in batter, calf's tongue and stewed kidneys and veal rose over Onion Road. The cornucopia of food was washed down with sarsaparilla, Eagle Brewery lager, grape juice, minted water and, as the party reached its loudest stage, homemade corn whiskey. Archie himself had one too many tips of the jug and became maudlin. How he envied them all their sense of belonging! A family rooted in blood, shackles and newfound freedom. The true Josephs were they, not he. Tricked and sold into slavery but rising, building a community, being a part of something bigger.

Later in the evening, Archie was drunk and only vaguely aware of the little girl sitting on his lap, playing with his eyelids—"snake eyes," she called him. He ignored her prying and chatter as a horse does an importuning horsefly. Eventually, Miss Lydia came to his rescue and shooed the girl away.

"She can be a pesky child, that Bridget."

Archie felt lightheaded, exhausted and vaguely ill. As usual, Miss Lydia understood the origin of a problem and doled out the right remedy.

"Joseph, child, I think you're doing the right thing. Life is a current. Its whole purpose is moving on. Even the Bible is about *going*. Setting out, searching, finding, losing, going, wandering, and starting the cycle again." She touched his hands affectionately. "You will always have a home here, dear."

3

Archie went to work for the Central Pacific Railroad Company of California, out of Sacramento. For the next two years, he labored alongside and served as translator for the ten thousand Mandarin Chinese coolies employed at a pittance to drag iron rails and lumber up and down the towering passes of the High Sierras. He bunked with the Chinese but often drank and gambled with ex-soldiers—both Union and Confederate—as well as sundry other cutthroats and thieves. Archie's expertise at cards and superior knowledge of the English language often got him in trouble with liquored-up card cheats who threatened to gut him like a rainbow trout. But Providence, in the form of hired bodyguards, always intervened. Such was his value to the company as a translator.

On May 10, 1869, as the last spike was being driven into place with a silver hammer at Promontory Summit, Utah Territory, Archie collected his wages and examined the four cardinal points of the compass. He was free to go anywhere and do anything he wanted. He had no responsibility to anyone but himself. He could hop the Transcontinental and return east to fight Terrence Finley for his inheritance, or take the Overland back to San Francisco and sail to Shanghai to see his family, or buy a horse and head south to Texas or north to Montana. It was a quandary, but a delicious one.

His pockets lined with cash, Archie set out for the Washington and Idaho territories. The next few years saw him in a number of odd jobs: trapping, mining, herding, farming, cleaning stables and enjoying some success as a small-time saloon gambler. "I quite enjoy the freedom of moving about, taking opportunities as they come," he wrote Randolph Osborne in the autumn of 1871. "I didn't think I could do it at first. I was petrified. But Miss Lydia said something I shall never forget: life is a current. And I've taken to travel like a fish to water. Maybe movement for its own sake is the overriding moral of any life. I believe it's mine."

Four years later, Archie had grown less enamored of the open road: "To be quite honest, I'm fed up with the cold, the critters and my own stink. I've hired on with an

English outfit out of Victoria, and I am Shanghai-bound, returning home like any salmon or homing pigeon worth its salt!"

A year on, another letter arrived from Shanghai. "There's a martial cloud hanging over my old city. European and American navies occupy Shanghai. My father is dead, my second oldest brother Zhou, too. My mother lives and works in another man's house and has put me out of her life. Everything moves, even one's old life. What one calls home moves on when one leaves it. I can find no trace of a Finley ship, but I shall sail for Neespaugot when I find another outfit that will have me."

Archie returned to Neespaugot in 1877. He was twenty-seven years old, with pockets so deep they echoed. It had been ten years since his departure, and the city had changed. The world's first suspension bridge now spanned the North and South bays. A train station with lines to Boston, New York, Baltimore and Washington, D.C., sat at the mouth of the Neespaugot River. Finley Sons had changed, too, for the worse. At Grover Wharf, he saw more Finley ships out of water than in it. Twelve ships, two complete fleets, in dry dock. When he had set out for California, a grounded Finley boat was as rare as a Chinaman in New England.

Two longshoremen sat idly on the dock, flinging seashells at the Finley sign. Archie asked them what had happened.

"Terrence Finley happened! The cocksucker scuttled the affair."

"We should've tarred and feathered the bastard when we had the chance."

Archie hoisted his bag and started the long haul out to Pickworth Point to see for himself just how desperate the situation was. Maybe being taken down a peg or two had rendered Terrence a little more reasonable about the terms of the Master's will.

The Finley maid left him standing under the portico while she went to announce him. To pass the time, Archie hummed a few bars of "Old Black Joe."

Gone to the shore where my soul has longed to go,
I hear those gentle voices calling Old Black Joe.

The maid returned. "Mr. Finley says go away." And she closed the door in his face.

By late afternoon he was back at the Old Port, heading down Onion Road. In his time away, his mind had forged an idealized version of the house where he had spent the best two years of his young adult life. But the mythic gold he'd concocted on the prairie collapsed into a heap of dreary reality. The house he remembered so fondly was withered and depressing. The widow's walk looked ready to slide off the roof. Wrens and sparrows nested in the eaves, the garden was overrun by thickets, and the Tuscan birdbath lay in three pieces beside the weed-cracked walkway. Archie recalled a line from *As You Like It*, read in Mr. Osborne's class: *"And so from hour to hour we ripe and ripe, and then from hour to hour we rot and rot, And thereby hangs a tale."*

Miss Lydia was sitting by herself on the porch, hunched up, grizzled as an old sea bass and muttering in communion with herself. She had a brown cane in her trembling hand. Her failing eyesight no doubt made him an approaching blur, so he called loudly. "Miss Lydia, it's Joseph Finley!" Her leather face sprung to life. "Dear Lord, Joseph!" With the help of her cane, she worked herself out of the chair and wiggled down the steps to greet him. Eighty-plus years and physically diminished, the old caregiver still had spirit. "Welcome, sweet boy, welcome!" She kissed his cheek. "Lordy! Lordy! Clara!" she called back to the house. "Sweet Joseph Finley has finally come home!"

They were still sitting on the porch—Clara had gone back inside to bathe her toddler Sarelle—when Randolph Osborne came up the walkway, ten years heavier in the belt and thinner in hair. Beside him walked a beautiful young woman, distracted by some tune she was humming, and terribly distracting to Archie—who was smitten on the spot. Her butter-colored wasp-waist dress seemed not so much to clothe as unclothe her, and Archie found himself ogling.

As if sensing his ardor, Miss Lydia asked, "Remember her?"

"I'm afraid not," he said. "Should I?"

"Why, it's Bridget," said Miss Lydia, chuckling. "She's all grown up!"

Archie was dumbstruck. The little pest had become a buxom, auburn-haired, emerald-eyed manslayer.

During dinner, he heard himself speaking like an imbecile, trying to impress her with his travel stories. But the girl he once couldn't get off his lap now treated him and his adventures with a distance bordering on disdain. She yawned as he described fending off a mountain lion, sighed as he was treed by a grizzly bear, pouted when he survived a massacre at the hands of Shoshone Indians and brushed her hair at golden sunsets over the Pacific.

"My word, I envy you, Joseph," said Randolph. "How I would have loved to experience your adventures. Thank goodness I can do it vicariously through you. What do you intend to do for an encore?"

"Get a ship's commission," he said with an emphatic glance at Bridget. She had put her brush away and was back to yawning. Archie continued his narrative, a bit deflated. "At least, that's what I was hoping. You recall that the Master's will gave me a choice, job or money. But with Finley floundering and all…"

At the mention of the name Finley, the young beauty shot up. "You know the Finleys?" The Finley name did what lions, bears and wild Indians could not. "How do you know them, Joe?"

Randolph upbraided her. "His name is Joseph, Bridget, and of course he knows them. He *is* a Finley. Weren't you listening?"

She challenged her big brother more out of spite than curiosity. "And how could he be a Finley? He's Chinese."

It was the first time Archie had ever seen Miss Lydia express a negative gesture. She pinched up her face and spoke quietly but firmly to the flippant belle: "Joseph was adopted, dear, same as you. His race is inconsequential."

"Is it?" she asked, her tone confrontational and coy.

"And what's that supposed to mean?" said Randolph.

Bridget smiled and let it drop.

4

To fight Terrence Finley for his rightful inheritance, Archie hired a lawyer willing to work for a percentage of the final inheritance settlement, a fellow named Leadbetter, who warned him, "These battles can take years."

Archie didn't understand why. "Aren't the terms of the will fairly cut and dry?"

"They are indeed," said Leadbetter. "But your stepbrother is arguing that his—um, *your*—father wasn't in his right state of mind when he drafted his will, having lost a son and his wife in short order. He's spending a pretty penny in legal fees on what is, if you'll forgive me, a trifle in regard to the family fortune. It's spite to the point of irrationality."

"It's on account of my race."

"Yes, I'm afraid so, and I'm not sure what will sway him to call off the battle."

In the meantime, Archie found employment at United Shoe Machinery and moved into a one-room flat in the industrial park. His excuse to the Osbornes was that he wanted to be closer to work, but the real reason was to be farther from Bridget. He lusted after her, and she didn't help matters. When the household was fast asleep, she would sneak half-naked into his room and flirt with him, working him into a tizzy before spiriting herself away, leaving him literally high and dry. "No hanky-panky *yet*," she told him, carrot-and-stick-like. She ran him in so many circles that his head spun the length of the day and into his sleep, when he got any.

Nonetheless, Archie still crossed the Neespaugot River several times a week to see his paramour. He called on her with niceties and trinkets that he could ill afford. "Why, Joe, how thoughtful!" said Bridget, acting surprised in front of her family, though she herself always specified beforehand the gifts she expected him to buy. Then, as per the protocol, Archie would ask her family's permission to promenade with the young woman. They would stroll up Sentinel Hill to Revolutionary Park, and sit on a public bench to watch sailboats in the Old Port. Any attempt on his part to snatch a kiss landed a handful of fingers between his lips and hers. "The courtship," she told him, "must remain chaste." Yes, he thought, and lucrative for her and hopelessly platonic and enervating for me.

One Sunday as he waited on the stoop for Bridget to return from church, Miss Lydia came around the corner of the house, holding the hand of her granddaughter Della, who'd only just begun to walk. Occupying the opposing extremities of life, grandmother and toddler did share one trait: each waddled like a duck. Archie stood to embrace Miss Lydia, then picked up the squealing little creature and swung her around like a sparrow. When he sat back down with the toddler on his knee, he pretended not to have a care in the world, but Miss Lydia could read him like a book. "How are you holding up, dear?"

He told it to her straight. "Like a submersible, floating and sinking at the same time."

"Ha!" She was tickled by the metaphor.

"I'm anxious all the time, Miss Lydia."

She labored to a seat beside him. "Can I share something with you, Joseph? It's sure to make you think

I'm a babbling old coot, but here goes. Once upon a time, I worked for your American family. I don't mean as their health-giver. For a good decade, I was their chief financial advisor. They didn't know it, of course. All of my dealings with them were by mail. I hoodwinked the board of directors into thinking I was my husband. The good doctor owned a number of shares in the company. Well, all good games come to an end, and when mine was up, your adoptive father was fit to be tied and hell-bent on closing our clinic.

"So, why am I telling you this, Joseph? Because it so happens that while I was playing advisor to the gods, I managed to convince William Finley, the man you call the Master, to go to China. Many years later, he brought you back here. Thus, I feel I have some responsibility in your being here. I consider you my *spiritual* son, Joseph. And everything I'm about to say from here on out has only your protection in mind. Bridget…"

Archie stiffened. "I know she's young."

"It's not her age, dear." Miss Lydia's voice was more solemn than critical. "It's her ancestry."

Archie straightened like a dog catching a scent. "Her ancestry?"

The old lady reflected for a moment, deciding on the best angle from which to broach the subject. "I'm just going to come out and say it, Joseph. Bridget's daddy was a thug, and her mama was worse."

"Worse than a thug?"

"Her mother murdered people, Joseph. With her bare hands. Slit their throats."

"Gadzooks!" Archie groped for reassurances. "But you raised her, Miss Lydia."

"I did indeed. G.O. and I raised her as best we could. But who knows what percentage of a person's character is nurtured and what comes free of charge, as it were. Now, don't get me wrong. Bridget is no thug or killer, but she does share something with her natural mother. Call it flashes of a dark calculation."

"You're scaring me, Miss Lydia."

"Good! It's my duty to put you on guard. If you're going to be smitten with my daughter, you need to have your eyes wide open, dear Joseph. I can't tell you what to do. Matters of the heart play out in the heart, where reason never gets much purchase. But I do ask that you think over very carefully what I've said, before making any commitment."

"I shall, Miss Lydia. I shall be on the lookout and will terminate the courtship if I discover anything untoward. You have my word."

5

Archie being Archie, he went ahead and married Bridget anyway. It was a small gathering at the First Baptist Church. On his side of the aisle was a mate from work; on hers, the Osbornes and a few relatives of Clara's. After a brief collation in the Osborne living room, the newlyweds adjourned to Archie's one-room flat in the factory district and consummated their union on a bare mattress. The bride, now eighteen years old, lay inert on the bedding, her sweet flesh buried within a confusion of crinoline and stiff petticoats. She was beautiful to behold but as stiff and coarse as her garments, and she seemed eager to get the business overwith as quickly as possible. The groom toiled away patiently, eventually turning her aggravation to pleasure. When he was done, she said, "You touch better than you talk, Joe." Then she rolled over and immediately fell asleep.

The following morning, Archie awoke to find her straddling him naked, which made him smile at first, until he saw what Miss Lydia had termed a "flash of dark calculation." Her green eyes went almost black, and her explosion of red hair coiled over his face like descending snakes. "Morning, Joe. How about some more, eh?" she asked.

As he wiped the sleep from his eyes and tried to fathom what was going on, she stuck her left breast in his face. "Go on, grope me," she said. Too slow for her tastes, she seized his hand and clamped it between her thighs. "Rub some more, Joe."

He still didn't get it, so she gyrated on his hand. "How's it feel? I want you to remember my feel, my smell, Joe. It'll be the last piece of me you get until you get us your inheritance." She pushed off him and returned to her side of the mattress, brooding.

He shook his head in disbelief. "We've only been married twelve hours and—"

"And nothing! It's been thirteen years the Finleys have owed you. You may not give a damn, but I do. I'm your wife now, and we need the money."

"And what do you think I can do that the lawyer cannot?"

"The lawyer can't grow you a pair of balls, Joe! Only you can march your measly hide out to Pickworth Point and demand what's yours. Go prove you're a man."

He didn't like being blackmailed, and he cared even less for having his manhood called into question. "I recall this saying from my boyhood in China. *What the superior man seeks is in himself. What the mean man seeks is in others.* That's my answer."

Confucius cost him a month's worth of bunking on the hardwood floor.

When Bridget finally did invite him back to the conjugal mattress, he chalked it up to good sex trumping greed. He made the false assumption that his young inexperienced wife had seen the errors of her ways and was now desirous to have more of what he, an experienced *older* man, could offer in carnal knowledge. He had opened the flower, and now the flower was thirsty.

His mistake was in thinking that she was like him and thought with her loins. She didn't. Greed, and some serious financial anxieties, resonated stronger in her than carnality ever would. In fact, the sweet balm of money *was* the turn-on, always titillating, usually frustrating and only occasionally gratifying to the likes of her.

So what had changed? Why had she relented? Simply put, she had come into some money of her own. Two months after her eighteenth birthday, a letter arrived for her from a lawyer named Arondale. A trust account in her name, set up by Miss Lydia Freeman, had come due. Her nurture-mother had been depositing five dollars a month for eighteen years into an account that now totaled $1,369.

Of course, it would be a cold day in hell before she'd share the knowledge of her windfall with her husband. He didn't have the smarts to claim his own damn money, and she'd be screwed if he got his mitts on hers. The problem was her mother. Mama Lydia appreciated Archie and would, sooner or later, spill the beans to him. Somehow, someway, Bridget would have to separate the old woman from the young Chinaman.

So Bridget began begging off from Sunday get-togethers with the Osbornes, replacing them with more intimate affairs, meaning just her and Archie and maybe a workmate or two from The Shoe. She played the good wife, cooking nice meals, pretending to take an interest in her husband's shop talk and, if they were alone, granting him unlimited access to her body. The latter privilege bore immediate consequences, and she fell pregnant with their first child, born a year after their wedding. They named her Maureen.

Another mouth to feed revived Bridget's money worries. Hence, she was back at badgering her husband to do something about his inheritance. All the hectoring, hers and the baby's crying, which to his ears sounded awfully similar to hectoring, rekindled his yearning for open water, the boundless spaces, the road less traveled, movement for its own sake. The tangle of responsibility was tightening around him like kelp around a shark, suffocating him in a bed of stasis. In short, Archie was seeking a way out of the marriage.

Nothing moves a person like self-interest, and this time, when the subject turned to doing something about his inheritance, husband and wife were of the same mind, working together to free each other of each other. He tied up his bootstraps and marched out the door, ready and willing to face Terrence Finley man to man.

Not surprisingly, on his way to Pickworth Point, he got cold feet and settled instead for the warmth of the North Bay Post Office, where he drafted and sent a letter proposing a compromise: he would take only half of his $3,000 inheritance if Terrence offered him a traveling position with the company. He knew that Bridget would be furious, but once he had appeased her with all $1,500, she'd see her advantage. Not only would she have the money but he'd be on a mission away from home—thus, out of her hair.

A week later he had his answer.

Dear Mr. Ching Archung,

As litigator for Mr. Terrence Finley, I address on my client's behalf your letter of the 12th March of this year. Mr. Finley would have you know that he has only one brother, Rutherford Finley, who, alas, has been dead now some sixteen years. Your ethnicity being unquestionably Chinese, Mr. Finley suggests that you solicit your Chinese family for money and whatsoever inheritance you may expect from them, in your country of origin. Moreover, he would remind you that the Chinese Exclusion Act, recently enacted and now signed into law, renders the deportation of Chinamen a simple formality, and that you should heed this warning should you choose to importune Mr. Finley again with your outrageous claims of brotherhood and inheritance.

Your faithful servitor,

Colin Reed, Esquire

Archie's face drained of blood and he felt sick. The only reason Terrence would blackmail him with the Chinese Exclusion Act was that the son-of-a-bitch had his adoption papers. Archie had left them in the Finleys' attic the day Terrence had given him the boot in 1865. Terrence now owned him.

"I'm fucked," he told his wife. "I don't have a leg to stand on. He's got the matter all tied up. I can't go after my inheritance with this damnable Chinese Exclusion Act dangling over my head."

"Two can play at that game," she said, her eyes darkening again with calculation.

"What do you mean?" he asked.

"You'll see. It could take a year or two, but be patient. I *will* skin this bastard."

Whatever she meant by that was put on hold by the birth of their second child, Olivia. Then along came a third, Rebecca. She was pregnant with their fourth when, in March of 1883, Miss Lydia died. A few days after the funeral, when Bridget knew that Randolph was teaching and Clara was out on the Commons with her three little girls—Sarelle, Della and newborn Hattie Lawrence—she broke into Osborne House and into her defunct parents' bedroom. There she found her mother's medallion laid out nicely on a lace doily on the nightstand. She thought about stealing it but changed her mind. The coin was useless and would only get in the way of the bigger prize: the chest. She spirited it out of the house, much like her natural father Sean Griffin had carried it in, held in both greedy hands like an ancient treasure. With any luck, no one would even know it was missing.

"There!" she said, setting down on the table a cakebox-sized chest engraved with the initials "FST." "Have yourself a gander, Joe. It beats feeling sorry for your damn self."

"This is your mother's," he said with an accusatory look.

"Yes, my *natural* mother's. She stole it from the Finleys. The lawyer told me all about this box."

"What lawyer?"

She realized she'd said too much. "Never mind what lawyer. All these documents," she said, opening the chest as much to change the subject as to show what was inside. "They prove the Finleys were in the slave trade. And these letters here, they're even more damaging, since they were written by Mama Lydia. She fucked the Finleys good for ten years."

"How can we prove Miss Lydia wrote them?"

"We don't have to prove anything, Joe. That's the beauty of it. They're all signed *George Osborne Jr., MD*, the so-called Nigger Doctor."

She had a point.

"There's your fucking leverage, husband. Chinese Act, my ass! Write that bastard stepbrother of yours and tell him to pay up or this goes public."

"And what about this?" he asked, extracting from the box a thin, pistol-colored book wrapped in an oilcloth. Its pages were so desiccated they seemed like the wings of dead butterflies.

"Worthless," she said. "Take it with the chest to the river and burn them."

Archie read the title: *Blue Devil: the Trials of a Wampanoag Woman*. Waffling, he said, "Maybe you should sneak *this*, at least, back to Onion Road."

"And risk putting Randolph onto me? Over some dumb old book? Do you really *not* have a brain in that head of yours?"

Baby Johnny's cries took her out of the kitchen. Archie remained seated, weighing the book in each hand as if judging its fate. At last he rendered his verdict, wrapped the book in its cloth and set it inside the empty chest. Then, he carried both items down to the marsh, located an area well-concealed behind a row of reeds, and built a fire. A moment later, a small plume of smoke rose above the marsh, followed by a brief but intense skein of flame.

The blackmail letter went out that day, with "a small sampling of what the newspapers will receive if you don't comply." In the envelope was a Finley billing ledger dated 1764 for the sale of one hundred fifty-seven Negro men, women and children, and a Finley stock report highlighting Doctor Osborne's earnings for the fiscal year 1843.

Two days later, a courier on horseback delivered a note summoning Archie to the Pickworth Point mansion for a "talk." Along with the note was a silver dollar for horse-car fare.

6

Terrence's scornful wife showed Archie into the Master's study, a deep, high-ceilinged hall with a grand bay window facing east, framing open water that stretched all the way to Greenland. Closer to shore, the turbulent Atlantic crashed white against the dark cliffs of the peninsula. Terrence came bursting into the hall via a side door, shouting at his wife to get out. She hurried back down the hall, her anxious footfalls marking an interminable beat against the teak floorboards.

Archie hadn't seen Terrence Finley since he'd been given the bum's rush seventeen years earlier. The president and chief executive of the floundering Finley affair had aged badly. A fake tuft of unnaturally tinted hair crowned a puffy face decomposing into a puddle of jowls. He was as round as one of his Chinese father's remedies, animal penises mashed in mortar-and-pestle and rolled into honey balls. Terrence, of course, was anything but honey, not even on a good day, and this was decidedly not a good day. Once his wife had closed the far door, Terrence came at Archie as if he meant to tackle him. He stopped just short, the tip of his nose so close to Archie's that a sheet of paper wouldn't have slid through.

"You filthy little muckchuck!" The raging words came with flying spit and cigar breath. "You think you can blackmail me. *Me!* I will shoot you dead here and now if you don't give me every single one of those documents. I'll blast your yellow ass from here to Shanghai!"

"Be quick about it then," Archie said, holding his ground. "If I leave this house without a deal, those papers go to the *Neespaugot Times*."

"*If* you leave here alive, it'll be to jail, you thieving bastard. When I think of everything Papa did for you—"

"Put me in jail and see what happens to your nasty little secret. Anyway, you *know* I didn't steal anything. Why would I take those papers, yet leave my own papers behind?"

"Then how did they wind up in your yellow hands?"

"That's none of your business. Do we have a deal or don't we?"

"All right, you tight-eyed bastard. One thousand in cash and consider yourself lucky."

Archie put the kibosh on that. "Do I still look fifteen to you, Terrence? You should have accepted my first proposition when you had the chance. Now it's different. You'll give me every last penny of the three thousand the Master left to me *and* a ship's commission. Oh, and I want a twenty-percent stake in the company, a seat on the board *and* my adoptions papers."

Terrence turned red as sunset. "You cudmashed-chumball piece of dung. I'll show you what you'll get." This time, the curmudgeon drew a derringer from his waistband. He stuck the point of the barrel against Archie's forehead. "You'll take what I give you, you sniveling fish-head!"

"Fuck you, Terrence." Archie turned on his heels, tossing over a shoulder, "I can see the headlines now, 'The Finley Who Buried Finley.'"

Instead of a gun blast, he heard a begrudging grunt. "Hold on, damn you!"

The terms of the deal called for Archie to deliver into Terrence's hands all documents concerning the company's business in the slave trade and all correspondence of a professional nature between Finley and Doctor Osborne.

In exchange, Terrence agreed to pay him three thousand dollars, give him a captaincy and return Archie's adoption papers. But Terrence drew the line at part-ownership. "There will *never* be a fish-head on my board."

"Of course not. That would be as bad as a woman or a Negro. Oh, wait a minute…"

"Get the fuck out of my house!"

The next afternoon at Finley headquarters on Pier Five, the stepbrothers and their respective lawyers dipped ink, plumed terms, signed, stamped and sealed binding contracts. They did not shake. From the company office window, Terrence pointed out Archie's new commission, a suspiciously impressive frigate named the *South Pacific Belle*, sitting in dry dock. "She sails in three weeks, *captain*," said Terrence, snickering.

Archie crossed the pier to East Gaines Street and entered Kelly's, pushing into the crowd of swabbies and stevedores finishing off their day at the bar like a herd of barking seals. He mounted the staircase to Mabelle's room. The door was closed, so he waited outside. A moment later the door opened, the client exited and Archie entered her small, disheveled, malodorous room, barely big enough for the unmade bed she was trying to straighten. "Hey, Archie."

"Hey, Mabelle. Here's for your trouble." Archie peeled a sawbuck off a roll of banknotes freshly printed at Neespaugot National Bank. Mabelle, a young dark-eyed *métisse* of French and Indian extraction, had no pocket in her sheer garment, so she set the ten-dollar bill on the floor as she reached under her bed and pulled out the strongbox Archie had given her for safekeeping. He sat on the bed to open it and placed his stack of money on top of a bundle of documents.

"What's all that stuff?" asked Mabelle.

"Insurance," he said. "Actually, slave ledgers and Osborne-to-Finley communication. The bastard paid up, but you never know. And there's this book." Archie mumbled guiltily, reached inside the strong box and drew out *Blue Devil*. "Can't say why I kept it. But I couldn't bear to destroy it, either."

"What will you do with it?"

"I don't know. Can't entrust it to the wife. She'll just burn it and wouldn't know how to give it back to the person she pinched it from. I'll think of something."

Mabelle lay on the bed on her elbows, her knees up, her gown and thighs open for business. She operated her knees like sex levers, converging and spreading, cranking him up. "You can leave the stuff with me, Archie," she cooed.

"Nah, too many comings and goings around here."

"Whatever you say, sweetheart," she said, switching the levers to the wide-open position, licking her lips and wetting her labia. "How about one for the road?"

Archie nodded. "What the hell. I deserve it." He peeled off a bill, then peeled off his britches.

7

When Archie was a boy, the Master had taken him to the Seaman's Cottage. The boy had been expecting a cozy public house out of the public eye, where privileged sailors could drink in peace, maybe even get laid. What he saw instead was a solitary fieldstone tower overlooking the sea from the east ridge of Neespaugot Cemetery. The "cottage" had no windows nor floor, either, other than earth trampled over the years into a somewhat solid base. Nor was there a door to speak of, or even the intention of one. Visitors entered through a cramped aperture and found themselves inside a giant stone funnel, fifty feet in diameter and climbing in an ever-narrowing concentration thirty feet into the sky. It was chilly, it was windy, and there was a constant whistling that seemed to spiral down from the afterlife. Nearer the ground, the interior walls bristled with thousands of crude bogwood pegs, each slanted upward in erectile anticipation of memorial offerings: cards on a string, crucifixes, children's drawings, flowers, any kind of memento that would dangle. The Seaman's Cottage was a public mausoleum, constructed in the early 1800s of Bronze Age cairns and dedicated to local sailors who had gone down with their ships.

On a warm spring evening in 1884, Archie hauled a pick, shovel, lantern and strongbox into the Seaman's Cottage and began digging into the topsoil at the base of Rutherford Finley's peg. It took a full night, but the hole he'd dug finally met his satisfaction: a good three and half feet down through granite and shale, deep enough to bury a corpse. Into the hole Archie lowered the strongbox and all it contained. Then he covered it over.

The *South Pacific Belle* was composed of 110,000 pieces of beautifully handcrafted wood, all of it having rotted in dry dock for better than two years. Like an alluring woman standing alone under a streetlamp, the ship was suspect, the circumstances dirty. A little digging on Archie's part uncovered the truth about the fragile frigate. She flew the colors of a weighted past, twenty-five years of bad luck stretching back to the first time the wind had inflated her glorious sails.

Originally christened *The Sea Fairy*, she had sunk off the Massachusetts coast in 1868. Rechristened *The Ipswich*, she had caught fire in Jamaica in 1874. Under yet another name, *The Crystal Moon*, she had returned from Indonesia with half her crew dying of typhoid fever. Sailors are a notoriously superstitious lot, and few cared to work on the newly christened *South Pacific Belle*. Finley couldn't outfit her, so she had been consigned to dry dock.

In the incompetent hands of Terrence Finley, the company still did the bulk of its business as it had in the early 1830s, shipping raw materials—train oil, furs and bushels of cotton and tobacco—to a world evermore fixated on finished products. The company's staple commodity, whale oil, was dying a fast death due to kerosene, yet Terrence persisted on putting his money in harvesting an ever-dwindling population of hump, right and sperm whales because the product of the future, paraffin oil, was still relatively unknown in the South Seas.

The third week of May 1884, a "Notice To Seaman" was nailed to the pilings on Grover Wharf, announcing the recruitment of one hundred eighteen hands under the guidance of Joseph "Archie" Finley to transport whale oil to Australia aboard the *South Pacific Belle*. Reactions ran from cocking a snook to profanity. No self-respecting mariner would sail across the globe on a cursed ship with a Chinaman at the helm—sooner jump from the Neespaugot Bridge and save oneself the trouble.

The notice had been up ten days, yet only four men had signed on: a stone-deaf first officer, a septuagenarian navigator of questionable eyesight, an adolescent boatswain and one sailor before the mast, a rough scalawag with a knife-mutilated face by the name of Miggs. Terrence Finley had hired all of them personally. Their respective presences aboard were "non-negotiable."

Archie accused Terrence of sabotaging the mission in order to deprive him of his commission. Terrence got a chuckle out of that one. "I want nothing more than to see your yellow ass sinking beyond the horizon." To prove it, he had his company offer triple the going wage to anyone with the guts to sail. Suddenly, takers poured in, most of them desperate, craven characters.

Both to legitimize the undertaking and to offset the increased wages, the company also advertised discount passage on *The Belle* for research scientists and artists. Unlike sailors, scientists weren't superstitious, and seven men purchased passage: two naturalists, two botanists, a geologist, an astronomer and an illustrator.

In preparation for the voyage, Archie pored over seafarer manuals borrowed from Captain Osborne's collection. Bridget would drag herself out of bed to the kitchen to find the gas lanterns empty, the candles melted and her husband himself a puddle of shapeless wax stretched across his readings.

Bridget couldn't understand why Archie was still determined to sail despite all the shadowy details.

"Joe, you must realize it's all a ruse to get rid of you. They'll cut your throat and dump your body in the deep blue sea, just as Terrence paid them to do."

"You're imagining things."

"And you're as gullible as the day you were born. Look, if you don't want to tell me where you put the rest of the papers, fine. But at least let Terrence know you still have some proof against him. What the hell good is insurance if you don't use it?"

"I told you, I don't want you and the children mixed up. I can't risk Terrence coming after you once I'm gone."

"Then just don't go, you imbecile!"

It was too difficult to explain to her that if he didn't go, he'd suffocate. "Look, I thought this was what you wanted. Me out of the way."

"Out, maybe. Not dead."

The morning of her husband's departure, Bridget broke down in tears. Archie hugged her and thanked her for caring. Petulant to the end, she pushed him away. "Go on and good riddance to you." As he started out the door, she threw herself back into his arms a last time and wept some more on his chest. "You're a scalawag, Joseph Archung-Finley, but I shall miss you. *Bon voyage*!"

It was the first time since their wedding vows that she had said something kind to him.

8

The *South Pacific Belle*'s last known port of call was Port Moresby, Papua New Guinea. After being unloaded, the ship set back out across the Coral Sea, destination Samoa. It was never seen again. Months of waiting only confirmed what the Neespaugot boating community had known from the start: a cursed ship always met a bad end. For the rest of the year, solemn vigil was kept at the First Baptist Church. Mourners flocked to the Seaman's Cottage to hang *triste* memorabilia.

Winter 1885 was one of the harshest in living memory. There was a stretch of a few weeks when sea travel of any sort in and out of Neespaugot ground to a standstill, and Grover Wharf was a veritable ghost port. Terrence Finley, bundled to the ears in warm clothing, reached his dock office, the howling wind practically snapping his arm off as it took the front door out of his hand and slammed it against the building. The whole structure shuddered. To get the door shut required two pairs of hands, his and those of his office manager. "Jehoshaphat!" he said, closing the wind out. Trailed by the manager, he went into the inner sanctum, where it was warm and cozy from the coal stove going full blast, and removed his thick wool coat and scarf.

"How'd it go at the Sea Trade Commission?" asked the manager, a burly ex-stevedore whose job profile was more muscle than management.

"Good. The affair is closed, everyone's been ruled dead, and that fucking Chinaman is now officially a resident of Davy Jones's locker. Mathews, I swear, I could do a jig!"

"Well, don't let me stop you, boss."

"Tell Scranton to send a leg of mutton and a bottle of port to each grieving family. And let the shysters know our legal obligations are done."

"You got it."

A moment later, the manager put his head inside. "Ah, boss, there's some gal out here requestin' a word."

"What gal?"

"Maybe the kind to help you with your jig," said the big man.

Terrence had her brought in but kept her standing. She was a *metisse* in her twenties, poorly clothed but her face richly painted in the shades of her profession. "So, it's door-to-door now, is it, miss?"

"Oh, no, sir, I ain't come about that. I brought you something *important*," she said, opening her threadbare bag on his desk and handing him a grimy oilcloth containing an old thin book. "It's *the* book."

"I can see it's a book," he said, seizing it and scrutinizing its dog-eared cover and pages as flaky as old cigar leaves. "What in blazes does this rubbish have to do with me?"

"You can pay me for it, sir."

"Can I now? And why the fuck would I do that?"

She was confused. "You paid Archie handsomely for it. Don't you want it back? Archie took your money but kept the book, sir."

Behind the desk, the big boss said nothing for the longest while, until the girl realized that he was heating up like a full pot on a high flame. "I'd best go, sir," she said, trembling and backing away.

"Tell me, girl. Were there other papers with this?"

"Archie had a strongbox full of them, sir. He called them his insurance."

"Don't suppose you have that strongbox?"

"No, sir, just the book. It was all I had the time to take while I was doin' him."

"Mathews!" Terrence exploded. "Round up the boys!"

9

The years descended through the deep like sunken ships bound for the ocean floor. The *South Pacific Belle* mystery disappeared into the murk of oblivion. But the currents of life have a way of dredging up the past and, in the spring of 1890, a large piece of the tragic puzzle resurfaced. In the pearl fog of pre-dawn, *L'Etoile Filante*, a Belgium craft out of Antwerp via Hong Kong, docked at Grover Wharf. A federal inspector came aboard and perfunctorily read the new Scott Act to captain and crew. "Any attempt to smuggle a Chinese into the United States, even one legally residing here, will result in your prosecution and imprisonment and the immediate impounding of your ship." The inspector then looked to the ship's captain to assure that he had been well understood. The ship's captain nodded and placed a large cash settlement into the chief inspector's outstretched hand. Thus, eighteen unprocessed Chinese and Malaysian prostitutes were herded down the gangplank and into the custody of hired thugs. One of the women, swaddled in a burqa, dragged a wooden leg across Waterfront Alley. The thugs distributed the women to the brothels of East Gaines Street, and it was only while making the counts that the thugs realized they were short a woman. The peg-legged bitch had ditched them.

At sunset, having ditched the burqa, Archie reached his old flat and peeped through the window. His wife and children were huddled around a pot of stew like feeding animals, just as he had left them, frozen in time, a Rip-Van-Winkle scenario in reverse, him awake and aging, his former world asleep and awaiting his return. All an illusion, of course. The one eye still remaining in his head began to focus on evidence that the world had inexorably turned despite him. Kids, like dogs, are the most cogent markers of time, and his one-year-old son, John Thomas, was now seven, with hair the tint of flame and facial features much like his father's. His eldest child, Maureen, a young lady who seemed more in charge than her mother, served stew and disciplined her younger sisters and brother, while the mother listed on an elbow, slack-jawed, vacant and nursing a flask of whatever spirit was in it. The wall behind them had changed as well, being now bare of his prize possessions: the Ute and Cheyenne furs and spears, the whalebones, the silver railway stake and various other mementoes brought back from the Wild West. If the wall's emptiness was any indication, his family had neither waited for nor memorialized him. Instead, they had obliterated his memory. Well, could he blame them?

Too hungry and desperate to bother easing back into their lives, Archie gripped the sooty knob and walked inside. His sudden appearance caused the children to leap out of their chairs and almost upend the table. Because he had come to endure his physical misfortunes, he did not fully appreciate the effect his state might have on his family. Now, he saw himself through their eyes: a sun-and-sea-withered forty-year-old crustacean with a two-foot-long pigtail sprouting from under a dirty green turban, a butchered face—a crushed left cheek, a brown patch over an empty right eye socket—a faded jade tunic, Tartar britches, a canvas-and-hemp moccasin on his right foot and no left foot to speak of, only a wooden peg extending from his knee to the ground. He stood before them, feeling like the scum of the earth and hoping beyond hope that one of them would run into his arms, hug him and shout out, *Welcome home, Papa, we accept you as you are!*

One of his children did, in fact, take a run at him: Maureen. She charged him like a bull, wielding a baker's roller. "Thief! Pauper!" she screamed. "I'll crack your miserable skull!"

"Stop, daughter!" Bridget's stern order, though slurred and diminished by alcohol, stayed the girl's attack. "Can't you see it's your father come home at last?"

Maureen lowered the roller, but not her hostility. She had her mother's thick, red hair and freckles, but was more like him in frame—lanky and sinewy. He could sense that whatever femininity she might have claimed had been distilled out of her, boiled down to a black-hearted spite, poisoned even against her own blood and procreator. No doubt it was the fear for her family position that sharpened her tawny eyes, steeled her lipless arched mouth and honed her pointy jaw. He was the despised nomad, come to mooch, meddle and modify a codified life, and she wished him gone, back to the deep where he belonged. "I don't care who you are, you're not wanted here. Go away."

"Let's be civil, child," said her drunken mother. "Well now, look what you've gone and done to yourself," Bridget said, chuckling, apparently no more surprised by his reappearance than by the grime on the windowpanes. "What a pity. You were a right good-looking man when you left us. Maureen, get him some stew."

"Mama!" said the girl.

"Daughter, a little food isn't going to change anything. Do as I say."

Archie drew Maureen's chair, sat and served himself in her dish and began to eat with her spoon. He gobbled the stew faster than his mouth could accommodate, and spoonfuls of it ran down his chin and fell back into the bowl for a second chance. The three younger ones gave him a wide berth, like harpooners circling a wounded whale. He beckoned them, but none would attempt an approach. "It's all right, children," he said. "I don't blame you."

"You can leave the table," said their mother. "Go on outside while I catch up with Black Beard here."

Maureen would have none of that. "Whatever he has to say, Mama, he can say in front of us."

Bridget shot her daughter a look, and Maureen took the others outside.

His once-voluptuous wife had taken on much weight and was now as hefty as he was scrawny, her face and forearms flabby as whale blubber, her breasts so ample they pushed away bowls as she leaned into the table to have a better look at him. "So you're still alive, husband…

but *barely*, from what I can see. Look at you, a chair with five legs, a man with one. You smell like—what's that smell?"

"Chinese mugwort. I burn it over my stump. It dulls the pain."

"Smells as dreadful as my menses."

"Yes, the menstrual smell served its purpose in getting me back home."

"Do you plan to regale me with your mighty adventures?" she asked.

He made no comment.

"Good, because you're about to get an earful from me."

She started with the Finley henchmen who broke down her door in the middle of the night looking for a strongbox of documents. "They ransacked the place, found the money you left me and skedaddled. You might want to know they did the same to my brother's place—all on a tip from some whore. Bravo, Joe! You trusted a whore more than your own wife."

Archie swallowed the news better than the stew, for whatever was in his mouth stayed in. But Bridget could see that she had wounded him, and she kept twisting the blade. "Yeah, you might want to think twice about ever showing your face around Osborne House again. The next morning Randolph stormed over here yelling his fool head off about Mama's chest and that damn book, how important it was, and how he would never forgive me—or you—for stealing it."

His response, raspy and pitiful, came out whispering. "I didn't steal it."

"But you burned it. Or should have. Anyway, who cares? It's because of *you* that Randolph got barred from teaching. As for me, I got dragged into court to get me to cough up the remaining documents, which I couldn't hand over, of course. And all because you're a shiftless, sorry excuse for a man who couldn't keep his dick in his pants and his tongue in his mouth."

"I'm sorry, Bridget."

"Fuck your 'sorry,' Joe! Why'd you even come back? Whatever could you want here? What could you possibly expect of anybody?"

"I mean to honor my obligations."

"You? Honor something? Now that's a good one. Look at you, you crippled bag of bones. Commerce ain't exactly crying out for one-eyed Chinamen in pigtails clopping about on a stool leg. Besides, Terrence Finley will have you thrown in jail the minute he knows you're in town. Need I remind you what a vindictive bastard he is? You should've stayed dead, Joe."

"All I ask is a chance."

She shook her besotted noggin. "No. Not here. Not in this house. We've been through enough. Maureen would never allow it."

"Maureen? She's still a child. She doesn't have a say."

"That girl is more father than you ever were. She stood up to them Finley thugs when they broke in here. Only eight years old and swinging a broom at those thieves. Since you've been gone, she's looked after the household. Lord knows I couldn't. I fell sick, and we had to live off some money I had put away. When it ran out, things got so tight I had to sell off your wall junk just to put food on the table. Now Maureen works at The Shoe, a steady six-day-a-week job. She's the breadwinner around here, and you're just another mouth to feed. She'll tell you we can't afford you, and she's right."

"I can pull my weight, I tell you."

"Yeah, tell *her* that."

The children stampeded back into the apartment, shouting in unison, "Begone, get out, through the gate and out of the state, to China return your sinner's fate!"

Bridget ordered them to stop, but the chanting went on until Maureen quieted them and led them back out.

"There's your answer, Joe. Maureen runs the show. Back before you were officially dead, she told me she hoped you were dead. She was fearful you'd come back and get me pregnant. Can you blame her? All she ever knew growing up was a knocked-up mum and more mouths to feed."

"It doesn't have to be like this."

"Damn you, you're the one who couldn't stop yapping about moving, about discovering the wide world! Well, begone, Joe. We're a damn sight better off without you."

He bowed to her wishes and walked out. On the other side of the front door awaited an angry gauntlet of twenty kids, egged on by his eldest daughter. On her command, they beat him with the same chant: *Begone, get out, through the gate and out of the state, to China return your sinner's fate!* When he broke through their ranks, they pursued him like harpies down the alley and across the industrial park, the racket raising windows, bringing the curious to their sooty sills, mouths still chewing Sunday stew and potatoes, collecting other urchins like sharks to a wounded whale, the crescendo of their collective cry crepitating out of the slums and traveling all the way to Grover Wharf. *Begone, get out, through the gate and out of the state, to China return your sinner's fate!* He clopped up the coastal road toward town, cowered by the fury of a resounding rejection.

10

Archie awoke on a bug-infested beach, alone, the sun high over the water. He slipped his bowie knife back inside the peg, brushed the sand from his stump and reattached the wooden leg. It was a trial to rise, but walking wasn't so bad. He could cover ten miles in a day without too much bother. And walk he would, straight to Onion Road to speak with the Osbornes. He intended to give them an explanation and an apology, though nothing he could say would ever undo the damage he'd done. He took heart in the fact that he could at least return Miss Lydia's book. In retrospect, preserving that book was the best decision he'd ever made. At the time, however, little separated the good decision from the bad. He was sickened to recall that it could have gone either way. The width between destroying and not destroying that book had been as diaphanous as one of its pages. Archie had merely lucked into the right decision, much as he had lucked into surviving his shipwreck.

Later that day, he reached the old medical clinic and clopped up the walkway to the front door. A dark-skinned girl answered his knock. "What do *you* want?" she said, her sangfroid as shocking as her rudeness. She looked to be about the age of his only son Johnny, seven or eight, making her Miss Clara's third girl, born the year Archie sailed on the *South Pacific Belle*.

"Would your folks be in, princess?"

"That's none of your business, Mr. Pirate Man."

"Look, I need to speak to your father. I'm an old friend."

"Get lost." The little imp shut the door in his face.

He remained standing there, wondering how he had managed to offend every tyke in the universe. A moment later Miss Clara opened the door, the silver striations in her dark cotton hair like veins in a rock. "Can I help you?" she asked, failing to recognize him.

"Clara, it's me."

His voice did the trick. "Joseph Finley? Dear Lord, it cannot… But they said you were…"

"They were wrong."

"Randolph!" she cried toward the hall. "Randolph, you must come this instant!"

11

As a youth, Randy Osborne had seen his fair share of shattered souls stagger into his parents' clinic. But now, forty years on, he was having a difficult time getting his head around the miserable scarecrow sitting in his living room. The left side of his face was caved in like a tin of beans, the brown patch over his right eye was as abject as the emptiness it covered, and it hurt to hear the man butcher words spat from a mouth full of broken teeth.

There was more weight in the wood of his wretched prosthesis than in all the rest of him combined. Surely this scroungy wharf cat wasn't the bright young Chinese student he'd invited into his home twenty-five years before. No, Joseph Archung-Finley would have remained wholly dead rather than resurrect into the fragmented pieces of the man now littering his settee.

Randy had many sound reasons to hate the visitor, starting with the fact that the fool had burned his mother's book and that his filthy frequentations had cost Randy his livelihood. Why then was it an *unsound* reason that Randy most held against Joseph Archung-Finley? The longer Randy looked at Joseph, the more the visitor's broken body repulsed him. Randy had always entertained a quasi-religious belief that what moves improves. But Joseph's status seemed a slap to Randy's own self-esteem, if not his sense of classic heroism. The wandering hero wasn't supposed to return home an *actual* bum, abandoned by the gods, unable to draw his own bow and save his wife. The beggar's disguise was meant to be removable, not remain mutilated and scarred for life. There was no happy end here. The visitor's condition turned Randy's stomach.

For once, the host's bratty seven-year-old did him a favor. The child, Hattie Lawrence, kept pelting the visitor with disrespectful piques about his dastardly looks. Her mean-spiritedness proved therapeutic for Randy, so he let the abuse continue. The visitor took the pestering calmly, like some kind of Zen master whose mind flees a body under attack. Clara finally ordered the pest upstairs to her room.

With fresh teenage exuberance, Randy's well-mannered girls, Sarelle and Della, moved the conversation from the visitor's appearance to the hole in his history. Each tried to familiarize Joseph with every end-of-century novelty and innovation that had come along since he'd been gone: the new generating plant in South Bay, supplying the rich with electrical lighting. The electric trolley that could carry people up Sentinel Hill. The six new states added to the Union—North and South Dakota, Montana, Washington, Idaho and Wyoming—making it forty-four stars on the flag. These were territories the visitor knew well from his ten-year sojourn out west, and Randy fully expected an anecdote or two from Joseph. But not a peep came from the bum.

The presentation of the nation's progress eventually lost steam and ground to a head-scratching halt. Whereupon the twelve-year-old Della, who liked to play hopscotch with the line between familiarity and impertinence, asked the question that no one else would. "Captain Finley, won't you share your story with us?"

To that point, the visitor's silence seemed proof that his youthful need to impress people and set himself at the center of a conversation was long gone. But Della's calling him "Captain" had stirred something in Joseph. His eyes glimmered, his mangled face took on color, and the man, this human shipwreck, raised his spirit from the depths.

"All right, I owe you that much," he said for Randy's benefit, before turning back to the inquisitive daughters. "So, my pretty young ladies, it's my story you want, is it? So be it. But a word of caution," he said. "There are always risks when someone tells his tale. Aye, maybe he steers you clear of the rocks and maybe he crashes you into them. And nobody comes out of the recounting the same as they went into it. Are you two girls willing to take that risk?"

"Yes!" The girls giggled, enthralled. No matter what else he might have lost on the high seas, Joseph had obviously preserved his storytelling ability.

"All right then, I'll start with this. There is no such thing as a cursed ship, only an incompetent captain and crew. We had precious little discipline aboard. And then came the typhoon…"

The night long, the crew hunkered against nature's wrath. The ship was pounded by winds so powerful they lifted hull from water and sent it careening down swells as steep as canyons. The rain was relentless and so ferocious that it splintered wood. A gale snapped the foremast like a toothpick, and the *South Pacific Belle* was helpless, barreling uncontrollably toward a reef lying two miles off the Navigator Islands.

The ship was dashed to pieces against the rocks, its crew cut to bits in the razor-edged maelstrom. Packs of sharks did the rest. The screaming, gnashing and chewing rose above the roar of the surf. The Captain was attacked from below. Something like a bear claw snapped around his leg and shook him like a rag doll until it stopped. He caught sight of a fleeing fin, and the pain worsened, as if the jaws of the fish were still clamped on. The smell of his own blood mixed with that of the brine.

The surf carried him to the beach, and soon afterward, daylight broke over a shore littered with limbs and lumber. His left pant leg was gone, as was most of his calf. He considered himself lucky. Of the one hundred twenty-six souls who'd set sail on the *South Pacific Belle*, only fifteen had made it alive to land.

Over the following days, the survivors salvaged bits of wreckage with which to fashion a boat. The Captain was of little use to the enterprise, being both lame and diminished by fever. His shark-bitten leg, black and misshapen, needed to come off below the knee. Of the seven learned passengers who had sailed aboard the *South Pacific Belle*, only the illustrator had survived—a cruel irony indeed. The fellow declined most insistently to perform the surgery. "I assure you, Captain. I am the very last soul you'd want removing your leg," he said, shaking like a sail.

Another problem was the instrument for its amputation. Within reach was a most suitable bowie knife, sharpened daily to quarter a twig, but it rested firmly on the hip of its owner, Mr. Miggs, the scalawag hired by Terrence Finley to insure the Captain never returned to Neespaugot. Miggs was, of course, most stingy about lending his implement. After many hours of wrangling, it was clear that the shady fellow had no intention of improving the Captain's predicament. Miggs admitted as much. "I was hired to do a job and I'm going to relish watching you and your leg rot." The temperature was high and heavy, tempers were hot, and everyone was miserable with hunger. The crew pounced on Miggs, who drove his knife through a man before he himself was beaten to the ground and had his brains dashed with a length of *South Pacific Belle* planking.

The Captain's lower leg was hacked off, along with much of his sanity; such was the duration of the ordeal, the extent of the pain and the vehemence with which he cursed them. His screaming diatribe came in Chinese, his mother tongue, dredged from deep memory like sea-bottom flotsam disturbed by a tsunami.

In the ensuing days, the illustrator sculpted a wooden leg from deck railing, catgut and sails. It was a most crude creation but quite serviceable, with the added distinction that the hollow peg was large enough to store Miggs' bowie knife.

The crew had the island to themselves for several weeks. But then a war party of seaborne Samoans came ashore and invaded their settlement. In close hand-to-hand combat, the natives killed the illustrator and five other white men with spears, before losing two of their own and fleeing. The nine surviving sailors roasted the two dead Samoans over a pit and ate them. Sickened with their cannibalism, the Captain and his men launched their single-mast compendium against the island breakers, sailing for the next island as if they could simply leave their unsavory past behind them.

But guilt is not a question of geography. And for the better part of a month, they migrated from island to island, gathering food, consumed by shame and loathing. Every fruit, every fish tasted like man-flesh. They didn't stay anywhere for longer than a few days.

After a great while, they ran out of islands, and the eight of them—the ninth had died from a seasnake bite—found themselves adrift on a boundless sea, baking and thirsting to death under a withering sun. Their salt-wasted lips and calcified tongues became a burden to breathing. Two men fought over an invisible pot of water. Their delirious dispute took them and a third man overboard. No one lifted a finger to save any of them, and that left five. It was now every man for himself, survival of the fittest, as the Naturalists had been wont to say.

In the wee hours of a day among countless others, the Captain awoke, startled to discover a seaman named Carmichael trying to sink teeth into his neck, vampire-like. Fortunately for the Captain, the vampire's teeth were too rotten and they broke against the Captain's sea-hardened flesh. The Captain struggled for his peg, seized the bowie knife and shoved it through Carmichael's throat. He died gagging on his blood. The Captain and the three remaining crew drank Carmichael as dry as pressed fruit. Then, they sliced him open, eviscerated him and consumed him warm and gooey. What was left of him, they tossed into the ocean and stood whooping on the bulwarks like sated ghouls, their chins agleam with gore under the brilliant doldrums, mocking the trailing sharks as the creatures ripped into a bloodless meal.

A sailor named Stokes was next. He keeled over and shuddered a few times. It took a full day before anyone mustered the energy to crawl over to him. By then, Stokes was already shrunken and dry, mouth slack, eyes wide open, a paste of brown excretion drying around his ankles. The Captain cut open his neck but discovered only hardened arteries. Stokes was good only for feeding the fish. They threw him over, and now there were three.

The Captain decided to die next. His spirit deserted him. He lowered his guard and waited for his two companions to finish him off. He drifted into unconsciousness.

When he came to, he no longer smelled the ocean but rather the stale confinement of close quarters and caulked wood. He was in the forecastle of a large ship, lying in the bottom bunk of a crewman's infirmary. A limp arm dangled over the side of the bunk above him. It belonged to a big man, a white man. The Captain studied its coarse, mangled fingers and thick wrist. The arm was not attached to a dead man, for it moved independently of the sway of the ocean, a woeful herky-jerky motion. The Captain meant to say something to this arm, but he could not make his tongue work. He had forgotten how to speak. Tired, deathly tired, he made up his mind to speak to the arm at some future date. Then, he fell into another profound sleep.

They kept him alive on a diet of broths. Unable to move, he lay in his excretions and passed his moments of consciousness staring at the dangling arm, at the heavily bowed bunk pressing down on him. Twice a day, a coarse wet cloth was scrubbed across his soiled loins, but he had neither energy nor desire to raise himself to see who was cleaning him. He could not recall when he first noticed that the arm in the berth above had disappeared. The heavy body to which it had been attached no longer imprinted the thin bedding above his nose.

A face finally appeared, belonging to a steely, mustachioed Englishman leaning over his bunk, speaking at him clinically. "Chief Petty Officer Harry Shelby, Her Majesty's Royal Navy. What's your name, port of origin and destination?" The Captain could not muster a word. He had lost his voice. Shelby reddened with impatience and informed the Captain that he was aboard the HMS *Colston* on its way into the port of Hong Kong. "We will leave you there unless you give us just cause not to."

The Captain could not give them just cause. He could not speak.

On Paddar Quay, he was placed in the hands of the local authorities, who didn't know what to do with him. A Chinese riverboat merchant carrying Canton silk and porcelain from inland to the coast via the Pearl River agreed to transport the castaway upriver. The junk sailed along the lowlands of San-Shui to the town of Tsing-yane, where the Captain was offloaded at the monastery of Fi-lai-sz and put in the care of Buddhist monks.

He spent the next three years convalescing at Fi-lai-sz, trying to make sense of dreams that dissipated in the morning light. Pieces of memory flitted in and out like fireflies, a swarm of nonsense. Sometimes he would see a room of glass in many colors, a bespectacled Mandarin in clean tunic and skullcap sifting through dried roots, a woman with a mouse-eared chignon scrubbing his arms. He glimpsed a liquor palace of subservient courtesans, a redheaded white woman lying naked beneath him, babies with bright red heads and green eyes screaming at him. He was unable to put a name, time or place to any of his visions. He had forgotten his own name.

The monks invited him on their retreats into the heavily wooded Mang-Asz-Nap, the Blind Man's Gorge. Only through meditation, they said, could he lift the veil of darkness and attain spiritual bliss and a healthy *qi*. The Captain followed their instruction, but his progress was minimal.

Then, the Japanese came. With rifles and bayonets, they crashed through the Gate of Virtue into the courtyard, seeking the pirates who had intercepted a gift bound for the Guangxu emperor. Two monks tried to bar the soldiers from entering the Hall of Righteousness and were impaled with bayonets. A riot of monks took to the courtyard and were shot or clubbed to death. In the melee, the Captain was rifle-butted in the face, a blow of such violence that it caved in his left cheek and popped his right eye out of its socket. His orb hit a soldier in the face. Disgusted, the soldier mashed the eye under his boot.

Severe nose bleeds, earaches and a throbbing skull joined his miserable band of afflictions. Insects darted in and out of his empty eye socket, now as hollow as his wooden leg. A constant buzz that had nothing to do with bugs nearly drove away the few senses still belonging to him. He decided that death alone would bring him peace. So he set out alone into the Tsing-yane Valley. On a sacred hillside toothed with a hundred thousand white tombstones, he knelt and propped the bowie knife between the ground and his belly. As he steeled himself for the liberating blow, a butterfly alighted upon his hand. He let go of the knife and caught the creature by its colorful wings. A vision bubbled up from another time, another world. He saw butterflies clustered in a tree, eating leaves. Birds of prey circled overhead but did not attack the butterflies because they were feeding on poisonous leaves. The butterflies were poisoning themselves so as not to be eaten. Later, those butterflies would die, but first they would produce offspring which would complete the migration for them. *California,* he said to himself.

The Captain set aside his suicide and continued wandering upriver. He came to Canton, one hundred miles inland. The city had a deep-water port with many grand vessels anchored there, most of them American. Their language sounded familiar to the Captain, so he decided to stay there. He went to work for a tea maker on Pharmacy Street, in a quarter that provided some clues to his past, with its scent of incense and colorful banners dangling in front of each shop, bearing Chinese lettering. On the banner out front of the Captain's tea shop was written "Yun-Ki." *Transcendence.*

He lived on a dinner of rice and fish every night. After eating he would pray at the temple of Kouan-Yin, the Goddess of Pity. Prayers led to frustration, frustration to the taverns. The Captain finished each night curled up on a bench, puffing opium. One night, through a cloud of smoke, a Chinese cobra reared its head, black sails fanning, pitiless yellow eyes peering into the Captain's soul. The snake was too close to escape, and the Captain, expecting instant death, thanked the Pity Goddess for answering his prayers. But the snake did not strike.

"If you wish to die now," spoke the snake, "mix a mud cake of opium ash and water. It's less painful than my venom."

"Why have you come to me, Master Serpent?"

"I need your help, Captain. My snake family is trapped in a box bound for Neespaugot. You must bring them back to me. Agree, here and now, and I will answer three questions."

"Done," said the Captain. "First, who am I?"

"You are two people, Ching Ah Chung of Shanghai and Joseph Archung-Finley of Neespaugot."

"How can one be two?"

"It can't. But it is."

"Can I ever be fulfilled?"

"Fulfillment is an illusion, created by a sense of purpose, which is also an illusion. The only constant in life is change. One can only navigate the waves of change, doing one's best to preserve those aspects of our lives that deliver spiritual balance and energy."

"Where do I belong, Master Serpent? China or America?"

But the three questions had been answered and the snake was gone. When the Captain awoke, the buzzing in his head was also gone. His confusion, like a morning's fog, had burned off, and he saw his mother and father in their pagoda the day the Master came to take him away to America. The guano and barnacle-covered atolls so dear to the Naturalists. The North Bay steeple welcoming boats into the old port of Neespaugot. Miss Lydia and Randolph. The coolie campfires illuminating an entire mountainside. The Gold Rush armada left to rot in San Francisco harbor and, a continent away, the Finley armada left to rot in dry dock. His wife, his children, his own name: *Ching Chung Joseph Archung-Finley.*

The Captain began spending time at Canton Harbor, in particular the speakeasies and saloons that fed off the port like pilot fish. His eyes were always open, his ears pricked up and listening, ever on the lookout for a way back to Neespaugot. He meant to honor his promise to the snake.

Clara and the girls said goodnight to the storyteller and left the room. Randolph stayed on, saying nothing, pacing in front of the visitor, his anger building like a storm, sucking out the air, before he cut loose. "You *burned* my mother's book. Do you have any idea, any damn idea at all, what you've done? You think your few years of amnesia were bad? Try multiplying that by ten. My mother suffered for sixty damn years, stuck in the dark. That book was *her* snake, *her* moment of clarity, and you *burned* it. Some spiritual son you turned out to be. You betrayed her. You betrayed me. You betrayed my ancestors and my descendants. What the devil do you have to say for yourself, Joseph?"

"The book is safe."

Randy was so caught up in his anger that he almost missed it. "I— What did you say?"

"I said I have the book, Randolph. You'll have it tomorrow."

Randy's mouth continued to emit a senseless whir, like the sound of air escaping a balloon. He deflated quickly and flopped down at his father's desk. "Kindly fill me in because I don't know who or what to believe anymore."

"Look, it's simple. The book belonged to Miss Lydia, and that was a good enough reason for me to save it."

"I... I don't know what to say. I was... misled..."

"Not intentionally. Your sister thought she saw me burn it. *I* misled *her*."

"Are you the one who broke in here and stole the chest?"

"Look, friend. I'm guilty of weakness, selfishness, irresponsibility and a hundred other crimes of character, but I'm no thief."

Randy slumped, conflicted, into the Doctor's armchair and tried to sift through his avalanche of emotions. He'd gotten used to cursing Joseph Archung-Finley. In the past hour, he had convinced himself that Joseph's physical plight said less about the risks of stepping out and more about what happens to those who are rotten to the core. But Randy now understood that this was not the case. He rose and walked to the liquor cabinet where he removed a bottle of port and two small crystal goblets. "I guess we could both use a drink," he said, pouring two glasses and handing one to Joseph. Before he could catch himself, he'd said, "Here's mud in your eye."

Joseph took no offense. "I guess that makes me blind."

Randy was chagrined. "Goodness gracious, I didn't mean—"

"Forget it," said Joseph. "Don't take it to the stump, so to speak. At least you didn't say let's get tipsy… Yeah, I've heard 'em all, Randolph."

The men chortled, clinked and quaffed their drinks. Randy filled their empty glasses. "It's my turn to make a toast," said Joseph. "Reach your glass back over here before I make a mess. Here's to good port!"

"To good port," said Randy. "And bottom's up!"

"Now that's just vicious."

"My goodness, I just keep putting my foot into it. How about 'down the hatch'?"

"Still an insult."

They clinked and quaffed and started again.

"To destiny!" said Joseph.

"To coincidence!" countered Randy.

"To preservation!"

"To movement!"

"To immigrants!"

"To freedom!"

"To refusing to accept anything less of life!"

"To Chinamen and mulattoes!"

"To America!"

"Hear, hear!"

They clinked, indulging each other in the illusion that a clean slate might be cut between them. But once the visitor had gone and Randy's high had dissipated, he recognized that contempt was like wet paint. Once it had sunk in, you either lived with the color or tried to cover it up. In the interest of retrieving the book, Randy played cover-up. As he had been showing out Joseph, Randy repeated, "Please, Joseph, come back tomorrow with the book."

"You have my word. By the way, could I borrow your pickax? I'll explain tomorrow."

And the morrow laughed.

12

Randy waited all day, but Joseph never turned up. To calm his temper, he walked the length of Cabot Street to Grover Wharf. And that's where he learned of the murder. The newspaper hawkers were up and down the docks and byways, shouting, "Read all about it! Terrence Finley, shipping magnate, brutally assassinated! Throat slit as he slept! Only one muddy footprint at the scene! Rumors of a dead Chinaman's ghost! Read all about it!"

Randy rushed back to Onion Road, gathered his family in the room where, just the night before, the storyteller had described killing and eating another man, and informed them of the news. The entire night, he expected the police to bang down his door just like Mad Dog Griffin and Terrence Finley's thugs had done. *Randolph Osborne, you are under arrest for the murder of Terrence Finley. We have apprehended the other suspect—* how many one-legged Chinamen could there be roaming Neespaugot?—*who has confessed to drinking here the night before. Terrence Finley had you blackballed from teaching, and that's motive enough for us. You will be tried as an accomplice, convicted of murder and hanged like your namesakes Runinniduk and William Running Duck!*

Randy spent a week of sleepless nights and anxiety-ridden days expecting a knock at any moment. Then, a second week came and went with Onion Road remaining eerily quiet. In the third week, Randy ventured out to Neespaugot Bridge, then kept walking and didn't stop until he'd reached South Bay's industrial village. He hadn't spoken to his sister in five years. For that matter, he hadn't planned on speaking to her ever again. But these were exceptional times, and he had to know what she knew and what she planned to do with the information.

She answered the door drunk and as fat as any of Pharaoh's seven cows. "Bloody hell!" she said, noticeably relieved. "It's just you. I thought it was the police. Come in."

He didn't stay long. She was still dead to him. But by the time he left, he was relieved to know that Bridget was of the same mind as he. No one in their respective families could breathe a word to anyone of Joseph's recent passage. "So, brother, do you think he did it?"

"Of course he did. But we're safe until they find him. Legally, he's dead, and dead men have no accomplices."

"But why did the fool go and commit murder?"

"You're the only fool, sister. He did it for us."

Several weeks more and the murder, like the *South Pacific Belle* disaster, moved to the inner pages of the *Neespaugot Times*. The investigation was pursuing new leads into disgruntled ex-employees, of whom there had been many over the years, as the company had made its slow but inevitable descent into ruin and bankruptcy. There was no more talk of Chinese specters. According to the chief of police, "We never took seriously the rumors of a one-legged ghost."

Yet, the community at large preferred spicy sensationalism to dry mundanity, so the rumors stayed afloat, founded on the sketchy testimony of the victim's wife. From the window of her bedroom, which was a floor and a wing removed from her husband's, Mrs. Finley had glimpsed "a shadow crossing the yard." The intruder had a peg leg, wore breeches and sprouted a pigtail "a yard long." Incredible to Randy was the fact that neither she nor her believers or detractors ever put two and two together that the Finleys once claimed among them a Chinese boy. Everyone had forgotten Ching Ah Chung, alias Joseph Archung-Finley.

Time pursued its inexorable pace, and the case went cold. Randy applied and was re-instated as a teacher at South Bay Public School. Eight months after the murder, he returned home from school to find a letter in his mailbox, return address unknown, stamped out of New York.

Dear Randolph,

By now you know that I have let you down once again, dear friend. I write you not to offer up excuses, but to explain myself, so that you are not left wondering and guessing. Leaving someone in the dark is the cruelest form of spite.

I wasn't completely honest with you. I didn't fully comprehend the importance of the book. I never even read it. I came close to getting rid of it for my wife's sake. In the end, I preserved it simply because it had belonged to your mother. I saved it because of an inkling, not a heroic epiphany. My appreciation changed once we'd had our talk, and when I left your home, nothing on earth could have stopped me from returning it to you. That is, all except one: its disappearance.

The site where I had buried the strongbox had not been disturbed. I found my documents and money exactly as I had left them. But the book was gone, and there was only one conclusion. It had been stolen before I'd buried the box. There was only one person capable of performing the deed (whom I so gullibly trusted), only one reason she'd have done so (venality) and only one person to try to sell it to (whose name shall remain anonymous).

Believing the thief had left town, I sought out the buyer. One thing led to another, and for reasons of which you are now aware, I had to leave Neespaugot. In the weeks and months thereafter, I have sought out the thief, with no success. At this stage, I am of the belief that the buyer either sold her into foreign bondage or dispatched her to the depths of the ocean.

It sickens me to abandon the hunt, dear friend. Your mother was my Potiphar, and finding her book would have been the least I could do to honor her memory. Perhaps one day it shall resurface. I have that hope. In the meantime, do not lose sight of the fact that you still possess that which is most important to your family, the Indian's coin, which remains the heart of your history. It was worn by so many of your ancestors, and it gave them pride, hope and succor in times of great trial. The coin is the symbol of your family's transcendence.

For my actions, I shall never again be able to step foot in our beloved city, never see my family again, never toast with you again. But by my actions, I hope to have removed an impediment to your livelihood. If this proves the case, then the sacrifice was worth it and I am content. I have hurt and disappointed you, my friend, and as a small consolation, please accept this money, for your pain and suffering. Your sister is receiving the same sum.

Your less than faithful servant,

J

Inside the envelope was five hundred dollars.

As the nineteenth century wound down, an urban legend grew up around the tale of the one-legged Chinaman. A fellow of that profile was purported working in Pullman, Illinois, fighting on behalf of the American Railway Union against the robber barons of the railroad industry. Sometime after that, there was a report of a one-eyed Chinaman working in Chicago, taking tickets at the West Side Grounds for the Chicago Colts, the city's championship professional baseball team. At century's end, a sailor returning from Canton claimed to have seen a peg-legged Chinamen killed in a street riot during the Boxer Rebellion. Shortly thereafter, a man fitting the same description was hanged on the Chisholm Trail, while another was seen washed over Niagara Falls. A one-eyed Asian was witnessed performing in Buffalo Bill's Wild West Show. The sightings slowed to a trickle in the first years of the twentieth century and, by Teddy Roosevelt's second term in office, went as dry as the Death Valley salt beds.

Della

April 19, 1953

"Turning to national news, President Eisenhower has refused a stay of execution for Julius and Ethel Rosenberg. The execution is scheduled for June 19. In a statement to Congress, Senator Joseph McCarthy said that the number of Communist sympathizers and spies in the United States was at a critical level and spoke of the necessity of rooting them out, along with homosexuals—"

Angrily, the old woman snapped off the radio. *Watch out! Commie spies and homosexuals behind every bush! Blacks invading the neighborhood! Jews running Hollywood!* Give me a break! Reactionary thinking was still running the show and had been for twenty years despite a world war against it. Momentum was clearly with the mopers and against the forward-thinkers, the movers. Would it ever end, this Dark Age of Moperdom?

She tried to remind herself that history was a weather report, and that mopers and movers, like clouds and clear skies, eventually traded places. Still, understanding the cyclical nature of the world's psyche did little to assuage her current frustration and depression. She had done battle her entire life with mopers. She had been a print journalist, a suffragist, an activist, a defender of civil liberties, a person of strong convictions and a pen that couldn't be bought. Mopers had attacked her race, her gender, her sexual preferences, her beliefs—you name it. Back in the days before the "c" word, mopers had slung the word *agitator* in her face. They had chased her out of Neespaugot, out of the state of Massachusetts and finally out of the United States of America. She had spent the past thirty years in Europe, up close and personal with the worst scourge of mopism in the history of humankind: Nazis, Fascisti and Bolsheviki, from the Russian word for greater—always that word, *greater*, and its inherent meaning of a return to racial purity and dominance.

Della, now a seventy-four-year-old colored lesbian, was back in her own country, just in time for a new age of blacklisting, jail and deportation for speaking one's mind, government-sponsored infecting of poor black men with syphilis, and women still dying from illegal abortions. She lived like a hermit in the South Bay, in a small duplex on Crawford Street, in the heart of Little Italy. Her neighbors were Italian Catholics with strong opinions concerning her skin color and beliefs. Della figured she could croak, rot and be eaten by rats before any of them would lift a finger to complain about the smell.

"My, my, how you blather, you bitter old fool," she said to herself.

Using her cane, Della rose from the edge of her single bed and tapped across the cheap parquet floor to a rickety rocking chair angled toward her one window on the second floor. She sank into the chair and began her daily cadence of rocking, reliving better times while gazing blankly down to the street.

Death scared her. Well, not so much the notion of death as the actual act itself: the seizing up, locked in agonizing contortion, sucking for a last gasp of life. It haunted her waking hours. Perhaps her real fear was of dying alone. Her soulmate Gillian had gone graciously in bed at high noon, surrounded by their Parisian friends. When Della's time came, she'd have nobody.

On the small round table next to the rocker was a framed photograph of her and Gillian taken by some passing chap at the Café Flore in Paris. They were so happy, with their hands intertwined in the middle of the tiny café table, between liquor-coated glasses and aperitif. Those were bad times for the world, but good times personally. Della had just bought Gillian a watch for her birthday. The Della in the photo was wearing a silver chain, below which dangled the Indian's coin. Della reached into the frame and removed the chain from around her neck. The old coin was worn almost smooth, just a few grooves and lines to remind the onlooker that something had once been engraved there. This apparently worthless piece of metal had sustained the movers in her ancestry through moments of crushing anguish, solitude and despair, and it would carry her, too, through the night.

Aggressive chatter filtered into the bedroom. Della looked out the window and saw two boys arguing on the street corner. The taller boy, East European by the looks of his rough, red face and honey-colored hair, was bullying a smaller toothpick of a boy who looked like he was from the neighborhood. He had an olive complexion and straight, ink-black hair. Della lifted the window and shouted a word of warning. "You two scoot or I'll hex you!"

The boys moved up the street. Being known as the Witch of Crawford Street had its advantages, thought Della, but she closed the window with small satisfaction and sat back into the rocker.

Her house was enclosed by tenement houses and lorded over by The Shoe, an Industrial Revolution-era factory pumping its last gasping waste from twin stacks rising above the horizon like giant goalposts. The Shoe was scheduled for closing near the end of the year. In the meantime, Little Italy wasn't far from the shore, and her twice-daily strolls removed her from the stultifying cement and miasma of her immediate neighborhood to the freedom of the Atlantic Ocean.

In her rocker, Della began to doze off when she was roused by the sound of footsteps in her hallway.

"Who's there?" she called, seeking a voice of authority but managing only an unconfident caw. The creaking of the floorboards ceased. "I'm telling you, if you've come for money, you won't leave empty-handed. I'll put more welts in your palms than you can carry."

There was no response. She wondered if she was hearing things again.

She placed the chain around her neck, tucked the coin down her bosom and pushed out of the rocker. Wearing a raggedy dress and men's socks, she slid into a pair of men's leather slippers, threw on a housecoat and caned into the hall.

The hallway was empty, but she could hear water running in the bathroom. Time, that infernal runaway train, suddenly braked and was compressed into a moment's clarity where the stains on the wall became the spots on her hand and the images of her life. Was this the end of her? She jabbed open the bathroom door with the rubber end of her cane. The sink faucet was running.

"Who's in here? I'll give you until the count of three to get out. One! Two! Three!" She entered the bathroom, pounding the toilet seat with her cane as much to steel her nerves as to influence whoever was in there. The bathroom was empty. She turned off the tap and felt helpless. Her telephone had been disconnected a year ago, and who the hell was she going to call anyway? She hadn't spoken to either of her sisters in thirty-three years, and the few friends and acquaintances she'd had back in those times had turned their backs on her when she was being railroaded out of town on trumped-up charges of public indecency. (She had been photographed on the Commons holding Gillian's hand.) And the Little Italy police department didn't give a hoot about her complaints. Whenever boys broke into her yard, the cops mocked her with racially coated jargon and side-glances.

She gimped back out of the bathroom and hurried down the hall. If she could reach the bedroom, she would lock herself inside. Then, let them take what they wanted and be damned.

Just as she reached her bedroom door, the intruder sprang out at her.

"Boo!" he yelled.

Della banged into the opposite wall and knocked out her own wind. She slumped splay-legged to the floor and wheezed. Death had come for her—it was time. As she groped for breath, she was lucid enough to notice that the brigand was the honey-haired bully she had shooed away earlier. She heard him swear under his breath. "Aw fuck, c'mon, lady. Lay on ya back. It happens to me all the time. Ya just got ya wind knocked out." He straddled her and put his arms under her pelvis and lifted. "Ya breath'll come." Della could smell cigarette smoke on his breath. Only a boy, he had a raw, pimply face and the pesky hazel eyes of a sprite. Oxygen flowed back into her chest. She was still alive.

"That's betta," he said, propping her up against the wall.

"How the devil did you get in here, boy?" she said, rasping it.

"Ya basement. The padlock on ya trap door's busted."

"So what gives you the right to come in?"

His tone hardened. "I'll ask the questions, old woman."

"And I'll answer them, you impudent rapscallion." Della swung at him with her cane, batted nothing but air. She got to her knees, staggered to her feet and stumbled after him down the hall. The boy found it some kind of game and baited her. "Aw, c'mon, you can do betta than that, you biddy!" He stayed out of reach. She wouldn't catch him in a million years.

When her coughing started, she abandoned the chase and staggered back inside her bedroom. The scamp followed her in, where she took another swing at him but then had to sit on the bed to catch her breath. "You have some nerve," she said, wiping the tears out of her eyes. "What must I do to get you out of my house?" Her voice was hoarse.

"I want infahmation."

"Information! What could I possibly know that would interest you, boy?"

"Stop calling me 'boy.' I'm fourteen."

"Well, it's a devil of an age to wind up in jail. Leave now and I won't press charges."

"Nobody in Neespaugot gives a damn about you or ya complaints."

"Well, you're right about that, so I'm done talking to you."

She took a book from her nightstand and pretended to read.

"Fine. I'll just give *you* infahmation."

Della studied his face for telltale signs of bluffing, but his raw complexion, scabbed with scarlet buttons, burned with conviction. So she dared him. "Go on, then. Give me your 'infahmation.' What is it? I'm a witch? I'm a communist? I'm a lesbian?"

"Nah." He grinned wickedly. "Any wop in Little Italy can tell you that. I'm here to give you greetings from my grandmothah, Hattie Lawrence Ozbum."

Della reared off the bed with such determination that she managed to catch the urchin off guard. She landed a blow on his arm with her cane. "Get out, I say! You get out!"

"You crazy old bitch," he said, wrenching the stick out of her hands, ready to bash in her skull. "I oughta brain you."

"Go on then!"

"You'd like that, wouldn't you?" he said. "I got a betta idear. Hattie Lawrence Ozbum!"

"Hush your mouth! Don't you say that woman's name in here. I won't have it, not in my own home."

"Hattie Lawrence Ozbum!"

Della lifted the window and yelled for the police, but the only one on the street was the bully's scrawny Italian accomplice standing behind her sycamore tree. Meanwhile, the rogue in the bedroom was jabbing her buttocks with the rubber end of her cane and taunting her with the name of her younger sister. "Hattie Lawrence! Hattie Lawrence! Hattie Lawrence!" Della retreated from the window and switched on the radio full blast. But he kept jabbing her backside with her cane.

Defeated, she turned off the machine and fell into the rocking chair, instinctively fingering the contours of the coin under her robe. The boy tossed the cane on the bed and stared contemptuously at her. "Y'know, you look nothing like what they say. Everybody says you were some kind of beauty, but people always lie and exaggerate. You ain't nothin' but a sack of brown potatoes."

"And you are the most brazen child it has ever been my displeasure to meet. When I think that you may be family—"

"No way we're family," he said. "I'm a Roxxmott. You're just an Ozbum, a losah."

"And that makes you what?"

"Smaht!"

"You'll be the smartest person in prison."

"Prison!? I'm going to M.I.T., like my dad. I'm already doing college-level math."

"So what do you want from me, Mr. M.I.T?"

"I told you. Ansahs."

"You seem to have all your answers. I'm an Osborne, a loser."

At that moment the second boy leaned his head into the bedroom. His sudden appearance had a curious effect on her attacker, who went apoplectic with anger. "What the hell are you doing up here, fuckweed? I told you to stay put and be my lookout."

"I thought she was killing you, Ezra."

"Do I look dead? Get the fuck back outside, you brown bastahd."

"Hold on," Della said. "Come in, boy." The younger fellow stayed clinging to the doorjamb. "It's all right, child, don't be afraid. For the moment, you're the only one with an invitation."

But he wouldn't move. He was more afraid of the bully than of her.

"Young man," she said, "there are two sorts of people in this world, movers and mopers. Are you a moper?"

He approached, too frightened to look at anything but the peeling rubber toes of his sneakers.

"That's a good boy. Come closer to my chair. I won't hurt you. That's it. Now, tell me your name."

"Zeke."

"Zeke what?"

"Zeke Roxxmott."

"Roxxmott? Like this devil here?"

"Yes, ma'am. Ezra's my brothuh."

"But surely you don't have the same mother and father, Zeke."

Ezra said, "Of course we have the same parents, you crazy old bat."

Della gave the two boys another looking-over. One broad and muscular, the other short and wiry. One Slavic, the other Mediterranean. Brothers. Interesting.

"All right, you two. You've come here to know something, so here's my deal. I'll answer your questions if you promise to leave me in peace for good. Do you agree?"

"Yeah, sure, whatevah," said Ezra.

"Good. Now, you, the little guy, you go first."

Zeke nodded. "How old are you, ma'am?"

"Seventy-four. How about you?"

"Eleven."

"Anything else?"

"How come people say you're a commie?"

"Because labels are simpler than the truth, young man. I was a newspaper editorialist for many years, defending those without a voice against those with more than their fair share. In particular, I wrote against federal anti-immigration laws aimed at Southern and Eastern Europeans, Middle Easterners, East Asians and Asia Indians. In short, anybody who wasn't a WASP. My enemies labeled me an agitator, a Bolshevik—that's a communist with an attitude. None of it was true, but that's the thing about smear tactics. In this country, when it comes to race, religion, gender and politics, the label always sticks. I hope you'll never have to learn that hard lesson, Zeke. Now, I'll give you one more question, and then we'll let Mr. M.I.T. have a go."

The boy vacillated. His brother started to speak for him, but Della tapped her cane on the floor to silence him. After turning it over in his mind, the smaller boy blurted proudly, "Do you know our ma?"

"You idiot," said Ezra, groaning.

"Hush, you. No, Zeke, I don't know your mother, not really. She was born at the end of the First World War, by which time I was no longer having anything to do with your grandmother. I moved to France shortly thereafter. Okay, Zeke, normally it's your brother's turn, but due to his rudeness, you can have another."

"No way!" said Ezra.

"Says the boy who broke into my house. Proceed, Zeke."

Zeke looked to Ezra for a clue but got shut out, so he was on his own to come up with a question.

"Oh, yeah. Are you a lesbian?"

"Do you even know what a lesbian is, Zeke?"

"Women kissing each other?"

"It's an orientation, child, a sexual orientation. A woman feels a pull towards other women. But I have never felt a pull towards other *women*—or men, for that matter. The fact is that I have only ever known one passion for another human being in my entire life, and she happened to be a woman. Before meeting her, I had no interest in a relationship of any kind. Since her death twelve years ago, I have lived comfortably and gratefully alone. So, my answer to your question is no, I'm not a lesbian. I'm not a label of any sort. I'm, well, nothing at all."

"How did your friend die?"

"Sorry, Zeke. You're moving off the subject. Your turn, M.I.T.," she said, turning a critical eye on Ezra.

"Well, I don't give a rat's ass about ya dead girlfriend, that's fah sure. My Ma's a big fat liar, so I need you to put somethin' straight for me. You got the Indian's coin?"

The question, totally unexpected, hit Della sideways. "Who put you up to this? Your grandmother?"

"My turn, my question, lady."

"All right, then. The answer is yes. Your mother is obviously not the liar you make her out to be."

"So, when you croak, this coin is supposed to get passed on to a worthy family membah. How does that happen if you're a damn hermit?"

"I don't know, Ezra, but if I do manage to keep it out of *your* hands, I'll die in peace."

"I got one more."

"All right."

"Where's Septimania?"

Della was flabbergasted. "How would you know that word?"

"How else? I read your shit. All them newspaper articles you wrote are stuffed in trunks in the Osborne House attic."

Della gave Ezra a long inquisitive stare. "Septimania is a metaphor."

"A metaphor fah what?"

"A metaphor for come back tomorrow because you've used up my patience today."

"That ain't the deal, old woman."

"Don't push it, boy. Your time is done and I owe you nothing. Still, I'm willing to afford you an answer *tomorrow*."

"Yah, like I trust you."

"Like you have a choice," she said.

Defeated, he changed his tone. "What time tomorrow?"

Della waited all day, but the scamp never showed up. What irked her was that she was irked, and she chalked it up to vanity. After all, Al Capone might have gotten an invite just for *mentioning* Septimania. She rationalized that his no-show was all for the best. Her grand-nephew was an Osborne, and Della wanted nothing more to do with any of them. Osbornes—and she included herself in the list—were loners, outliers and third-partyers indoctrinated from a young age in the creed that happiness, or even its pursuit, was as out of reach as white skin and a WASP ethos. To survive, the racially mixed Osbornes needed to be the self-involved, self-indulgent egomaniacs they were. And Ezra Roxxmott, name and appearance to the contrary, was a perfect example.

The following afternoon, Della was reading in her rocker when the clacking of the door knocker disturbed the early spring mellow. Aw, fiddlesticks! She'd forgotten all about him. Before going downstairs, Della thought it best to hide the Indian's coin, as there was no telling what that boy was capable of. She dug Gillian's brown-leather Longine watchcase out of the closet and popped the lid. It was the first time in twelve years that she'd had the courage to open the box. Her dead lover's thin silver watch was strung across a palm-sized pink pillow, hands frozen at 11:35. Della's thoughts flashed to that mild September afternoon, 1938, Rue Faubourg, Paris. The kind jeweler in his glass shop saying he knew just what Gillian wanted and slipping the watch on her wrist. This happy image got scrambled with the painful one at the morgue: unclasping the band from Gillian's wrist and setting it in its funereal case, untouched until now. Della stuffed the coin under the case's silk lining, put the watch back in its place and the case back in the closet.

By the time she got downstairs, the knocking had ceased. She hoped the boy had lost patience and gone. She opened the door. Standing on the stoop was a tall, elderly colored lady, dressed in a fusty coarse skirt suit. Della noticed that Time had been kinder than Fortune to her visitor, whose physical homeliness had been transformed into a third-age distinction.

"Hello, dear," her older sister said, smiling and placing a gentle but grossly misshapen hand on Della's shoulder. Sarelle Osborne had inherited the Doctor's deformed limbs. She also had Lydia Freeman's kindness. Della neither dislodged the hand nor reciprocated the gesture.

"How did you find me?" The question came out colder than she'd intended.

"After thirty-three years, that's your first question?"

"What do you want, Sarelle?"

"May I come in?"

Della hesitated.

"Please."

Della stepped aside and gestured her six-foot-tall sister into the kitchen, a space so narrow that opening the fridge barred the passageway. They passed into the living room—a confined area without furniture, only some stacks of old newspapers and a disconnected daisy-wheel phone lying unplugged in a corner. "Take the stairs ahead," she said. "We'll talk in my room."

The two sisters climbed on stiffened joints to Della's bedroom.

"Go on, sit on the bed," said Della, settling into the rocker. "Let me guess. Those ragamuffins told you where to find me?"

Her sister nodded. "The one beats up the other. The other tattles. And on it goes. Nonstop contention and conflict. In this case, so much the better. If it weren't for those two rascals, I wouldn't have known you were in the country at all. We all thought you were still in France. Honestly, Della, you could have said something. I didn't know if you were alive or dead. How's Gillian?"

"Dead."

"Oh, dear. I'm so sorry." Della stubbornly refused to acknowledge her sister's condolences. Sarelle continued, "I don't suppose you can let bygones be bygones?"

"You want to know the funny thing about living outside your country for so long? When you come back, it doesn't seem like time has passed at all. What you call a bygone is still pretty fresh news in my mind, *sister*!"

"Della, dear…"

"You let that shrew turn me out to the wolves."

"What choice did you leave me? I never agreed with Hattie's spite or her methods, but she had young children and a home to protect."

"Spin that malarkey to someone else, Sarelle. It had nothing to do with protecting anyone or anything. It was contempt pure and simple. I was bold enough to live my life and speak my mind—and you, my own sisters, despised me for it and took the side of my attackers."

"That's your version, dear. But you forget how provocative you could be. Your reputation—"

"Enough already!" shouted Della, rising angrily from the rocker. "We went through this thirty-three years ago. If that's all that brought you here, you can show yourself out."

"Age has not settled your temper, dear. I didn't come to fight. I'd like you to come home."

"Surely you're joking. Has *she* kicked the bucket?"

"That's not funny. Would you at least consider coming to dinner next week?"

"Is *she* going to be there?"

"Of course she will."

"Forget it, Sarelle. Don't you get it? If she's around, I wouldn't come if it were the last supper before the entire frigid universe crumbled and collapsed into the pit."

"Papa always said your stubborn pride would be your undoing."

"And you were always Papa's little negotiator. Good, safe, spinster Sarelle. And now you're doing Hattie's bidding. I pity you."

"No, dear, it's you who's deserving of pity. Living a self-imposed exile in this cold empty cubicle of a house is a terrible punishment."

"I'd live in a tomb before I'd kowtow to that lying freak."

"You know, you're not very consistent, Della. I recall a headstrong young woman snatching up the Indian's coin and vowing to pass it on to the appropriate family member. How can you do that, divorced as you are from your family?"

The familiar reek of angry pride burned in Della's nostrils. It was an attitude as much as a sense, but it sickened her nonetheless. "I'm not worried," she said. "The coin has always found its way into the appropriate hands. I don't need to prostrate myself before the likes of Hattie Lawrence."

"Very well," said Sarelle, standing and opening her handbag. She took out a card and set it on the table, beside the picture frame. "Our telephone number changed years ago. Call me. Stubborn pride never brought happiness or peace to anyone, sister. I will leave you to your solitude in the hope that you will change your mind."

"I won't."

Her sister had almost made it to the bedroom door when Della lashed out with what she knew to be *orgueil*, a French word summing up the sinister, self-destructive side of pride. "Maybe the coin has already chosen someone."

Her sister paused. "And who might that be, dear?"

"Ezra Roxxmott."

Sarelle looked shocked. "That willful child? He's trouble on two legs."

"You always did see willfulness as a flaw," said Della, contemptuous of her sister's properness. "Vulgar as he is, he strikes me as intellectually honest. The other one, Ezekiel, I suspect that under all that sweetness is a twisted mind."

Sarelle shook her head, a gesture of good sense in the face of intractable contention. "Dear, you've made some questionable decisions in the past, but taking Ezra Roxxmott under your wing would be the biggest folly of your life."

"You'll excuse me, sister, if I don't take the advice of an old spinster who hasn't taken a chance in her entire life."

A lambent spring morning scented with jasmine, Della returned from her daily stroll to find Ezra waiting for her in her front yard, holding a standard-sized envelope. She was glad to see him but loath to show it.

"Oh, you again," she mumbled, ignoring the envelope and letting herself in without extending an invitation to him. He wasn't waiting for one. The imp followed her inside and tossed the envelope on the kitchen counter.

"Aunt Sarelle thought you'd like some pictures of the littah," he said with remarkable brass. "She has all kinds of old photos. She's got dagger-types dating back to the mid-nineteenth century."

Della nodded. "Yes, Sarelle is a photo buff. Incidentally, the word is *daguerreotype*, Ezra. The inventor was Mr. Daguerre."

"If you say so," he said, like a wise-ass.

She picked up the envelope, smudged with axle grease. She glanced at his hands, also blackened with grease. "What have you been up to now?"

"Robbing trains." For the slightest instant she believed him. "C'mon," he said. "You're too easy. I do auto mechanics."

"At school?"

"A bit. They don't give you much space at school." His eyes teemed with something unpredictable and predatory. "I work down in our basement. You got an old dish rag or somethin'?"

She pointed first at the cloth on the oven-door handle, then at the sink. "Scrub your pistons first, Mr. Mechanic. Use the dish soap. Aren't you a little young for auto…" She let it drop. What was the point?

As Ezra soaped his hands in the kitchen sink, Della dug out the contents of the envelope. There were two Kodak pictures. The first had been shot in the Osborne House front garden, beside the century-old ruin of a marble birdbath. The man in the picture was as diminished as the decaying Gregorian house in the background. His wrinkled Asian face was twisted with worries and illness, and age had turned his once-red hair tawny. "My, goodness! That's Johnny T!"

"Yeah, it's Grampy all right," the boy said, lathering his nails and knuckles.

"Did the poor man ever get to California?"

"Grampy nevah went nowhere. He dropped dead on Onion Road a couple of years ago."

This insensitively delivered information struck Della harder than she might have expected. "In this life," she said, "we have time for one dream and then it's over… Did anyone ever tell you how we Osbornes first met your Grampy?" The boy's shrug seemed to indicate that, if she wanted to tell him, he'd listen. "It was several years after the Chinaman disappeared."

"You mean the guy who killed someone."

"Yes. Joseph Archung-Finley. I mean, nothing was ever proven, but, yes, *he* probably did the murder. Anyway, one snowy winter's night about thirteen years after the murder, we saw the Chinaman's ghost standing on Onion Road."

"Get outta heeah!"

Della smiled wickedly. She had nabbed the little bastard.

The year was 1901, and the ghost invested the evening shadows, darting under the electric lampposts recently installed on Onion Road. "There it goes again," shrieked Sarelle. "The ghost of the Chinaman!" Mama, Sarelle and

Della rushed as one to the window facing the road. Papa set down *Moby Dick* and said, "Thar he blows!" He went to fetch his coat.

The spook, weary of its habitual game of hide-and-seek, chose to linger a little longer under the lamplight. Snowflakes swirled about him, accumulating on the brim of his black cap and the shoulders of his navy-blue pea coat. Papa went down to the road and entreated the ghost to come inside and get warm. Finally, the ghost crossed Onion Road to the front gate. He was a young man, not yet twenty but exceedingly tall, a good head above Papa, who was taller than most men his age. But it wasn't the stranger's height that threw Papa. It was the fact that the young man was a dead ringer for the Chinaman. "Well, I'll be damned!" declared Papa. "You're your father's spitting image."

In the entry, the young man removed his cap, releasing a fine wet powder of snow and a shock of carroty hair that definitely hadn't come from his father. Joseph Finley's petroleum-black hair had hung off his bony skull like kelp from a keel. "Sorry to wet up your place," said the redheaded Chinese, handing over his coat but not the cap, which he gripped with both hands, nervous as a schoolboy. He followed Papa through a beat-up velvet curtain into an electrically lit parlor to be introduced to the lady of the house and her two smiling daughters.

"This is my wife Clara," said Papa. "And my daughters Sarelle and Della."

Mama was petite, perky and black as slate, in contrast to Papa's light-mustard and freckled complexion. Sarelle and Della were both in their twenties, husbandless and dressed for the evening in snug wasp-waist dresses. Sarelle, almost as tall as the stranger, was a sweet, homely woman with a blunt nose, mare-like earthen eyes, frizzy copper hair and Papa's golden complexion. She taught at the local elementary school. Della was more the color of cinnamon, a classic beauty both of face and figure, and she had a sparkle of mischief in her bright almond eyes. She had recently started work as a journalist for the *Neespaugot Times*.

"Won't you sit, cousin?" Della asked him.

Papa stood at the potbelly stove, reloading it with logs from a scuttle. "Son, what are you, six foot three?"

"And a half, sir."

"That's your Irish grandfather's doing," said Papa, returning to the sofa. "A big brute of a fella who almost threw me off the roof. It's John Thomas, I believe?"

"Why, yes, sir, but the fellows at The Shoe call me Johnny T for short. That's where I work... as a machinist..."

Mama informed Johnny T that her youngest daughter would be down shortly. "Hattie's your age, dear. I know this because your mother and I were both pregnant the year that your father..."

An awkward silence fell, and Johnny T survived it as best he could by continuing to wring his cap, as if expecting to squeeze a little confidence from its coarse wool. "About my father," he began. "I was thinking, um, that maybe you... could, um..."

Papa came to his aid. "You'd like us to tell you about your father?"

"Yes, sir!" he said as if believing Papa could read minds.

"Only if you stop with this 'sir' business." Everyone laughed. "I'm your Uncle Randy and much prefer that title to sir. What would you like to know about your dear dad?"

"I don't know where to begin, sir—I mean, Uncle Randy. The only bits I know come from my mam and my sister Maureen, and neither speaks much or kindly of him. What was he like?"

Papa thought for a moment, seeking the right tone. How to tell the young man that his father was an abject disappointment? "Your father was a gentle, friendly fella, but a bit of a transcendentalist, if you get my meaning. A free spirit. A wanderer. Don't get me wrong, I admired his gusto, but his blood burned to move. I think travel was a compulsion for him." Papa paused with an idea, and then hurried to the Doctor's desk in the corner of the parlor, loaded down with old papers and utensils. "Somewhere in this clutter I've kept some letters…"

After some moments, a much-contented Papa returned with the sought-after correspondence. "Your father sent me these while he was out west." As Papa skimmed through the epistles, it was clear to all but Johnny T that Papa wasn't picking out the letters he was willing to share but searching for the one he couldn't share, the last letter the Chinaman had ever written to him, the incriminating one. "You see, after his railroad stint, your father stayed in the west for a good ten years— Ah! Here we go," said Papa, removing the forbidden letter with a cardsharp's sleight of hand and placing it at the bottom of the pile. "Take this one, for example, dated May 2, 1871: 'I quite enjoy this moving about. It makes me wonder if movement for its own sake isn't the overriding moral of my story.' And then there was this one: 'I'm fed up with the cold, the critters and my own stink, so I've hired on with an English outfit out of Victoria for Shanghai. Maybe I'm not the shark I'd supposed myself to be, needing to move to breathe. Maybe I'm just some sort of migratory creature that knows when enough is enough and decides to wind its way home.'" Papa handed over his own pick of letters to the young man. "Have yourself a gander, my boy. You can see for yourself that your father could set out at the drop of a hat, often without a clear plan or objective. But I don't judge him."

Papa drew out a cigar and lit it just as his third and youngest daughter made her entrance like a primadonna about to miss her second act. Overdressed in stiff layers of white taffeta and sporting a mask of thick white paste, the young woman seemed by all appearances to be striving for a phantom self-effacement at complete odds with the numbing strike of her bossy cords. "Mama! This stupid thing came apart." She showed her mother a thread dangling from the neckline of her dress.

Johnny T quickly set down his father's letters and, nervous to the point of shattering, stood to make her acquaintance. The spoiled little hussy ignored him.

"Can you repair it now, Mother? I just can't go around half-naked."

Mama took her to task. "Hattie, show some manners and greet your cousin, John Thomas Archung-Finley."

The brazen girl sprang a critical eye on the awkward fellow. "Ah, the skulker," she said, giving the word the sound of something to be dumped or buried. He offered to shake her hand, but Hattie declined. "A young man must wait for the lady," she said. "Put your hand away." When he did so, she reached out her hand. He went to take it, but she suddenly withdrew the offer, leaving his hand dangling. She sat on the divan, leaving Johnny T standing alone. Della politely nudged him and motioned him to sit. Hattie resumed her onslaught on the weakened boy's defenses.

"So, you really are part of that family with the dreadfully hyphenated last name. Archung-Finley. Sounds like a fit of sneezing just to say it. Are all of you redheaded and slanty-eyed?"

"No, miss. I'm the only one like this," he answered.

"I met that Chinese father of yours once."

"Truly?" he asked, naively opening himself to a counterpunch.

"Yes, *truly*, ninny. Do you think me a liar? And let me tell you, to this day he is positively the scariest man I have ever met. The afternoon he came rapping on the door with his wooden leg, I thought I would die of fright. He growled at me to let him in and thanked me for it by lifting his eyepatch and showing me a hole that went clean through his head."

"Stop exaggerating, Hattie," said Papa.

"I had nightmares for years."

"You had no such a thing, Hattie," said Mama.

Della added, "As I recall, Hell, you tortured that poor man as you're now torturing his son."

"Mama, make her stop calling me 'Hell'!"

Della grinned. "Well, it *is* your name. Hattie Lawrence. HL. *Hell*."

"Very funny." The little tyrant turned to Johnny T. "You see how it is for me around here, Mr. Sneezy? No one believes anything I say, and I am constantly insulted."

It turned out that the poor boy was no stranger to this kind of manipulation. Johnny T cohabited with six siblings—including a domineering older sister—and a hard-hearted mother. Between his mother's wrangling and his sister's contrivances, he was always being tugged one way or the other like fresh dough, pressed and rolled by conflict. But it seemed he had learned precious few lessons from his prior experiences, and remained ever gullible and willing to please those who did not deserve it.

"I believe you, miss," he said.

"I am not asking to be humored, Mr. Archung-Finley."

Johnny T was bamboozled by this slap in the face. Papa intervened, seizing the opportunity to change the subject. "Suppose we set aside your dear dad, and you tell us something about yourself, Johnny T. What are your aims, son?"

The young man didn't skip a beat. "I aim to go to California, like my dad did."

Papa's demeanor turned dark. He stopped puffing and snuffed out his stogie in the ashtray. "Ambition is good, young man, but it should be your own."

"And who but a fool would choose to go to such a place?" said Hattie Lawrence.

"O hush, you," said Della. "You know nothing of California."

"I know there are savages out there. I read it in a magazine."

"And did the magazine happen to mention that those savages are your own ancestors?"

"Bite your tongue. Don't believe a word of it, Mr. Archung-Finley. In case you don't know, my grandfather was a Scottish-American doctor."

"And your grandmother was who?" asked Della.

"Girls," said Mama.

Hattie sent Della a scowl full of buckshot and, to get even, fished out of her neckline a silver chain and dull coin. To the innocent eyes of Johnny T, the object seemed harmless enough, but its sudden manifestation sent Della into a fit of rage.

"You hussy! You take that off!"

"Calm down, Della," said Papa.

"It's pure provocation, Papa. You know she doesn't give a damn about the Indian's coin. She calls it a 'filthy lobe of lechery.'"

"Only to bait you," Hattie Lawrence replied with mock sincerity.

"All right, that's enough," said Mama. "Hattie, return the pendant to your father."

Papa pointed an incriminating look at Johnny T. "This, young man, is what happens when you start talking about wanderlust."

"Why did Grampy ever marry that bitch?" Ezra said now.

"Times were different then," said Della. "Opportunity, scarce. And Papa could be very controlling. He steered Johnny T into the marriage because he felt guilty about the way he had treated the Chinaman."

"How did he treat the Chinaman?"

"Papa's favorite motto was: 'what moves, improves, and what stays, decays.' All well and good, except that Papa never moved an inch in his life, being that he suffered from misoneism, as did his own father, Doctor Osborne."

"Miss *what*?"

"Misoneism. It's the fear and loathing of change. The Puritan disease. Papa had it in spades and never put a foot outside the North Bay. The Chinaman, on the other hand, gallivanted recklessly from one corner of the globe to another. They were opposites, mover and moper, and Papa was jealous of the Chinaman. Buried deep in Papa's heart was the desire to see him brought low. When that day arrived, Papa made him pay."

"How?"

"Papa was clever with words. He knew how to inject venom and retract his fangs before you even knew you'd been bitten."

"Sounds like my grandmothah."

"As they say, the fruit doesn't fall far from the tree."

"So you snatched the coin for yaself," said Ezra with spiteful glee. The comment wasn't accusatorial in the least, but Della felt a rush of shame. The blunt non sequitur struck her like a slap in the face.

"Another time, perhaps," she mumbled and quickly changed the subject. "Suppose you tell me about this second photograph. Who are these three lovely people?" Two young men and a young woman, obviously related, stood in front of a soda shop on Cabot Street. The men were tall, lanky and Asian, while the young woman, clearly a bit Asian herself, also had mocha skin and a mane of frizzy orange hair. "Tell me about them."

"Well, this one heah," said Ezra, pointing a finger at the older male who had the look of an intelligent rake. "That's Uncle Bobby, the oldest brother. He's kinda like what ya said about the Chinaman, always taking off fah pahts unknown."

"Maybe the genes skipped a generation."

"And that's Uncle Gil," said the boy, fingering the other brother, who displayed the vacuous expression of a simpleton. "He was born retahded. Nowadays, Uncle Gil is a seven-year-old in a man's body. He lives with Grandma. She doesn't take care of him, he takes care of her. He's her goddamn servant."

"Hattie always used somebody… And the young woman?"

"That's Ma, their sistah."

Ezra's mother was wearing a vanilla-pleated dress, tight at the waist, wide at the shoulders and descending to the midcalf of very nice legs. "Well, I must say, she's a lovely woman."

"Are you daffy?"

His opprobrium surprised Della. "Young man, are you embarrassed by your mother's exoticism?"

"If that means looks, ya damn right I am. I mean, it ain't her fault if she's too brown fah this town. Nitwits are always giving her a hard time about her flavor. Is she Harlem brown? Muhammad brown? Tongatabooan brown? It's like she's some kind of rice."

"Let me guess. You feel you have to defend her, because she's your mother, but you can't defend her from the world, and that makes you feel helpless and you don't like that, so instead you take it out on her in order to work through your guilt. Am I right?"

"I don't have a clue what you just said."

"Listen to me, young man, and listen good. All real Americans are brown. Brown means castoff, exiled, mixed, *different*. And that's what makes this country special. It's also what these racist, separatist, isolationist, exclusionist mopers don't get. All Americans are mongrels of some type, and mongrels aren't stuck in the past. We move, like electricity, like waves literal and transmitted, right down to our DNA. Look at her, boy, look at your mother. She has the eyes of great China, the noble brow of the native people, the flesh of grand Africa, the hair color of the Celts. My word, the beauty of history and progress is embodied in her every feature, child. There's your *real* American. How could you not be proud to call yourself her son? Your grandmother, that self-deluding fool, she never could understand that the noblest dog in the street is and has always been the non-pedigree— Why are you grinning like a fool, boy? I'm serious!"

"Nah. I just like the way ya talk. Like ya got hand grenades comin' outta ya mouth. Gimme hand grenades ovah handshakes any old day."

"Careful, Ezra. You're talking about scorn. I'm talking about transcendence. Do you understand that word? Transcendence means looking beyond yourself, beyond your own small, pitiful existence. You came to me seeking answers about the Indian's coin and a long-dead place called Septimania. Well, their common denominator is the notion of transcendence. So let's get to it, shall we? Septimania?"

Ezra

May 7, 1955

By the age of fifteen, Ezra Roxxmott knew as much about automobile engines and transmissions as most mechanics. He had already built a car before he could legally drive it. And even that restriction was about to fall. "Happy birthday," he said to himself, releasing a pearl-handled stick shift from a vice grip.

Ezra was standing under a naked lightbulb in his parents' basement, where his workbench stretched the length of the east wall, below a hatch window just brightening with the day's first light. The basement smelled like the dump, but he wasn't complaining. The dump had coughed up every tool he owned: a high-powered drill, all manner of bit, a soldering iron, blowtorch and protective mask, hammers, screwdrivers, cutters, clamps and coils of wire. Plus, there were cans of screws and nails, oxygen bottles, broken rifle barrels, a collection of steering wheels and, for company, the mounted head of a black bear missing its nose.

The upstairs floors rumbled, shaking the steering wheels hanging from mounted hooks on the rafter. He could track the urgent footfalls across the kitchen. Finally, the back door slammed and the house went quiet. "Fucking family," he said. Two parents, four kids with a fifth on the way, all of them stuffed like sardines in a two-bedroom, rat-infested dump house. Every butt cheek shared the same fucking toilet seat.

The only privacy he had was down there in his "Rat Cave," his sanctuary. Ezra had walled off a quarter of the basement with plywood, plastic, fiberglass and one large padlock. If it weren't for the rats and mildew, he'd be sleeping down there as well. But today, his sixteenth birthday, it was goodbye aggravation and hello freedom!

His impending liberation from family bondage dredged up a tale his mother liked to tell, the only one he had ever enjoyed because it wasn't one of her lame family histories. The yarn opened in late fifteenth-century London. Sir Calvin Finley and his wife Dame Clare were both scientists. Sir Calvin had built a reflecting telescope, dabbled in alchemy, did historical research and studied theology. Dame Clare was attempting to dissect light into its component particles. Sir Calvin was a far-thinker but also a member of Star Chamber, a reactionary body of scientific nincompoops with whom he was constantly at odds. The Chamber hardliners intended to rid the assembly of dissenters like Sir Calvin, and they finally lucked upon a pretext.

In May of 1498, John Cabot—the second-most successful navigator in the world after Columbus and the most popular gentleman in England for having navigated to Newfoundland and back in eleven weeks in 1497—set out on another expedition with five of King Henry VII's best ships and was never heard from again. The mopers of Star Chamber declared that the Cabot disaster was proof that God was against such expensive foolhardy missions and, knowing Sir Calvin's views on Divine Will, tricked him into presenting his opinion of the tragedy to the entire tribunal. Sir Calvin didn't disappoint them. He declared that Cabot's disappearance had a numerical—not an ecumenical—explanation: "Sea travel is many pluses and minuses with no greater law save the law of probability. I'm afraid that God is in the odds, gentlemen."

For that apostasy, Sir Calvin was excommunicated, then axed.

Dame Clare was next. She was dragged into the archdiocese tribunal to explain her theory that white light was actually composed of every color in the spectrum. Her discourse sounded like so much hocus pocus to the nincompoops, so she was tried as a witch and burned. Their son Devon was put under house arrest. Devon understood it was only a matter of time before someone concocted the means to execute him, too, so he familiarized himself with Da Vinci's plans for an "air screw," had sails and pine wood smuggled into his chamber, constructed a wing called an *aviavessel* and glided out the high window to freedom. Ezra had always liked the end: flying the coop in a machine of his own doing.

He snapped off the basement light and loped up the cellar steps two at a time. Zeke was in the kitchen, stuffing his face with cereal. His younger brother, now thirteen, had sprouted over the past year and was now taller than Ezra. As Ezra passed, he jostled his brother's shoulder, causing him to drop his spoon. It gave him nasty pleasure to watch the weasel squirm, to see his cheeks twitch and his eyes nictitate and avert. You skinny shit, you better be scared, thought Ezra. It doesn't matter how tall you get, I'll always own your ass.

"Who went bangin' outta here just now?"

"Pop took Ma to the hospital," said Zeke, squealing like one of the rats in the basement. "The baby's coming."

"One kid more, one kid less," Ezra mumbled.

"Whatcha mean?"

"For me to know and you to find out, dickwad." As he looked at Zeke, he recalled some words of his Aunt Della, who had seen right through the weasel: "Do not underestimate your brother. His insatiable need to replace you as the number-one son in your dad's eyes will know no bounds. He will lie and cheat to get what he wants. He will deny everything he is and fabricate everything he is not to get ahead. He is very much like my younger sister."

As Ezra banged out the back door, Zeke called after him. "Where you going? You and me are supposed to look after Miriam and Joey Snots."

"You look aftah them. I got plans."

The spring morning was ripe with sweet nature. At curbside waited his 1953 Studebaker Commander Starlight, fresh silver paint glistening with dew. The body, which had taken him the better part of a year to pound out and sand, was the only thing Studebaker about his hot rod. The insides were a mix. The chassis, frame and drivetrain were from a 1950 Chrysler De Soto, the engine was a 1947 Ford V8 flathead engine and crankshaft, and the carburetor had come out of a Chevy. For good measure, he had stuck on some Coker Classic whitewall tires, silver Rambler hubcaps, ten gallons of easy-drying Duco lacquer paint and now one pearl-handled stick shift. Everything but the stolen cans of paint and the stolen tires had come from the dump and various junkyards around town. His means to freedom had cost him practically nothing but elbow grease.

Ezra eased into a leather bucket seat and screwed in the shifter head. Then, he sat back and luxuriated for a moment, letting the sweet balm of empowerment seep in. He inserted the key and started her up. The V8 turned over and growled like a deep-chested giant. He backed her out onto Indian Hill Drive, set it in first gear, stuck both hands on the padded steering wheel and gunned the son-of-a-bitch, burning rubber all the way to the Neespaugot Turnpike.

He pulled off The Pike into Little Italy and parked in front of his aunt's place.

"Hey, Aunty," he yelled up from the kitchen. The habitual closet stink of her house had a new odor today, one of warm pastry. On the kitchen counter was a small pink box containing a baker's cake with "Happy Birthday, Nephew" writ in red icing. She hadn't forgotten. What Ezra *really* wanted to know was if she planned to give him the only gift that counted: the Indian's coin. "Aunt Deller," he shouted, "ain't you ready yet?"

After a while of nothing, Ezra bounded up the stairs and found the old gal sitting glumly in her rocker, still dressed in the rags she always wore around the house.

Her silver hair was a mess. Her barky face was puffy and haggard.

"Geez, Aunty, what's up?"

"I don't want to do this," she said, flinging her words like accusations.

"I meant it as an honor."

"No, you did not! You just need me, is all."

What bug had climbed up her ass? Ezra hadn't prepared himself for this stonewalling. "Aunty, I could've asked Pops, but I wanted to celebrate my freedom with you," he lied. He did need her to get his driver's license, and he hoped that once she understood he was leaving for good, she would hand over the Indian's coin to the only person worthy of it—namely, himself. Just the other day she'd been trying to convey something to him, rather guiltily, that she hadn't "snatched" the coin. She had "saved it from that ungrateful unworthy shrew Hattie Lawrence in order to give it to somebody worthy." Not wishing to contradict her and ruin his front-runner status, Ezra simply nodded, though to him a snatch was still a snatch. Whatever.

He leaned against the doorjamb and waited her out. He straightened his glasses—black-rimmed frames that his aunt said made him look meaner and more intractable, but which were, as far as he was concerned, merely geeky. His jeans and t-shirt were stained from his morning labor. He tapped his shit-kicker boots against her parquet floor, anxious. Tick tick tick. There was no going back now.

But the stubborn old cow was still equivocating. "How," she asked, "are we supposed to get to the

Department of Motor Vehicles?" It was a rhetorical question meant to remonstrate.

"A space craft," he flung back at her. "Damn, how do ya think? My cah!"

"And you realize that if the police stop us between here and the DMV, you can kiss your driver's license goodbye?"

"Aw, c'mon. For someone who preaches movement, I can't believe you're hung up on a little thing like driving to the DMV."

"It's not a 'little' thing. It's an illegal thing."

"Ooh, illegal! Look, if you're not interested, just say so and I'll drive home and get Pop," he said, bluffing. Ezra would rather a complete stranger vouch for him at the DMV than ask either parent for a favor.

"All right," she said, rising and grumbling to her dresser. "It's not like I didn't ask for this. Shame on me. Now, go out and give me some privacy."

He waited outside her bedroom door, in that narrow fusty corridor where, two years earlier, he had knocked out her wind. Funny to think that the mean old hag who had come after him that day with a walking cane was now his role model. Ezra admired no one as much as Della Osborne. She had told the world to fuck off. He dug that she had preferred exile to suffering fools. And her brand of sarcasm was right up his alley. None of his grandmother's hogwash about being Scot-American. His great-aunt called it as she saw it. "Some people get facelifts. Your grandmother gets *fact* lifts, the facts she doesn't like. Cosmetic sleight of hand," she had said. And when Ezra had confessed to not understanding history, she assured him that it was easy. "History, Ezra, is ballroom dancing, with swings and shifts. Just remember that as the music goes on, some people move with it. But most just hold it back and clog up the dance floor."

Della Osborne was the one person in his life he felt he could trust. So, for the previous eighteen months or so, he had been confiding in her. Sometimes it was goofy stuff: girls he was banging, teachers he'd socked, his exasperation with fading eyesight and not growing taller anymore. But there was serious stuff, too. He had told her why he hated his family and his ancestors. "Pop coulda been a scientist, but he quit and now look at him, a no-account dungeon workah. As fah Ma, what's she evah done except spit out stories of losahs?"

"Well, she did give you life, young man. Anyway, it sounds to me you think your parents have failed *you*. Tell me if I have this right. In your eyes, our family history is a long list of losers—*ergo*, colored equals shame, alpha white male equals winner, and because you can never be an alpha white male, you hate your genes. That certainly puts you in good company with your grandmother. Except, she never agonized over any inconvenient gene, she simply refused to recognize it. Instead, she built her life on the myth of an immaculate conception, the Scotsman who, without need of a woman or a womb, birthed a bloodline."

"Ha, now *that's* funny."

"Do you see me laughing, nephew? The genes of privilege might count for something in older societies, but they have no place in America, leastwise not the America I've always defended, where status must be *earned*, and no generation is ever condemned based on genes and the struggles of its parents. That's the promise of this country. Those who work the hardest are rewarded. But reality isn't so cut-and-dry. The truth is that the non-alpha types usually do fail. But then their children carry on. And then their children's children. Because it's transcendence that counts, Ezra. I'm not talking about one individual overcoming adversity. I mean a transcendence occurring over many generations."

She had had him read a book called *The Myth of Sisyphus*. The protagonist, a poor sap named Sisyphus, goes to hell, where his eternal punishment is to push a boulder up a hill. He fails every time. The boulder always rolls back down the hill, and Sisyphus has to begin anew. The gods intend to suck him dry of any hope. But Sisyphus turns the tables on them. He voluntarily relinquishes hope and replaces it with scorn. *There is not fate that cannot be surmounted by scorn.* Sisyphus stops thinking about beating the hill and focuses instead on the task of rolling, in full knowledge that he will never get his rock over the hill. And so he goes about his daily and futile toil with something approaching contentment, turning eternal punishment into a kind of salvation.

It was scorn the way Ezra liked it. But to his dismay, his aunt's lesson was just beginning.

"Now, try to think about the story from an American perspective."

Ezra was lost. "What d'ya mean?"

"Well, as an American, do you believe in a fate that can hold you back? Is that why you're building that car of yours? Because you don't think there's anything you can do about your future? My point is that, sure, scorn beats fate if your fate is to be a miserable moper. But scorn will also keep you in hell. Transcendence is only possible through a genuine belief in ultimate possibilities. And that, until now, has been the American way."

Ezra got mad. "How can ya talk about America like that aftah getting run out of the country on a rail?"

"Dear, we're still the only country to elect a self-educated hillbilly as president. One day, I'm sure we'll see a person of color in the White House, and a woman. If you can imagine something, the impossible becomes possible."

"I ain't interested in that positive-thinking crap."

"All right, I respect that. So let me ask you this. If you admire what Sisyphus did, why don't you respect your dad's life? From what you've told me, he's a modern-day Sisyphus. A dungeon worker. Rolls midnight missiles up an arsenal hill. Sleeps all day to wake up and do it all again."

"It ain't the same."

"You're right. Sisyphus is dead, and hell is just a self-contained, self-centered timelessness where nothing he does matters to anyone but himself. Your dad, on the other hand, he's alive and toiling for a life for *you*, your brothers and sister."

"He's just goin' through the motions."

"Maybe. And maybe he can also envisage something beyond himself, beyond the gods and fate and their tricks. He sees his kids moving ahead, and even if it's only self-vindication and triumphalism, who cares as long as you kids get your shot?"

"That's rich talk comin' from a mothahless hermit."

"Yes, but a hermit who has the Indian's coin." She winked.

The nasty bitch, Ezra remembered thinking. And he had never been more proud of her.

"Get a move on it there, Aunty! The longah we dally, the longah we'll be waitin' in line at the DMV."

"Five minutes," she called through the door.

The Indian's coin. To his aunt, the coin was a symbol of transcendence. To Ezra, its possession would represent a personal vindication vis-à-vis his family, a kind of anointment setting him apart for all time from his loser relatives. He'd only seen it once—which was once more than anyone in his mother's generation. One day, Aunt Della had handed him a watch case and told him to open it. Inside, strung to a silver chain slotted through a crude nail hole, was the coin. It was nothing special-looking, just a dull brown piece of shit. But it was the prize, so he wasn't about to spit on it. "There it is," she'd said, in the solemn tone of a rabbi. "Passed on from one generation to the next, one generous heart to another. Go on, touch it. Feel the spirit of your ancestors."

The only thing he felt was the power of one-upmanship.

"Okay," she'd said, taking back the coin and closing it away in the box. "Suppose we get to the subject that earned you a return trip to my house. Septimania."

His great-aunt explained to him that Septimania was a territory in southern France, existing from the fall of the Roman Empire to the Middle Ages. Blind to color and creed, Septimania was the most enlightened place on earth. The territory was united by a code of laws called *Lex Visigothorum*, laws that abolished the separate and unequal treatment of races and religions. Goths (who were Arians), Gauls (who were Trinitarians), Baghdad Jews and Moors—all were treated equally under those laws. Immigration was welcomed, integration encouraged and intermarriage celebrated. Without prejudice, suspicion or scorn, the people of Septimania advanced medicine, art, ethics and technology. Courtly love was invented in Septimania. Women were granted rights thought unbelievable—even blasphemous—in the mad orthodox kingdoms surrounding Septimania. For example, women were entitled to their deceased husband's property. Women also had the right to be priests. "Some of the community property and family laws we have today are descended from *Lex Visigothorum.* Now that's transcendence, child."

"So what happened to this Septimania?" he'd asked.

"What always happens to movers? The mopers eventually rode in and chopped them to bits."

At long last, his aunt caned from her bedroom. She had done herself up in a fancy-cut knee-length dress, high heels and a classy hat from her Parisian days. She'd even thrown on some makeup, highlighting her cheeks and eyes, and for the first time Ezra caught a glimpse of the beauty everybody said she once was. In her free hand was a gift-wrapped package the size of a watch case, and Ezra's face lit up. Was this really going to be the moment she gave it to him? He reached for the box, but she tapped his hand with her cane. "Patience," she admonished. "I also bought you a cake, which we'll have when we get back."

"Yes, ma'am!"

As they exited by the kitchen, she set the gift beside the cake.

Out on the curb, he was curious to know what she thought of his car. She shrugged. "I've seen it before."

"But never painted," he said, disappointed. He opened her door. "It was only buffed out then."

"If you say so," she said, party-pooper-like, and set a hand for support on the roof as she strained to make her knees bend. Her rear end went in fine, but she could do nothing with the legs. Ezra reached under her calves and swung her legs into the tight foot compartment. Her calves were softer than young breasts. Ezra had never touched anything softer. "Geez, that's nice," he said with a lascivious wink. She slapped his hands away and tried not to smile.

"You could have put in some lap belts," she said, trying to get comfortable.

"Lap belts are fah losahs."

"I read somewhere that one day most cars will have them."

"Not if I can help it, Aunty."

So as not to scare her, Ezra kept his speed down, leaving her neighborhood. At the end of Crawford Street, United Shoe Machinery popped up in the windshield, its dead stacks like permanent signs to heaven to go fuck itself. "Must be nice havin' The Shoe closed down, eh, Aunty?" She shrugged. He flipped the right-turn signal and picked up Boston Road before taking another right and motoring up the shore on Route 128.

Along the way, he kept expecting her to compliment the car or his driving. But all that interested her were the scenes outside the car—or in her old head—and none of it was having a positive effect on her. He could tell she was tense and cranky. She mumbled something about outer space and grumped that there was a time, and not all that long ago, when the entire South Bay was primal marshland and coastal plains, home to all manner of creature, large and small, serving as food for the native peoples. "Now look at it. Fabric factory and the storage plant, home to petroleum, cereal, dog food, automobiles and modern appliances. Commercial buildings and giant billboards blocking the view of the ocean. Everywhere a road. Driveway, lane, avenue, boulevard, highway, tunnel, turnpike. Everybody owns a *cah*."

"Geez, Aunty, what's with you today?"

"Does it have a name, your *cah*?" she asked. "People christen their boats. Soldiers give names to their bombs. Maybe you need a name *fuh yah cah*."

To make her less crabby, he turned on the radio. *"...with trouble brewing in the Near East between Nasser's Egypt and the state of Israel..."* He switched it off. The world was in a bitchy mood today, too.

"Why did you cut that?"

"Ya really wanna hear that crap, Aunty?"

"Why wouldn't I?" she said. "I can identify with what's going on ten thousand miles away from Neespaugot. It's what's going on two miles from my home that depresses me."

"Y'know, Aunty, sometimes ya sound just like Grandma."

Oops, he was going to regret that. And sure enough, he got the silent treatment all the way to the DMV parking lot.

But she warmed up after that. She came inside and followed the plan, giving the authorities her address, swearing under oath that Ezra lived with her and the Studebaker was hers. Everything was flowing until she said Ezra was her nephew. *That* was the part that raised suspicion. Those saps were willing to believe that a seventy-six-year-old invalid owned a souped-up hot rod but didn't buy that she, a colored woman, had a white-skinned nephew. Transcendence, my ass! What kind of transcendence could you expect in a world populated by such assholes?

Anyway, his aunt tore into them with enough of a history lesson that they let him in just to shut her up. He tested out of the written and driving exams, and an hour later they were back out in the DMV parking lot with what they had come for.

"That's what I'm talking about!" he said, kissing his shiny new driver's license.

Aunt Della congratulated him. "And now that you're legal, stay out of trouble."

"And now that you're pretty again, gimme some love!" He threw a bear hug on her and grabbed her ass.

"You rogue!" She pushed him away, grinning.

He chuckled and unlocked the Studebaker.

On the drive back, Ezra was on top of the world. He had his car, his license and his freedom. As he motored back down Route 128, his fingers thumping the steering wheel to the beat of "Bo Diddley," he was even ready to admit that his aunt's transcendence malarkey deserved a chance. Life was that good.

"Ezra, turn off the music."

He turned the knob and glanced at her. Her cheeks were wet. She'd been silently crying. "Yo, what's up, Aunty? Ya cah-sick or something?"

She placed her hands on the dashboard. She was trembling. "I saw your mother yesterday."

"You what? My Ma? Why?"

"I went to your house… It wasn't the first time."

She might just as well have stuck his head under water. For a moment Ezra couldn't breathe. "What the f— *Why!?*"

"The first time was simple curiosity. Then, I realized I'd missed out on something. It isn't your mother's fault who *her* mother is."

Ezra banged the steering wheel in disgust. "I can't believe this! The family gave you the shaft."

"Your mother had nothing to do with that. Neither did my dear Gillian, but I made them both pay for my dark pride, my *orgueil*. Gillian never wanted to live the life of an exile. She was happy here in Neespaugot. She had a wonderful relationship with her family and friends. But she gave it all up to follow me and my stupid pride into limbo. Oh, she never complained, always the brave face. But the misery of exile ate her from the inside out. Her sickness was my doing. *I* killed her."

He watched his aunt break down in full-blown sobbing, and it disgusted him, her weakness. "Fuck that! You were right. *They* were wrong."

"No, *I* was wrong, Ezra. Scorn cannot surmount fate. *Orgueil* is no substitute for happiness. I allowed spite and stubborn pride to hijack my career, my country and my relationship with your mother's generation—and yours. I'm a fine one to talk about transcendence." She shook her head and tried to recompose herself. Then, she got about her real business, which was the fucking *coup de grace*.

"I've given your mother the Indian's coin."

"You what! But that gift box you had—"

"Oh, dear, no! You misunderstood." The blood drained from her face, leaving it waxen. "Oh, good Lord, it's a watch, dear. I bought you a watch for your birthday."

He screeched to the side of the road and let the car run as he jumped out and began stomping on the shoulder of the highway. *Fuck fuck fuck fuck fuck fuck fuck fuck fuck fuck!* History! What good is it if you're destined to play on the losing side all the fucking time? His spiritual mother had just kicked him in the nuts. Aunt Della was a loser like the rest of them—the Osbornes, Freemans, Griffins, Archungs, Finleys, Roxxmotts—all a bunch of lowlife spineless gutless specimens. That hell-walking Sisyphus had it right. Scorn was the only medicine!

Ezra got back behind the wheel and threw it in gear, tearing off the shoulder.

The late-morning sun hung diffuse and sickly behind the dull veil of muggy weather. The incoming tide was making its inexorable bi-daily sweep across the South Bay. Ezra opened his window and let the sea air cool his nerves.

After a long silence, his aunt tried to explain her actions.

"Ezra, I know it's cruel to hear, but the Indian's coin is not for people like us. It's more than transcendence.

There's the continuity as well. You and I, we're rebels. I have been a mere caretaker in search of the person to carry on the legacy of Runinniduk and Melba and Lydia. When I met your mother, I knew I'd found that person. I saw my grandmother Lydia in your mother."

Another fucking word and he'd bust her chops!

"Hey, guess what?" he asked, his voice full of ice. "You suggested this cah deserved a name. How about Septimania, eh? Y'know, that transcendent shithole over in France?" And he hit the accelerator, enlisting all the power under the hood.

Startled by the roar and frightened by the speed, his aunt demanded he slow down and take her home. But he laughed. "Aw, c'mon, Aunty, we're movin'! That's what you preach, ain't it? Be a movah, not a mopah?"

"Stop your nonsense this instant!"

"Oh, I ain't playin'. And I sure as hell ain't gonna be sorry like you about flipping the world the bird. Not me. My history's my own. Nobody gets in my way. Not even those cops chasing us."

She arched her head to have a look and saw the trailing cop car in the rear window, its red light flashing.

"What do they want?"

"I'm speeding, woman. They want me to stop so they can give me a ticket."

"Then pull over."

"Not on yah life." Instead, he went faster, and the flashing light was joined by a siren.

"Don't be a hothead, Ezra!"

"My advice to you, Aunty, is hold on to yah girdle."

The high-speed chase covered four counties. Just past

Cowlick Cove, Route 128 looped and dove at a ninety-degree angle, a virtual rollercoaster plummeting through woods of red, black and white spruce, birch, elm, conifers, chestnut, maple, moosewood and oak, some pussy willow and poison sumac, toward the Merrimac River. It felt like flying…before they actually did fly.

The speedometer showed a hundred miles per hour at the bottom of the steep grade, as the car blew through the guardrail into the ravine along the river. Had they hit a tree or any other obstacle thereof, well, that would have been curtains. As it was, they landed in a meadow, contacting the ground sideways. He felt the axle crack, saw the passenger door being ripped from its hinges, and then his aunt was gone, disappeared, like she'd never been there to begin with. Ezra's side of the vehicle rushed in and smashed him and nearly knocked him out, but he stayed alert long enough to witness his car finish in a brook full of cat-o'-nine-tails.

Dizzy but alive, he crawled from the wreckage. He had no idea where his aunt was, but he could hear the sirens coming from an elevated point a good half-mile away from where the car ended up. He didn't lose time and headed on foot away from Route 128 into the same forest where Melba had buried Runinniduk almost three centuries before. His aunt had been right about one thing: time was a tricky devil. His three-day sojourn seemed to pass in a moment's daze, and three centuries was no time whatsoever. The authorities eventually caught him sitting at a diner counter, licking yolk off a twenty-five-cent plate of eggs.

As for his aunt, when the police got down to the base of the ravine, they found a mangled car and, some one hundred fifty yards from it, the corpse of an elderly colored woman. Estimated age: mid-seventies. Cause of death: a broken neck. One of the cops was quoted in the *Neespaugot Times*: "Man, they sure were moving."

Zeke

November 5, 2008

Getting to where he got took guts and booze. Teetering three hundred feet above the ground on the metal band of a Plexiglas high-rise, icy wind whipping and no coat to speak of. *Screw the coat*, he thought. He'd tough it out. A gust buffeted the building, almost dislodging him. *Whoa! Jesus!* He clung harder to the wall. Amazing to think that only an inch of polymethyl methacrylate separated his ass from the spacious penthouse office on the other side. But life is a game of inches, and right now five inches of ledge arbitrated between his life and his demise.

He had been inching along that damn ledge for two hours. The back of his six-hundred-dollar loafers were worn to the nub, and his neck, back, shins, calves, toes and fingers were all cramping. He was half-crocked and not a young stud by any stretch of the imagination, just a sixty-four-year-old overweight dude with knees shot to shit, outfitted in a seven-thousand-dollar navy-blue suit, a flask of whiskey in one hand, a book in the other. But at least he'd made it to the front of the building, where his name was stenciled in six-foot copper lettering. There would be no going out the rear for Zeke Roxxmotto, chairman and CEO of Roxxmotto Capital Industries.

Zeke took another swig of whiskey and looked down. People were gathering like ants clustered around a scrap of bread. How long would it take? Three seconds? Then splat across the flagstone entrance like gull guano.

The ground wasn't the only place astir at that moment. The winter-gray heavens were abuzz with police, rescue and news helicopters overflying South Bay and its frozen industries. Zeke had rebuilt most of the waterfront. More than any other entrepreneur in town, he, Zeke Roxxmotto, was responsible for the South Bay economic miracle. Ever wonder what the equation of a life passed by was? Here's the formula: forty years plus a twenty-four-hour net loss of two hundred fifty million dollars equals three seconds of hang time to the flagstone entrance of your own financially gutted building.

Well, it wasn't just about the money, but whatever. Now that it was almost over, he realized his life had passed like a fart in a gale. Damn, it was only yesterday that he was still Zeke Roxxmott (without the "o"), a young high-school English teacher putting himself through law school at night, passing the bar on his third go. He'd borrowed enough money to set up a practice in Little Italy, a two-room locale squashed between a Filene's Basement department store and an A&P supermarket. He had added an "o" to his last name to fool people into believing he was Italian. It was 1971. Nobody checked anything or gave a fuck. One day the Canavales, owners of this small South Bay fishery, hired him to sue Exxon Neespaugot for disrupting the local fishing waters. A fool's wager, but what the hell. Somehow he bumbled his way into a seven-million-dollar settlement. Sometimes it *is* better to be lucky than good. He sank his earnings into a construction project to rebuild the waterfront. Big score again. Now he was lucky *and* good, and he rode the boom times of the 1980s into great wealth. The Roxxmotto Capital Industries building went up in '88. He invested left and right, and was courted by politicians, entrepreneurs and gangsters. Guest-speaking his ass off. Spending more time with his chauffeur than his wife and girls. Then, the Republican Party came calling. They had him run for mayor of Neespaugot, and damn if he wasn't elected in 1994. First fucking Republican town hall boss in seventy-five years. First "Italian" since the late '50s. In his first term, he raised the city's economy, lowered its crime rate and curbed its spending. His approval rating was off the charts, and he demolished the opposition in the '98 election.

Then came 9/11. The dust was still settling around Ground Zero when his enemies smeared him with the "m" word: Muslim. He got his ass handed to him in the 2002 election. Still toxic to his own party in 2006, he ran as an independent and was crushed again by both major parties. Fine. No more politics. At least he had his business.

Then, the second 9/11 hit—September 11, 2007. Lehman Brothers stock took a seventy-three-percent nosedive, and Zeke lost eighty percent of his fortune. His remaining assets dried up. His wife was gone, dead of cancer. His two girls, grown with families of their own, still blamed him more than the cancer for their mother's death. What would they know about what it takes to reach the pinnacle of Neespaugot? Their mother understood that you can't make an omelet without breaking some eggs.

Zeke finished off the last of the whiskey and released the flask. He counted aloud as it tumbled end-over-end down the side of the building. His cell phone vibrated against his chest. Without losing his grip on the book, he fished the phone out of his pocket. The cell's screen read "caller unknown." Maybe God? Ha ha ha!

"Yeah, who's this?"

"Mayor Roxxmotto, it's Lynn Chalmers of the *Neespaugot Times*. Please, sir, don't do this."

"What'd you say your name was?" He heard his voice trembling from the cold, the shock, and it didn't bother him.

"Lynn."

"Okay, listen, Liz, you cannot believe the difference in perspective between being *in* your office and standing on a ledge *outside* it. I gotta tell you, it's like the difference between thinking about doing something and doing it. Just fucking diametrically opposed, know what I mean? Rather invigorating, if you ask me."

He heard a loud whoosh and saw a rescue helicopter landing on the roof. Zeke's position made it impossible to lower someone by chopper. The rescuers would need to rappel down to him.

"Mr. Mayor, are you there?"

"I'm sorry, who are you again?"

"Sir, it's Lynn Chalmers of the *Neespaugot Times*…"

"Ah, yes, the *Times*. My great-aunt Della worked for your paper back in the day. She had a saying: 'People are either movers or mopers.' Just so you know, and you can quote me on this: I don't mope."

"Sounds like a worthy comeback speech, Mr. Mayor."

"Not on your life! To paraphrase Nixon, Neespaugot won't have Zeke Roxxmotto to kick around anymore. I'm flying out, as it were…without the chopper, of course."

"Sir, just— Let me get your take on the election of President Obama."

"Nice try."

"Well, you were Neespaugot's first non-white mayor. Many people still believe you gave the nation's second-oldest city the same feeling of hope as the country's experiencing today."

"Come on. We both know that's baloney. Everyone drank the Kool-Aid that I was Italian."

"In the first election. The second time around, you were more popular as a colored mayor than as a faux Italian. Your brother's book—"

"His fucking book painted me into a Muslim corner." Zeke's outburst almost caused him to slip. His interlocutor, watching live, gasped so loud that Zeke's ear itched. He steadied himself and continued. "The book was right about one thing, though. We're all profiled as 'this' or 'that'—and 'other' be damned! Listen, Leah, I gotta go now, but your relentless good timing deserves a reward. How would you like an exclusive?"

"It would be an honor."

"Listen carefully then. This is the sound of me hitting the ground."

Zeke let his cell phone go. It twirled to the ground and splintered into fragments. Good riddance!

A police chopper buzzed him, indifferent to his aggravation. In the distance, an oil tanker plied the waters between the North and South Bays. That fucking brother of his. It was all his doing!

Zeke spat on the hardcover book in his hand. The slug of saliva snailed down the volume's pine-green cover, over its title, *The Onion Road Legacy*, and down the copper insignia of the Indian's coin, that stupid piece of tin that had caused his foolish mother such anguish after his older brother stole it. But it was his youngest brother, author of this fucking book, whom Zeke blamed the most. His tell-all story had done more to ruin Zeke's life than the entire subprime mortgage crisis. The crisis hadn't tarnished his name and reputation. The crisis hadn't hijacked his self-esteem. But this book…

"I'm running for mayor of this city, damn you! What do you think is going to happen if it comes out I've been lying about my heritage?"

"Maybe it's time you stepped out of the mulatto closet and came clean."

"You vindictive bastard! This is payback for Ma and the house."

"It has nothing to do with that."

"What do you want, Oz? Money? I'll pay your price not to publish this."

"Screw your money, Zeke. This is for our ancestors."

"They're dead, damn you! I'm alive and this crap will bury me. At least change the names and write under a pseudonym."

"It comes out as is."

"We'll see about that."

Zeke had instructed his staff to buy the small publishing house. Once that was done, he had the book's publicity campaign squelched. And, for a time, it worked. The book flopped. But after the second election and owing to Zeke's notoriety, the book gathered steam again. The most damning part was about Uncle Bobby. The idiot converted to Islam in the late '70s and came to Zeke seeking a handout to finance an organic farm he ran with his girlfriend Fatima Hamid out in California. Zeke, rolling in cash, pride and arrogance, said what the hell. The entire family should know who the real paterfamilias was.

Pre-9/11, only wackos would have called the mayor of America's second-oldest city a jihadist. But post-9/11 times were not normal. Neespaugot was situated only fifteen miles from Logan International Airport, where two teams of five al-Qaeda terrorists had boarded American Airlines Flight 11 and United Airlines Flight 175 and crashed them into the North and South Towers of the World Trade Center. In the aftermath, word spread of the book, particularly the part about him having a Muslim uncle. Local radio talk shows accused Zeke of "playing hush with his racial and religious mush." Listeners called in to vent their hysteria. "If the bastard can lie about being Italian and Catholic, he can lie about *not* being a camel jockey!" "He's been planted here like those other bastards!" Posters around town portrayed the mayor riding a camel and wearing a turban.

The whiskey was wearing off, and tremors of fear were setting in. If Zeke didn't act soon, the rescuers would be upon him. He dangled the book over the abyss, ready to let it go the way of the flask and cell phone. Suddenly, he changed his mind and decided that the book, a chronicle of losers, was coming with him.

Zeke tried to think of a religious passage to smooth the ride, but what sprung to mind was something from his schoolteaching days, the diatribe of a religious fanatic from Puritan times: "You have no interest in any Mediator," wrote Jonathan Edwards, "and nothing to lay hold of to save yourself, nothing to keep off the flames of wrath, nothing of your own, nothing that you ever have done, nothing that you can do, to induce God to spare you one moment…"

Amen. Zeke closed his eyes and, clutching the book, stepped from his building.

Ruth

June 8, 2015

In the dead of night, the young woman drove north on Spider Leg Road, navigating the long, winding coastline by moonlight. There being no streetlamps anywhere, she had been driving with her high beams for the past twenty minutes, which was how long it had been since she'd come across another vehicle. The car clock read 4:23 a.m. About fifteen miles north of Neespaugot, she cut her headlights and engine and let momentum carry the car another one hundred fifty yards along the darkened shoreline, where she rolled onto a soft shoulder and braked. The only sound was the whoosh of the surf. She stepped out, setting off the car's interior light and her own stifled curse. *Damn you, you'll give yourself away!*

Ruth Roxxmott was dressed head to heel in black spandex, and even her running shoes and laces were black. She felt a little silly, like some kind of pantomime artist, commando or comic-book superhero. But this *was* indeed a black ops moment, and she didn't want to risk being detected. She set out quickly toward the beach.

Half a mile across the opaque wetland plain, she took cover behind a knot of driftwood. Once in position, she trained a pair of binoculars on a beach shack, the only habitation for miles around. And she waited for darkness to transition into crepuscule.

With first light, the gray landscape slowly came into focus: dunes, shrubs and driftwood stretching to a steely sea swirling with riptides and undertows. The beaches up there were wretched, the ocean glacial. She saw candlelight grow in the shack's only window. Through her binoculars, Ruth could see her target making himself comfortable at his breakfast table. He had long, disheveled gray hair and a white Old-Testament beard spilling down the front of his shirt like a vomit of purity. A Moses on Medicaid, she mused. She watched him raise his black eyeglasses to rub his nose, before digging into a bowl of algae and sprouts, his homegrown remedy for the disease that plagued the twilight of his existence.

Sunrise would come quickly now. Ruth set down the binoculars and braced for her daily cataclysm. "Ten, nine, eight, seven, six, five…"

The sun, blood red and distinct, lipped the horizon, and Ruth felt her world tilt like a dustpan slanted over a bin, all of existence seeming to tumble toward oblivion. She went dizzy, lost balance and fell back as the saltwater creeks filled with incoming tide. The screams of cormorants and gulls shattered against her skull. She felt swarming insects trying to eat through her full-body Lycra. Nature was stirring, but Ruth could only lie there and wait for the spell to pass.

Baffled that her bouts only happened at dawn, doctors called it insomnia-induced vertigo. Her inner ears had been examined, her blood pressure checked and pills prescribed to help her sleep through the new day. But none of it had helped. One psychiatrist had called it "battle fatigue," and there was certainly some truth to that. When she was three years old, Ruth had awoken to find her mother, a measured, articulate woman, lying prostrate on the kitchen floor, sobbing inconsolably and incapable of putting two words together. The small television beside the toaster was tuned to a news program, and the journalist was squawking her dad's name over and over. Ruth's big sister Melba, just nine herself, tried to explain to Ruth why an army of paparazzi was bivouacking up and down Onion Road, and why crowds were amassing outside Osborne House, gawking and pointing fingers at them.

"A crazy man killed Daddy," said Melba.

The only thing Ruth understood was that her dad was never coming home and that something ill-boding hung over the new day like a cloud.

A year later, the cloud turned into real plumes of smoke pouring from the tops of great twin buildings collapsing live on TV. In the aftermath, once-friendly neighbors and total strangers threw bottles at Ruth's house, calling her mom a filthy Arab terrorist. Ruth was four and had no idea what a "camel jockey" or "rug head" was. She stood in the front yard by the old birdbath, mesmerized by the sight of her mother dressed in an ugly black robe and hijab, pouring gasoline over her beautiful Western clothes and shoes and lighting the pile on fire. The heap went *KABOOM!* and ash swirled into the sky.

The community did not care for her mother's hijab. They called it "provocation." Her mother agreed with them: "You have provoked me. Now I shall provoke you." One day on the wharf, a mob of both sexes harassed her mother and threw things at her. A man ran after her and punched her in the back and she fell. Then, late one night, they broke into Osborne House. Her mother held Ruth and Melba close to her side as the mob tore down her dad's family-history museum. They dragged the wax figures out to Onion Road, decapitated them and impaled them in their genital areas.

That was Ruth's environment through the first five years of her life.

At age ten, the crowds were back. Onion Road swarmed with curiosity seekers wired on someone else's misery. Her rich uncle, the former mayor, whom Ruth knew only by reputation, had committed suicide. He had thrown himself from a building in front of helicopter news cameras and was splattered into every home in the country. His suicide became a hit on the nascent YouTube site. Kids at school teased her for having an omelette for an uncle. Ruth had little understanding of the human comedy being played out. Talking heads on the radio and internet proclaimed that her uncle had been unable to bear the guilt of being a jihadist mayor. Others said he had killed himself in a spirit of revenge against the town and his brother, Ruth's dad.

What troubled Ruth most was that only one person from her dad's immediate family bothered to turn up for her uncle's funeral. The defunct's own daughters, Willa and Kerri, both in their late thirties, boycotted their father's funeral. The only family there were Ruth, her sister Melba, their mother in her hijab and their Aunt Esther, who lived in California and was a state senator.

Ruth asked her famous aunt why there weren't more mourners. "Family quirks," said Aunt Esther. "One day it'll all make sense to you, Ruth. Just promise me you'll honor your father's memory. He felt responsible for this family. And when I say 'family,' I include all who came before and those still to come. Perhaps you or your sister will end up carrying his torch."

The shack door swung open, and the old man stepped out in a t-shirt, shorts and sandals, ready for his morning exercise. Ruth had been spying on him for the better part of a month, and she had to admit that, despite the involuntary twitching of his left arm, he was in darn good shape for a guy who had just turned seventy-five—not an ounce of flab on him. He was the same age as Runinniduk the day of his hanging. In fact, that very day marked the three hundred fortieth anniversary of the medicine man's execution. Which, of course, was no coincidence. Ruth had expressly chosen the occasion for retribution.

She had first read her dad's book, *The Onion Road Legacy*, in the ninth grade. Then, in what turned out to be a very bitter, and cathartic, book report, she expressed her indignation that "after close to four hundred years of social progress, the good still die young while the bad pass away in bed." It galled her that her father was dead, yet the villain who had dispatched Aunt Della, stolen the Indian's coin and set in motion a chain of events leading to her father's death, her mother's anguish and her own sunrise malaise had puttered along sweet as you please.

Four years and multiple readings later, Ruth's thirst for retribution had only hardened. She held her Uncle

Ezra accountable, and not just as a rogue and thief but also as the personification of a historical injustice that cried out for correction. She had considered breaking a few of his bones, even killing him, but that was a rather stupid and whimsical idea. Instead, she had settled on a more appropriate response. Her dad's book claimed that Uncle Ezra's rapport with the Indian's coin was not affective but spiteful: "Ezra didn't care about the coin itself, only the fact that no one else could have it." In snatching back the coin, Ruth would be striking a blow to her uncle's self-esteem, recalibrating family history and perhaps even liberating herself of her morning vertigo, all in one fell swoop.

She watched her uncle disappear down the beach, then set her stopwatch. She had timed him on multiple occasions, and it was always a forty-minute speed walk to Wampanoag Beach and back. He would then practice tai chi on his own beach for an additional twenty minutes. That gave Ruth about an hour to get in, find the coin and get out. Judging by the state of the shack, she was going to need every second.

The shack was raw cinderblocks erected on a slab of concrete covered by corrugated sheet-metal roofing rattling in the breeze. There were none of the tethers that connect regular people to society: no power or telephone lines, no running water nor a sewage-evacuation system. Once a week a water truck backed up and filled a plastic tank propped between the shack and an outdoor latrine ripe with infestation. The only visible sign of modernity was a small battery-operated generator behind the house, which her uncle used primarily to run a satellite hookup. Yes, in that sense, the bastard was "connected."

Through the Internet, her uncle ran a successful website catering to the soft-porn/art scene. He shot nude pictures on the beach, developed film in the shack— this in a time when most photographers had made the transition to digital—then scanned and uploaded the images onto his site. Ruth had visited the website and was disheartened to discover that her uncle's work was considered tasteful and popular, garnering rave reviews from professionals in the art industry. His pictures were "erotic *and* masterful," a fact that had probably kept his ass out of jail. His models, exclusively young women, came in all shapes, sizes and colors. Some were pretty, others not so much, but their looks and plastic were immaterial to him. What he craved was their innocence. First, he stole it, and then he hoarded it, exactly as he had with the Indian's coin.

To capture purity is to sully it, and her Uncle Ezra was the devil's artist. Armed with camera and tripod, he would troll the beaches for gullible and susceptible models. Spotting one, he would swoop in, all debonair and articulate—he could be exceedingly charming and alluring—with his avuncular white hair and beard, his Whitmanesque artiness and his gleaming professional business cards. Often, all it took to entice a prey out of her bikini and waiver rights was a few bucks and a shot at fame.

Ruth remembered that, when she was nine years old, a pretty mocha-skinned young woman had come knocking on their door, asking to visit Osborne House. Her mom said the house hadn't been open to the public since 9/11, but the young woman was insistent, so her mom let her in. The young woman asked if the late Hosea

Roxxmott was related to a hermit who lived on the beach, name of Ezra Roxxmott. "Yes, they were brothers," said her mom. "Why?"

The young woman told her story carefully. She had been snuggled up napping on the warm dunes when the hermit sent a quarter of the dune hill avalanching down on her. She reached for the knife in her cheap synthetic shoulder bag. "Whoa, I'm just a photographer," he said, showing her his cameras. He gave his spiel and asked if he could take nude pictures of her. It was an odd request, but she liked doing things she shouldn't. He arranged her legs and arms and head the way he liked against the white sand, and spread her Rastafarian jet-black tresses just so, and snapped away. As she put her clothes back on, he counted out some bills, told her where she could see the photographs and started to leave. She pulled out a joint and said she'd trade him a few puffs for a warm cup of tea.

The wind had whistled through the shack. The tea kettle itself had raised a racket, and the young woman had made plenty of noise of her own during sex on the hermit's couch, under the gaze of numerous cats. "You're good for your age," she gasped, out of breath.

"How old are you?"

"How old do you think I am?"

"Jailbait."

"Well, I'm nineteen, but most guys take me for thirty."

"I'm not most guys."

"I can see that," she said. "How come you live like this?"

"I'd rather live in my own crap than everyone else's."

"That's just talk. Everybody lives in everyone else's

shit. Chernobyl, Operation Desert Storm, the L.A. Riots, 9/11, Al-Qaida madness."

"Doesn't mean shit to me," he said, staring at her supple backside. "I've managed to shut myself off from the affairs of the planet. Even Alice can't find me."

"Who's Alice?"

"From the song— Aw, forget it. Where you from?"

"Haiti. I came to New York when I was a girl."

"Let me show you something."

He showed her the picture of a beautiful colored woman from 1901. "Now, she was a great woman."

"She is black. Are you black?"

"Do I look black?"

"I meet white people all the time who tell me they're black."

"That's because they want to fuck you."

"Yeah, maybe."

"So what brings you to Neespaugot?"

"I want to visit the house of that author who was shot. Hosea Roxxmott. You two share the same last name, and I thought you could ask the people who live there."

"You thought wrong, kid. Now, why don't you beat it. I got work to do."

Ruth found her uncle's shack unlocked, which didn't bode well since she'd always seen him lock his door. Gingerly, she eased it open. A tornado of screaming cats lunged out and whirled into the rushes. Ruth collected her nerves and gave it another shot, but once again she was driven back, this time by the stench, which was so caustic it made her gag. Finally, holding her hand over her nose and steeling herself for the olfactory onslaught, she stepped inside the premises.

A half-dozen plastic litter boxes were strewn around the room, each overflowing with feline urine, feces and flies. Open cans of rotting cat pâté littered the cement floor. The sea breeze whistled like a teakettle through the shack, but the stench hung in place like something nailed down. That Haitian girl must've really wanted that cup of tea, she thought.

The room was small. Good. That meant less to have to deal with. There wasn't much in the way of amenities to encumber her search. No wall adornments, practically no furniture and, other than a flea-bitten rug under the couch, just a bare cement floor. She turned over a small portable radiator, rummaged through a chest of drawers and found a pair of binoculars—vindicating her decision to dress like a ninja to escape detection—and rifled around in a flimsy cabinet. She looked under the chair and patted down a cat-clawed leather couch, which she assumed served as his bed. She upended the couch and found a midden of rodent and fish remains and mounds of fur balls piled on the rug. But no coin.

Next, she went through a rack of cheap shelves bowed by stacks of old photo magazines. There was a collection of flotsam from the beach: a rose window pane, an urn, a whale bone and a shark jaw—the cumulative litter of an Apollonian diet gone sclerotic.

There was no kitchen per se, just a corner of the same room set up like a kitchen, at the window. He had a fold-out camping table and plastic chair. A plastic washbasin full of dirty dishes also contained a toothbrush and nail clippers. The basin sat under a hand pump connected to the outdoor water tank. But again, no coin.

Ruth tried outside. She checked the water tank, gave a cursory look inside the foul latrine and finished by inspecting the small greenhouse where he grew his comestible plants. She came up empty.

Time was pressing, her temper rising. She tore off the suffocating spandex hood, releasing a panache of long, dark curls, and checked her stopwatch. Thirty-three minutes eclipsed just like that. Where the fuck did he put it? She knew he didn't wear it around his neck, and she doubted he carried it around in his shorts. Had the bastard gone and lost the Indian's coin? Ruth felt an onrush of panic and sat down to weather the emotion. As she gathered her breath, she tried to take stock of the situation. All right, this is what she knew: the ceiling and roof were the same bare covering, so she could rule them out. And the floor was a concrete slab. The walls were uninsulated, and the furniture was unsuitable for hiding anything. Ergo, the coin was not in the shack. So why was her instinct screaming it was? What was she missing? What was the blind spot?

And then it hit her. The coin wasn't the only object missing from view. In her mad dash to find the coin, she'd completely overlooked the most obvious: his cameras! Where were they? And, for that matter, where was his darkroom? And what about the tool essential to running his website? Where was his computer?

Ruth rushed back inside, yanked up the couch and pulled away the rug, fur balls and all. "Oh, the rat bastard!" she muttered, staring at a hatch door flush with the floor. She lifted it by its embedded ring latch.

Her persistence was afforded the discovery of a concrete stairway dissolving into a black pool of obscurity. She would need a light. She didn't have her iPhone, but her uncle had candles.

The steps were steep and narrow like a ladder, and Ruth descended them backward, gripping the burning candle in her teeth until reaching the bottom. She held up the light and found herself crouched within the confines of her uncle's squat darkroom. The subterranean space was roughly the size of a storage container and, compared to the utter chaos above, a model of orderliness. Metal shelves were neatly stocked with chemical vats, clean wash trays and stacks of paper and film. A tidy workbench contained all the tools of the trade: brass plates, framing boards, scissors and cutters, rulers and pencils. In the half-light, Ruth saw a cupboard of cameras, both state-of-the-art and relics, spool and digital, apparatuses requiring two hands and ones the size of cigarette packets. She presumed he must have run some generated power down there for light, and she began searching the back wall for a switch. While she was splashing candlelight against a wall, a crowd of dead people popped up and spooked her worse than the cats had done, almost causing her to drop the candle. It was a gallery of blow-ups, some from hundred-and-fifty-year-old daguerreotypes, all in black and white, men and women born pre-twentieth century, ancestors of hers she had read about in her dad's book. Luckily, each image was named and dated. Otherwise, Ruth would have been clueless. There was a middle-aged Lydia Freeman (1840). An elderly Doctor Osborne (1855). Archie Finley in the High Sierras, standing among a group of coolies (1868) and out front of the Neespaugot town hall with his young bride Bridget (1878). Randolph and Clara Osborne, posing in the parlor with their young daughters—Sarelle, Della and Hattie Lawrence (1886). The newlyweds Johnny T and Hattie Lawrence standing out front of the First Baptist Church on Cabot Street (1903). The Russian Roxxmotts outside their Cabot Street tailor shop (1904).

Her dad's book said that Ezra had ripped off his mother's picture collection, same as he had the Indian's coin, and this trove proved it. It dawned on Ruth that her uncle's gallery was a version of her dad's family-history museum. It also didn't escape her that the two shrines couldn't have been more different. While her dad's museum was intended to share the family's legacy, her uncle's subterranean exhibition was meant to hoard it. This stash was a tomb, a legacy erected to his monumental insecurity. Photographs couldn't run away or die like the people themselves.

Hot wax dripped on Ruth's hand, a stinging reminder to continue looking for a light switch. Searching high and low, Ruth located the switch on the north wall and flipped it. The generator hummed, and gradually the room turned vermilion from an energy-efficient infrared lightbulb. From out of the red haze appeared a second photo gallery. It was so creepy that Ruth was sure her eyes were playing tricks on her. "It can't be," she mumbled, moving in for a closer inspection of the pictures. But it was true. Every single photo was of *her*. Each picture had been shot from a distance with a high-powered zoom lens. There she was, a three-year-old seated between her mom and sister at her dad's burial. Then, again at the cemetery, a little older, sitting next to Aunt Esther at Uncle Zeke's funeral. And at the center of bunches of school events: plays, award ceremonies, athletic contests. He had taken a series of photos from every one of her judo competitions and track meets since she was twelve, including shots of her rounding the final curve on her way to winning the Massachusetts State High School championship in the four hundred meters, which had taken place only two months before. But the photo that actually made her skin crawl showed her hiding at daybreak out front of his beach shack, spying on him through a pair of binoculars. The picture was snapped less than a week before. The bastard knew who she was and why she was there. It's why he'd left the door open. He was toying with her. The whole thing was a setup.

Ruth continued ransacking his workbench until she found his laptop. And sure enough, there it was, proof that she'd been played. He had left her an envelope, pinched between screen and keyboard, inscribed with *Ruth*. She tore it open and read: "Congratulations! You're as clever as I thought you'd be. I have a pretty good idea what you're after, and I believe we can work something out. Meet me on the beach, and we'll talk about it."

Her uncle was standing near the surf, doing tai chi on a shelf of gravelly sand glimmering with quahog shells. Ruth's sudden appearance from his shack had no impact on the man whatsoever. After brief eye contact, he continued doing his *kata*. His slow-motion movements were more a lyrical dance than simulated fighting and a far cry from Ruth's judo and mix martial arts. Set against the scintillating sea, her uncle seemed to be fending off millions of sparkling darts, like a scene from *House of Flying Daggers*. Ruth sensed he was showing off. We'll see about that, she thought, hustling back into the shack and fetching the fullest kitty litter box. She hoisted it out and heaved it in his direction. The plastic box split apart on impact, slewing slop every which way and sending up the stinging stench of cat waste. But her hope of making him uncomfortable failed. Her uncle was more amused than miffed. "Do me a favor and take out the others," he said.

His nonchalance infuriated her more, and, with menace in her heart, Ruth strode over to him and glared down, hands clenched into fists. She had a good five inches on the old man. Still, he showed no signs of being intimidated by her. On the contrary, he stood his ground, cool as ocean spray. "What now, kid? You going to hit me?"

"It's looking that way."

"You really want assault and battery charges added to breaking and entering?"

"Yeah, right. A pedophile is going to complain to the cops."

Her pedophilia accusation stripped a little shine off his varnish. "You're in the wrong TV series, kid." He scowled, pushing past her and entering his shack.

When he came back out, he had a bottle of water and two folding beach chairs. "Grab a seat," he said, opening a chair and setting it beside her.

"I'll stand," she said.

"Suit yourself." He shrugged, easing into a beach chair and sipping from his bottle. The shakes caused him to spill whole gulps down his beard. "Go on and take a load off," he said, patting the other chair with his troubled hand. "You're here now. We might as well talk."

Begrudgingly, Ruth sat, but not before making one thing perfectly clear. "I didn't come here for small talk."

Her guff made him chuckle. "I'm not offering any… unless your dad is small talk."

"No, unh-unh! You don't get to talk about my dad, buster."

"And why's that?" he asked, scratching his whiskers. "Afraid to hear something you won't like?"

"You're the one who should be afraid, old man. A sick fuck like you doesn't get to tell his side of the story."

"Relax, kid," he said in a low, mildly offended voice. "No one's going to say anything bad about your dad. He had his issues but, all in all, he was a stand-up guy. And just for the record, photography is my vocation, not avocation, so cut the sick-fuck and pedophilia comments."

"Photography? You mean *pornography*. You feed the lust of freaks like you."

His green eyes got dark and squinty. "For a teenager, you're pretty uptight. Still a virgin?"

"Fuck you."

"You're a knockout, but no thanks. I'm not into incest. And I'm *not* into what you think I am. I don't do nude kids."

"And what about the kid on your darkroom wall?"

"What about her? What's indecent about that?"

"It's voyeurism, and if you think otherwise, you're delusional."

"*I'm* delusional, am I? I'm not the one who built a tower of lies to jump off. I didn't write a book that got me shot. I never tried to sell anybody on anything."

"Bullshit. I've seen you on the beach, pimping for flesh. Your site exploits those girls."

"Oh, is that right? Did you ever see me force anyone to do anything she didn't want to do?"

"You forced *me* onto your wall."

"Aw, pshaw! You didn't know those pictures existed until a few minutes ago."

"And only in your fucked-up universe would that make it okay."

"In any universe."

He had an answer for everything, and arguing with him was pointless. But like it or not, Ruth would have to stick around and butt heads with the sonofabitch until she determined whether or not he had the coin.

As gulls screamed in the distance, Ruth goaded him. "You must be so proud, outliving those two upstart younger brothers of yours. And you have so much to show for it. I mean, just look at you, man. Bitter. Unloved. No good to anyone but perverts. Forgotten. Dead to everyone who knows you."

His countenance darkened, but his voice remained surprisingly even. Ruth witnessed, without fully appreciating it, the result of seven decades spent battling for self-control. "Ah, yes." He sighed. "*Love, family, friendship, remembrance.* The Hallmark guide to a fulfilling life. Woe unto me for not partaking of the ice cream of saccharin sentiments. Sorry, kid, but I don't like having to lick my sentiments fast before they melt down my hand. Count me among the lactose-intolerant."

"Sure, your taste is more for bile. The Sisyphus guide to life."

Her uncle puckered his lips and nodded favorably. Ruth had scored a point. "Good girl. You did your homework. But here's the thing. We're all Sisyphus, with varying degrees of recognizing it. Even Aunt Della knew that. By the way, she would've taken to you like a warm bath."

"I wouldn't have killed her in a selfish fit, that's for sure."

"Yet here you are, breaking into my place, threatening to kick my ass. And with the right blow, who knows? You could end up being me."

Point for her uncle, Ruth acknowledged.

"Your Aunt Della was a great reader," he continued. "Which I hear you are, too."

"Is that another fun fact you picked up sleazing around corners?"

His left arm rattled involuntarily against the aluminum chair frame. He quieted the movement by steadying it with his good hand. "Suppose we stop trading barbs and I give you a fact you maybe weren't aware of. While Aunt Della was having me read *The Myth of Sisyphus*, she was having your uncle Zeke read *The Great Gatsby*. She meant it as a cautionary tale, not a road map. She was prescient, your great-aunt. She knew that, one day, that ambitious idiot would try to pass himself off as someone he wasn't."

"And what about you?"

"What *about* me? When did I ever try to be somebody I wasn't?"

"When did you ever try to be who you are?"

"Every day of my life. I never denied being Jewish."

"My point exactly. That makes two idiots who didn't learn their lessons."

Her uncle, patience thinning, hit back with sarcasm. "I wonder what Aunt Della would have had your dad read. Maybe Marcel Proust. That way he could've made up the past without getting out of bed."

"Watch it!" she said.

But he persisted. "I find it funny that my brothers ended up darting off in opposite directions, Zeke towards a fictive future, your dad chasing a presumptive past, yet both were squashed like bugs against the same windshield."

Ruth booted her uncle's beach chair out from under him, and he fell on his bad side. Her uncle prized the air with his good arm, trying to turn himself over. "Now that's funny," Ruth said. But as she watched him struggle, she felt a twinge of compunction. Blindsiding an old guy with Parkinson's wasn't as satisfying as she had imagined it would be. She grabbed hold of his flailing forearm and hauled him to his feet.

Chagrined, he brushed off the sand and walked away. "I have something you'll want to see," he called over his shoulder before disappearing inside his shack.

Her uncle returned to the beach carrying his laptop and a rickety parasol. He handed Ruth the parasol. "It takes some pinching and pushing."

Ruth got the parasol open and sunk its nib deep into the sand, between the beach chairs. Her uncle sat and began scrolling through his computer files. At last he found what he was looking for and handed her the machine. "Just hit play."

"What is it?" she asked, fearing some cheesy clandestine footage of one of her childhood birthday parties.

"An important video."

Ruth pressed *Play*. And there was her father, footage of him in his mid-thirties, crossing the set of a recording studio toward a sound booth where an interviewer was waiting in front of a softball-sized recording microphone. As Ruth watched her dad move, she remembered her mom telling her how much she took after her dad physically. The facial structure. The cambered back. The round tushy and long legs. At that moment it hit Ruth that, but by some mystery of nature, she had also inherited her dad's way of walking—something between moonwalking and highlining. How, she wondered, had she learned to move like a man who had died when she was barely three years old? She tapped *Pause*. "How did you get this?"

"I asked the studio, the day it was recorded. I knew a woman there."

"Why would you want a video of my dad doing an interview?"

"To share with you, dumb-ass. I knew this day would come and you'd be sitting right where you are, wondering why he died."

"Bullshit. You didn't know he was going to be shot."

"Everyone knew it. Your dad was poking the wrong people, kid. See for yourself." He reached over and hit *Play*, and for the next seventeen minutes Ruth became lost in her father's world.

Host: *This is Jim Tucker live from New York. Our next guest, ladies and gentlemen, is a former professional football player and current history professor whose book,* The Onion Road Legacy, *is selling like Korean cars. Let's give a warm welcome to Dr. Hosea Roxxmott! Dr. Roxxmott, would you describe* The Onion Road Legacy *as an immigrant story?*

Dad: *No, not really. After all, the story does begin with Native Americans. Call it a melting-pot story, the pot in this case being one family, a stew of Native American, Black, Scottish, Chinese, Irish, Russian Jew and, most recently, Spanish and Pakistani people. Above all—and this is what I hope readers relate to—it's a story of transcendence, of parents and ancestors who've made enormous sacrifices for the well-being of their children and children's children.*

Host: *We'll take our first caller. Go ahead.*

Caller: *Hi, I'm Marilyn Shepherd from Westchester. Dr. Roxxmott, would you call your book timely, seeing as last year was the five-hundredth anniversary of the failed John Cabot expedition?*

Dad: *Great question, Marilyn. But no, that was a coincidence. The fact is,* Onion *was first published back in 1993, a year after the five-hundredth anniversary of Columbus's discovery of America, but back then it didn't have much success—the book, not the discovery of America, ha ha.* (Ruth's dad had a nice smile, a wholesome laugh. He seemed fulfilled.) *Five years later the book got a second shot.* (He turned to the host.) *Marilyn is referring to one of history's great mysteries, the disappearance in 1498 of five English ships under the command of the Italian navigator Giovanni Caboto. Not a soul was heard from again. It was the Challenger explosion of its time, but that didn't stop the Crown from laying claim to large chunks of the New World based on the supposition that Cabot reached North America. In fact, my wife Peggy, an accomplished historian, speculates that the*

Cabot fleet probably made it as far south as Delaware and that one of its crew may have been the ancestor of the patriarch of my story, Runinniduk.

Host: Let's talk about your book's second life. Your detractors claim that it owes its newfound success to the controversy surrounding your brother, who was elected mayor of Neespaugot under false pretenses. Would you care to elaborate?

Dad (chuckling): As they say, there's no such thing as bad ink! I can't help it if certain people went out of their way to stomp out the book and only made it into a bigger fire.

Host: Meaning your brother's political staff?

Dad: Look, the book is what it is. It came out before the election. In fact, I'd been writing Onion *in my head from the age of ten. For me, it's never been about personal fame and glory, just a desire to honor some of my ancestors and family members.*

Host: To the detriment of certain other family members?

Dad: The truth only harms those who deny it. Onion *is not about settling scores or disparaging anyone. On the contrary, it's a tribute.*

Host: We'll take our next caller. This is Jim Tucker live from New York, you're on.

Caller: This is, dah, Richie. I din't read yer book, but my cousin did, and he says you was lyin' 'bout that black woman havin' a kid when she was seventy-eight. Them things ain't possible 'cept in the Bible.

Dad: I don't know what story your cousin read, Richie, but in mine, the woman, Lydia Freeman, is fifty, not seventy-eight. Though I'll give you that birthing a first child in your fifties in 1844 was today's equivalent of a seventy-year-old giving birth.

Host: *This is Jim Tucker live from New York, with Dr. Hosea Roxxmott, who's written a book that's catching on across the country. Hosea, your book seems to touch only peripherally on the plight of minorities in America. Why is that?*

Dad: *I disagree. The story deals almost exclusively with the plight of a minority: multiracial people, or what my mother used to call "meat stew." We're a minority among minorities and probably have more in common with multicultural people than with monoracial minorities. We have no fixed anchor, are constantly being tugged one way or another and never feel entire. It's complicated. Sometimes for expediency we choose a camp. But you know, deep down, it's not the whole truth. It's like wearing a shirt with one sleeve.*

Host: *Yet, you can understand why people take you for African-American?*

Dad: *If beauty is only skin deep, what's that say about the importance of skin color? How much do we glean of a book by looking at its cover? Or, to use some examples from* Onion, *did Melba Blue Jay's fair skin make her less of a native? Did Lydia Freeman's dark skin make her less of a doctor? More recently, the good people of Neespaugot stared at my brother's election posters and believed he was Italian-American. The importance of skin color should go the way of the dodo and die out.*

Host: *But surely there will always be racial profiling.*

Dad: *And there'll always be cancer, right? Well, I'm not buying it. A strong, forward-thinking society like America doesn't give up just because the disease is intractable. Racism is no different. The antidote is already written into our Constitution. A government of the people, by the people, for the people. These aren't just words. Root out racial profiling and it'll wither on the vine. Life is too complex for labels.*

Host: *Jim Tucker live from New York. Good morning.*

Caller: *I ain't got a name. All I gotta say to this half-breed is I don't see nothin' wrong with callin' a spade a spade. Where I come from, we're white. In Harlem, they're niggers. Up yuhs, mooladdo!* (Click)

Dad (smiling, shaking his head): *Come on, that guy was a plant!*

Host (also smiling): *We don't plant or filter. It's life in the fast lane.*

Dad: *Life in the fast sewer.*

Host: *This is Jim Tucker live from New York with Dr. Hosea Roxxmott. You're working on a new book?*

Dad: *I'm researching modern-day immigration.*

Host: *And?*

Dad: *Well, it's pretty much the same cast of characters. Mr. and Mrs. Spite, Contempt, Fear and Hatred making things tough for Mr. and Mrs. Hope, Faith, Will and Love. The history of the world is one of movement, and where there's motion, there's friction. Go back to Moses and you'll find conflict not just between the Pharaoh's slavers and Jewish slaves but also between the Israelites themselves, between those brave enough to accept the necessity of crossing the Red Sea and those who can't stand unleavened bread. Then again, where there's movement there's hope, and America is still a major draw. It's still the country of opportunity despite being uncivilized.*

Host: *Wow. You're calling the greatest democracy in the world uncivilized?*

Dad: *It's a caldron where molecules clash, where real justice and freedom collide with utter barbarity. I'm talking about turf wars, drive-by shootings, public executions, mass murders in schoolyards, and let's not forget the drugs and guns hidden in Mickey Mouse lunchboxes and Jack raping Jill up a hill and Jack on crack breaking his shades and pregnant Jill tumbling down with AIDS. The bottom line is too often about profit, and it's amazing that freedom and justice exist here at all. But they do, and that's a testament to our Constitution and our history of not being a prisoner to history.*

Host: *This is Jim Tucker live from New York with Hosea Roxxmott, provocative author of* The Onion Road Legacy. *It's time to ask our listeners this question. What race is Mr. Roxxmott? Call 1-800-RACE, with your answers. That's 1-800-RACE, and win an all-expenses paid trip to...*

The video went blank, and her dad's image was snatched back into the ether, his voice replaced by the sounds of the incoming tide. For a moment, Ruth was lost in a time lag, like exiting a movie into daylight. She had the impression that her dad's murder had yet to happen and there was still time to warn him. She almost said aloud, "Don't meet Aunt Esther in Orange County."

Her uncle burst the bubble. "What you just saw was a typical interview for your dad. He was doing them all over the country, and stirring up hornet's nests of hardcore fanatics and racists. His very last one was similar, the one out in California."

"Dad wasn't shot for anything *he* said. The target out in California was Aunt Esther. He took a bullet for her at that political rally."

"Don't be gullible, kid. That was just the ice cream they were selling. When the security team killed the extremist, the identity of his real target went with him. It was your aunt's political team that rushed in and refocused the narrative. In fact, your dad was still bleeding out when they announced to the world that your aunt was the intended victim. It's what got her elected."

Ruth's temper boiled over. "You just can't help it, can you, pissing all over your own family? You're a piece of shit."

"Think what you want, but whatever I am, you are, too."

"Just because you took my picture doesn't mean you know me."

"Yeah, I do, smart-ass. The first time I saw you wasn't behind a lens. I was as close to you as I am now."

"You're lying."

"Look, I knew your dad was heading for a bad end, so I passed by Osborne House to talk some sense into him. The front gate was open. There were some dolls in the middle of the lawn. I hadn't had any contact in years with your dad and knew nothing about his family situation. I heard the sound of a vacuum cleaner coming from upstairs. I called but nobody answered. So I tried the doorknob and stepped inside. And there you were, sitting in a playpen set up in that stupid museum of his. You were real little, maybe a year old. You hadn't even started walking yet. I picked you up out of the pen. You were warm as baked bread, sweet as fresh flowers. That impish expression of yours, it told me right away who you were."

"Who was I?"

"A Roxxmott, that's who. Your mother came running into the room, trailed by your sister, both of them yelling at me to put you down. Your mother cussed me out and told me that the museum was closed on Wednesdays. I ignored her and spoke directly to your sister Melba. 'Kid,' I said, 'does your mother let you play on the widow's walk? Me, I used to drag your no-good crybaby uncle up there, and now he can't get enough of high places.' That's when your mother figured out who I was. 'Ezra?' she said, like she was trying to stomach snails in polite company.

"I asked her where my brother was. 'On a book tour,' she said. 'Best to keep that kind of information to yourself,' I said. 'How so?' she said. 'Because you're the attractive wife of a muckraker, alone in a big house with a child and a baby,' I said. Your mother shot me a look like I was the predator she needed to fear. That pissed me off, so I retaliated. I propositioned her to model nude for me, and she kicked me out."

"Why be such a dick to her?"

"Like I said, I was offended. Besides, neither of us felt like pretending we were family."

"So once again you decided what was best for everybody."

"Aw, don't turn it into a referendum, kid. You know damn well what I'm talking about. I've filmed you plenty of times feeling awkward, out of place, and then the flash of anger and the biting off of people's heads. It's really just about being pissed off at yourself."

"Thanks for the psychoanalysis, but I'm nothing like you."

"You keep saying that. So, how about a fact check? You're a loner. Check. People always disappoint you. Check. Trying to communicate with all but a select few frustrates and tires you to death. Check. Face it, kid, you're an emotional recluse just like me. You distill your insecurity the same way I do. You boil it down to one-hundred-proof perverseness, especially with those you care about. I pushed away everyone who meant anything to me. My father, Aunt Della, my mother. Because they failed to rise to my expectations."

"And my dad?" Ruth asked. "He was just a kid when you screwed him over the Indian's coin." Her thrust pierced his armor, and she twisted the blade. "You never gave him a chance. And for one reason. His skin, you spiteful bastard."

"Wrong. I cheated him because all that counted was the coin ending up in the right hands."

"Sure, *your* hands."

"The right hands are the ones that pass it on. Nobody's designated, kid. The coin ain't a crown."

"It ain't a relay baton, either. There's also the responsibility of transferring what it stands for. The coin comes with a user manual, old man. Didn't you read the damn book?"

"Yeah, punk, I did, and I recall the coin bouncing around like a ping-pong ball. First, it was cut off a putrefying corpse. Then, it was found around the neck of a nameless African girl. Aunt Della absconded to Europe with it, yet it wound up back here in Ma's hands. I took it, and here you are, fifty years later, ready to steal it. All the book's baloney about the Indian's coin being a symbol for inclusion, transcendence, universality and whatnot, that's just baloney. The coin stands for life, and life, as they say, always finds a way."

"Great. So, hand it over."

Her uncle grinned devilishly. Leverage was obviously one of the few pleasures left to him. "What makes you think it's yours? What about your sister Melba? She's older, and she's got the name recognition. You're just 'Ruth.' That was the name of a lowly Moabite convert."

"Who became the great-grandmother of kings."

His green eyes twitched with approval. "Again, I'm impressed, kid."

The sun at this point was high in the cloud-veiled heavens, and the heat and humidity were starting to oppress Ruth in her tights. The mission, as it were, was never supposed to have taken this long. "Look, old man. Suppose we stop the games and you tell me exactly what *you* want in exchange for the Indian's coin."

Her uncle grunted out of his beach chair and had her follow him to the latrine. He flapped open the door and they were both blown back by the pungency of lime and twenty-five years of his bodily wastes. "Go for it," he said. "It's yours for the taking."

Ruth was bemused. "What are you talking about?"

"The coin is down the chute, under all the swill."

"Get out of here!"

"What!? That surprises you, 'great-grandmother of kings'? Even the great Melba Blue Jay was forced to conceal the coin in her own shit to keep it hidden from the sugar baron and pimp. I thought you were up to the task. Maybe I was wrong."

"All right, give me a pail and shovel. And if this is a trick, you're going down that hole."

He started laughing. "Forget it, I'm just messing with you, kid. Call it payback for breaking my kitty litter box."

"So cut the crap and tell me what I need to do."

"Fine, but it's dirtier than digging in my swill."

"I'm listening."

"I can see you're burning up in those tights. Strip, liberate yourself and let me shoot you naked."

"Up yours, you lech!"

"Come on, kid, you read the book. There's always a sacrifice. Clarisse was willing to drown in a tub to preserve the coin. The Griffin woman killed herself to save her baby and loot. The Chinaman killed that Finley bastard to protect the Osbornes. Della chose exile over compromise. Your own father accepted death in exchange for a book. And me… well, you see how I live."

"And you're comparing those things to what you're asking me to do? You're as sick in your head as you are in your body."

"It's all a question of sacrifice, and your prudery is evidently what's hardest for you to let go of. So, yes, that's my deal. If you want the coin, strip and pose."

Ruth stood there in her heated garb, trying to decide her next move. Agreeing to his terms was out of the question. Prudery wasn't the issue. She couldn't stomach the notion of his winning again. Which left either beating the coin out of him and possibly killing him with nothing to show for it, or retreating to fight another day.

"Goodbye, uncle," she said and turned to leave.

"Lightweight," he said to her back. "I thought you were a Roxxmott. You're just an Osborne and whatever kind of Muslim your mother is. Loser!"

"Yeah, whatever," Ruth yelled back and kept walking.

She hadn't reached the first dune before a realization struck her. She turned around and loped back to her uncle. He was still standing there, waiting, his left arm twitching, his elfin grin triumphant and expectant. "Forget something?"

"No, I remembered something."

"And what would that be?" he asked, amused.

"I need to make a sacrifice, right? Well, I know what that is now. It's you, old man. You're my sacrifice. I'm going to tend to your needs until the day you croak."

Her uncle's steely demeanor faltered, and for the first time Ruth thought she caught a glimpse of fallibility in his eyes.

"You're bluffing."

She shook her head. "No, you're wrong. If Melba Blue Jay and Lydia Freeman could make the kinds of sacrifices they made over so many years, I can put up with you for a while longer."

He was incredulous. "You'll just get tired and give up."

"Then you don't know me. Yes, I'm a Roxxmott, but not only. I'm also a Native American and African and Chinese and Irish and Russian and Jew and Muslim, and we don't give up."

Silent for a long lapse, her uncle recovered, tugged on his beard and smiled. "Well, I didn't see that coming. Good for you, kid." He held out his hand, palm up, and there was the Indian's coin. "Go on, take it, no strings attached. It's yours now."

Ruth reached into her uncle's palm and retrieved the dull copper coin between thumb and index finger. "Where were you hiding it?"

Her uncle lifted the bottom fringes of his beard perpendicular to his chin. "Tied up nice and safe, day and night, always with me."

Ruth held up the coin, turned it over, inspected it for something extraordinary but found little to recommend it. "It's really not much, is it?"

"Kid," said her uncle, quite composed, even serene now, "it's like any work of art. Its value is in the eye of the beholder. Anyway, you earned it and can go home now."

Ruth nodded. "You're still a bastard, you know. Your solitude is still what's dearest to you, and that's tragic."

"Better solitude than selfishness, I'm sure you'd agree."

"In your case I don't see much of a difference."

"That depends," he said softly.

"On what?"

In her uncle's pause, Ruth detected nervousness and, more remarkably, trepidation. "On if you'll give me a chance. You know, come by now and then. Spend some time… together."

Ruth was dumbstruck. After all of this, the guy wanted to hang out. "I'll have to think about it," she stammered.

"Yeah, sure," he said, his voice trailing off.

"I have to go." She sighed and moved away, distancing herself. "Thanks, for this." She flashed the coin.

He called to her. "Having it is more work than getting it."

"We'll see," she answered.

"So, maybe we'll be seeing you?" He sounded desperate but resigned.

Ruth threw up her arms noncommittally. Damn it, she owed him nothing. Now that she had what she'd come for, she had every right to walk away and never come back. To hell with him. He deserved nothing. The bastard had pushed everyone away. You reap what you sow, as they say.

Yet, who was she to judge and sentence him to exile? And wouldn't such a judgment prove that she was every bit like him—a cold and calculating Roxxmott? That was his point all along, and he had intended to prove it even if it meant sacrificing his relationship with her. As Ruth looked at him standing barefoot in the sand, his left arm twitching, she realized that no matter what she chose to do, her uncle would feed off it like a suckling baby, his sense of victimization the tit that never stopped giving.

"Uncle!" she shouted. "Maybe tomorrow. We'll see."

He nodded without emotion, signaled goodbye and walked back toward his shack on the beach.

About the Author

John Mugglebee is a racial and ethnic jigsaw puzzle. His heritage, in chronological order, includes Native American, African American, Scots-Irish, Chinese and Russian Jew. Growing up, John was told family stories that had been passed down for generations. *Neespaugot* is loosely based on those stories.

John has said there were two major factors that shaped him as a person and a writer. One was "being *colored* but not knowing which color." The other was upheaval. Born in Salem, Massachusetts, at age eleven John was uprooted and moved to Southern California in the midst of the '60s race riots. It was through sports and academics that he found stability and integration.

John attended Dartmouth College and received a master's in creative writing from Colorado State University. He currently lives in the South of France, where he heads a language laboratory for French Civil Aviation. His previous novel, *Renaissance in Provence*, was published in 2004.